**High praise for the Matador series,
Steve Perry's stories of intrigue and honor, including . . .**

*The Man Who Never Missed, The 97th Step,
The Albino Knife, Matadora, Black Steel,
The Machiavelli Interface,* **and** *Brother Death*

"A crackling good story. I enjoyed it immensely!"
—Chris Claremont

"Heroic . . . Perry builds his protagonist into a mythical figure without losing his human dimension. It's refreshing."
—*Newsday*

"Perry provides plenty of action [and] expertise about weapons and combat."
—*Booklist*

"Noteworthy." —*The Magazine of Fantasy and Science Fiction*

"Another sci-fi winner . . . cleanly written . . . the story accelerates smoothly at an adventurous clip, bristling with martial arts feats and as many pop-out weapons as a Swiss army knife."
—*The Oregonian*

"Plenty of blood, guts, and wild fight scenes." —*VOYA*

"Excellent reading." —*Science Fiction Review*

"Action and adventure flow cleanly from Perry's pen."
—*Pulp and Celluloid*

THE
MUSASHI
FLEX

STEVE
PERRY

ACE BOOKS, NEW YORK

THE BERKLEY PUBLISHING GROUP
Published by the Penguin Group
Penguin Group (USA) Inc.
375 Hudson Street, New York, New York 10014, USA
Penguin Group (Canada), 90 Eglinton Avenue East, Suite 700, Toronto, Ontario M4P 2Y3, Canada
(a division of Pearson Penguin Canada Inc.)
Penguin Books Ltd., 80 Strand, London WC2R 0RL, England
Penguin Group Ireland, 25 St. Stephen's Green, Dublin 2, Ireland (a division of Penguin Books Ltd.)
Penguin Group (Australia), 250 Camberwell Road, Camberwell, Victoria 3124, Australia
(a division of Pearson Australia Group Pty. Ltd.)
Penguin Books India Pvt. Ltd., 11 Community Centre, Panchsheel Park, New Delhi—110 017, India
Penguin Group (NZ), Cnr. Airborne and Rosedale Roads, Albany, Auckland 1310, New Zealand
(a division of Pearson New Zealand Ltd.)
Penguin Books (South Africa) (Pty.) Ltd., 24 Sturdee Avenue, Rosebank, Johannesburg 2196, South
Africa

Penguin Books Ltd., Registered Offices: 80 Strand, London WC2R 0RL, England

THE MUSASHI FLEX

An Ace Book / published by arrangement with the author

PRINTING HISTORY
Ace edition / January 2006

Copyright © 2006 by Steve Perry.
Cover art by Christian McGrath.
Cover design by Judith Murello.
Interior text design by Stacy Irwin.

ISBN: 0-441-01361-9

ACE
Ace Books are published by The Berkley Publishing Group,
a division of Penguin Group (USA) Inc.,
375 Hudson Street, New York, New York 10014.
ACE and the "A" design are trademarks belonging to Penguin Group (USA) Inc.

PRINTED IN THE UNITED STATES OF AMERICA

10 9 8 7 6 5 4 3 2 1

*This book is for Dianne, as they all have been and
if I am fortunate enough to keep writing them, ever will be;
For the grandsons: Zach, Brett, Cy, and Dex;
And for the Eclectics, who have a point,
but who also miss a larger one:
Now and then, deep and narrow beats
wide and shallow all to hell and gone—
and you ignore this at your peril.*

SP

Acknowledgments

I'd like to thank *Maha Guru* Stevan Plinck, who is, in my opinion, the world's best player and teacher of the esoteric Javanese fighting art *Pukulan Pentjak Silat Sera*. Guru Plinck is a kind and gentle man, which is good, because of that which he is capable. I owe him much for taking me on as a student, and for the nine years I've been privileged to study with him. (A special thanks goes to writer and martial artist Steven Barnes for introducing me to Guru. When I started writing about the 97 Steps, I thought I was making it all up, until I discovered that silat had beaten me to it.)

Thanks to: Ginjer Buchanan, at Penguin/Ace, for all the years of help as my excellent editor, and to Jean Naggar and the good folks at her agency for making it possible for me to pay the rent.

Thanks to: Master Shiva Ki, who made the *kerambits,* and Chas Clements, who did the leather for them. Men of character, both.

Thanks to: Todd and Tiel, for the read—and the Swahili.

Martial arts are a lifelong journey for some, and I am happy to count myself among those long on the path. I hope my readers find my latest foray into this arena interesting. It's all pure fiction, of course—but it's all true, nonetheless.

The only thing necessary
for the triumph of evil
is for good men
to do nothing.

—EDMUND BURKE

When you know who you are,
you know what to do.

—GEORGE EMERY

Batur arek uring enggeus.

(When they get ready,
we are already done.)

—SUDANESE FIGHTING PROVERB

1

Death came for him from the shadows, as it had so many times before. This time, his would-be killer bore a dagger. Lazlo Mourn recognized not only the type, he knew who had made it. The distinctive layered-damascus steel was the giveaway: Angel's Wings, created by a smith who was well regarded by Flex players for knives that were virtually unbreakable; high-carbon stain-free plexsteel cryonically tempered in liquid nitrogen. You could bend one those blades ninety degrees without snapping it, and it would spring back, good as new. That was a blade worth having.

He wondered how old man Kiley the knifemaker was these days? Was he still living on Koji, the Holy World? That might seem an odd place for a man who made killing weapons, but not if you had turned smithing into a religion as Kiley had. In one of his deposit vaults, Mourn had two of the old man's knives. They were worth half again each what he had paid for them, and they had not been cheap. He expected to be using them again—assuming he lived to do so.

He was mildly amused at himself for wandering off on such a flight of fancy while looking at a man who planned to kill him.

Amused, not afraid.

He could remember exactly when it had happened. During a duel with slap-caps four years ago he had realized that losing—and dying—were not as important as doing his technique properly.

How far gone was that? *Better focus here, Mourn.*

He breathed in through his nose, using the Ayurvedic method. This alley was, save for the two of them, deserted, just another of the tens of thousands of building gaps like it all over Jakarta. The afternoon was hot, tropically so. The air had a faintly rancid, spoiled-fruit odor, as might be made by some small bit of garbage fallen unseen behind a bin to rot in the cloying heat.

The man with the dagger was short, wide, and muscular but not so much so that he couldn't move well. His hair was cropped tight in a spacer's buzz, and while sparkle-dyed a hideous, almost pustulant, glittery yellow, had dark roots. He was maybe twenty-five, and of course, Mourn knew him. It was Harnett, and ranked probably around Twentieth, Twenty-First or so, that due to his work with short-edged weaponry. You got more points for weapons. So his challenge would be legit; he was within Mourn's cohort.

Harnett wore stretch leathers and flexsoles, and to suffer the leather in this heat almost surely meant spidersilk armor was part of the weave. He was young, skilled, and quick—and he knew it. But he was not well seasoned yet, despite his rank. Mostly, Harnett had been lucky. Some had it, some didn't. Luck could take you places, but She could never be trusted to stay in your bed once you got there.

"Hello, Mourn. Fancy meeting you here." He waved the knife like a pointer.

Mourn shook his head. Jesu. He'd probably been working on his delivery of that line for days.

Mourn was taller, probably weighed about the same, and was at least twenty years older. *And ranked higher— though there were never guarantees in a knife fight.*

Of a moment, despite the yogic breathing, he felt tired.

"Harnett. You sure you want to play it this way?" He nodded at the dagger. Technically, it was Mourn's choice— he was the challenged party—but if the man wanted to slice, it was all the same to him.

"Unless you just want to, you know, hand over your tag?"

Mourn smiled. At this level, nobody gave up their tag.

He uncrowed the flap of the paddle-holster tucked under the belt on his left side, a sheath of pebbled gray curlnose leather. The case, custom-designed by a grizzled old artist named Clements, was a nice piece of art in itself, made to look like a transponder case. Had to be disguised, since what was in it was illegal in this city. He slipped his forefinger into the rings of the twin *kerambits*.

He pulled the two short knives free but held them together in his left hand as if they were one thick blade, points down and edges forward in what knifers called the ice-pick grip. The *kerambits* were claw-shaped single-edge weapons whose curved inner edges were only about the length of his crooked little finger. The other end of the all-steel knife bore a ring that would allow it to be worn like a brass knuckle. It was a slashing weapon rather than a stabbing one, though the thick and heavy ring also allowed striking. Like Harnett's blade, these were layered pattern-weld steel, done by a local artisan named Shiva, and had not been cheap. You never stinted on your weapons; you always bought the best you could afford. He had been practicing with these every day for the last year or so, and he was quite comfortable with the little knives.

Held the way he had them, the two should, from Harnett's viewpoint, look like one.

Harnett grinned. In a knife fight, size mattered, his dagger was easily four times as long, and would cut going and coming. If he had been smart, he would have wondered: Why did a fighter like Lazlo Mourn, at least six or eight ranks higher than he was, feel that he needed nothing larger than a little hook blade?

If he had been smart, Harnett wouldn't have followed Mourn into this alley.

Harnett edged in, but was still more than three meters away. He lowered himself slowly into a knife fighter's crouch, blade leading in a saber grip.

Mourn turned his body so that he was angled at maybe fifty degrees to Harnett, his left leg forward, his right leg back, feet just under a meter apart. He held the knives low, by his groin, his other hand by his face.

Mourn had mostly been on Earth for more than a year, training under a little old man named Setarko, who was a master of one of the *pentjak silat* variants called *Tjindak*. *Silat* was a weapons-based system, which meant that the unarmed moves were derived from those with blades, and not the other way around. Mourn had been pretty quiet while he trained, only a few challenges, most of those off-world, and the ones he'd fought here had been unarmed. The way the Flex ranking system worked, as long as he was minimally active and he didn't lose, he wouldn't drop off the map.

Harnett wasn't local. He might not know about the blades and the system that taught their use.

Silat wasn't Mourn's only art, of course; he had trained in others, from *Teräs Kasi*—"steel hands"—to combat *Changa* grappling, to the bonebreak system of *Maumivu Matunda*—"the Fruit of Pain." He was still in pretty good condition at a hair over forty-five years T.S., but he wasn't getting any younger. You could count the number of top-rated Flex players past his age on your fingers—with one left over to scratch your nose.

He had considered retiring. He could open a school. Lots of players would seek him out to see if they could learn what had kept him alive for twenty-five years against some of the best in the galaxy. Once, he had been full of fire, striving to reach the top of the Flex. Now? The game was week-old bread. You could still eat it, but it was dry and hard, and there was no real taste left to it. He was tired, he was old, he should quit.

Whatever happened here, this kid wasn't going to go much farther up the ranks. He just didn't have enough fire. Luck was not infinite.

Harnett stole a half step closer.

Mourn waited. Attack had its advantages, but first to move ran the risk of being first to err.

Harnett darted in, threw a quick slash, and jumped back. A feint, to check his reaction more than actually to do damage, but Mourn swiped at the attacking arm, deliberately slow, knives still held together as one.

Yeah, the kid was fast, but that was not nearly as dangerous as smart. Fast you could deal with.

Harnett circled, shifted his weapon from hand to hand, showing off. He jumped in and slashed again.

Mourn sidestepped, easily avoiding the attack, but he didn't follow up as Harnett retreated.

Harnett circled in the opposite direction.

Mourn stayed where he was.

Harnett must have figured he had what he needed. He switched grips from saber to ice pick, and began to bounce forward and backward, getting almost within range, but not quite, going up and down, slapping his body with his free hand, his moves increasingly jerky.

Ah. *Peepah*-style, a tribal art developed in prisons for

assassinations. It looked something like *kuntao,* maybe even a little like *silat. Peepah* was a hodgepodge, but not dangerous if you knew what it was—and if you had a blade of your own, it was nothing—no real principles in it, only technique.

Harnett got ready to make his run, and Mourn figured he knew how it would play out. He must have figured he could give Mourn his arm, take the cut, even if it punched through the armored leather sleeve, and gut him before Mourn could recover. A little orthostat glue and the arm would be good as new, only a small bragging scar to show for it. *Yar, that's the one I took when I sent Mourn over. He was pretty good for an old guy, you know?*

No, more likely with somebody like Harnett, it would be: *Mourn? Nah, he wasn't shit. Way past it, an easy kill.*

It might have been a good strategy if Mourn had held but the one blade. But as Mourn switched his hand position, reversing them to cover high and low line, he palmed the second *kerambit* into his other hand, covering it with the angle of his body.

Harnett lunged, stabbed, and when Mourn went for the slice and block, to "defang the snake," Harnett did a neat border shift, tossing the dagger from his right to his left—

—Mourn cut the right arm, snagged the point in the armored sleeve, and Harnett grinned—

—but as Harnett caught the dagger for the true strike, Mourn stepped in and punched with the second *kerambit.* The move was called "the helpful waiter" stance, because it looked rather like a waiter holding a serving tray balanced on one hand, palm held up and at throat level.

The little blade bit into Harnett's neck, just under his chin below his ear. Right where the carotid artery pulsed within a millimeter or two of the skin.

The talon snicked through the great vessel, hardly slowing, and Mourn did a short follow-through, then swung his fist back and used the thick ring to smash into Harnett's temple.

Harnett stumbled, shock and surprise painting his face. He went down. Blood spewed from his neck, pulsing in great gouts.

Mourn backed off quickly. A wounded killer was a danger.

Harnett came back to his feet. He brought both hands to his wound, still holding the knife, but the blood coursed between his fingers, leaving his face dead pale. It wouldn't be long before he bled out enough to lose consciousness. Even with immediate medical attention, it would be iffy if he survived, and there weren't any medicos around. Mourn prepared himself for a final desperate lunge, but Harnett didn't have enough left.

"What—?" he managed.

Mourn turned his hands around, palms forward, to show both *kerambits*.

The great sin of youth was to be so full of your own ability you couldn't see another's. Mourn had been there, and had been lucky enough to survive his own stupidity.

"Shit," Harnett said. His voice was barely a whisper. "You cheated!"

"No. You didn't pay enough attention." He didn't say he was sorry. He wasn't. When a man came at you with a blade, it was his karma if he ate your steel instead. That was how the game was played.

The younger man stood there for another few heartbeats, then his eyes clouded, and he collapsed.

The tag, a thumbnail-sized carbon-fiber computer-chip embed bearing a holographic image of a samurai sword, was stuck to the inside of the dead man's boot, between the insole and the outer, which was where most players who hadn't been hassled too much by cools kept them. Mourn usually wore his clipped to his pubic hair—if a cool found it, he would have to be getting very personal. And if somebody dropped him, they'd spend a while looking for it, a small revenge from the final chill.

For just a moment, as he looked at the strip, Mourn considered leaving it with the body. He wasn't worried about getting rid of the corpse—Jakarta was a violent city, dozens of homicides every day, and the local cools weren't going to search real hard for whoever had tanked an offworlder that nobody was going to file a report on. The cools would look at Harnett and figure it out when they saw the knife, the armor weave, the other weapons he surely had hidden on him. Yes, dueling was illegal, but *Fuck it,* they would say. *Just another dead Flex asshole and good fucking riddance!* None of his DNA to connect him to Harnett, if he stayed careful.

Someday, if he stayed in the game, it would be him lying dead in some dank alley like this. That was how it went if you walked the Musashi Flex. You either retired, went to jail, or wound up dead.

He stuck the tag into his pocket, wiped the blood from his blades, sheathed them, then turned and walked away. He'd dump the steels and the sheath into the ultrasonic cleaner he had in his hotel room, to rid them of any Harnett's DNA, just to be sure.

The air seemed fresher now, sweeter, and the tropical warmth was not as oppressive as it had been. Fights to the death did that. Life was briefly, a little sweeter. He was still tired, though.

2

Ellis Mtumbo Shaw was not a happy man.

He sat in the richly appointed office of his company's headquarters in Chim City, on Tatsu, the main world of the Haradali System, staring at Martin Snow Owl's sculpture *Two Wrestlers*. It was the original, of course, one-quarter life-sized, carved from a single, two-hundred-kilo chunk of black opal unearthed decades ago in the Cody Brothers' Marissa #3 Opal Mine, on Thompson's Gazelle. Shaw considered it priceless, though his insurance company, being somewhat more pragmatic, valued it at 12 million stads, plus or minus a little. Normally just looking at it put him in a good mood. The opal itself was full of fire, with wide harlequin and Chinese-writing patterns, brilliant, multicolored flashes across the spectrum, reds, greens, blues, yellows. Hell, it was worth 6 million uncarved as a doorstop. With Snow Owl's magnificent work, it was, and would be, forever one of a kind. More than one museum had offered him a fat credit cube and told him to deduct the amount he wanted. He had just laughed at them.

Today, however, the piece was not enough to lift his spirits. Another group of the fucking rock apes had died, five of them, all within hours of each other. Dammit!

The formula had been working, otherwise. Theoretical reaction times should have been at .65, myoconduction enhanced proportionately, and there had been no reason for significant loss of fine motor control at full speed. It would have been amazing—

—except for killing all the patients. The pathologists were at it now, but Shaw already knew what they would find. The apes had cooked in their own juices, the fucking HRE—the hypothalamic regulator enzyme—that was a big factor, and it was off, every fucking time, it was off—

"Sir?"

Shaw waded back from his sea of impotent rage and looked at the door to the office. It was Cervo, his head of security and primary bodyguard.

When Shaw spoke, his voice was cool, a vat of liquid helium, betraying none of his anger. One did not let the help see how one was feeling, a lesson first pounded into him at his father's knee. "Yes?"

"The Tomodachians are here." Despite his size—Cervo was a heavy-gravity mue, two meters tall and 120 kilos heavy—his voice was soft and not much more than whisper.

Shaw nodded. "Of course. Send them in."

Shaw had a secretary and a personal assistant, of course, but anybody he didn't personally know had to get past Cervo.

The medico-research group from Tomodachi, in the nearby Shin System, were on a different track than Shaw. They were trying recom DNA, piggybacking viral packets on common gut bacteria. It didn't work yet, but in the long term, it might, and if it did, it would have some advantages over his company's method. Bacteria could be trained like tiny dogs to do all kinds of things, not the least of which would be to self-replicate for a predetermined time. You could tailor a strain to keep delivering its payload for days, weeks, months—even years, then have it hayflick out. Of course, you had to charge enough for that to make it worthwhile; and you had to build in a fail-safe to keep some clever competitor from taking it apart to see how it worked, but those were minor problems.

Shaw was content to let the Tomodachians play with the biologicals until they solved the larger issues. Meanwhile, he would continue to fund them. When you owned 51 percent of ShawPharm Inc., the largest pharmaceutical company in the galaxy, with branch offices on forty of the fifty-some planets and many of the more substantial wheelworlds, money was not a worry. The contingent from Tomodachi had come to report on their progress, and they'd have their hands out when they finished. He could give them half a billion without having to call the accountants, but they'd only ask for a few million; they really had no idea how valuable their work would be when it finally got to market. Of course, that might take five years, but no matter. As long as he could keep all his options covered.

If you could make something go away by throwing money at it, it wasn't really much of a problem. Too bad hormones and glands couldn't be bought off so damned easily . . .

The meeting ran longer than Shaw had expected and now he had to hurry—Baba Ngumi absolutely did not like to be kept waiting. If Shaw was even a minute late—sometimes even if he was on time—the old man could just decide to up and leave, and if he did, nothing could coax him back for today's lesson. As rich as he was, Shaw's stads were, past the agreed-upon fee, worthless as far as Baba was concerned. That he could have bought the man ten thousand times over, gifted him with more money than the gross national product of some countries to do nothing but teach Shaw for an hour a day, meant exactly nothing to Baba. And no excuse was acceptable—you either wanted to train enough to get there, or you did not.

Shaw had rearranged his workday around his *Kifo Mokono* instruction. His life, actually. He practiced on his own for an hour in the mornings, two hours in the evenings, plus the hour five days a week of private lessons, those last determined by Baba's schedule, which was capricious at best. If Shaw did not drop whatever he was doing for the time upon which Baba decided the stars or planets or whatever were right, then he was out of luck. The old man was a mystic—cranky, and inconsistent, among other less cheerful virtues. But Baba was the galaxy's foremost expert in the little-known martial art of *Kifo Mokono*—"Death's Hand"—and if you wanted to learn it from him, you did it on his terms. End of discussion.

As he hurried across the compound to the private *skuli* he had built for his training, Shaw already knew that the art was not going to be the magic carpet he had hoped. It offered a lot, and he would stay with it for a while longer, but it wasn't going to take him where he truly wanted to go. For he had a secret desire, one he had never told to anybody: He wanted to be a player in the Musashi Flex, that loose agglomeration of close-combat artists who traveled the stellar systems fighting duels with each other. More, he wanted not only to be ranked, he wanted to be the best player of them all.

He wanted to be the deadliest man in the known galaxy.

He smiled at himself. There was a good reason he had never told anybody this desire. They would surely mark him as mad. You are a fucking billionaire a score of times over, and you want to risk getting your head bashed in or your body sliced into bloody ribbons by some psychotic killer? Can we get a psychiatrist over here, stat?

The problem was that he wasn't a natural. Yes, he had

trained so that he was better than good. He had rank in four arts before he had come to Baba Ngumi, but at the top levels, the fighters had something more than training. They had some kind of innate . . . *something*—talent, drive, whatever—that made them more than the sum of their fighting arts. He had seen the best, and they all possessed it, whatever it was. And Shaw knew that this spirit, be it *ki,* or *prana,* or *tenaga dalam* or whatever, was not part of his makeup. He could beat nine out of ten men or mues he was apt to meet on any street on any planet, he was good, but he was not *great,* and that was what it took to be a Top Player in the Flex.

Greatness. Whatever it might be called, you had it or you did not, and if you didn't, you could not buy it. That had been a hard lesson, one he had fought against learning for fifteen years. He was young, only forty T.S. He was in outstanding physical condition. He was smart and he was rich and he *wanted* it, God, he wanted it! He had believed he could not be denied. He could afford the best teachers, and he had never failed at anything he had truly desired. Business, women, whatever, he set his sights on a goal and he, by Jesu, *achieved* it! Always had, no matter what the odds against it; always would—so he had thought. He had never had reason to think otherwise. He'd really believed that.

He had paid some of the best Flexers to come and spar with him, offered them small fortunes to do it. Men who were ranked in the Teens had come to his private school. Beat me and double your fee, he had told them.

They had all left twice as wealthy as they'd expected. All of them.

It had been painful. Physically, to be sure, but bones could be glued, torn tissues mended. What had hurt more was learning that he was not going to be able to defeat the Top Players no matter how much training he had. No matter how much he wanted it. Training and desire weren't enough. He needed something they had that he didn't. And it wasn't for sale.

There had been a time of despair.

But because he was smart and rich, he came to realize he had other options. There was a way to give himself an edge. If he couldn't do it one way, he could do it another. And if the fucking rock apes would stop dying, he would get it . . .

Baba was waiting when he got to the *skuli*. Just standing there, not doing anything, staring at a blank wall. He was a short, wizened, dark-skinned man pushing eighty-five; if you saw him in a market or at a restaurant, you would not have a clue that he had once been among the deadliest fighting men alive, retired at his peak—Third, amazing for a man his size—and that he *still* was more dangerous than a bagful of Mtuan vipers. Appearances were deceiving—if you believed this little old fellow was innocuous and thought to push him around, you would regret it—assuming he let you live to do so.

Without turning to look at him, Baba said, "Position One."

Baba did not believe in warming up or stretching. If you had a scheduled duel, yes, you could do that, but if you were attacked suddenly, if you saw a situation coming that was only a matter of seconds away, then you had better be ready to deal with it immediately. You would not be able to hold up your hand to an attacker bent on smashing your face and say, *Hold up there, fellowman, I need to loosen up first, okay?*

Knives? Oh, but I left my knife at home—wait right here, I'll go fetch it . . . Shaw had to smile at the thought.

"Something is funny?" Baba said. Given that his back was still turned to Shaw and he couldn't possibly see Shaw's face, this was, despite the number of times similar things had happened, still amazing.

"No, Baba."

"Then do not break your concentration. Position One."

Shaw nodded. "Yes, Baba."

Shaw slid his feet into the pose, right forward, left back, parallel and square with his shoulders, knees slightly bent. He kept his back straight, circled his hands so that his left was low, in front of his groin, and his right just under his chin, both clenched into tight fists. He took a deep breath, expelled half of it slowly, and began the dance with an imaginary opponent. Later, Baba would have him hammer the hydraulic bag, the wooden man, and dance through the small forest of hanging bleakballs. And if it went well, maybe Baba would show him a new combination. But he had best concentrate on his form, first. If he messed that up, Baba would walk away, and that would be that.

As much as he respected the old man, he also hated him. Once he had learned what Baba had to teach him, Shaw was fairly certain he was going to have the old bastard killed. Not only would that keep anybody else from learning Baba's tricks, it would be personally most satisfying . . .

3

In the run-down section of Madrid the locals impolitely called *Ciudad de las Putas,* Cayne Sola crouched behind a recycling bin where the two fighters couldn't see her. The bin was heaped full of scrap plastic, mostly clotted food containers and beer bottles gone alcoholically fragrant in the summer sun. Not the most pleasant combination of odors, though she had smelled worse. She was, as usual, a little excited and a little afraid, but not so much so that she wasn't doing her job. The two men were only ten or twelve meters away, the holoproj pen-cam she had quikstik-mounted on the bin's rim fed its narrowcast digital sig to the loup mounted on the left lens of her shades, and she had a fairly good view. Even if they happened to see the cam, they likely wouldn't mark it for what it was.

The cam, with one of the new photomutable-gel lenses, was voxax-controlled by a wireless patch mike on her throat. The whole system had cost her three months' pay. She subvocalized the words "medium-wide angle," and got a better shot.

The larger of the two men was very big, pushing two meters and probably over a hundred kilos; despite that, his moves were lithe, almost snakelike, as he circled his hands up and down, back and forth, forming and re-forming strange, hypnotic gestures that looked to her almost as if they were some kind of sign language.

The smaller man, who was exceedingly fair, nearly an albino in his paleness, though he had jet hair and eyebrows, laughed, and said, "You don't really think that old *kuji-kiri* weave is going to work on me, do you, Al?"

"Who knows? You could be almost as stupid as you look."

She had always found that part interesting—that these guys knew each other well enough to joke, but that they would fight until one or the other was too injured to go on. Or was dead.

Pale chuckled and circled to his left, his right side forward. Snake—that would be Al—moved an equal amount to his left, keeping the distance between them identical, not quite close enough to cover with one jump. It was an exacting dance, the intricacies of which Sola was only beginning to be able to see, even after almost two months of investigation. It was like watching chess or maybe *Go* between two masters; each step, no matter how small, had meaning. A misplaced foot, and the response would be fast and maybe deadly.

Snake shuffled forward a hair, then back.

Pale held his ground, his hands raised in front of his chest. Neither man had weapons. She was glad of that. They bled enough when it was fists and boots and elbows; with weapons, it was much worse.

Sola looked at the blinking diode on the loup's heads-up display. Still green, so the batteries were good for at least another hour, way more than enough time. It wouldn't do to run out of power in the middle of recording—that had happened during a duel on Mtu last month, and she'd missed some spectacular footage. She wasn't going to be able to ask those guys for a reshoot, since one of them was dead and the other had gone straight to a medical center to be glued back together. Too bad for them, but she was more concerned for what she'd lost.

Another few matches, and she'd have enough for the whole documentary. Yeah, it was all spec, but she was sure she could sell it—the entcom market was like a starving monster, it was always hungry for the new and different, and nobody had done an in-depth work on the Musashi Flex before—bits and pieces, sure, but nothing nearly as deep as what Sola had. A primecast hour-and-a-half, easy, and with any luck at all, she could get a miniseries, three, maybe five segs, system syndications, maybe even GalaxNet—wouldn't *that* be something? She could write her own ticket then, direct, produce, she'd be set, and only twenty-eight T.S. years old. That would give that fucking father something to think about, seeing her name on the 'proj.

It was a nice fantasy, being rich and famous. She'd have to stop chasing it pretty soon, because she was gonna be out of stads. And if she couldn't sell this, she was going to have to get a *job,* and *there* was a sad prospect . . .

Pale and Al, the giant snake, continued to circle, and while she had learned the moves all meant something, if not always what, a general audience wouldn't know that much, so she'd better spice things up some.

"Two-shot, closer," she subvocalized.

The cam's POV snapped in tighter. What a great toy. It should be, it cost enough.

"Solarize, refield, refade to previous shot," she said.

The color washed out to a bright monochrome, then faded back in to the same image. Yeah, she could do all this on the editing comp later, but the more you could do in-cam, the better—it saved you a lot of work when you did EFX on the fly, plus in the moment, your instincts gave you a better flow. Usually. And hell, if it didn't work, you could always fix it later—

Al lunged, moving in very fast, and fired a punch at Pale's face—

Pale didn't back up, but angled to the outside of the incoming strike—

"Wider!" she said, louder than she'd intended. "Include both!"

The cam's field expanded, to include the fighters' feet. Yes, yes, she needed that—

Pale ducked and shot a punch under Al's incoming fist, hit him under the armpit, hard. Sola heard something break—whether it was Al's rib or Pale's hand she couldn't tell, but it was another sound she had learned to recognize, that wet snap of bone cracking—

Al grunted with pain, then dropped lower and brought his elbow down, trapping Pale's hand against his injured ribs. With his other hand, he slapped at Pale's ear, but continued past, shoved his hand under the man's jaw, and wrenched his head backward—

Pale tried to step away from it, but Al hooked his left heel behind Pale's ankle, and Pale went horizontal suddenly, falling straight back. He was going to hit the plast-crete hard—

—but no, somehow, Pale twisted and turned the fall into an angled dive, hit on one shoulder, rolled, dived again, with Al chasing him. Pale came up, spun, and was ready when Al got there. He kicked, his left boot connecting with Al's knee. Another gristlelike *pop!* and Al wobbled to the side, turned, awkwardly, and put his weight on his good leg.

Pale stayed back. "That's the lateral ligament, Al. Plus the rib. Time to pack it in."

Al shook his head. "Fuck you, Timson!"

"You wish. Come on. Lose gracefully. It's only a few

points. You could maybe dance the rib, but you can't win with that knee fucked-up."

"You might be surprised."

"Hell, we'd both be surprised, you more than me. Come on. It's not like you have to give me your tag. We'll catch a hack to a medic, and you can call it in. This is a done deal. No point in suffering any more damage, hey?"

Al didn't say anything. He was apparently thinking about the offer.

Take it, Al, Sola thought. *I don't need footage of another guy getting beat to a bloody mess, I got plenty of that already. Show some class, that'll look good on the holoproj nets—*

"Tell you what, take the deal, and you can have first turn with the girl hiding behind the bin. She looks like she's got plenty enough juice for me when an old crip like you gets done."

Sola went cold, as if a bucket of liquid nitrogen had splashed on her. *Shit!*

She didn't hesitate. She grabbed her cam, broke the quik-stik loose from the bin, and ran, terrified.

Behind her, she heard loud laughter. From both men.

Shame blended with her terror. The bastards! She wanted to go back and give them each a blast from the hand wand she had tucked into her back pocket. Let them wake up with nasty fucking headaches in half an hour to regret having frightened her that way. But she was angry, not stupid. Flexers who fought unarmed did so from choice, not necessity. They certainly carried more weapons than she did, and were unquestionably better with them. Both of the men were bigger and stronger than she, and she had no desire to wake up in an alley naked and sore, her body abused and her valuable cam and gear gone. They could do that without a second thought, use her and steal her stuff. She knew about men, violent men. Local authorities wouldn't have much sympathy for a loco woman who wandered around the City of Whores alone, spying on duelists. Got robbed and raped? *Siento*. Too bad.

Fuck. She hated being afraid, but she wasn't suicidal. She would go back to her hotel, dump today's footage into the editing comp, fiddle with it a little. It was getting pretty warm out here anyway, and the local custom of *siesta* didn't sound so bad . . .

The raw recording was good, but nothing spectacular. She reviewed it on the loup as she walked toward her hotel. Well. That didn't matter so much by itself. She had lots of medium-level fighter stuff to go with it. Hours and hours and hours, maybe sixty, sixty-five all total. All she really needed was a climax, something really righteous to point it all toward. A crux.

The gods must have been listening. She was crossing a new retroplaza with a high-tech shopping kiosk surrounding it when she saw Lazlo Mourn coming out of a shoe store.

She knew it was him, she didn't need to check her records, she could ID all the current—as of three days past, anyway—Top Twenty Players by sight; she knew their bios, their match histories, everything that was available on the ed- and entcom nets about them. So far, she hadn't seen any of them fight, though she had just missed one between Orleans Plinck and Monroe Rouge on the frontier world Greaves, in Orm System, three weeks earlier. A chance to see Top Five Players clash, and she had gotten there too late. By two fucking minutes.

There had been witnesses, a couple of Confed troopers who happened to be passing by, and she interviewed them, got some pix, but they weren't much help. Plinck, who was ranked Third, and Rouge, Fifth, had taken all of five seconds from start to finish. The Confed troopers, two wet-bottom conscripts just out of basic on their first tour, couldn't begin to tell her how it had happened. One second, the two were squared off, maybe two, three meters apart, the next thing they saw, Rouge was down and unconscious or dead, and Plinck was searching him for his tag. They had been blurs to the Confed watchers, despite whatever basic fighting skills they had gotten in training.

Damn!

That was as close as she had come to the best working. But Lazlo Mourn was consistently in and out of the Top Twenty. *His current rank, as of, let's see, two days ago, was . . . Eleventh?* She'd have to check that to be sure, but it wouldn't be a place or more away in either direction. Could be Twelfth. Maybe even Tenth.

This was a blast of good luck, like a cool breeze on a hot day. Mourn, here. He might not have anything going at the moment, but sooner or later, he would. A few years back, Mourn had really liked to mix it up; he fought three or four times a month when he could find players worth his effort, though he had been quiet lately. If she could stay with him, she'd get a capper for the documentary, almost certainly.

She watched him pass by, a clear plastic tube with a pair of flexsoles in it under his arm. He didn't appear to be paying any attention to his surroundings, but she knew better than that. You didn't get to be among the most expert hand-to-hand fighters in the galaxy by sleepwalking. She would have to be very careful following him, else he'd spot her pretty quick.

She had an edge. She had spent three weeks learning sub-rosa surveillance techniques from Carl "The Shadow" Denali, an expert security agent formerly with Confederation Intelligence and now in the private sector, who, it was said, could track a black gnat at midnight in a sootstorm. We're So Glad Entertainment, for whom she had been working at the time, had paid for the course—she'd have never been able to afford it, and it had been worth it as far she had been concerned. She had gotten footage of several dirty pols using that training, crooked politicians being one of We're So Glad's prime exposé subjects. Fortunately, after they had parted company, Denali's training was hers to continue using. They could take your company ID chit, but they couldn't take what was inside your head. Not yet, anyway.

You could, Denali had taught the class, secretly tail a man who checked to see if he was being followed—if you were very careful. Sola had practiced the techniques dozens of times since she'd learned them, seeing what worked and what didn't, and she had gotten pretty good at it, so she figured. A lot of it had to do with attitude. You had to be focused in such a way that the subject couldn't feel you watching him. You had to be elsewhere when he looked for a tail. He looked behind himself, you needed to be across the street; he looked across the street, you needed to be in front of him; he looked in front of himself, you needed to be behind him. You had to dope out his patterns before he spotted you, and if you could, he wouldn't know you were there.

She allowed Mourn to get twenty meters ahead, then she angled across the street to parallel him.

The first time he checks, it'll be behind him, Denali had taught her. *It's almost instinctive. If he doesn't see anything there that trips an alarm, next he'll look to the sides. Then if he's savvy, he'll scope any pedestrians or vehicles in front of him. You need to be one shift ahead of him all the time. And the tricky part is, you need to be able to rotate it randomly, because he won't look back, sideways, and to the front sequentially after the first time, he'll mix it up. But a good shadow will figure out what he is going to do before he does it. It's a skill, an art. It takes constant practice . . .*

She grinned to herself. Jesu knew she had done enough of that. When you were a freelance investigative journalist in a very competitive market, you either got good at what you did or you went on the dole. So far, Sola had managed to keep from having to do that. This guy was canny, and he'd be alert, but he was just a man. Put his pants on one leg at a time like everybody else did. She could do this. She *would* do it—and if she pulled it off, it would help make her rep. The woman who tracks professional killers. Cayne Sola, ghost-at-large, the wraith, the invisible girl . . .

It was all in your attitude.

Yeah, well, if you are so hot, how come those two dim-bulb midthirties-ranked Flexers back in the alley spotted you, hmm?

She shook her head. A fluke. They had been so easy to tail, she had relaxed too much, that was all. Probably they had heard her when she did the cam command was all.

Uh-huh. Sure.

Okay, fine. She'd be more careful.

She moved her position several times as Mourn walked down the street. Now and then, he'd slow or stop to look into a shop window. She was certain he hadn't spotted her.

He went into a flickstik and smoke shop a few blocks up the street, a small storefront place. She parked herself at a cafe across the road so she could look out the window, ordered a drink, paid in advance, in case she had to leave in a hurry. The smell of the city was a mix of dust and exhaust and dried herbs from the shop.

She saw Mourn in the doorway a few minutes later, and she stood to exit. Just as she did, an electric bus pulled to the curb across from her, blocking him from view.

When the vehicle left, there was no sign of her quarry.

Shit! He got on the bus!

She hurried down the street. There were enough traffic signals so the bus wouldn't be able to get too far ahead too fast.

She looked around for a hack, but of course, there weren't any empties in sight. Always worked that way.

At a speed somewhere between a fast walk and a slow jog, Sola managed to keep pace with the bus for two blocks. It stopped twice, people got on or off, and she didn't mark Mourn among those leaving. As it pulled over to pick up and disgorge passengers the third time, she crossed the street and watched. She couldn't spot Mourn through the windows on her side, nor did he appear to have alighted with the half dozen or so others who just got off.

Damn!

She ran to the bus, got on, waved her credit cube over the reader, and started down the aisle. He hadn't seen her, and she hated to give him a chance to mark her so quick, but there was no help for it. Traffic signals or not, she couldn't keep up with a bus on foot for much longer.

She walked all the way to the back and no two ways about it, Lazlo Mourn wasn't here.

Well . . . fuck!

Luna Azul—a name she had invented—stood in the shadows of a warehouse in Chambee Town, on Wu, in Haradali, and watched the Confed's Assault Team storm the building across the street. It was cold, and there had been a dusting of powdery snow earlier in the day, just enough to make everything look clean and fresh.

Beauty, before the beast arrived . . .

The CAT unit steamed in, no finesse, just raw power: Fifty troopers in full body armor, using .177 Parkers, pop-grenades, puke gas, and polarized smoke. A four-person CI team ran the op—they were not in front, but they weren't at the back, either.

The spookeyed troops could work in near darkness, and with her own spookeyes up and running, she had no trouble seeing them hit the place.

Doors blew in, walls crumbled, and the would-be terrorists inside would be going down like weeds in front of a power mower, cut to bloody shards before they had a chance to mount any kind of defense.

Score another one for UO—undercover operative—what was that name? ah, yes, Luna Azul, of Confederation Intelligence. The cell was wiped out, and the lesson plain—conspire against the Confed and get caught, the price was exceedingly expensive—it would cost you your ass.

Why did people risk it? The Confed wasn't the most benevolent organization, to be sure, but overall, it kept the galaxy stable, and it probably did almost as much good as harm, give or take. It damn sure *was* a giant, and no handful of malcons meeting in a run-down goods storehouse on some back-rocket world was going to knock the Confed down. How could they think otherwise? It's one thing to sling a rock at a giant and catch him by surprise. It's another thing to try throwing stones at an M-Class tank tracking you on Doppler with smart guns locked, moving in at speed. Best say a final prayer quickly, because you were about to leave this life for whatever was waiting in the next . . .

That there were fourteen people dead or dying in the wreck of a building and that she had sent the ones who'd done it? Not her problem. Once upon a time, she worried about it: The dead people had children, spouses, maybe parents who loved them, and all of that . . . went away, because of her. But those worries had eventually faded to twinges, and the twinges were few and far between. If you want to play, you have to be willing to pay. If you had small children at home, what the fuck were you doing plotting against the Confed? It wasn't as if there was anybody with a working brain who didn't know that treason was a mind-wipe-punishable crime. Dead or brainless in a medical kiosk, what was the difference? Probably not a lot

of spouses wanted to bring the kiddies by to visit Daddy in
stasis, where he was waiting to be cut up for spare parts.
The dead and dying here weren't spitting on the sidewalk
or shoplifting, they were planning revolution. They knew
the risks. They might not think anybody would catch them,
but that was a big mistake, wasn't it?

She pushed the spookeyes up onto her forehead and
turned away, suddenly a little tired. It always had a same-
ness to it. People could be so fucking stupid. They deserved to be removed from the gene pool.

A few minutes later, Marky, the Lead Operative, came
over. "It's a done deal," he said. "Twelve klags DOA, one
more on the way there, one alive enough to maybe har-
vest a bit more intel from before he goes in the box. Good
job, op."

She shrugged. "What they pay me for."

"We'll have it clean in a few minutes. Where you off to,
next?"

"Classified, LO," she said. She gave him her professional smile.

"Of course. Sorry."

She wanted to shake her head. These Assault Team Ops
were always so stick-up-the-ass deadly serious. No jokes,
all business.

And where was she going next? Vacation. She'd earned
it. She'd done twenty-five ops in the last eighteen months,
one for every year she'd been alive, lacking one. She had a
thick bank account, and she needed a break. Maybe she'd
try one of the pleasure casinos. Or do some sight-seeing on
one of the scenic planets. Get herself a boytoy and hole up
in some hotel with silk sheets and room service, not get out
of bed for week.

Or maybe it was time try to find her brother. She had
been thinking about tracing him for a long time, just never
had gotten around to it. Her parents were dead, and her

brother was her only blood kin in the universe—assuming he hadn't died—and she was curious. She had been a late baby, an accident, and her brother was twenty years older than she was, two years gone from their rabbit hole of a home by the time she'd been conceived—they'd never actually seen each other. He hadn't looked back, and she couldn't blame him for that. Far as she knew, he didn't know she'd ever been born.

Of course, he could be long dead like their parents, too. Did she really want to know one way or the other? If she didn't look, she could keep thinking he was still alive out there. Mated, maybe, a couple of kids, a good job, a happy life. Wouldn't that be something?

Or he could have been cooked robbing a casino. Or maybe in one of these revolutionary cells—maybe she had sicced the CATs on him herself?

She shook her head. Not likely, given the breadth of the galaxy, but possible. Did she want to know *that* if it was true?

Well. She didn't have to decide today. First thing, she was going to go sit in a hot soak tub, have a stein of good beer, then go sleep for about thirty hours. Undercover work was stressful. Yeah, she was good at it, as good as anybody, but you never could truly relax when you were down in the trench—an offhand and thoughtless remark could get you chilled. That was part of the game, too. A caught spy didn't fare well.

Rest, first. After that, she'd see.

She caught a hack, gave it directions, and leaned back in the seat. But before she was halfway to her kiosk, her com vibrated against her hip. Nobody had the code but her bosses, and there was no way not to answer the call—they'd have her on sat-track, would know where she was and that her com was on. She lit her confounder to scramble any electronic eavesdroppers and voxaxed the comm's ear implant.

"What?" She kept it subvocal; even somebody sitting in the hack next to her would have had trouble hearing her.

"Chim City, on Tatsu," the gravelly voice of Commander Pachel said without preamble. "An op will meet you at the boxcar station with details up when you get on-planet."

"Fuck they will. I'm on vacation as of ten minutes ago. Send somebody else."

"Can't do it. You're the only op in the system rated for this, and it's just the next world over. There's an e-ticket on file at the uplift station three klicks ahead of your hack."

Yeah, they were tracking her. Knew to within half a meter exactly where she was.

"I quit."

He laughed softly. "You can't quit, girl. This is an A-dash-one-slash-A directly from Wu's PR Newman Randall Himself. All leaves are canceled, all excuses dust in the wind. You *will* catch the next boxcar up and hop over there and see what the Planet Rep wants, end of discussion."

A-1/A. As high as things ever got in her biz, though that didn't always scan. "Does this asshole have a clue what that kind of rating means? What is it about?"

"His family is rich enough to buy the planet you're on, plus the one you're going to, and burn them to warm their hands if they feel like it. It doesn't matter if he can't tell the difference between a top priority code and his left nut. You didn't just fall off the vegetable hauler to town, Luna. When money calls, the Service answers. I don't know what he wants, I don't *want* to know. Go, see what it is, handle it, call me when you are done and tell me all about how clever you were fixing it. Take your vacation afterward."

"This sucks."

"Well, if it did, at least it would be useful for something. I didn't write the game, I just move the pieces."

Pachel cut the connection and the com shut off.

Fuck. Fuck, fuck, fuck . . .

Wu. She'd only been there once or twice. Best she brush

up on the place. She lit the com and called the Confed general information computer. "Wu," she said. "Sixty-minute encap. Include history, politics, geography, sociology."

"Wu," the computer began. "First planet settled in the Haradali System . . ."

She leaned back and listened.

4

From the inside of a two-passenger fuel-cell hack directly behind her bus, Mourn watched the woman discover that he wasn't on the pubtrans vehicle. The hack's windshield was polarized so he could see her, but it was opaque from the other side. Even if she looked this way, she wouldn't make him.

She was surprised and irritated that she'd lost him, he could see that much in her face and body language.

He smiled. She wasn't bad, but you had to be very good to walk in his tracks without being seen. There were always a few stupid players who weren't above backshooting a high rank and trying to claim they'd beaten him fairly. They thought they could beat the stress scanners or face readers, and, of course, nobody did, but you didn't want to be the man they assassinated for their two-minute bragging rights. There were cools and Confed intel to worry about, and other legit players. You walked in a fog, didn't pay attention, you wouldn't survive long.

He was curious, though not particularly worried. The woman's shadowing technique was good enough so he knew she had training. She could be some kind of terran or Confed agent, a local cool, maybe even private op, but somehow, it didn't feel as if she were any of these.

Maybe she was a player, though if she was, she wasn't ranked in the Hundred. There were plenty of fems in the game, though only a few were in the Hundred; he knew most of the currents by sight, and most of those specialized in armed stuff. The ones who went bare tended to be fairly big and strong, they had to be. It wasn't as if a woman couldn't get the same skills as a man, she could, but small men didn't fare that well in the top ranks, either. In hand-to-hand combat, just like it did with knives, size mattered. The toughest competitors tended to be in the light heavyweight class—big and strong enough to deliver power, not too big to move well. A featherweight might be fast, but his—or her—skill had to be extraordinary to keep up with somebody who was thirty or forty kilos heavier and much stronger. At the highest levels, *every*body was well trained. There had been some little guys who were that good, so their skill could overcome the size disparity, couple of them fems, but only a relative handful. The odds were against it. Last time he'd looked, of the current Top Twenty players, thirteen were light heavies; there were four heavies, an ultraheavy, a middleweight, and only one lightweight. Two of the light heavies were women, one of them an HG mue. The lightweight, Tak Houghton Clar Besser, of Mti, was a master of weapons, and had cut his way into Eighteenth, last time Mourn checked.

As the woman made her way to the bus's exit, he shook his head. No. She didn't have the look of a player. She was young, reasonably fit, had red hair trimmed short, wore middle-class clothes—a loose green silk shirt over snug pants, flexsoles, and had a big carry bag on a shoulder strap. Attractive enough, midtwenties or so. He saw what he took to be the somewhat-disguised outline of a hand wand tucked into a back pocket, so she was armed, but a lot of cits carried in the big cities on the old worlds, even if it was against local laws. The thinking went that it was better to have explain your illegal weapon to the cools than it was for them to have to tell your family you were dead.

She didn't move like a fighter, though.

A fan, maybe? There were plenty of those floating around, and more than a few had wanted to lie next to him. People who got off on what they thought was the danger of being with a player. Star-fuckers. He had bedded a few of those. Not any lately. It seemed to be more trouble than it was worth.

A lot of his life seemed more trouble than it was worth lately.

He sighed. Maybe he really should give serious consideration to retiring. Start a little school, train the wanna-bes, get drunk now and then, maybe find a comfortable woman . . .

She alighted from the bus and started walking back the way the vehicle had come, a tight anger in her moves. No, he decided, she wasn't a fan who wanted to swap fluids. You don't get invited into a man's bed if you take great pains to keep him from seeing you, now do you?

There were other possibilities: A thief, stalking him? A relative, bent on vengeance for somebody he had taken out along the way?

He made it a point to look like everybody else, no flashy jewelry, no expensive clothes, nothing to draw attention to himself. Just Art Average on his way from nowhere to no place special. Not a target for the Confed, the cools, nor the bents.

Not an op, not a player, not a fan or a thief, he decided. Maybe somebody's sib or kin or spouse, come to pay him back for her loss. But not a real threat if so, now that he had marked her. And, somehow, the wounded spouse didn't feel right, either.

Did he really care enough to worry about it?

He directed the hack driver to the curb, paid him with a couple of hardcurry coins, and stepped out onto the sidewalk. He watched the woman walk away and decided: Yes, he did care—at least enough to tail her and find out who she was. It had been a while since anything had made him really curious.

Shaw would have spent a few minutes in the spa, with the mint-scented hot water swirling over his tired body, stuck a pain patch on his deltoid, and gone to bed after his lesson with Baba. The old man had thumped the hell out of him today, and he was physically spent and sore, but he couldn't relax yet. His secretary called to tell him that the Confederation Planet Representative, Newman Randall, was waiting in his office, and you didn't just tell the Confed Rep to go home and come back tomorrow, even if the sucker showed up unannounced. Not a man who could shut down your business on this world with a wave of his hand, were he so disposed. Not that he would—big money didn't fuck with other big money, generally speaking, but he *could,* so power respected power.

So Shaw had settled for a quick shower and clean clothes and headed back to his office.

It was a beautiful late-spring afternoon. A big thunderstorm gathered itself a few miles out from Chim City, flashing and grumbling, working its way toward the metroplex. The air was warm, but not overly hot, and the smell of mtawbi blossoms, that cedar-trunk-and-musk scent, wafted over him as he walked across the company courtyard. The gardeners did a good job here; everything was trimmed and neat, a man-made and -maintained riot of color and pleasing odors.

His staff knew he was coming, and the security cams made certain they knew when he'd reached the building.

Everybody was alert, doing their jobs, attentive. They smiled and nodded as he passed.

Being the boss did have its perks.

He met Randall as he entered the outer office.

"Ah, Newman. Good to see you again."

"And you, Ellis."

Of course they were on a first-name basis, the richest man on-planet and the Confed's highest-ranked rep on this world, who was also considerably well off. Randall's family was old money, and he had gone into the diplomatic corps as had his father, uncles, aunts, and sibs before him; it was part of what one did if one didn't have to take over the family business. One served.

"Come in, come in," Shaw said. "Lillie has offered you a drink, some smoke or dust?"

"Yes, of course."

"Sorry to have kept you waiting."

"Not to worry. I should have called for an appointment. I just happened to be in the area and thought I'd stop in."

Shaw fought the urge to smile. Just happened to be in the area? *There* would be a cold day in the tropical regions of Hell.

Once they were in the inner office and his assistant had come and gone with tea and silver trays bearing tiny spirals of kick-dust, a legal version made in his own labs, Shaw smiled and they made small talk. How were Newman's spouses and children?—he was in a group marriage, five men and three women—matters of Confederation concern, the state of business and the markets. He did not look at his chrono, but Shaw knew that this chitchat would last four minutes. That was enough to be polite, not so much as to waste time.

When the niceties had been covered, Shaw got to it: "So, what can I do for you, Newman?"

"Sorry to hear about the rock apes," he said.

Shaw's smile didn't falter. He inclined his head in a slow nod. "Thank you," he said. "I appreciate your concern."

To admit surprise at Randall's knowledge or his revelation thereof would have been a weak move. To pretend he didn't know what the man was talking about would have been impolite—and useless anyhow. If you are caught, his father had taught him, at least have the good grace to acknowledge it like a man.

Inwardly, he cursed. Randall was adept at diplo-speak, a kind of verbal fugue in which much was meant while little was actually *said*. His comment about the apes spoke volumes. The research involving those creatures was secret—nobody outside of the labs was supposed to know anything about it, save for Cervo and Shaw himself. It was his private project. So Newman Randall had a spy in the labs, possibly bioelectronic, but more likely one of Shaw's employees had been socially engineered.

That Randall knew of the project *and* what it was meant also that the Confederation was interested in it, and not just because Shaw's particular line of research was technically not quite legal. Such an interest of course, Shaw would expect. A drug that would speed human reaction time and physical movement without major side effects? The Confed military would drool. A well-trained soldier who was a third or half again as fast as an enemy? That would be worth enough to put it on a restricted schedule and limit production for official Confederation uses only. Not that such a thing would be a problem; nor would it keep the opposition from eventually getting its hands on it, either. Shaw hadn't been working on the stuff to make stads anyway. If he went up and down the streets shoveling thousand-stad notes out of the back of a van all day every day forever, he'd still be making more in interest on his principal than he could get rid of shoveling it into the street. At his level, you didn't even need to keep score any longer; that much money was a force unto itself.

That Randall had given up his spy by speaking of the apes meant that either he thought the man—or woman— was untouchable, or that he didn't care if Shaw removed him or her. Mazes within mazes, gears meshing with gears, this was how the game went at this level, though none of it was a threat to his own purpose. Still, he would have to root out and eliminate the spy. Traitors couldn't be brooked.

The pause for these thoughts was short, broken by Randall: "I'll get right to the point," he said. "We are willing to overlook, um, the *irregularities* concerning the CDA protocols of this new pharmaceutical. But we would like to be kept up to speed on its development."

"You don't slap me on the hand and you get first shot at it," Shaw said.

"Just so."

"And when it is perfected, if you like what you see, you will grab it for the Confed military in an exclusive run."

Randall smiled, leaned back in the form-chair, and sipped at his tea.

For the sake of form, Shaw knew he had to protest. Such was expected. He was rich and powerful, and if he didn't kick, Randall would be quick to wonder why. "This drug could be worth a great deal of money to my company."

"If it works, it certainly shall be. But you won't miss a meal if it never turned a demistad. And we would want to keep the production limited to those who would not misuse it."

"Which, of course, the Confed would never do."

"Oh, of course not."

They both smiled at that one.

"And if I decide to stand up for my rights to the free market, I suppose my CDA approval might be particularly taxing. Might not be forthcoming at all?"

"It is always a pleasure to deal with a man of the galaxy about such matters." He sipped more tea. "What are you calling it again? The drug?"

If he knew about the rock apes, he fucking well knew the name, but there was no point in being ungracious. Randall thought he had the upper hand; let him continue to think so. "Well. We haven't decided on a marketing strategy, it's much too soon. We've been calling it 'Reflex,' though that's just a working name."

Randall nodded. Nothing new to him. "My. Look at the time. I must be off, my spouses will be wondering where I am. So good to see you, as always, Ellis." He stood.

Shaw stood and gave the man his best fake high-wattage smile. "And it's good to see you again, Newman. My best to the family."

After he was gone, Shaw said, "Cervo."

The bodyguard seemed to materialize from nowhere, though he had actually been watching through a one-way panel from a hidden room behind Shaw's desk. "Sir?"

"You heard about the spy."

"Yes, sir."

"Find out who it is. Don't do anything to them yet, just find out."

"Yes, sir."

Cervo left, a human tank in whose path you did not want to step.

He had to do that, it would be expected, and the fucking Confed would try to slip somebody else in to replace the spy, even though there was no real need. Besides, he might get some good use from the spy, whoever it was.

As for the Confed, it could take all the Reflex it wanted. He'd still make a profit, and all he needed was a personal supply and exclusive use of it for long enough to achieve his goal. That wasn't going to be a problem. He owned more than half of the company. When he said "Jump," there was a thundering chorus of "How high?" in return. This was as it should be.

He would have his drug. The Confed wouldn't start bleeding it all over the galaxy until human protocols were finished, at least a couple of years, so that was plenty of time. Assuming, of course, the rock apes stopped dying. And that the humans brought in for the next round of tests didn't themselves *start* dying.

The Confed could be a pain in the ass, but for men like Shaw, the balm of great monies could soothe things. What the poor people did when the Confederation slapped them? Well, life was unfair. That wasn't his worry.

Sola, feeling hot and irritated, made it back to her hotel room and fell on the bed. She was sure Mourn hadn't spotted her. It was just bad luck she had lost him. Damn! That was twice now she had fuzzed an opportunity to get material that would focus her project. She might be able to cast around and find Mourn again—it was a big city, but she might be able to run him down.

Or not. If she couldn't, something else would turn up. She was too close to victory to lose. Something would turn up.

But before she did anything else, a cool shower would be good. Fresh clothes, something to eat, a glass of wine, and she would be a new woman, ready to kick the planet's ass, by Jesu!

She stripped, chucking the sweaty shirt and pants into the hamper for the maid, and headed for the shower. They had pretty good water pressure here.

She passed in front of the mirror and took a critical look at her nude body. Not too bad, she decided. She could lose a kilo or two from her hips, which had always been a trifle wide. She did enough walking and gym work to keep pretty toned. She was a little taller than average, maybe 170 centimeters, and probably went fifty-eight, fifty-nine kilograms, and none of it too jiggly.

She turned around, looked over her shoulder at her rear end. Definitely needed to drop a kilo and tighten that part up, though. You couldn't let fat get ahead of you. She had been chubby as a little girl, and had worked hard to slim down. It was a lot easier to maintain shape than it was to get there in the first place. Well. When she got rich from selling her documentary, maybe she would hire a good-looking trainer to travel with her, to keep her fit. She grinned. Another pleasant fantasy.

She spent ten minutes enjoying the needle spray and emerged feeling much cleaner. She dried herself, wrapped the towel around her hips, and went to find some clean clothes.

She jumped and almost screamed when she saw the man sitting in the chair in front of her computer. The holoprojic image above the unit showed a pair of men facing each other with a jungle backdrop. Footage she had shot on Rift? Or was it Lee?

"Nice work, Fem Sola," Lazlo Mourn said. He looked at her and smiled. "Nice shape, too."

5

She was aware that she was bare from the waist up, but having him see her half-naked was the least of her worries.

"What are you doing here?"

"Watching part of your documentary," he said. "Waiting for you to finish your shower so we could talk."

She shook her head.

"You aren't going to call security and have me thrown out?" He gave her a small grin. A smile that said he was very much aware that there wasn't enough security in this hotel to remove him if he decided he didn't want to go.

"Asshole," she said under her breath. Louder, she said, "Wait right there." She went to the closest, found a robe, slipped it on and crowed it shut, then wiggled out of the towel and came back to face him. Well. She wasn't slow. He had spotted her, turned the tail around, and followed her, and he already knew who she was and what she was doing.

Sola didn't much like any of that, but it was what it was. You had to admire his skill.

"You wanted to put me in this?" He waved at the image, now frozen into small statues in the air.

"Yes."

"I'm flattered."

"I think maybe you're not so easily flattered, M. Mourn."

"Well, if truth must be told, no."

She nodded.

"Generally, it's not a good idea for players to be *too* well known. I'd hate, at my age, to have to start wearing a skinmask everywhere I went. Why would I want to be in your entcom?"

"I could pay you when it sells."

He smiled again. Had a lot of wrinkles at the corners of his eyes. No surgery to look younger that she could tell. He said, "I have a fair amount of stads tucked away I'm not using. See this?" He pulled a hand wand from his pocket and waved it. "The maker of this little toy pays me a couple thousand a month to endorse it. I also have armored clothes, slap-caps, blades, and a particular medical service I use when I can, all of whom also pay me so they can put my name in their ads. Just my name, not my face. There are a few big-time gamblers who cover the matches that like me enough to let me in on their action. I actually do real well. Probably a lot better than you."

She knew that. "How about my undying gratitude?"

He laughed. "There was a time what an offer like that from a beautiful woman would have been irresistible."

"Not now?"

"Not for a while, no."

"What would it take?"

He smiled again. He stood, moving with the grace of a professional athlete.

"You're leaving?"

"Yes. I found out what I came for. Good luck on your project, fem." He started for the door.

"Wait. Don't go."

He paused. Raised an eyebrow.

She looked at him. He was an attractive enough man, she was an adult. She started to make the offer: "What if I . . . ?" She stopped. Shook her head.

He chuckled.

"You knew what I was going to say?"

He shrugged. "I believe so. Why didn't you finish it?"

"Would it have done any good? Offering to sleep with you?"

"I expect not."

"That's why I didn't say it."

He nodded. Started to turn away again. He didn't need money or fame. A man like him wouldn't have any trouble finding company for sex. He had traveled the galaxy, seen its wonders, pitted himself against men and women in hand-to-hand combat, won many times, and lost a few—so what could she offer him that he didn't already have?

"I'll tell your story," she said.

He looked at her. "For your own ends."

"Of course. But for yours, too."

"Why?"

"Because it matters."

He stood there for what seemed a long time. "You think?"

"Yes." She smiled. She had him!

Then he laughed softly. "This one work for you a lot?"

She had to smile in return, despite herself. "Well. A couple times it has."

He nodded. "You sounded almost sincere."

"I almost was. You don't think people would find your story interesting?"

"Actually, I expect that many would. I'm just not interested in telling it. Nice to have met you, F. Sola. Have a nice life."

Aw, shii, she thought, as he left.

6

The trip to Wu's orbit from Tatsu's was fast and uneventful. Azul caught a boxcar for the drop from the orbital station, and that was just as dull. Half an hour later, she breezed through the checkpoint, courtesy of her priority alpha visa stamp. The ID was as real as anybody's, given its source, but under a different name with a thick, fake background. She smiled as the clerk saw the shimmering hologram appear over his cube reader, watched him raise an eyebrow. They called it DFWM, the stamp. What that meant was, "Don't Fuck With Me," and they didn't give it to you unless you had mondo clout, big stads in your wallet, or high Confederation connections. Sometimes all three. A small perk, and she enjoyed it. Not that she had any such desire, but if she wanted to smuggle sunstones or psycho-erotic drugs, she could, because no customs agent in his or her right mind would dare stop somebody with the stamp. Whoever you were, you had to be important to rate it, and fucking with important people could easily cost you your job. Or worse.

Hey, have a great day, Citizen, and enjoy your trip!

She was ten meters past the checkpoint when an op approached her. He was tall, handsome, probably her age, and built like a gymnast. Nice.

He handed her a marble-sized info ball, smiled, and walked away. Never said a word.

She pocketed the ball. Soon as she found a private spot, she'd pop it into her reader and see what was so fucking important.

But: She saw something that gave her pause. There was a thin, small woman to her left, trying to be invisible.

You couldn't really *be* invisible, not even in one of the state-of-the-art shiftsuits—in those, you could blend into the background pretty damned well, but somebody really looking could spot you, and any decent LOS motion sensor would point right at you. With the right mind-set, however, you could become effectively harder to notice. People's gazes would slide past—sure, they'd *see* you, but they wouldn't pay any *attention* to you, and that was almost as good as being invisible, at least in some circumstances.

The little woman was trying to project that energy, and Azul knew it because it was one of her own tricks.

Now, maybe the little woman didn't have anything to do with her; maybe it was just a coincidence, or maybe she had been set to collect somebody else, but Azul didn't put much stock in coincidence. A top UO blows into port, and there's somebody who is, if you know how to look, a watcher, just standing there?

You might not get to go home if you let one like that slide more than once or twice in your career.

So, assume the little woman was here for her. Okay, no problem, she'd been tailed before, and probably would be again, but the bigger question was, who had sent her?

Not her people. Pachel was a dickhead, but he knew that

if he got caught spying on his own, it would be bad. In her case, she might not be able to pack it in and walk away, but she damn sure could drag her heels on whatever assignment she was on and do it in such a way they'd never be able to prove it for sure without a brain strain. At this point, she was worth more to the Confed with her mind intact, and she knew it, so past a certain point, they wouldn't fuck with her.

So. Who *had* sent the surveillance? And why? Get one, she'd get the other, but she needed to figure that out before she moved too far along in her assignment.

Could be the watcher was from the Confed's Planetary Representative, though that didn't make any sense either. Why bother? She was here by his call, it wasn't as if she was gonna turn around and walk away. The handsome op who'd delivered the info ball was enough. He could have crooked his finger, and she'd have gone with him.

Who did that leave?

Nobody else on this world ought to know who she was. None of the six names for which she had IDs were more than a couple days old, and the newest one she was using for herself? She'd never spoken that one aloud. She was a nonperson to anybody outside CI, and none of her tags should draw any interest at all.

What made sense was, the watcher was connected to the reason the PR had called her here. Maybe somebody had figured out that he'd put out a sig for an undercover op, and they wanted to see who it was.

If that was the case, if she was burned before she ever got out of the fucking groundport, then she might as well turn around and get back on the next boxcar up to the orbital, because the only way she could effectively work was if nobody here knew who she was. Hard to be a sub-rosa op if you are carrying around a big flashing sign that says "Spy!" in glowing letters.

The watcher had probably attached herself to the pretty

boy who had come to give Azul the info ball, and if that
was the case, then the little woman who was trying to be invisible now knew who she was, and it was game over.

Azul kept walking as she considered all this, trying to
look unconcerned. Abruptly, the solution to this last problem welled up in her thoughts. If there was but one watcher
set to find her, if there wasn't another one dogging her
tracks, then maybe things could be . . . repaired.

First, she had to determine what the situation was, vis-à-
vis being shadowed. If the woman was alone, then she had
an option.

*Okay. Let's see who you are and what you got,
flo'man . . .*

Mourn smiled at the encounter again as he exited the hotel. It wasn't as if he didn't do that fairly frequently—
smile—but it was rare these days that there was any real
amusement in those expressions. Long ago and far away,
there had been much more of that, but not lately. He had
liked Sola. The woman had nerve. Of course, she was
young and ambitious, and with her beauty, that was a dangerous combination.

He spent thirty minutes making sure he wasn't followed,
including a check for hidden transmitters in his clothes. He
hadn't brushed up against anybody, nor had he felt the tap
of a blowgun burr hitting him, but it was always better safe
than sorry.

When he was sure he was clean, he worked his way
back to his primary house. He always rented two places
whenever he moved to a new city, under different names.
They were usually close enough so he could walk from one
to the other, and sometimes in the middle of the night, he
would arise and do just that.

Caution was automatic after all the years.

The primary residence was a small single-family condo with a yard, in the suburbs of the city, with the secondary being a room in a megaplex a couple of blocks away. Whenever he could, he liked to get a place with a yard, preferably one with a tall privacy fence. He liked to train outside.

A quick transponder check of his bioelectronic telltales showed that nobody had come calling—the locked gate for the everplast fence had not been opened, unless the person who did it was an electronics genius. Once inside with the gate locked, he did a scan of the yard, in case somebody had managed to make it over the two-and-a-half-meter-high fence. Apparently nobody had. Then he checked the house. He was alone.

He went to the com. He seldom carried a personal unit, it was too easy to locate somebody who was tied into a planetary communications net. Some planets were not above bugging personal coms so that they would send out a position sig even when the thing was ostensibly turned off. Could make for a nasty surprise if somebody got globesat codes and decided to pay you an unannounced visit. Yeah, he ran below the Confed's Doppler, at least most of the time, but it was a big dog, and if it got on your trail, you'd be hard-pressed to outrun it. Why open yourself to any more risk than you had to?

The com unit he had in the house wore a scrambler and a detector to tell him in case somebody tried to tap into it. He set it for vox-only and instructed it to access the number he had memorized. He didn't bother to rascal his voice.

"Yeah?"

"I'm looking for Theo Popper."

There was a pause. That would be Popper running Mourn's voice through his ID program. "Mourn," he said. "I thought that was you. Nice to hear from you."

"Always my pleasure," Mourn said.

Popper made some money as an information broker, but

mostly he was a handicapper, a bookie for those who wanted to bet on Flex matches. For this reason, he kept track of ranked players who showed up in his sector.

"What can I do for you, Mourn?"

"Just checking in. Anybody in the sector I should know about?"

"Not really. Been fairly slow here on the homeworld the last few months. You're the only Top Twenty guy still alive on-planet. Well. Except for Weems."

Weems? Jesu!

"You just loved dropping that on me, didn't you?"

Popper laughed, a rough, ragged sound caused by too many flicksticks smoked over too many years. Man always had one lit.

Z. B. Weems was the top of the heap—the Number One Ranked Player in the Musashi Flex, *El Primero*. A man who could kill with either hand—or a foot or elbow or a head butt—without bothering to resort to his favorite weapon, a plain old carbon-fiber cane. With that in hand, he pretty much could beat the crap out of everybody—at least he had so far—nobody could touch him with anything short of a firearm, and even that would be iffy if he was within ten meters when they reached for their weapon. Weems was a light heavy, but as fast as a flyweight, unnaturally fast, and as hard as a leather sack full of granite. He had been the best for more than a year, and that was impressive these days.

"I don't suppose you want to have a go at him?" Popper said.

Mourn laughed. "You don't suppose right. I couldn't anyway."

"Yeah, you could. After Harnett, you made it to Ten."

Interesting. Among the convoluted rules of the Flex and its intricate scoring were several that laid out who could challenge whom. Basically, you could theoretically go up against anybody who was ranked lower, but you didn't get any points unless you beat somebody who was within ten of your own rank, and even then only a few points, if you were lucky. Going the other way, you couldn't challenge anybody in the top hundred who was more than ten ranks above you without a dispensation from the Rules Committee. As a practical matter, the RC didn't give those out. This was to keep the high ranks from having to deal with every dim-brained kid who thought he had a hand that was better than his rank. If you tried to jump too many levels, the higher-ranked player was allowed to stop you by whatever means possible, and even if he didn't, and you somehow won, you wouldn't get the victory. If you were stupid enough to try, the Enforcers would chill you. That tended to keep the fool count in the game down somewhat. He'd made it to Ten once before, briefly, but that had been a couple years back.

"I'll pass," Mourn said.

"Too bad. I could have made some stads."

"Really? Who'd bet on me?"

"Give high enough odds, they come," Popper said. "Always some dweeb who's got a system."

"Anybody else?"

"Nobody who can challenge you. And unless Weems is bored, he probably won't go looking for you."

"He knows I'm here."

"I might have mentioned it. He wasn't impressed."

Mourn laughed. "Thanks for the info, Popper."

"Hey, it's what I do. Let me know if you mean to thump somebody I might have missed."

"I will."

Business concluded, Mourn shut off the com and went to the yard to begin his workout.

Luna Azul was certain that she had but a single watcher as she left the port and began to walk. Unlike the last world she'd been on, it was warm. Different hemisphere, different season. Not unduly hot, but enough so that a brisk walk quickly caused a sweat to break. At least it wasn't so humid that the sweat didn't evaporate. She hated climates like that, where the perspiration soaked your clothes and kept them wet, and when it pooled in your shoes . . .

If the watcher was surprised that she didn't catch a commercial transport, she gave no sign of it. The little woman immediately crossed the street and began a side tail, staying out of Azul's peripheral vision. If she hadn't known who the woman was, she would have picked her up eventually, but the tail was good enough so it might have taken a little while.

It didn't take long to find a place she liked. A cut-through from this street to the next, not really an alley, but not really a road, either, more like a wide driveway.

Azul took the turn, and as soon as she was out of her watcher's sight, she began a sprint. A hundred meters in, she spotted a trash bin. It was sealed, a truck-lock on it, so people too cheap to pay for haulers couldn't dump their garbage into it. But it was also far enough from the building wall so that somebody could slip behind the heavy, dark green plastcast container, which was two meters tall and twice that wide, set upon four squat wheels.

Azul hid behind the bin and breathed deeply several times to catch her breath. She needed to do more aerobics—that little sprint shouldn't have cost her that much effort.

After half a minute, she heard the follower's footsteps coming down the driveway. From her boot, Azul removed a onetime shot tube. It was not much more than a big firecracker—a charge of compressed gas behind a wad and a couple dozen expoxy-boron pellets set in semiperm gel, with the barrel only six or seven centimeters long. The whole thing was made of spun carbon fiber, and the outside was coated in something that wouldn't take fingerprints or hold DNA residue. It wouldn't pass an HO scanner, but it would slip past metal detectors. It was a throwaway weapon, useful for close range. Outside of five or six meters, hitting a target would be iffy—the thing had no sights, and you pointed it like you would your finger, squeezed it in the right spot, and it went off.

Azul didn't particularly want to use it, but she was glad she had it. It might facilitate a conversation.

If the tail had any smarts, she'd be wary approaching the trash bin.

Azul stood on a thin rim that formed a lip that ran around the bottom of the bin. If the watcher bent down and looked under the thing, she wouldn't see anybody's legs.

She assumed the watcher would look—Azul would have—and she also assumed that not seeing anybody hiding there wouldn't be enough to convince the watcher by itself.

The footsteps slowed. Stopped close by.

Azul edged along the back of the bin toward the far end.

She heard another couple of tentative steps away from that end. Azul got there, stepped down. She took a deep breath and made sure of her grip on the shot tube, then stepped out of concealment.

The watcher was looking the other way, but the movement caught her attention, and she spun quickly toward Azul.

"Who sent you?" Azul asked.

The woman jerked, surprised, and clawed for something in her back pocket.

Crap—!

Azul squeezed the shot tube. There was a loud *whump!* as the gas charge went off. The gel held together for a couple meters, then the shot started to spread. It was still clumped into a pattern no bigger than Azul's hand when it hit the watcher square in the face.

The woman's own weapon fell from her grip and clattered onto the plastcrete. A spring gun, Azul saw, as deadly as the shot tube in the right hands.

Not the watcher's hands, though.

Azul looked up and down the driveway. Nobody in sight. *Shit.*

There was little point in searching the body—the watcher was certainly good enough so she wouldn't have a folded note in her pocket with her employer's name on it and directions to his home—and being seen with a corpse was not the way to start a new assignment—especially when you had caused the death. Still, you never knew.

She pulled a pair of thinskin gloves from her pocket.

Aside from the gun, the dead woman had a credit cube and an ID. That was all. The cube held two hundred stads. Azul tucked it into her pocket—she would lose it as soon as she could, but she might as well make it look like robbery.

The ID bore the name "Kat Brant" and a local address, but Azul guessed that one or both of these bits of data were probably false. She took that, too—no point in doing the cools' work for them.

She'd wanted her alive, to find out who'd sent her. There hadn't been any real choice, not once the woman had gone for her gun; but if she was dead, well, that would also serve. Sorry, fem.

At least Kat there wouldn't be carrying any descriptions back to her masters.

The game was back on.

Mourn liked to break his workout into three or four chunks, rather than one long session. He would practice an hour in the morning, another hour or two in the afternoon, and if he had the energy, an hour before he went to sleep. He had been doing this for so many years that it had long ago ceased to be a matter of discipline. It was what he did, a part of the biz, training, and while there was only so much you could manage by yourself, you had to do it if you

wanted to stay reasonably sharp. Every player of rank he
knew trained every day. If he missed a day for any reason,
it felt really weird.

One of the first things he did when he got to a city of
any size was find a martial arts kiosk to get supplies—bag
gloves, bandages, unguents, odds and ends. Mourn moved
light, no more than he could carry. When he stepped off a
ship or a boxcar, he had a travel bag and his guitar, that was
it. When you had stads, you bought what you needed along
the way and left it behind when you departed. In his game,
you had to be ready to move at a moment's notice—you
never carried anything you couldn't leave behind. Although he would hate to lose another guitar, better that
than some of the options.

Mourn did a series of stretches and plyometrics to warm
up, some shadowboxing and kicking. Then he went
through the *silat* forms he had learned, eighteen short
dances called *djurus*. The *djurus* contained in them all the
fighting moves one could efficiently make with one's upper
body, so he had been taught. There were separate exercises
for the lower body, using various geometric platforms—
straight line, triangle, square, cross pattern—and he did
those, too.

Sufficiently loose after forty-five minutes, he lit Bob's
power and waited for the gyros to get enough spin.

The standard martial arts fighting/training dummy was
old-tech—a sodium borohydride fuel cell that powered bio-
electric motor-driven arms and legs made up of rods and
pistons, all covered with a biogel and skin that mimicked
human flesh. It was kept balanced by a trio of heavy and
high-speed gyroscopes, and could kick, punch, knee, elbow, or head-butt. You could program it for specific attacks
or set it on random mode. The basic models had sensors and
software sufficient to tell you how hard a strike was when
you tagged the dummy. The dummies ran about a thousand
standards each, which was spendy, but most of the time,

except the ones he cut up too bad practicing bladework, Mourn was able to sell them back for half or three-quarters what he paid, so it wasn't that bad a deal, and it was just part of operating expenses.

For some reason, somewhere back in the mists of history, the training dummies had come to be known as Bobs.

This unit was controlled by a covered panel in the middle of the back, or by voice-activation.

"Hey there, Bob. What say we spar? Random single or double attacks, full power, full spectrum."

Bob said, "Acknowledged." Then, "Up yours, punk ass."

Mourn grinned. This Bob was one of the vox-equipped models that would offer taunts, to simulate an opponent who tried to rattle you. Mourn was long past the days when anything anybody might say would do that to him. "Bob, Bob. You are so crude."

Bob said, "Your mother sucks mue dick. Your sister eats large animal turds."

Mourn laughed. Somebody must have had fun programming this chip.

Bob bent his knees, the hydraulics whining slightly, then stepped in, not the most graceful of moves, but quick enough, and fired a straight punch at Mourn's throat.

Mourn did a stop-kick to the groin, angled out, slammed a hammer fist into Bob's temple, and did a fast *sapu,* a sweep, on Bob's right ankle.

The gyroscopes kept the dummy upright, but a small *ting!* from Bob's computer told Mourn that he had done the sweep with sufficient force to have taken a normal man down. While he could have programmed the unit's balancers so that Bob would have toppled from the sweep, he preferred not to—Bob weighed nearly 150 kilograms, couldn't get up on his own without a crabbing, complicated process that took a while, and lifting him to his feet got old real fast. You had to shut off the gyros, lock the legs, haul him up, then restart him. Life was too short.

Bob shuffled around in a turn to face Mourn again. "My grand mam hits harder than that, elbow-sucker. I am going to fornicate you up the rectal orifice."

Mourn laughed. "Oh, Bob. You are *so* bad."

After thirty minutes of sparring with the dummy, Mourn headed for the shower. Another ten minutes of the hot water cleaned away the sweat and relaxed his tired muscles. He stood under the blowers until he was dry, put on a robe, and went to practice his guitar.

His guitar travel case was of spun polycarb fiber, strong as titanium but considerably lighter. The ad for it on commercial entcom showed four large men sitting on it without producing a dent. Inside, there was a small compartment for accoutrements—picks, an electronic tuner, a silk cleaning cloth, and enough plush lining to protect the passenger.

He thumbed the lock open and carefully removed the antique instrument.

The guitar itself was an unamplified hollow-body classic a couple of hundred years old. Named after the maker—Bogdanovich—it had been designed for players of classical or flamenco-style music, and was sans electronics. The back and sides were made of wood, black walnut, the front of red cedar, and the head and neck were of Spanish cedar, with an ebony fretboard. Over the years, the instrument, which hadn't been that expensive to start, given what a concert-level guitar had cost in those days, had developed a rich, warm, full tone, and was now worth probably fifteen times its original cost. For what it was worth, you could get a nice flitter or a so-so house.

The guitar was his most prized possession, the third instrument he had owned. He had started out with an electronic, Stratocaster-style, and that had been adequate for the simple-chord pop music he could play. Later, he had found a cutaway classic that also allowed him to reach twenty frets, and he began learning to play blues and lead. The second guitar had been a honey, a carbon-fiber hollow-body with electronic pickups, and a very fast action. It was a handmade piece, produced by a woman who used the name Jade Blue, on Spandle, in Mu. He would still be play-ing the Blue, if he hadn't had to bolt to escape the cools on Tembo after a match in which a citizen bystander had acci-dentally been killed. Mourn hadn't chilled the guy, his op-ponent had, when the cit had stepped in and tried to stop the fight. You couldn't blame the player the way it went down, but local cools took a squinty-eyed view of Flexers taking out their cits, and getting offworld fast was the only alternative to being arrested.

Somewhere on Tembo, some cool was probably still playing that guitar.

He had come across the Bogdanovich shortly after he lost the Blue, in a music shop in Star City on Alpha Point. A long way from home for the instrument. How had it made the trip? Who had brought it, how long ago? It was expensive, but after strumming one E-chord, he was sold. Given his life, money didn't matter much.

Because the classic style had only twelve frets you could comfortably use without contorting your hand, Mourn had found himself getting into that kind of music. He did pieces arranged by Segovia, Parkening, John Williams, Django By-ers, and El McMeen. He could still do twelve-bar blues and high-on-the-neck pop, but since he didn't play with anybody else, lead wasn't as useful without a rhythm machine to pick against anyway. And it wasn't as if there was a lack of reper-toire for classical music . . .

He sat in a straight-backed chair with his left foot on a fifteen-centimeter-high rest. In classical-style playing, the guitar was propped on the left leg, the neck angled up, and the thumb of the fret hand always stayed behind the neck. Notes were generally plucked and not strummed. Because he trained in the fighting arts using his fists every day, long fingernails on his right hand were out; they dug into his palm, so he used carbon-fiber finger and thumb picks, skeletonized jobs worn like thimbles. Not as purist as his own nails, but the sound was not too far off.

Mourn tuned the instrument, strummed a few chords, and started his practice with Pachelbel's *Canon in D*. After that, he ran through a couple of Bach pieces—he liked *Jesu, Joy of Man's Desiring* and the *Lute Suite IV Prelude*—then some Harrison—S. Yates's transcription of *Here Comes the Sun,* segueing right into an intricate tremolo work by Fernando Sor.

He didn't fool himself into believing he was a great musician. While he could probably earn money with his playing in some club or pub, he did it because it was relaxing. When you made your living by dueling, sitting and quietly playing music by yourself was restorative.

Done with the Sor piece, hands warmed up as good as they were going to get, he finished the practice set with Jeff Carter's *Etude for Venus,* the most difficult guitar work he could play. It had a lot of minor sevenths and ninths, and required very fast changes up and down the neck. Even with the flat-wound-coated-gold bass strings, the low E and A still squeaked when he did the long run at the end, going from the twelfth to the first fret and back doing triplets. He shook his head. He'd been working on that piece for three months, and while most people he had heard play it also squeaked the low strings somewhere on the final sliding chords, there were some who didn't. If they could do it silently, he could—assuming he lived long enough.

When he was done, an hour had slipped by. He wiped the guitar's fingerboard and neck with the silk, put the instrument away, and locked the case. Food. Food would be good. He had trained his body and calmed his spirit. Supper would work. And then bed.

It was something of a spartan existence, but it suited him well enough.

When it turned out that Stefano Bashnik was the spy, Shaw had felt mixed emotions. Bashnik was top-grade, one of a handful of biomedical specialists who could run at speed, and losing him would be a pain. He was the number two man on the project, nobody but Renoir ahead of him, and the most hands-on of the senior players. Which was the shits. Men of Bashnik's caliber were hard to find, and usually sufficiently self-aware that they knew what they were worth. It wasn't as if Shaw couldn't *afford* a new team member, just that he'd have to find him, interview him, convince him that he should leave whatever important project he was currently working—and the really good ones all already had important work to do—and then wait as he was brought up to speed.

On the other hand, Bashnik was young, a fitness buff, and while not a fighter per se, had played contact sports along the way.

It was indeed an ill wind that blew no good.

It was late, they were alone in the training hall, and Cervo had taken care, which included jiggering with security cams, to make sure no one had seen him bring Bashnik here.

Shaw, who was dressed as if he were going to work out with Baba, smiled.

Bashnik returned the smile. "All right," he said. "So you know. Listen, it wasn't personal. You might just want to let it slide—we're close to a breakthrough, you know. Kicking me off the project will only slow things down. I know how close this is to your heart."

"You have balls, Stefano, I'll give you that. You are a spy, feeding the Confed rep the details of a protocol I really wanted to keep a secret, and you think I should just . . . let it slide? Dock your bonus a little, maybe?"

THE MUSASHI FLEX 61

"It's a thought."

"What did our friendly planetary rep give you to betray me?"

"Head of the new Confed Military Research Laboratory on Earth."

"Nice plum."

He shrugged. "So I'm fired, right? Fine. You're the one who loses, M. Shaw. Me, I go off to my nice new job now instead of later. Doesn't bother me."

Shaw smiled again. "Well, not exactly. I'm afraid you won't be spacing to Earth to work for the Confed."

"I have a written contract with M. Randall saying otherwise."

Now Shaw laughed. "Stefano, Stefano. You don't think a man with my weight can squash such a deal without raising a sweat? All I'd have to do is tell my good friend Newman Randall that I will cut the Confed a little slack on any of fifty chems they buy from me wholesale, a point or two on some of those would save the military ten, twelve million stads. You think he wouldn't invoke the MPA and zero out your contract in a heartbeat for that?"

Bashnik frowned. "You would do that?"

Shaw shook his head. "No, I won't. But I *could*. You're a brilliant scientist, but not very smart in the ways of business and politics. I could also use my influence and money to make sure you never get a job any more complex than washing test tubes, if I so desired. It might cost a small fortune, but hey, I have a large fortune—a million here, a million there, if it falls out of my pocket, it isn't worth my time to bend over and pick it up. I could ruin your life forever and get up smiling about it every day."

"But you aren't going to do that, either," Bashnik said. He began to look worried.

"Nope. All I am going to do is terminate you."

"I don't understand."

They were two meters apart. Shaw took a lazy step and

slapped Bashnik, a nice swat that caught the younger man on the left ear. It didn't knock him down, but it did rock him. He grabbed at his head and backed away. "What the fuck are you doing?"

"Just what I said, Stefano. No more. No less."

The man's eyes went wide as, finally, he understood.

Terminate.

Shaw had six cams recording. He looked forward to seeing the show later, but for now, he wanted to enjoy the feeling of the experience.

Bashnik cursed loudly.

The thrill that Shaw felt was almost orgasmic.

Afterward, Cervo cleaned up and delivered some news: They'd lost one of their ops, one assigned to cover one of Randall's people. She hadn't reported in, and the cools had found her body in an alley—she'd been shot to death.

What was dear old Randall up to? Best to find out, Shaw knew. Knowledge was not only power, it was survival at this level.

7

Sola was about to pee herself she was so excited. Weems! Weems was here, on Earth!

When she'd gotten the tip, it had seemed a gift from God.

She had never seen the man in person, only in a couple of short and fuzzy clips, but she had no doubt that she would know him when she found him. And she *would* find him—he was on the same *planet,* for God's sake! How much better could it get than that? She would pay whatever it cost, if she had to sell herself on the street to get the stads, she would run him down. This was the chance of a lifetime—she might never get another shot at the number one, *numero uno, nam- aba moja* player. Even a short interview or some nonfighting footage of Weems would *make* her documentary!

Of course, she had to find him first.

As a freelancer, she didn't have the contacts of a big news organization, but there were ways to tap into those. If you had been around a while, you learned how.

She commed the Freelancers Media Guild, gave them her ID, and asked for the Membership Secretary.

"This is Brinker. How may I help you?"

"I would like a list of Associate Members on Earth who are within twenty hours of Full Member Status."

Brinker said, "Let me guess—not from around here, are you?"

"Nope."

"And too cheap to hire a certified Researcher."

Of course the Secretary would have heard this request a time or twelve before. He knew what she was up to. "Do I get the list?"

He sighed. "I'll download it to your com."

"Thank you." It was a legitimate request, and she was a member in good standing; still, he could have been a slop-ass about it and made her come in and pick up a hard copy if he felt like busting her boobs.

Once she had the list, Sola would start making calls. Associates who were getting close to Full usually had work, else they wouldn't be that close; still, there were always a few who weren't getting there as quick as they wanted. As a Full herself, Sola had just enough clout to be useful to somebody trying to climb the ladder. She could sign off on their hours, up to twenty, and while the deal wasn't techni-cally legal, it was a fair trade for the right person. An AM who could find the information she wanted, whether it took twenty hours or twenty minutes, would get her signature for the full score of hours' credit. No money, which was against the organization's rules, but since FM status was right off the mark an automatic rate increase of 50 percent, a few hours of research time was a cheap price to pay for it.

Somewhere on the list that her com now held was a hun-gry young reporter with local sources who would hustle his or her ass off to find out where Zachary Bretton Weems was. The faster the AM could do it, the better for both of them.

She could hire five and give them four hours each—twenty hours being her limit for any three-month period.

Or if she felt like being a real bitch, she could take ten or fifteen names on the list and offer them all a whoever-finds-it-first deal, winner take all. That could be a fast turn-around, but it was an ugly way to do biz. She'd hustled a few of those deals herself when she'd been an AM, and for the one winner who was happy, you pissed off a bunch of reporters who might someday be in a position to fuck you over. Media workers had long memories. There were a couple of fairly well known ones that she would shove over a cliff, figuratively, at least, should she be given the chance, and she didn't want to give anybody reason to want to do that to her. You made enough enemies along the way without working harder to do so.

No, the fair thing was to offer it to one, give them a shot at it, and if they scored, reward them. Yeah, it was cheap, but she didn't have the stads, and for a young and ambitious media worker, it was a good deal. Nobody lost.

She said, "Com, display downloaded list from Free-lancers Media Guild."

The small holoproj lit with the names. She scanned them quickly, looking for some reason to choose one over the other.

"Com, call Rasha Llew Aileen." Rasha needed twenty hours exactly. She'd likely be a little hungrier than somebody who needed only three or four. And she liked the sound of the name—as good a reason as any . . .

Shaw watched the recording again, with an eye to editing it. Blending the shots from the various angles was something he could have turned over to the cambot's computer, which would have done a decent enough job, but he liked to do it himself; he fancied that he had a good eye, and that his editings were more dramatic than the bot's.

It was not every day you killed a man with your hands and feet. You wanted to get the doing of it down as best you could—

"Sir," came his secretary's voice.

"Yes?"

"Your next appointment is here. The team from Portable Medical Systems."

He frowned. Ah, well. He could do this later. It would keep.

He locked it away under his personal code.

"Send them in."

"It looks like a suitcase somebody tipped onto its side," Shaw said.

"Low center of gravity," the CEO of PortMed said. "Henry?"

The R&D VP nodded. He was tall, lean, his hair shaved into a tight maze pattern. "Almost impossible to turn over, the wheelbase is so wide for the weight. If it does get flipped upside down . . ." He stuck his boot toe under the leading edge and heaved—it took some effort because the thing was apparently heavy—and the device landed on its "back."

There was a high-pitched hum, and the device extruded a spring-loaded arm and flipped itself back onto its silicone treads, which looked a lot like those on a military tank.

"Self-righting," the R&D guy said. "And the wheels are gyroscopic and on a frame, so if you come to some stairs, it can climb them as fast as you can, unless you are trying for some kind of record. On the flats, it can keep up with a jogger."

Shaw nodded. It wouldn't make any sense to have an emergency medical tracker called a "Vouch-Safe" that couldn't follow you around.

The R&D guy said, "There are ceramic plates on the belly, and spidersilk softweave just under the shell, so the thing is pretty much bulletproof. Waterproof, too—you can leave it in the rain for a year and it'll work just fine. Batteries are good for a month of normal use, and will automatically induce a recharge off any standard outlet; the fuel cell will last ten years, and you can switch it out in five minutes without tools, if you have the vault door codes. Same for loading RX."

Shaw nodded again. "All right. Tell me about the biological end."

The CEO said, "October?"

The woman, who was a little on the chunky side but quite attractive, with blond streaks in her red hair, said, "Everything is state-of-the-art. The main tracker uses the subject's brain pattern, via wireless pickups tuned to the subject's implants, coded sig, with an effective range of three hundred meters under ideal conditions—a walk in the country, say, alone—half that in a city's electronic flux."

"Implants?"

"Standard EEG transmitters used in seizure treatment. A primary and a backup, inserted into the trapezius at the base of the neck via intramuscular injection. About the size of a fat grain of rice each. Old-tech, nothing complicated, just like the first credit card IDs and dog-finder chips."

He nodded again. No problem with that.

"The main systems telemetry comes from another implant into the sternum that reads BP, heart rate, respiration, hormone levels, like that.

"In addition, the unit can do more extensive tests on blood, which it can draw either on command or automatically upon readings that are below normal limits."

"If the subject passes out, the unit works on its own?"

"Yes. It will roll up, query aloud, and if there is no response to trigger the voxax circuit—which can be limited to the owner and any designated others—then the vouch does a hypo stick, draws blood, and runs a full SMA chem. It can detect three hundred poisons and administer antidotes for the most common ones. If the ECG shows cardiac illness, it will administer appropriate medications or electricity. It has antibiotics, analgesics, stimulants, relaxants, clot-busters, diuretics—treatments for the most common diseases. It can detect and orthostat a simple fracture. It will use its built-in communications gear to call for help from the nearest medical facility if it detects anything beyond its capability to repair immediately. It can also analyze urine, fecal, and tissue samples."

Shaw smiled and shook his head. "A mechanical doctor that follows you around like a dog. What a great toy."

The VP, R&D, and Medico all smiled in return.

"How much do you need to go into full production?"

The Sales VP said, "Tooling and supplies, labor, marketing, we're thinking we could get by on eighteen million for the first year, though we'd be more comfortable with twenty. If we can get five from you, we believe we can get the rest from several other venture-capital parties who have shown interest."

"No," Shaw said.

He let them worry about that for a few seconds, just because it amused him. Before they could do more than frown and raise their eyebrows, he said, "I want to be the exclusive investor. I'll put up twenty-five million—you can walk out of here with a transfer cube for the entire amount—provided you will sign a contract making me your sole angel."

The CEO smiled, the three VPS looked stunned, and Shaw knew it was a done deal.

"One stipulation. How many prototypes do you have?"

"Half a dozen," the R&D VP said. "Three at full capacity."

"I want one." It was a great toy.

"You got it," the CEO said.

Shaw smiled again. It was good to be rich.

Azul rented a sleep kiosk, went inside, lit her confounder, and took out the info ball the op had tendered. She slipped it into her reader and watched the holoproj bloom over it.

ID CODE? blinked over and over in red.

Citizens had all kinds of codes—job numbers, communications numbers, travel and home addresses and medical codes, but there was no question but that the info ball wanted her Confed Operative Code. She used the keypad to input it—even with the confounder running to kill any electronic listeners, that wasn't something she wanted spoken aloud. A confounder wouldn't shut down a pair of human ears that might be at the keyhole.

The code was seventeen digits, and included numbers and letters. She changed it once a week. Chances of somebody figuring it out without a quantum computer dedicated to the task were between extremely slim and none. And if somebody wanted to bother wasting a QC unit on her? The code would be changed in a week anyhow.

Once she hit the return key, the three-dimensional holographic projection rippled, and she found herself looking at another set of numbers and words, no pictures:

4 SOUTH PARK NJIA YA MJI, SUITE 211, 1800 HOURS.

A street address, a room number, and a time. She memorized the screen. Ten seconds after she was done, the holoproj went blank, then shut down. The info ball ejected. She picked it up. It was warm. The data on it had been fried, it was just a little stainless-steel marble now, something you could present to the best computer recovery team out there and they'd find zip-zock if they tried to comb it. Whoever had sent this wasn't taking any chances that it would reveal who he or she was. Cautious, but since there had been a watcher on her when she arrived at the port, apparently not cautious enough.

She looked at her ring chronometer. Almost 1500. She had three hours to find the address and scope it before she walked into whatever was waiting there for her. Should be plenty of time.

8

Rasha Llew Aileen earned her twenty hours in a little under three—maybe less, depending on how long she waited to call Sola back. The verbal contract they had recorded wasn't technically enforceable, given Rasha's status in the Guild, but it was binding generally as a legal document, and Rasha, who sounded as if she was about twenty and SoAfrican, from her accent, tendered the information fast enough.

"He's at the Milner Hotel in New Orleans, NorAm, registered under the name 'Miyamoto Cyrus Dexter Carliano.'"

"Outstanding work. I am uploading the voucher right now. Thanks, F. Aileen."

"Are you kidding? Twenty hours puts me into Full status. Thank you, F. Sola. You need anything else done while you are Earth, call me first. Professional discount, plus ten percent."

"I will."

After they discommed, Sola called up a map on the room's computer and booked a boxcar for New Orleans. It was a city near the coast of the Gulf of Mexico, straddling a crescent-shaped loop of a large river, not far from the mouth. If she made the next connection, she could be there in a couple of hours. She grinned. *Yes!*

Mourn looked at the curve of the planet as the boxcar dropped from its high parabola toward the port. Earth was the bluest of all the worlds he had visited. There were a few others with more water-to-land ratios, but something in the atmosphere or the oceans made it a cooler color than those worlds.

He looked at his chronometer. They'd be down in another few minutes. He had never been to this particular city, in the southern section of NorAm, though he had done a search on its history and geography as part of the background check. A river port on alluvial soil, flat and mostly sea level, the place had changed hands more often than a demistad coin in the early years of its existence. Natives, Spanish, French, American Colonial, Confederate States, United States, World Union, Confederation. Even before space travel, the place had been a mélange of cultures and peoples. The place had been inundated a few times, drowning a lot of folks and destroying a lot of property, but had been rebuilt after each flood. Now, it was only a few miles from a large offworld port in a local gulf, which gave it more diversity.

He had but one reason to go there, and that was basic self-defense. While Weems had told Theo Popper that he wasn't interested in a match with Mourn, only a fool would accept such a statement at face value. You didn't get to be the top fighter in the galaxy without learning how to be devious. Maybe Weems was just taking a vacation and seeing the sights, sampling the native foods, whatever. Or maybe he was looking to get a little workout by hammering

Mourn into the ground with his cane. If you just sat around and waited to find out which was true, you could wind up dead. It only made sense strategically and tactically to check things out. If you had a potential enemy about, knowing where he was and what he was doing was basic.

He'd have to be very careful—if Weems spotted him, whatever he'd had planned might be affected. You looked up and saw a contender stalking you, you wanted to bring it to him on your terms rather than waiting for his. In this game, at this level, any and every advantage you could gain was to your benefit. Terrain, time of day or night, space, any or all of these might be the edge you'd need to walk away a winner. Put the sun in your opponent's eyes, take the high ground—or the low ground, if that was your preference— make the ring small if you were an infighter, larger if you liked to stand back—whatever. Like *Go* or chess, a move made early enough could influence the outcome a long way down the line. The fight, players liked to say, was not under your glove but under your hat.

Not that Mourn intended to challenge Weems. He was too good. Mourn had seen the recordings, he knew the stats. With a blade against a blade, maybe *ai-uchi,* mutual slaying, was possible, but that wasn't high on his list of ways to end a match. With a blade against that solid and heavy carbon-fiber cane Weems favored, Weems would win. He was a magician with that stick and hook. Bare? That was tricky. Weems was fast, and the new art Mourn had been studying gave him a positional advantage, wherein speed could be somewhat negated. But Mourn wasn't deep enough in it yet; he had the basics, especially with the short knives, but the basics weren't going to be enough to take out a man like Weems. Of course, he had other arts, but so did Number One, and he had beaten fighters who had beaten Mourn, and decisively. No, he wasn't quite ready to go head-to-head with Weems, bare or armed, not without a cheat, and of course, that would make it pointless.

Was it a fair match?

That would be the first question the showrunners asked—
it was *always* the first question they asked, and if you
couldn't answer it correctly—and the stress analyzers and
face readers and the brain strainers used were damned hard
to beat—then you didn't get the victory. If you cheated,
you were subject to immediate expulsion from the Flex.
And if you killed or even seriously injured the other player
using a cheat? The showrunners could zap you right there
and then for *making* it an unfair contest. No judge, no appeal, game, set, match, and final chill. Those were the rules
you agreed to when you entered the game. If you didn't
play by the rules, there was no point.

Cheats were for self-defense situations when some wa-
zoo street gang that didn't know better tried to mug you.
Them you could chill, at least as far as the Flex showrunners were concerned—you had to take your chances with
local and Confed law on your own. When you faced another player in a challenge, you played it straight, by the
numbers, or you didn't stay in the game. Or alive.

Below, the city of New Orleans grew in size as the ship
fell.

He wasn't going to challenge Weems. He was just going
to check him out. It was the prudent thing to do.

"We got a live one!" the medico Bevins said over the
comlink.

It took a second for Shaw to comprehend it. "Excuse
me?"

"Barry. Barry made it past the cutoff!"

Shaw was on his feet and heading for his office door before the tech spoke another word. He could be at the lab in
five minutes if he took the tram, less than that if he ran.

He ran. Didn't take the elevator, but ran down the stairs,
out the exit, and across the compound, sprinting. Cervo

would be behind him, even though they were in the protected compound.

"Barry" was one of the latest batch of rock apes. The term was not technically correct—the test animals were not apes, though once upon a time their ancestors had lived in a rocky environment. What they were in fact was a kind of creature more akin to lemurs, if somewhat larger, whose immune systems were a lot closer to humans than anything but H-DNA chimpanzees or revised bushmonks, both of which were hard to come by out here. That one of the animals had survived might be the breakthrough they had been hoping for.

The lab's door recognized and admitted him fast enough to keep him from smacking his nose into the denscris. Bevins, the Medico Team Leader, waited in the first positive-pressure room two locks in. Bevins wore sterile skins and held a second set. Shaw stripped to underwear and slipped into the skins. The white material covered everything from the head to the feet, and would protect the lab and its animals—and the people wearing the suits—from cross-contamination.

Shaw followed Bevins through the next pressure room, the vacuum room, and finally, was blasted by an eye-smiting actinic sterilizing light at the entrance to the main animal lab.

In the huge room, there were six people—four men, two women—working the monitors and the Healy, a medical coffin that could diagnose and repair most common human and mue illnesses and injuries. Barry was in a living-room-sized denscris cage, perched on a rock. The inside of the cage was as close to the animal's natural environment as possible, complete with sterilized plants and insects, and while the workers could see him, the view wall was one-way—Barry couldn't see them.

Barry was picking at his dinner, some kind of shellfish, and eating it with great relish. A viewer would think him healthy enough, and save for the small casters on his chest and head, he was unadorned.

"How long?" Shaw said.

"One hour and sixteen—no, seventeen minutes, mark, beyond Beatrice."

Shaw nodded. Beatrice had been the longest surviving of the apes thus far, the last to die on the previous rotation.

"Hour and a quarter is hardly conclusive," Shaw said.

"Look at him. He's happier than a dung beetle in curl-nose crap." Bevins waved at the bank of monitors. "All systems are normal—no hypothalmic inversion, no motor or CNS neuron shorts, cardiac system okay, blood pressure dead-on normal. Beatrice was falling apart six hours before she arrested. If Barry feels even a little bad, the best tools medical science has can't tell it."

Shaw allowed himself to feel a small thrill of victory.

"What did you do?"

Bevins went off on a technical lark, most of which Shaw tuned out as he watched the rock ape chew up river crawdaddy and spit out bits of the shell.

"—decided that the hormone regulator might respond to R-Enzyme if we used the viral-molecular fuser to blend them. It was a last-minute decision, and there was some argument as to whether or not we would go with it, but I decided it was worth the risk."

Bevins cast a quick glance at one of the women techs, Dr. Tenae, and Shaw made a mental note of that. Tenae was the risk-taker, Bevins the conservative, so it must have been her idea. Bevins was going to take credit for it, of course, but Shaw would see that Tenae was suitably rewarded—if Barry didn't suddenly take a header off that rock and croak on them.

An alarm of some kind went off, a strident ringing.

"What is that?" Shaw felt his bowels twist. *Come on, Barry! Don't you fucking* die *on me!*

Bevins frowned. "I don't know. Everything looks fine—"

"That's a security alarm," one of the other medicos said. "Nothing we're doing in here."

"Director Shaw?" came an amplified voice.

"Yes?"

"Sir, there's some kind of robot trying to get into the lab. It keeps bumping against the door."

For a heartbeat, Shaw drew a blank. Then he smiled. Ah. His vouch. He had forgotten all about it in his hurry to get here. The medical robot was lit, and it followed him. He must have gotten ahead of it on his run down the stairs.

He tried to reach into his pocket for the remote to deactivate the medical robot, then remembered he was wearing skins. "Nothing to worry about," Shaw said. "Tell Cervo to deactivate it, he has the code. Shut the door alarm off."

The noise stopped.

Shaw looked at Bevins. "Keep me informed. If Barry so much as sneezes, I want to know about it immediately—"

"Jesu, damn!" somebody said. "Did you see that?"

Shaw jerked his attention away from Bevins. "What?"

"Watch the holoproj to your left, sir," one of the monitor techs said. "I'll replay it."

Barry appeared in a small scale, floating over the 'proj. His arm flicked out, fast, and then he went back to picking at the crawfish.

"What am I looking at, Tech?"

"Sorry, M. Shaw, let me enlarge it and slow it down."

The image of Barry blinked, then reappeared, life-size. An insect buzzed around the ape's head, flying in a much-slowed-down spiral. Barry's arm came up in slomo. He pinched two fingers, caught the insect, crushed it, released it, and before the dead bug hit the rock, Barry had returned to his meal.

Rock apes couldn't move that fast. Not naturally.

Shaw grinned. *Yes!*

9

Finding the place where Weems was staying had been easy enough for Sola. He had a gated hotel cube near the river on the eastern edge of the old Casino District, past the floating city of faux–paddle wheel gaming houses that had sucked in people looking to lose their money for hundreds of years. The cubicle was on Dauphine Street, near the intersection with Mandeville, part of a new, high-tech renovation that gleamed like a dull mirror under the semitropical sun. It didn't look as if it belonged there, the renovation, among the older structures. It looked like a stainless-steel cancer.

Four hours after she had arrived, as she stood in the warm shade of some leafy tree she didn't recognize, Sola realized that bagging Z. B. might not be quite so simple. Apparently this section of the city was a mecca for tourists. To the west and slightly south were the French Quarter—Vieux Carré—Jackson Square, and all kinds of historical this, that, and the other that caused a fitful stream of outlanders clad in colorful, silly clothes and sporting expensive cams to mill back and forth among the sites like some kind of vapid herd animals.

The town here smelled of mold and fish, and the river, while probably much cleaner than it had been in centuries, was not a place you'd want to swim. The water was muddy, the flow was fast, and, so she had read in the hotel handout, was only still here through the grace of the local Army Corps of Engineers. Apparently the Mississippi would rather go to the Gulf of Mexico by jumping the levees men had constructed down its length and pouring itself into the nearby Atchafalaya River, which would have left New Orleans high and dry. Well, drier, at least. There was still the big lake, Poncho-something, to the north. And high wasn't really an option, since the place was so low and flat and the water table so close to the surface they couldn't even bury the dead back when that was in vogue—they'd had to entomb them above the ground. Apparently the first settlers here had tried planting coffins, only to see them bob to the surface after the first hard rain, of which there was plenty.

Why, hello, there, Tia Sarah. Didn't like it under the ground? Decided to come back for a visit?

Sola shook her head. She knew what Weems looked like, in theory. He could be disguised, of course, but she had his ear patterns and somatotype logged into her spotter scope, and the instrument was good enough to give her a dimension check, height, weight, morphologics, so—in theory—she could get past a simple skinmask. Unless he bothered to change his ears and wear padding to alter the look of his somatotype, she should be able to get a match if she saw somebody who looked like him.

But as another batch of lookielookies shuffled past her, the problem represented itself yet again. When you had a hundred people on foot coming or going every few minutes, it was a bitch to try and scope all the ones who might be her target.

Shit.

Sooner or later, she'd probably spot him. She had snapped still holos of everybody who had entered or left the building so far and none of them were him. But she had to pee, she was getting hungry, and she was cooking in the summer heat and humidity despite the tree's shade, sweat soaking into her clothes, making her sticky and stinky.

Ah, the exciting, glamorous life of a documentarian. Nothing like it.

If she left to attend to her distractions, that would be the moment Weems came or went. If she stayed put, then, of course, so would he. That was how it always worked. No justice in the galaxy. She had been around long enough to learn that. Timing was all.

At that thought, some deity apparently decided that she deserved a favor: From out of the locked steel gate ambled Z. B. Weems, easily identifiable from her images of him, nothing more to disguise him than a pair of dark glasses, and those probably for the purposes of eye protection rather than deception. He was fit, dressed for the weather in shorts, flex-soles, and a thinskin top, and looked just like thirty other men in sight at the moment. Blink, and he'd vanish.

There was a scar or a good facsimile of one on the outside of his right knee, visible across the street, which certainly would convince anybody not a medic that he needed the thin gray cane he carried. The cane had a rounded crook at the grip, with a black silicone cap on the other end, nothing fancy. It just looked functional. Something a man who maybe couldn't afford a regrow to repair a torn ligament might use until his fortunes improved.

Hallelujah! Thank you, Jesu!

Sola made sure she looked in another direction, quickly. She was aslant to him, and far enough away that he might not notice her at all on the crowded street, but that was not a chance she was going to take, not after her last couple of encounters with Flexers. This one wasn't going to spot her, no way.

She started walking, blended with a group of tourists, and watched Weems peripherally. As luck had it, he turned and headed up the sidewalk in the same direction. He touched the cane's tip down often enough so it appeared he needed its support. A good beginning, saving her from having to turn around or cross the street.

Her cam was inside her handbag, the gel lens peering through a tiny opening, and she subvocalized her commands to the instrument. The heads-up on the inside of her own polarized glasses showed a mob. She ordered the cam to stabilize and zoom, centered it on Weems, and started recording. It wasn't action stuff, but it was good background, and with him filling the frame, it was a sequence she could use under opening credits. At the very least, she would have footage of him more current than anything anybody else had. She was already ahead of the game.

Mentally, she started writing the voice-over: "Meet Zachary Bretton Weems, out for a stroll in the picturesque terran city of New Orleans. He looks just like any other tourist, maybe a bit less fit than most with his walking stick, and you'd never guess to look at him that he is the deadliest man in the galaxy, *the* champion player of the Musashi Flex, that loose agglomeration of duelists who fight for fame and sometimes money . . ."

Too sugary? Too pat? Well, that was the easy part, the writing, she could do that anytime. Once she had the visuals, the words would come. Anybody could write.

Later, she would figure out a way to approach him, get an interview, maybe even some scenes of him fighting, but she didn't want to rush it. She was platinum at the moment, and gleaming in the sun. Best to enjoy it while she could.

* * *

Mourn didn't know how long the woman had been following Weems. He didn't spot her until Weems sat down at
an open-air place called Cafe Du Monde and ordered coffee and one of the sweet confections the locals called
beignets, but it was her, Sola, the girl from Madrid. He
smiled at the memory. She was tenacious, he had to give
her that. She had found out that Weems was here, and was
now shadowing him. Being cautious about it, too, but that
was no guarantee she hadn't been spotted—Mourn had
tagged her, and he couldn't claim any more skill at detect-
ing tails than her quarry.

At the moment, Mourn was across the narrow street, inside a little shop, loading a handbasket with pecan pralines,
whatever the hell those were, with plenty of cover. He
could barely see the two, and if they looked his way, they
wouldn't be able to see him, not enough to ID him.

He did note that Weems had his cane with him. It was
hooked on the edge of the table a few centimeters away
from his right hand. He had gone to the carbon fiber, so it
was said, because he hated putting dings in his custom-
made hickory or snakewood sticks, made for him by a master canesmith and fighter named McNeill. McNeill made the
carbon-fiber jobs, too, but reportedly under protest—they
were just so . . . plain and ugly. Still, while the customer
wasn't always right, when you supplied the weapons for
the top-rated Flex player, it didn't hurt your sales, so
plain and ugly he wanted, plain and ugly he got.

Weems had bashed enough heads with the carbon-fiber
suckers and never broken one of the canes, so the old saw
about form following function seemed valid enough.

But here was the woman, who, far as he could tell,
didn't have a clue Mourn was here. Of course, she wasn't
looking for him, she was focused on Weems, that was her
error. Maybe Number One hadn't tagged her or Mourn yet.
He would, eventually, no question of that. You simply could
not tail somebody of his caliber for very long without being

burned, not unless you did it electronically and from a distance. One person alone doing a sub-rosa surveillance had only a limited time before a hinky target would see him. Or her.

Mourn himself had no intention of staying on Weems that long.

He knew what Sola was up to, given their visit, but he didn't know how she was going to play it, and it was a risky thing for her, though she probably didn't know how risky. Weems liked his privacy, more than most players. He lived for the contest, and all the rest of it was, as he had been heard to say, rat feces, as far as he was concerned. He might not take kindly to being watched by a spindoc, even one who planned to make him look good. He didn't care how he looked.

Well, it was not Mourn's biz. He had come to check Weems out, strictly strategic and tactical stuff, that was all. He'd mark the man's moves, try to get a sense of what he was about, and move on. Whatever happened to the woman was her problem.

Moving on meant to another world, too. He had gotten what he had come to Earth to learn, the art of *pentjak silat,* and the only way to get better at that was to go off and practice it for a couple hours a day for ten or twelve years. Along the way, he was sure to come across some other esoteric martial art that would call to him, and probably he would try to learn it.

Mourn grinned at the thought. There were some principles in *silat* he hadn't paid much mind to that he wanted to play with a little. When he had been young and strong, able to leap into the air high enough to kick a tall man in the face—and hit him three more times with both hands on the way down—he'd gloried in his speed and power. With the state of medicine, he could easily make it to 120 or 130, more if some of the newer treatments being researched panned out, but not with the reflexes and strength he'd had when he'd been 25. The idea that position and timing could compensate for what he was losing had its appeal.

Thing was, it was hard to give up the old ways. As long as the body would do what it used to do, putting that technique aside wasn't easy. Why would you?

Mainly because you might reach for it one day and it wouldn't be there, and *that* would get you killed. Best learn to fight smarter and not harder, especially when you yourself were getting softer and not harder.

Or, as the saying went: Old and treacherous may not beat young and strong every time, but that's the way the wise money bets . . .

But whatever principles he might eventually learn, they weren't going to be in place in this town on this day, and if he caught Weems crooked, the man would beat the crap out of him.

Mourn had a romantic bent now and again, but about some things he was a realist, and fighting was one of them. You didn't get to be *Primero* on luck, and while Mourn figured there were a couple, maybe three, possibly even as many as four people in the Top Ten he could take, or at least fight to a draw on a good day, Weems was not among them. Weems could hammer him down and be half a galaxy away before Mourn woke up inside a Healy, full of tubes and hoping nothing was permanent—and that was if Weems was feeling merciful.

It would be great to call Weems out and kick his ass.

So would being able to fly by jumping up and flapping your arms, and he had about the same chance at that as he did of taking Weems in a fair contest. Weems was the best. Mourn wasn't even close.

No, he had pretty much what he had come for. A few days to clean up his affairs here, he'd be on his way. He could stay out of Weems's way for that long.

He went to the checkout kiosk, pressed his credit cube against the reader, and had his purchases scanned and debited by the din running the kiosk. The din bagged the candy and heat-sealed the biodegradable plastic bag shut. No alarms went off as Mourn exited the store.

As he made his way along the walk, a transient approached him. "Spare a stad to help a hungry flo'man?"

"Here," Mourn said. He handed him the bag of pralines. "Sell these, they should buy you a jolt of whatever juice you need. About thirty standards worth, still store-sealed."

The man took the package, looked at the candy through the clear plastic. "I'd prefer hard curry, but I guess this is okay."

Mourn shook his head. Amazing how many times he had met beggars who were choosers.

What the hell, it didn't matter. He decided in that moment that he was done here, and he started looking for a hack to take him to the port. He didn't really need to wait at all. He'd go back to Madrid, sell his workout dummy and turn in his housing docs, grab his guitar and head for deep vac. Why not?

He saw Weems get up, collect his cane, and amble away from the table.

Something in the man's manner rang odd, and Mourn's gut-level instinct was that Weems had spotted his tail. Whether it was himself or the woman—or both—Mourn couldn't tell, but in that moment, he was certain *Primero* was burned.

Well, said the *atman* voice in his mind, *so what? Didn't you just decide you were done? Find that taxi and be gone. Whatever Weems does or doesn't do doesn't concern you, right?*

Then he saw the woman come to her feet and head for the street, and he remembered how he had smiled when she had tried to run that "I'll-tell-your-story" con past him. If Weems had spotted her, which, Mourn had to believe was more likely than Weems spotting *him,* then she could be in trouble. Weems's sexual preference was, from what Mourn knew, for women, though there wasn't a lot more than that floating around. Maybe he might decide to lure her down some empty alley for a little fun. He'd know she wasn't a Player from the way she moved, and like a lot of Flexers, Weems didn't have much respect for anybody who wasn't one. Would he thump the young woman around and then prong her, just for fun? His option.

And the little voice in his head said, *Which part of "So what?" didn't you copy, dink-brain? Somebody die and leave you in charge of rescuing women from their stupid mistakes? Because if they* did, *you are gonna be a busy, busy man from here on out.*

Weems was moving off, practically strolling, and that wasn't right either. Weems wasn't the kind of man who ordinarily *strolled* anywhere, from what Mourn knew of him.

So, he's setting a trap. No worry, you're leaving, remember? Can't catch what isn't here, can he? And she is not your responsibility.

Mourn shook his head. That wouldn't be right, to leave her to Weems. He could go warn her off. Tell her she'd been spotted. At least that much.

Aw, fuck. You are gonna get us killed!

10

"This is perhaps, uh...not the, uh, wisest course of action, sir," Bevins said.

Shaw grinned at the medico. They were in the infirmary, and Shaw was naked, sitting on the exam table, butt sunk into the biogel pad. Nice and warm, the stuff was.

"Don't you mean, 'This is extremely stupid'?"

Bevins looked uncomfortable but did not speak. It wouldn't be in him to make that kind of comment to the man who held his reins.

Behind him, Dr. Tenae shook her head slowly.

"Something you wanted to add?" Shaw said.

She glanced at Bevins, then at Shaw. " 'Suicidally stupid' would be closer to it, M. Shaw. 'Moronically stupid.' "

Shaw laughed. He liked this woman. Ass-kissers were a demistad a dozen, people with balls—they were worth their weight in platinum.

"Barry is still alive and happy enough, isn't he?"

"It's only been *one* day," Tenae said. "He could keel over

tomorrow, next week, next month, next year—we don't
have any idea how this will affect him in the long term."

"Dr. Tenae is correct," Bevins said, sensing which way
the wind was blowing here. "That the treatment did not
kill the creature immediately is, of course, a major breakthrough, but hardly conclusive. We are years away from
human protocols."

"Nope, we are about five seconds away from testing it
on a human being." Shaw picked up the skinpopper, a
small gun-shaped mechanical device that used high-
pressure compressed gas to inject medications through human or animal skin and into the muscle. Old-tech, but
sometimes the old ways still worked just fine.

"Don't do it," Tenae said.

"Who authorizes the credit transfers around here?"

"Who the hell is going to authorize *ours* if we let you
kill yourself?" she said.

Shaw laughed again. "Recorder, annotate and verify
this, please. In the event of my death, Dr. Isura Tenae is to
receive from my estate one million standards."

"Annotated and verified," said the recording computer's
deep voice.

"Happy? If I die, you get rich."

"It's still a bad idea," she said. "You're supposed to be a
smart man—you *know* better!"

He smiled again. He was going to give her the money
anyway, for that line. Because he wasn't going to die.

With that, he pressed the popper's muzzle against his
thigh and squeezed the trigger. The resulting *spat!* was
loud, it stung a little, and the stuff was cold, like being
stabbed to the bone with a blade of solid carbon dioxide.
He put the popper down and took a deep breath. "How
long?"

Tenae shrugged. "We don't have a clue. Nobody saw
Barry make a fast move until several hours after the injection. But maybe he didn't have any reason to hurry before

then. You're bigger, heavier, and a different species. We don't even know if the stuff will work at all."

"It'll work," Shaw said.

Both the medicos stared at him.

"All right. Let us hook you into the monitors—" Bevins began.

"Nope. It kills me, it will be while I am going about my business."

Both doctors shook their heads at this.

Shaw started to dress. Tenae said, "Will you let the vouch follow you around, at least?"

"Sure. I've kind of gotten used to the little fellow dogging my heels." He looked at his chronograph. "I need to get to a meeting. I'll keep you apprised of the situation."

As he walked away from the infirmary, the medical robot duly rolling along behind him a discreet three meters back, Shaw reflected that Bevins and Tenae probably thought he was insane. What billionaire would risk his life on an untried chem if he didn't have to? Maybe if he were dying of some dread disease and there was only one possible cure and it *might* be fatal, sure, anybody could see that. But to inject something that could kill you just because it maybe would give you reflexes and speed faster than normal? And not even be sure of that?

Oh, yeah. Crazier than a spazhead on suckle.

But it wasn't going to kill him. The little rock ape's vital signs were perfect, and while it was possible that there might be some long-term side effect, Shaw didn't believe that, either. Because he *knew*.

Sometimes he got these feelings. They were rare, had happened but four times in his life, he could remember each one vividly. There came a kind of tingling sensation in his body, as if he were being bathed in a mild electrical current. Combined with the physical effect was a sudden epiphany, a kind of *déjà verité,* a revelation of truth. It was the oddest thing. He had not read about anything quite like it in the medical literature; but each and every time it had happened, whatever it showed him, that thing always came to pass. When his mother died, when he took over as Chairman, when he *knew* a woman across the room would come over and say exactly the words she said. And now, not an hour past, with Reflex, that same certainty: The stuff was going to work. He'd bet his life on it.

He *had* bet his life on it, but he was not worried. If his gift let him down and it killed him? Well, fuck it, nobody lived forever. He had gone everywhere he had wanted to go, eaten the best foods, drunk the best wines, slept with the best women. He was a giant of industry, worth more than some wheelworlds, and the only goal he had not accomplished was to become a player and win the Musashi Flex. This drug was going to give him that. And afterward? Well, he'd worry about that later.

He was supposed to see Baba for his training in a few minutes. It was too much to hope for that the drug would kick in while he was training, allowing him to astound the shit out of Baba. The little old bastard would be impressed if Shaw did a drumroll on his head before Baba could blink; but if the rock ape hadn't come up to speed, so to speak, for seven and some hours, a few minutes for Shaw wasn't likely.

Well. Whatever. There would come another time.

Weems led them to a public schoolyard. Apparently the place was not in session, and there were only a few people around, kids playing on outdoor rec gear, swings, twirlers, bouncers, like that. It wasn't an empty alley, it was a big, open space, and the far corner of a playing field under some big oak trees was enough away from anybody so that it was effectively private. Even if somebody saw them and decided to head that way, Weems would have plenty of time to break Sola's neck and be on his way before help could get there. Not that there was anybody around here who, short of shooting him, *could* help her.

That left out Mourn, too, since he was too far back to catch her without yelling, and Weems wasn't deaf . . .

Nothing wrong with his eyes, either, so he could also see anybody trying to follow him across the schoolyard. Tailing somebody on foot across a tagball field unseen in the middle of the afternoon was pretty much impossible unless the person being tailed was blind or stupid, and Weems wasn't stupid, either.

Sola had some chops, Mourn already knew. She saw which way Weems was heading and circled away, using bushes and benches for cover, trying to flank him. But if he hadn't known she was behind him yet, all he had to do was glance back, and he'd spot her fast enough. She couldn't stay back far enough to be completely hidden and maintain surveillance. By the time she got to the edge of the yard, he'd be long gone.

Mourn, once he realized what Weems was up to, backed off and ran, circling around the schoolyard out of sight, hoping to get to a hiding place where his quarry would emerge. It was risky. If Weems stopped and turned back, he'd be gone before Mourn could pick him up again.

Mourn made it around. There was a gate in the expanded-metal fence that surrounded the school; it was open, and that was where Weems would emerge. Mourn's sense of time made it that he had thirty or forty seconds to find a hiding spot before Weems came through the gate. He spotted a big trash bin behind a cube complex and slid between it and the wall, crouched low.

Thirty seconds went by.

Sixty seconds.

Ninety . . .

Mourn swore softly. Weems could have hurried, gotten through the gate, and be six blocks away by now. Or he could have stopped in the yard, under the trees where he was hidden from Mourn's view. Or he could have turned around and headed back the way he'd come, to catch out his tail.

Or he could have fallen down and broken his fucking leg and be lying there on the grass in pain, hey? Really have a use for that cane he carries?

Mourn smiled at himself. *Yeah, right.*

Okay, now what?

Only one way to figure it out. Go look.

Mourn moved from his hiding place and headed for the gate.

Inside the schoolyard again, he saw them fast enough. Weems, with Sola, fifty meters away. He had her backed up against one of the thick-boled trees, not touching her, but close. She was talking fast, Mourn could see that even though he couldn't hear her, and maybe Weems was buying what she was selling—

Weems flicked a hand out and slapped her. It wasn't much, enough to sting and rock her head a little; he was playing with her, but Mourn realized that Sola was in deep shit.

He took a deep breath and headed toward them.

Weems caught the movement peripherally, spared Mourn a quick glance, realized who he was. He grinned, real big. Reached out and patted Sola's face where he had slapped her, a quick one-two. She swung on him, a hard right hand knotted into a fist. He blocked it, never taking his gaze from Mourn, slipped his hand forward and caught her by the throat. When she tried to punch again, he squeezed, enough to stop her struggles.

When he was five meters away, Mourn stopped.

"Hello, Mourn."

"Primero."

"She yours? Or are you just . . . passing by?"

"She's mine. Let her go. Dance with me instead."

"You aren't as pretty. And you don't have the steps."

"Maybe."

Weems laughed softly, released his grip on Sola's throat.

Mourn said to her, "Once we get started, you take off."

"You can call it," Weems said. He waggled the cane in his hand.

"Bare."

"Smart. But it won't matter, you know." Weems hooked the cane over a projecting nail or screw on the tree and took two steps to his left away from Sola.

"Want to warm up? Do a few push-ups?" Weems smiled broadly.

Mourn continued breathing deeply through his nose, reaching for the bottom of his lungs with each inhalation. He had the oxygen he needed, he had started as soon as he had seen them.

Weems moved toward him, as if he was walking over to turn on a light switch, no tension at all.

Mourn turned sideways, angling into the *silat* stance, right hand high, left low. Then he opened his right arm, giving Weems a clear shot at his head.

Weems laughed again. "Come *on,* Mourn! You came all this way to *insult* me?"

Mourn shook his head. How had he gotten himself into this?

The place on South Park Njia ya Mji had been a plain-vanilla office building, with a lot more security than it would normally rate. Azul discovered why when she got to the suite with a pair of heavily armed guards accompanying her: Newman Randall, the Confed's PR, sat behind a desk, smiling. He'd gestured at the guards, who vanished, then at the couch. She'd sat, and he'd laid it out.

There was a man, Ellis M. Shaw, who owned most of the largest pharmaceutical company in the galaxy. Randall

wanted UO Azul to get next to the man and find out everything she could about a new drug he was developing. It
was called "Reflex," and he wanted to know *every*thing.

She had shrugged. Fine.

He was conducting some personal inquiries into this
matter, he'd said. But he would keep any information he
gathered to himself and check it against what she learned.
He did not wish to influence her.

She shrugged again. Oh, by the way, did PR Randall
know that somebody had put a tail on her when she'd arrived on this world?

No. He hadn't known that. He would check into it. But
what mattered was her assignment.

"That's always what matters," she'd told him.

He would contact her again soon, he'd said. He'd smiled,
and she'd stood, nodded, and left. At least he hadn't told
her how to do her job. They sometimes did that. The more
money and power they had, the more they tended to think
that made them experts at everything. She recalled being
fascinated the first time she met a really rich man and realized that he wasn't particularly smart. You could be rich and
stupid—a good lesson in that realization.

A few days later, after a lot of preparation, Azul had
enough of a picture to begin working on ways to put herself into Shaw's path in a manner that wouldn't cause his,
or his security's, eyebrows to rise.

Having Confed Intelligence at your call to build you a
plausible background was invaluable. CI's ID Section
could produce birth, education, job, and hobby records;
they could fake holographs, a family, old friends; they could
produce souvenir place mats from the restaurant where you
ate lunch during your primary school trip to the San Carlos
Zoo when you were nine years old, suitably aged and wrin-
kled and with notes on it in your undeveloped handwriting.

This ersatz background would pass virtually any test because such history instantly became part of the official records available to anybody looking for them. The family or old friends were themselves operatives, and they would know your history and be able to offer it to anybody checking on you. It was as ship-hull solid as it could be: You became who you said you were, and nobody outside of CI who had set it up could tell differently. And if the CI op who had built your fake ID got into a traffic accident and died before she could log it into the proper system? You could become a whole new person and not even the Confed could see different.

Another good lesson to keep in mind against the day when you might need it . . .

For the moment, though, the trick was to build a character that would appeal to your target, and you had to assume that a man as rich and powerful as M. Shaw *would* check you out as a matter of course.

Shaw, it seemed, had an interest in the Musashi Flex. While Azul could certainly take care of herself in a routine physical encounter requiring self-defense, bare-handed or with a weapon, she was not skilled enough to fake being a high-level player. However, she could have a long-lost brother—she liked that idea—who had been, say, a Top Player in the Flex before he retired or died or whatever. Shaw was a student of martial arts, he had hired major players to come and teach him. It would be a connection of interest to him to meet a beautiful woman who was related to somebody he knew about. She'd never even have to make that claim, he would find it out on his own. And being beautiful? That was part of her biz. Normally, she could and did slouch around, dress down, and deliberately make herself less attractive. This was also part of the biz—you didn't want the attention all the time. But when she needed it, Luna Azul could be a drop-dead gorgeous knockout. It was a big part of why she had been hired, and while all of her beauty

wasn't natural—there had been a couple of discreet surger-
ies to complete the package—most of her looks were innate,
and such that, even unaugmented, they would open doors for
her anywhere there were men—or women—who had eyes
and lusts. It didn't mean anything to her in particular. It was
just a useful tool.

So, there were two things: a brother who was an adept
in something Shaw was into, and her own attractions. The
third would be to have some professional knowledge Shaw
might find of interest. CI could supply that. It could be in
the pharmaceutical biz. He was also an art collector of
some note. Maybe she could be an artist. CI had some of
those at its beck, they could produce some first-class paintings or sculpture, make them hers. She had a list of the major works Shaw owned; she could become an adept at
drawing or molding something that would catch his eye.
The trick was in figuring out what, not in the actual production of it. An up-and-coming artist from a world far
away, with a history, some shows, local glowing reviews in
news stats or entcom, some works that would be created
specifically to appeal to one man, this was another easy
task for Confed Intelligence.

Then there would need to be some public event at which
they could meet, through his action and not hers. A showing, some theatrical thing, charity event, whatever. She had
a list of charities Shaw supported, and of events he had attended, or was scheduled to attend.

It was all in the preparation and the timing. That he was
rich and well protected? Not a problem. She had done this
sort of thing many times before. She expected to do it
many times again.

Trolling for a particular fish might not be the easiest
thing, but if you had the right bait, it raised the chances of
your success. Azul was good at what she did, she had no
false modesty about that. If he could be hooked by anybody, then she would the one who could do it.

She would get her information and ID. She wouldn't tell ID Section what her mission was, nor would they ask. She'd be cleared for whatever she asked them to get, because when a PR wanted something, nobody downlevels wanted to stand in his path; neither did they want to be too close to it—if the deal went sour, better to be able to deny you knew anything about it. Covering one's ass in CI was practically an art form . . .

She smiled, not worried. If you had the will and you had the tools, it was just a matter of time . . .

When he was a step and a half away, Mourn jumped, bore in, and threw the fifth of the attack *sambuts,* a single beat broken into a triplet with a punch for each third— high, high, *low*—!

Even if you knew what was coming, it was impossible to block all three if the attacker sold them right. You had to short-circuit the attack with one of your own; pure blocking wouldn't work, no matter who you were.

Weems apparently thought he could manage it. He batted the first and second shots aside, but the third punch got through, hit him in the belly—

It was like smacking your fist into a wooden wall.

Mourn tried for the takedown, but Weems pivoted and hammered him with the edge of his fist, caught him in the ribs hard enough to break one or two. It drove him sideways, and Weems followed him in—

Mourn fired his right elbow, caught Weems on the left ear, staggered him, but when he tried to follow up, Weems ducked the next punch and slammed his fist into Mourn's solar plexus, knocking his wind out—

Mourn dropped to the ground and swept with his left leg. Caught Weems on the left calf and knocked him off-balance, but Weems dived away, hit in a shoulder roll, and came up—

Before Mourn could get to his feet, Weems jumped in—Jesu, he was fast!—and snapped a front kick. He blew through Mourn's block, caught him under the left armpit, broke a couple more ribs, and lifted him with the force of it—

Mourn went with the kick, rolled away, barely avoided the stomp to his head, and managed to get into a *siloh* squat.

Weems recognized the danger, circled to get behind him; Mourn scooted away and came up—

As Weems charged in, Mourn waited . . . waited . . . *now!* he dropped low, put his left hand into Weems's face, fingers spread, and went for the eyes. Weems slowed his rush, Mourn shoved at his face and reached for the leading leg, caught him behind the knee, to do *angkat,* the throw from the unweighted leg—

Weems dropped his weight, trapped Mourn's hand with his flexed knee, twisted, and drove a spear-hand at Mourn's throat—

Mourn blocked, deflected the attack enough so it drove into his shoulder instead of his throat, felt the muscle tear in a hot flash—

Weems kneed him, caught him on the back of the head, knocked him down, the blow enough to stun him. Mourn's vision blurred, he grayed out, but even half-unconscious, he tried to cover. He knew it wouldn't be enough, and knew he was more than a beat behind. He'd never be able to catch up, but he struggled to get up—

There was a sharp hum, and Weems suddenly collapsed, falling next to Mourn.

What the *fuck*—?

Mourn shook his head, trying to clear his vision. That didn't help, it only made his head hurt worse. He blinked. What—?

Sola came into view. She was holding a hand wand. Shaking like a woman with palsy.

He stared at her. "You *shot* him?"

"Goddamn right I did. He hit me."

He started to laugh, but it hurt his ribs, and he stopped. "Welcome to the club," he said. He managed to get to his feet. Man. He was going to be immobile once his injuries took hold.

"Thanks," he said.

"What are you doing here?" she said.

"I was passing by."

She was so rattled she let that go. "Did you see what he did? He was enjoying it, slapping and choking me!" Her voice was high and still full of fear and rage.

"Come on, we have to go. Once he wakes up, he'll kill us both if he catches us. We want to be far away from here."

Still holding the hand wand, she looked at Weems. "Why don't you just cut his throat while he's lying there unconscious? Stomp his fucking head in!"

"Can't," he said, shaking his head. *Ow.* Bad idea.

"Why not? You've killed men before."

"It wouldn't be fair."

She laughed, and it was on the edge of hysterical. "He would have stomped *you* to death! And probably raped me when he was finished with you!"

"That doesn't matter," he said. "Come on."

After a hurried trip to collect her gear and his—which included a guitar, of all things—they caught a local out of the region, then an uplight boxcar from the Central Mediterranean Terran Port to the wheelworld called Segundo, at the L-5 point between the Earth and Luna. There, they transferred to a liner heading galactic spinward, eventually to wind up in the Faust System, by way of Orm and Kar. Since those two systems had only one habitable planet each—Greaves, in Orm, and Makarooni, in Kar—it was as much as an express flight as they were apt to get. Even if Weems was able to track them, he wouldn't be able to get to their destination ahead of them. At least that's what Mourn told her.

On board, they stowed their gear in a fairly large cabin with two bunks, then went to find the clinic. Mourn seemed to be moving okay, but he said he might need some minor work. Given what she had seen, she had no trouble believing that. The two men had hit each other with fists and elbows and feet hard enough to break furniture, no question. Mourn was stoic, but he had to be in some pain.

He had purchased two open-ended tickets, paid for them—and they weren't cheap, since the flight was leaving less than an hour after they booked it. She'd thanked him, but he'd waved it off. "You saved my life."

"Well, you saved my virtue."

They both smiled at that.

"We can leave the ship at any of four destinations," he said. "Even if he tags us leaving, he won't know which world we drop on unless he can get the passenger manifest, which he isn't supposed to be able to do, but probably can. But we can catch a feeder and be off that planet before he can get there even if he does figure it out."

"And do what then?"

"It's a big galaxy," he said. "He isn't going to spend the rest of his life chasing us. I hope."

"Sooner or later he will find you, though, if you don't quit the Flex," she said.

"Yeah. Probably."

She raised an eyebrow.

He shrugged. "I'll have to up my game," he said.

"Just like that?"

"I didn't say it would be easy."

They made it to the ship's clinic, which was, like everything else on the starliner, sparkling new. The vessel, the

Ansel Park, was the size of a seagoing luxury ship, could carry three thousand passengers in comfort, and was essentially a small town in space. Starliners never touched atmosphere, they did all their travel in deep, most of it in Bender, only dropping out of warp near a feeder station.

The medico was a dour woman of sixty or seventy who took one look at Mourn and waved him toward the Healy. Mourn shucked his clothes without any false modesty, and Sola gasped at the size and colors of the bruises he sported. And at all the old scars.

He climbed into the Healy like a man who had done it more than a few times. The lid clamshelled shut, motors and pumps whirred to life, and there was a disinfectant smell when the bug-killer lamps strobed and flared actinically.

The medico went to the Healy's control panel and waved her hands over the sensors.

"So, what happened to you?"

"I fell down the stairs." His voice came from the device's amplifier and echoed hollowly.

The medico cackled, a hoarse, raspy laugh. "Yeah, you did, and I'm the fucking Queen of Charlene, too. You're a player."

"Good guess."

"I've seen a few fight injuries. And you didn't get all those old scars bumping down the risers, boy. How'd the other guy look?"

"Last time I saw him, he was out cold on the playground lawn."

"He fall down, too?"

"After somebody hand-wanded him."

She shook her head. "Well, let's see. You have five, six, *seven* broken ribs, none compound, fortunately. Torn obliques, torn intercostals, what looks like a bruised liver, a leaky spleen, interabdominal bleeding is going pretty good, not to mention some great contusions and abrasions. Your 'crit and hemoglobin are on the way down, and your left wrist is broken. Left fifth metacarpal, too, boxer's fracture. You should know better than to punch with that knuckle."

"I was in a hurry."

"Yeah, well, I'm surprised you walked away under your own power."

"I didn't want to be there when he woke up," Mourn said.

She cackled again.

"Well, you know the routine. Bones we can orthostat, I can transfuse enough oxyliq to make the blood flow okay, maybe a couple pints of whole, but I make your in-case time at, six, six-and-a-half hours for the spleen and liver. No way around it."

"I need to pee first," he said.

"After I got IVs set and running? Nope. You know where the catheter is. Oil M. Willie and shove it in, you are there for the duration."

Mourn sighed.

"Shoulda thought of that before you picked a fight with Goliath. He have a weapon?"

"He is a weapon."

"That's good, I like that one."

Sola walked to the Healy and peered though the clear lid. "You want me to stay and visit with you?"

"No reason to. Might as well get some rest yourself. It has been a long day."

"Boy, has it," she said. "I'll come back when the time is up."

"Okay. Doc, you got something to take the edge off so I can sleep?"

"Already pumping," the medico said. "Sweet dreams, M. Mourn."

Sola watched him fade into slumber.

"Is he going to be all right?" she asked the medico.

"Yeah, no sweat. He's a tough bastard, I'll give him that. On a scale of one to ten, he had to be hurting at least eight, and getting so anemic that if he stood up suddenly he'd have passed out. Man has discipline."

Sola nodded. Yes. She knew.

11

Shaw was in the middle of dinner when time slowed down.

The workout with Baba had been uneventful, the rest of the afternoon standard. He had felt fine, albeit somewhat more nervous than he had let on. The vouch followed him around, humming and whirring, and hadn't felt the need to rush forward and start pumping chem into him while screaming for medical help. Not yet, anyway.

But as he lifted a bite of hot and spicy dillnut noodle to his mouth, one of the strands slipped from the grip of the ivory chopsticks.

Shaw watched as the noodle fell. It wasn't like some entcom slomo effect, but it was definitely moving slower than normal in one gee. Without any particular sense of speed, he reached out with his free hand and managed to catch the falling bit of food.

Unless gravity had just changed the rules, the drug had finally kicked in. Son of a bitch.

He hadn't known how it would manifest, hadn't really thought about it, but here it was: The drug fired up, lit, and what it gave was the illusion that everything else had slowed, and that he was moving at normal speed. The truth was the opposite, but the effect was the same. An example of subjective relativity, so it seemed.

He took his water glass and heaved the contents straight up. The water stretched out in a fat globule and started to come down, and he was able to move the glass under it, catching most of the falling mass. Not all of it, he wasn't quite quick enough, but certainly he was faster than normal. Much faster.

Damn! This is great!

"Cervo!"

"Sir?" Cervo said.

"I need to see you in here."

"Yes, sir, right away."

Well, his speech hadn't been affected, that was good.

Cervo arrived ten seconds later and his movements didn't seem any slower than usual. Hmm.

"Sir."

"I need you to punch me," Shaw said. He pointed to his nose. "Right here."

"Sir?"

"Not hard enough to kill me, but fast, fast as you can."

Cervo nodded. "Yes, sir."

The giant stepped forward and snapped a punch at Shaw's face.

He had sparred with Cervo many times. The big man was quick, if not as quick as a flyweight. This time, the punch looked like a tai chi move, smooth, but maybe half the normal speed. Maybe the drug needed adrenaline to make it work?

Shaw slid to the side, deflected the punch with a slap block, and tagged Cervo's ribs with a one-two combination, not hard enough to cause any damage but enough to sting a little. He saw Cervo trying to react, but the man couldn't get out of the way.

"Yes!" Shaw yelled. "How did I look?"

"Never seen you move that fast before, sir," Cervo said. "Never seen anybody move that fast before."

"You were throwing at full speed?"

"Sir. Quick as I could."

"Yes, yes! Computer, mark the time, acknowledge."

"Time: 1847 hours, twelve seconds," the cube's computer said.

To Cervo, Shaw said, "Okay, let's see how long it lasts. Another punch, please."

Cervo nodded and came in, again moving as if he were a little better than half speed. Shaw waited, then just ducked and stepped to the side.

"Keep going!"

Cervo turned, slid forward, brought his right leg up in a muy thai kick, shin aiming for Shaw's thigh. Shaw waited, jumped over the attacking leg, came down, and danced behind the bigger man.

Cervo twisted, spun, and Shaw knew he could step in, smash the man with any tool he had, and be back out before Cervo could react.

Shaw dropped, shot his left leg out, swept, and caught Cervo behind the knees. He rarely could sweep the big man, his placement had to be perfect, but he went down this time.

Jesu, is this great, or what?

Things started to speed up for him after an hour. By an hour and a half, he was only slightly faster, and by the start of the second hour, he was back to normal.

He was also totally exhausted and starving. He had burned a lot of energy, and his heart rate was still elevated, up to 120, twice his usual resting pulse. What had it been at the peak?

He dismissed Cervo and called his vouch over and asked it for a record of his telemetry.

The device printed out a sheet and he looked at it. Only 170 beats per minute at the peak, that was high, but not dangerously so for a man in good shape. Respiration up to 26 per minute, but again, nothing beyond his limits. Blood pressure spiked to 160/90, no real danger there for an hour or two.

Body temp had spiked a couple of degrees, but if that worried the vouch, it hadn't said anything.

Already, his mind was whirling with ideas. An hour, ninety minutes? That was more than enough time for any match, though the timing to get to it might be tricky. He'd have to come up with some kind of faster delivery, to get the drug into his system quicker. If he could get the onset down to say, fifteen or twenty minutes, then he could track an opponent and stay with him long enough for the chem to kick in.

Even if they couldn't fix that, all he would have to do was be careful of his timing, make sure he didn't bump into another player until the Reflex had bloomed.

He laughed aloud. *God, this is fucking great!*

I am going to do it! Finally!

When Mourn awoke inside the Healy, the unit's clock showed that he had been asleep for four hours. He felt a little better, mostly due to the analgesics the machine had pumped into him. On the other hand, lying in a coffin-sized box unable to move, even with a clear denscris lid, full of needles stuck into your veins with a piss-drain tube up your lingam was not a situation he was ever apt to find pleasant.

He had at least two more hours before he could exit the medical unit, maybe longer, and since he was awake and couldn't move, thinking was his main option.

Since the reason he found himself in one of these bastards was usually the same, the first order of business was generally performance review.

Mourn replayed the fight with Weems.

First, he ran through his general impressions. What stood out, of course, were the strikes that Weems had gotten in, the bone-breakers being hard to forget even had he wanted to do so. What could he have done better to stop those?

Next, he went over relative positions during the exchanges, distances, angles, trying to imagine what it would have looked like from behind, above, Weems's point of view.

Then, he considered his own attacks, those that had landed, those that hadn't, and ways he might have better launched them.

He could have spent some time berating himself for his stupidity by challenging Weems in the first place, but done was done, and there was no sense in wasting energy on that, he couldn't undo it.

All in all, he hadn't done badly. Yes, he had lost, but he had known going in that he was going to lose. Weems was the best fighter out there, everybody knew it, and nobody knew it better than a highly ranked player such as Mourn. No dishonor in losing to a superior artist.

What could he have done to make it go his way?

After replaying it half a dozen times, Mourn knew the answer to that: Nothing.

Given the tools he had, which were not inconsiderable, he'd still never had a real chance of winning against a man of Weems's caliber, not unless *Primero* made a big error. At his level, players didn't make big errors. Yes, he had gotten a couple of good licks in, done some damage against the best player out there. He had marked him enough so he would remember it, and there was some small pride to be taken from that, but the end had never really been in doubt—and both he and Weems had known it.

Mourn sighed, realized he wasn't breathing properly and getting enough oxy. He concentrated on that for a few seconds until his heart rate dropped back to normal, around fifty beats per minute.

All right.

He looked at the clock. His review had taken only thirty minutes. He had time to kill.

He considered the woman who had probably saved his life, but there wasn't much point in trying to dissect that—he needed to talk to her again before he had enough information to think about her properly.

So he might as well work out. The painkillers were somato-specifics, they weren't making his mind fuzzy, and doing a mental workout, while not as good as doing one physically, was better than nothing. He'd start with the eighteen *djurus* from *silat,* first with blades, then bare, at slow speed, then fast, which would take an hour or so. After that, he'd see what else called to him.

Sola lay on one of the bunks and looked around the cabin. It was a large room, three meters by three meters, with a walk-in fresher that held a water shower, toilet, and sink. Business class, and a lot nicer than how she usually did vac travel, in the coach dorms. In the dorms, you had a narrow bunk, and your privacy, such as it was, consisted of a curtain-oval that nearly touched the edges of the bunk when pulled shut. Flop an arm out while lying asleep and you'd likely hit the passenger snoring next to you. Need to pee in the middle of the night, and you had to wend your way among the beds to the public fresher and hope nobody was in there with a long novel they wanted to finish . . .

Mourn had told her they could have gotten first-class accommodations, but that such travel attracted too much attention. Low profile was the way to go. Authorities kept better track of people who could afford first-class galactic travel than they did the rabble. Rich people could be trouble, they knew their money gave them certain privileges and that sometimes made them demanding. The Confed had been getting altogether too self-important of late, he'd said, and the brisk military walk it had once used when spacing out to civilize the galaxy had turned into a swagger. He didn't want them swaggering into his room in the middle of the night asking questions he'd rather not answer. He lived at the outskirts of civilization, and broke enough laws on a regular basis that he was hardly a model citizen. But even a junkyard dog knows better than to bark loud enough for the wolves to hear him.

She had liked that conversation. She'd find a place for it in her show, no question. One had to accommodate the Confed—it was everywhere, all the time.

She had already reviewed the footage she had shot of the fight between Weems and Mourn, gone over it three times, and that few seconds alone was enough to make her documentary. The top-rated player going up against the tenth-rated, and with the added drama of her own participation—real, first-person, I'm-part-of-the-story journalism? Sheeit, it was a free kick, no goalkeep, an easy score. It needed to be good, of course, it needed to be fucking great, so that when it aired, it would knock the pants off the audience and the critics alike; but it was going to air, that she didn't doubt.

To get rich and win big awards? That would show her father, yes, indeed, it would.

She had squirted a copy of all her existing footage into the ship's computer, paid a storage fee, and a copy of the Weems/Mourn fight was on its way, via White Radio, to the Guild Archives on the wheelworld of Alpha Sub. She wasn't going to lose this by having some yahoo rip her cam or computer with their copies, no fucking way.

She looked at her chrono. The old lady medic would be letting Mourn out in another hour or so. There was no hurry, but she stood and headed for the fresher. A quick shower—the only kind allowed even in business class, she suspected—and she'd get dressed and go see how Mourn was doing. The man had saved her, at the least, from a beating, probably from a rape, as well. She'd never have gotten that hand wand out of her pocket without Weems— the bastard!—thumping her. She owed Mourn, in more ways than one. He had taken a hard ride for her, she had recorded it, and the footage she had gotten was the core of her project. Was that lucky, or what?

Besides, she liked the guy. He had a manner about him.

"Everything okay?" Shaw asked.

"As far as I can tell," Dr. Tenae said. She waved her hands at the diagnoster and the holographic reader translated her gestures into rest-mode command. "You can get dressed."

He grinned at her. "Do you have a familiar name you like?" He asked.

"Lissie."

Sitting naked on her exam table, he felt himself stirring, and certainly that would be evident to her. He said, "Lissie. I like it. Let me ask you a question: Would you have sex with me for a million stads?"

She smiled and shook her head, as if she couldn't believe the question.

"I'm serious."

There was a short pause. "Yes, I would."

"Computer, transfer one million standards from my personal account into Dr. Tenae's personal account."

"One million standards transferred," the computer said.

He waved at the exam table. "Join me?"

Tenae raised an eyebrow. "Right here and now? And payment in advance?"

"No time like the present, and we've got this nice

padded table and all. And I'm sure you will be worth it."

"That's true. I am," she said.

She removed her clothes, efficiently and with only a trace of suggestiveness, enough to cause his attention to spring to full alertness. Under the clothes, she was built well, wide hips, lush breasts, thick, glossy, black pubic hair. She looked better naked than he had expected. That hadn't really mattered. It was her mind that had attracted him, her spirit. Good looks were a bonus, but not necessary in this case.

She stepped out of her panties, moved toward him, bent, and took him into her mouth.

Ah, yes . . .

Half an hour later, after they had taken turns bringing each other to two orgasms each, they lay side by side on the exam table, looking at each other. He laughed.

"Did I miss the joke?"

"Well, yes. After you told me you thought my taking the Reflex was a stupid idea, and I put that million into a post-death account for you, I decided I was going to give it to you anyway. So you see, the money was really already yours when I offered it to you to play lingam-and-yoni. I conned you."

She laughed, a soft and low sound.

"Pretty funny, huh?"

She gave him a bright smile. "Oh, that's not what I'm laughing at."

"No?"

"No."

"What, then?"

"Well, you see, I would have pronged you for free."

He propped himself up on his elbow. "You would have."

She looked up at him. "You're a good-looking man. Fit, smart, brave, ambitious, rich. Even a little foolish. Attraction to such alpha males is hardwired into a woman's genes, just as a young and shapely female form calls to men—to normal heteros, anyway. So you see, you could have saved yourself a million stads and had me for free. Who conned whom?"

He laughed again, a deep, really amused one this time. "Hell, that's worth the million right there."

"You can get another helping, if you want. On the house."

"I think I'll take you up on that." He reached for her.

12

Once she'd made her decision—to become an artist—Azul posted her request to Confed Intelligence through a secure pipe. Field-ops had a lot of latitude in such matters, but the request would have to be approved by the head of Operations. It was pretty much a dupe seal deal, but it would take a little time for the programmers to get the request and set up the background and history. And longer for some on-call artists to create her portfolio. She had been fairly specific in what she wanted: She needed to be a painter, working primarily in acrylics, and the kinds of pictures her alter ego would create would be of a certain heroic-socialist stripe. She knew that M. Shaw had many of those in his collection, even if CI did not.

Meanwhile, Azul could do a little more on her own. If she was going to be an artist, she probably ought to know the lingo.

She called up an art program and started to read.

She didn't have an eidetic memory, but she tended to

absorb and be able to recall most of what she wanted to remember. For several hours, she scanned art history and appreciation files, specific techniques for specific styles of drawing and painting.

After a few hours, she stopped. No point in exhausting herself, it would be a few days or maybe even weeks before she could move into a direct-contact situation.

Another round of education needed to be on the Flex, following the biography of her player brother. She'd let CI pick somebody and link her to him, they had such data at hand, so she didn't have to worry about that until they got back to her.

Why she needed a brother who was a Flex player? None of their business. All they had to do was come up with him.

The hotel suite she'd rented was large and expensive— she'd need that later, and it came with a big soak tub, into which Azul was about to step. If she couldn't get away from the job, at least she could relax a little while she was doing it . . .

The hot water enveloped her, fragrant vapors rising, and she instantly felt better. The tub's motors stirred the water gently, enough to relax her muscles without being obtrusive. *Ah.*

Being a high-level Confed operative had some advantages. A woman from her background, raised poor as dirt, would have had to do a lot of work to earn the money needed to stay in places like this. Life wasn't so bad.

Mourn and Sola walked through the biggest of the ship's four gardens, a pocket-park that, with clever design, managed at times to make it look as if you were nowhere near civilization, much less on a giant starship. This particular park's theme was tropical, and there was even a program that offered regularly scheduled rains, complete with lightning flashes and muted thunder. It had been but a few minutes since the last such artificial rain, and the greenery was still wet and glistening under the high overhead spotlight that pretended to be a sun. Amazing how good the illusion was, with just a little suspension of disbelief on your part.

"How are you feeling?" she asked.

"Better."

"You were injured more than you let on."

"I've been hurt worse. You learn to deal with it."

"I want to thank you again, for what you did on Earth."

He shrugged. "You returned the favor and then some. Weems probably wouldn't have killed you. He might have chilled me, he was pissed off enough."

The recorded sounds of tropical birds played over them. A turning of the path revealed a small stream under a narrow bridge. A couple coming from the other direction waited for Mourn and Sola to cross, smiled at them—until they saw his still unfaded bruises. He had some *dit da jow* and *balour* in his travel bag; he'd have to use the liniments to help those contusions along. With all that modern medical science had achieved, the centuries-old martial arts remedies for healing bruises still worked as well as anything.

"So, where are we in regard to you helping with my project?" she asked.

He thought about it for a few seconds. Then he said, "Do you know where the Flex's name came from?"

She said, "I know it was called that after some kind of swordplayer from ancient times on Earth. Southeast Asian tap?"

He nodded. "Yes. Let me give you the lecture. Musashi was Nipponese, Nippon being a country of small islands. He was born in the late 1500s, C.E. time scale. The family names back then were long and convoluted, but the short version was Miyamoto Musashi—the last name actually being the name of the province where he was from."

She nodded. He saw her make sure her recorder was collecting it, said, "Go on."

"His father was a professional soldier—they were called *samurai*—who was in the employ of the lord of the local castle. Apparently his wife was highly placed, maybe even the daughter of the local ruler, though that is speculation. The times and country were tumultuous and violent. The father seems to have left the picture when the boy was around seven T.S., and whether he was killed in battle or just took off is unclear. An uncle on the mother's side of the family more or less raised him, and Musashi learned the arts of stick and sword fighting from him and other *samurai*.

"Supposedly, he killed his first man in a duel when he was thirteen, using a stick."

"Thirteen. Lord."

"As I said, the times were violent. The *samurai* were soldiers, and wars and personal fights were common."

She nodded again. Made the keep-it-rolling sign at him.

He smiled. "Musashi was, according to various historians, a big, strong thug who would as soon cut a man down as look at him. He enjoyed hard drink and the company of whores, and was not fond of bathing—but he was also an accomplished artist, sculptor, poet, and a writer, all of which were considered appropriate behavior for soldiers in those times. A man who was able to lop your head off with a sword could also arrange flowers and recite haiku—a rigorous kind of poetry—as well as he could kill. Surviving examples of Musashi's art can be found in the Imperial Museum in Tokyo, and some of it is strikingly beautiful. Wood carvings, iron sword guards, ink drawings.

"The short version of his life is that he was a wanderer, and by the time he was thirty, he had killed sixty men in single combat. If he did not create it, he certainly perfected the use of the two-sword method, using a long sword in one hand and a shorter one in the other, and moving both constantly. Toward the end of his career, he was such an adept that he would face sword fighters with only a wooden blade, to even the odds, and he was still unbeatable.

"Eventually, he retired to a cave where he wrote *A Book of Five Rings*, a treatise on strategy and tactics of *kendo*, which is what they called swordplay there in those days. For hundreds of years, this was the most respected work about the subject, and it is still germane today."

"Interesting," she said.

"My first visit to Earth, I went to the shrine at Reigendo, the cave where Musashi spent his final two years. He was only sixty T.S. or so when he died—but given the facts that he was a duelist and living in a time when fatal diseases were common and the average life expectancy was well under forty, that was a ripe old age.

"Any of this useful?" he asked.

"Oh, yeah, this could all show up as an animation, easy to whip out a nice-looking CGI: 'Musashi, the greatest swordsman who ever lived . . .' I can get a picture, the VR actor will look exactly like him."

Mourn smiled at her enthusiasm. "Of course, he *wasn't* the greatest swordsman who ever lived, though he was certainly among them—there were a couple of others even in the same historical period and the same area who fought more duels—but Musashi is the one history remembers because of the book he wrote. In reality, he lost several practice fights to other swordsmen using wooden implements, and once to a man who was an adept with a spear. Several of his wins were surprise attacks, which was considered a legitimate tactic. If a man allowed you to sneak up on him, then that was his problem. Those tales were omitted from the registers. Nobody wants their hero to have any flaws. A man who never lost is more impressive than a man who lost a few times—or stabbed several of his unwary foes in the back from ambush."

He paused again. Ahead, a jungle primate hooted, its voice either computer-generated or recorded from some animal that was probably long dead.

"The best fighting men were often anonymous by

THE MUSASHI FLEX   119

choice—it was safer that way. When you were the man to beat, people came looking for you. If nobody knew who you were, you didn't have to sleep with one eye open all the time. Some killers were in the game for money and not for fame, though one often generated the other.

"Musashi had good press, much of which he generated himself. There were—and still are—a lot of people willing to buy a meal or drinks or offer you a place to sleep if you are a well-known bad man. A big enough reputation can be lived upon."

"You would know that," she said.

"Celebrity has its uses."

"So the patron saint of the Flexers is an appropriate one."

"Yes. Like him, at the top levels, somebody is always watching. Being as anonymous as you can is safer. But I like you. And I expect I'll be retiring in the not-too-distant future—it's a younger person's game, really. So if I am outed on galactic entcom, it won't be all that detrimental. Maybe even to my benefit. Famous ex-players get as much attention as some of the current ones, and your documentary will make me famous, won't it?"

"God, I hope so."

He smiled. Bare-naked ambition could be ugly, but on her, it looked, well, kind of cute.

"So, yes, I'll help you."

Her smile was radiant. "Great!"

Shaw waited a few days, to make sure he was physically recovered—it was very tiring to fly on Reflex—then tried it again. It worked the same way as it had before, so he lost no time in getting into the game. He called himself and activated his membership.

He smiled at the image of calling himself. Practically speaking, for any ranking below the Top Hundred, you could always find somebody who'd sell their identity, if you were willing to pay enough for it. There were professional placeholders, men or women who joined the Flex, worked their way into the low two hundreds, say, then sold that position to anybody looking to avoid taking the long road to get that far. A lot of the placeholders were named "Johnson," or "Wu," or "Muhammed," to make it simple. But he didn't have to do that. Years ago, when it looked as if it might be a while before he was ready to go play with the big boys, Shaw had sponsored several promising players who could work their way up the lists. He paid all living expenses, medical, and a generous allowance over that, with the stipulation that they compete under the name "Shaw," and that one day, he might want the name. He owned five officially registered Shaws at the moment, and the highest ranked among them was at 110th place. Not as high as he would like, but still, it would only take him a score or maybe two dozen fights to get to a match with the top dog. Something he could easily manage in a few months or less, even at galactic travel speeds.

Just think. A couple months from now, he would be *Primero,* the best fighter in the known galaxy!

And he could do it *legally,* because many drugs were acceptable adjuncts to matches. Everybody had access to them, so what one could have, another could get; therefore, there was a balance. If you chose not to use steroids or endorphins, that was your pick. There were a couple that were banned, but Reflex wouldn't be among them, because nobody would know about it but him—until it would be too late to do anything about it.

Shaw would have the monopoly, and nobody would even know what it was or that it even *existed* until he was on top. Would the matches be fair? Not really, but under the rules, *technically,* they would be. That was the beauty of it. When they asked, "Was it a fair match?" you could think of the technical truth and answer "Yes," because you were using a drug, *but it wasn't banned!* and not have it be a lie.

Even if they asked straight out: *Are you using any prohibited substances?* he could deny it. That was the beauty of it.

They couldn't forbid it if they had never considered that it even existed.

Eventually, they would figure it out, and eventually, put Reflex on the proscribed list, because everybody would have to use it to be competitive, but until then, there would be a window. Shaw would climb in, steal the title, and climb out before it was closed. He didn't have to stay on top forever, that wasn't the point.

He had fully intended to take another dose and deal with Baba Ngumi, and to extract a certain vengeance on the old bastard, but Baba hadn't shown up for his lesson yesterday, and all attempts to locate him, which included a tame police force and the best private operatives, came up empty—it was as if the old man had vanished. Such a thing was not possible in a civilized society, but for all his effort to find his teacher, Baba might as well have turned into smoke in a high wind.

It seemed awfully coincidental to Shaw that Baba would have departed just at the moment when his life was about to become forfeit. Maybe the old man had some kind of precognition, as Shaw himself had. Couldn't discount that.

Well. No matter. He didn't have to worry about Baba. He had enough training. Coupled with his artificially enhanced supernatural speed? He would be unbeatable.

"Sir," came his secretary's voice. "M. Newman Randall is here to see you. He doesn't have an appointment."

Shaw's joy soured. Randall. What did he want? "Send him in."

Shaw's smile didn't get above his lips, something that

Randall, who had certainly had face-dance training, would have seen. He could have thought of something amusing and faked it, but it wasn't worth the trouble.

They exchanged the usual mutterings, then Randall got to it: "So I understand that you have achieved success on your Reflex project."

Fuck! How could he know that? The man's spy was *dead*!

He didn't need to be a face reader to know that Randall's expression was genuine. He was amused, no question.

"Hardly," Shaw said. "We haven't even begun clinical trials on human subjects yet."

"That's not what I understand."

"Oh, yes, we had a volunteer take the compound and it seemed to work without immediate side effects, but it is far too early to tell if that will hold for a larger sample over time."

"Your . . . *volunteer* must have been pretty confident to risk his life."

Son of a bitch knew that was he who had taken the chem! Who was it? Who was his other spy? There were only a few people who knew. Either one was a traitor, or Randall had other ways of collecting his information. As soon as the fucker left, Shaw was going to have his entire compound swept for bugs . . .

"Let's not beat around the bush here, my friend. You have the chemical, it works, and we want it."

"Or else?"

"Ellis, Ellis. No need to be confrontational. We are reasonable men, aren't we?" He glanced at his ring chrono. "Ah, but look at the time. I just dropped round on my way to see the Confed Sector General, who is, as I am sure you know, staying at the Musali Game Preserve for a bit of a vacation before he spaces on to wherever he is off to next."

He looked Shaw right in the eyes. "He is expecting me, but I told him I had to stop by and see you first."

Shaw repressed a sigh and understood exactly what it was Randall was trying to tell him with that remark: If he didn't make it to the CSG's, they would come here looking. And he suspected—maybe knew—what had happened to his spy.

Well . . . shit.

Even so, Shaw was tempted. Kill the man, drop the body into one of the industrial-grade radioactive-leachers they had in the lab, grind him into atoms, even a DNA match would be impossible, somebody got that far. But—no. Not yet. He needed to find out how the man was getting his information. Then he would kill him.

"Give him my regards," Shaw said, smiling and meaning it this time. Let Randall chew on that and wonder what it meant.

"I certainly will. Oh. Say hello to that old gentleman martial arts teacher for me, would you? A delightful fellow."

Shaw's smile froze. Baba? It immediately made a certain kind of sense. Baba could come and go as he pleased, and—shit! Baba was the spy! The devious bastard! Somehow, he had figured out things he shouldn't, but it made sense. It had never crossed Shaw's mind that Baba . . .

Shaw was outraged; even though he had planned to kill the man, it really pissed him off.

And Randall saw that, too.

"One experiment does not a trial make, Newman. Even with all the Confederation can do to pave the road, there still need to be tests, and they will take time. Otherwise, our liability would be insupportable."

"Of course, old friend, I understand. We merely want to make sure the process begins as quickly as possible. That it might take a few months to get to the point where our own medicos are given a supply for testing is not unreasonable."

"It could take a year or two," Shaw tried.

"Oh, I don't think it will. I would guess three or four months. You know it works, and you must be very confident that it has no major side effects."

Shaw said nothing. He knew. No doubt of it. Had he guessed why Shaw had developed it? If so, had he *told* anyone? The CSG was expecting Randall *now,* but in a week or a month, six months, maybe something unfortunate might happen to him.

The PR stood. "I'll be in touch," he said, still smiling. And meaning it.

The asshole . . .

After Randall was gone, Shaw considered the situation. All was not lost, of course. He would still have a jump on the competition with his chemical crutch. Once it got into widespread military use, there'd be a black market, of course, and it would start showing up in the Flex, it would have to, eventually. The question was, could he get to the top before it did? He didn't plan to stay in the game once he won. He'd retire.

If he could do it before the Confed tripped him up.

Look there, that's Ellis Mtumbo Shaw. The billionaire who was also the number one player in the Musashi Flex, retired undefeated. They say he quit because there was nobody to challenge him, you know. Must be a helluva thing, to have all that money and to be the toughest fucker walking around on any planet in the whole galaxy. Some guys have all the luck . . .

That was worth another real smile of his own. Yes, indeed, it was . . .

13

A week later, when they were almost to Ago's Moon, in Faust, Mourn went to work the weights. Sola tagged along to watch.

The place was one of the smaller gyms, out of the way, and empty, save for them. It was early in the ship's day cycle, and this far into the voyage, most passengers had probably made the transition to ship time and were still asleep. She asked the question she'd obviously been considering.

"How *do* you get better?" Mourn said, repeating her question. He smiled, something he found himself doing more of when she was around. He said, "You know who Hébert Braun was?"

"Of course."

He waited a second, and she rightly took this for a challenge to demonstrate her knowledge. She said, "He held the number one position for two years. Had sixty-one matches while he was king of the hill, thirty-nine bare, twenty-two armed, *all* of which he won, retiring undefeated, if not uninjured, let me see, fourteen years past. He went to Mtu, where he got into politics, was elected to the planetary senate and served two terms. He retired from that four years ago. He owns a chain of pubs on Mwanamamke and Mtu, and he lives in a palatial estate on the Green Moon—Rangi ya Majani Mwezi."

"Good to see that you do your research," he said.

She didn't smile. "I take my work seriously."

"So do Flexers, if they manage to get ranked. Anyway, there's a story about Braun. The way he supposedly trained was to find the worst quarry or asteroid miner's pub he could, which if you know rock jocks, is apt to be a real hellhole. He'd walk to the bar, then in a loud voice announce that all the men on his left were pedophiles, and all those on his right were motherfuckers. Then he'd fight his way to the door."

Now she did smile. "That's a good story."

He walked to the weight bench and stretched out on his back. Said, "One hundred kilos."

The hum of the pressor field didn't change, but the bare bar on the rack it controlled was now effectively a lot heavier. He reached up, grabbed the bar, lifted it from the rack and lowered it to his chest. It was a warm-up weight, and he could continue talking as he benched it. He didn't lift real heavy anymore. He had all the muscle he needed, he just needed to keep it toned and flexible.

"Yeah, it's a great story, but it's pure *deeli*bird kark. Braun was tougher than a meter-thick wall of denscris. In his day, he was the best one-on-one fighter in the galaxy, no question, maybe the best ever. The first time he walked into a rock jock pub and said what he was supposed to have said? He'd have been dead before he got to the words 'on my left.'"

"The best fighter in the galaxy? Really?"

He lowered the weight, raised it, trying for smoothness rather than speed. Plyometrics was a different workout.

"No one man is a stand-up army. Hard as he was, skilled as he was, he wasn't invulnerable. Against a score of un-armed and unorganized fighters, yeah, he *could* probably carve a path to the exit. Once you get past four or five, opponents just get in each other's way. When you fight the ten thousand, you do it one at a time—but you do each one real quick."

He finished the fifteenth rep, racked the bar, and said, "Field off."

He sat up, wiped sweat from his face, look directly at her.

"In a pub full of strong, violent, proud men who make their livings pounding rock, probably at least half of whom will be armed, somebody will pull a blade or a slap-cap or a dart gun when you insult him, and that changes things.

"We have homilies by the barrel in the Flex. The weapons players like to say, 'You can butter your bread with your finger, but, why would you?' Or, 'You're not an ape, use a tool.'

"Facing a knife takes away your first five years of train-ing bare. A slap-cap does the same thing. Maybe if you are ten years into it, you have a chance. That's if you are look-ing right at him when he pulls it. A man with a needler or dart pistol or an illegal, overamped tightbeam hand wand three meters away and behind you? If he has a clue what he is doing, he'll kill you before you turn around, even if you've got a weapon of your own.

"*You* shot Weems, remember, and you aren't even a player."

"So what are you saying here, Mourn?"

He stood, headed for the hyperextension chair. She fol-lowed him.

"What I'm saying is, the meanest, baddest, toughest fighter who ever walked breathes the same air as the rest of us. Skill and training count for a lot, but they don't make you invincible. The fight might be to the death, but there are rules. It's one player at a time against another player. They agree to the venue, the kinds of weapons, they both have some idea of what they are doing and what they are up against. A duel isn't self-defense, and it isn't war. It is what it is."

She said, "Ah. The first question the brain strainers and face readers ask a player when he reports the results of a fight."

"Yes. 'Was it a fair match?' Meaning, did you adhere to the rules? If not, you don't get the win, and if the showrunners decide you cheated sufficiently much, they can punish you severely, on the spot. And they'll know if you are lying. You lie, you can die."

They reached the rack and he climbed up on it, put his heels under the support and leaned forward. His hipbones pressed into the padding. He bent at the waist until his head almost touched the spongy floor, then used the muscles of his low back and buttocks slowly to raise the weight of his upper body until his back was straight. He kept his arms folded across his chest.

"You're saying that you fight like you train," she said.

He nodded as he lowered his face back toward the floor. "Yes. There are plenty of martial arts that teach dealing with multiple opponents, some of them actually work, and you can learn that if you want—there may come a time when you need that knowledge. And you can learn a lot by training under experts who can show you things you don't know. But the way you get better as a duelist is to fight people who are your equal or your superior as duelists. It doesn't matter if you can kick multiple butts in a fighting class or a pub brawl. It's what you do in an alley when the guy standing in front of you understands who and what you are, is willing to come at you anyway, and knows as much about kicking ass as you do. Now and then, you'll surprise a player close to your rank with something he hasn't seen, but there are only so many ways to efficiently move when push comes to shove, and the guy you're fighting will have seen as many of them as you have. A technique a thousand years old will sometimes work as well as it did the first time somebody threw it; but, of course, you won't know until you try."

She didn't say anything until after he finished his set of hyperextensions, fifteen reps. When he climbed out of the rack, she said, "For a man who isn't interested in talking about all this, you sure talk a lot."

He laughed. *Touché.* "You asked," he said.

"Yes. And I am getting it all cammed and recorded."

"Good."

"So, how do you get better?"

"You study the best fighting systems from the best teachers—martial arts have been around as long as mankind—and some are simply better than others. That's not a popular view in polite culture, you might offend somebody by saying so, but it's the truth. You train. You practice."

"And that's it?"

He laughed. "You can learn enough technique to defend yourself against most people in most circumstances in an hour, maybe less."

She raised an interviewer's eyebrow.

"It's true. A handful of moves, drilled until you can do them in your sleep, and they'll buy you a pass nine times out of ten if somebody takes a swing at you. You have to practice them, and you have to do it against people who won't just stand there and *let* you do them; but if you are willing to put the time in, those moves will see you through almost every time.

"Learning how to face a first-rate opponent in a blood-and-bones or to-the-death, that's a different story. A foot crooked, balance off a hair, a quarter-second hesitation at the wrong moment, these things will cost you when you face an expert. A real expert, not somebody who gets a black pin or teacher certificate in some strip kiosk *dojo* or *kwoon* set up for kids outside a casino, and who has never been hit hard enough to know what it feels like. A fighter, not a dancer.

"Once you have the tools, you use them. Try them out against fighters who are good. You have to develop your sensitivity. Lose, you go back to the training hall. Win, you go back to the training hall—you're never done. But if you start winning, you move up to the next level when you fight again.

"If you are gifted—fast, strong, eyes full of fire—and you study hard, train right, pick your fights carefully, you can get the basics in five or six years, enough to make it into the threes or twos—that's the two or three hundred rankings.

"The top pros have all been at it for at least ten or fifteen years, some of them longer."

Like me, he thought. *Too long.*

"The *silat* you saw me use against Weems? It's one of the better arts from Earth—got weapons, boxing, grappling, and it is deceptive, a cheating art. Even if the guy against you is very good, you can sometimes still sucker him—sometimes. But it takes a long while to get good at it."

The gym had an ultrasonic shower. He headed toward it. She followed him.

"So that's it? You just learn a trick, then practice it until you can do it real well?"

He laughed. "Fem, you just described how life works in general, didn't you? Do it well enough, there's no limits to what you can accomplish. But there's another trick—what you do needs to have a set of consistent principles, things that you do every time you crank it up. There needs to be an underlying method to your madness."

"Meaning?"

"You can't just learn if-he-does-that, then I-always-do-this, because you might not be able to get to that weapon in time, or he might not come at you exactly as you've been trained. So basing your tricks on a more general principle gives you options. You could always block and counter, for instance. Or you could always take a certain stance, or always step back and counter. I haven't found those to be especially valid, but that's me."

She nodded, as if she understood.

"Might want to shut your recorder off," he said. "I'm about to get naked."

"This'll be running on the adult entcom channels, I am sure," she said. "Go ahead and strip, it'll add a little spice. I saw you go into the Healy, you don't have anything I haven't seen before."

He grinned.

As he started to remove his sweaty clothes, she said, "If there aren't any limits, if you don't think about losing, and if you train as hard as you do, how is it that you knew Weems was going to beat you?"

He started to pop off a stock response about Weems being the best, but stopped. A brief . . . *something* flitted through his mind, a startling thought:

She's right. You knew *you couldn't beat Weems; you lost before you ever moved. You know the old saying: The fight isn't under your glove, it's under your hat . . .*

"Mourn?"

He shook himself free of the surprising revelation. "What?"

"Where'd you go? You just blanked out there."

He sighed. "Getting senile, I guess. My mind wandered. Sorry."

"Where?"

"Where?"

"Where did your mind wander?" She had a bright, expectant look. Like a gator watching a small animal moving toward his pond. Or a shark about to bite a careless swimmer.

He looked at her as if seeing her for the first time. She was good at this. He said, "Just a stray thought about fighting. Something you just said."

"Give."

"Turn that off, first."

"Why?"

"Because it's something I don't want anybody else to think about if they haven't already. Something I can use."

"It's off," she said, touching a control. "What is it?"

"A way to get better, maybe," he said. "You game?"

"Me?"

"I'll need a student. You need to learn how to defend yourself anyhow. We might be able to teach each other something."

14

It was different than Shaw had expected.

He'd found his first opponent practically in his own backyard, on Haradali's other world, Wu. Wu was in the same orbit as Tatsu, but on the opposite point of the ellipse. A few hours in his personal yacht, he and Cervo were there. One of Cervo's ops tracked the man down, and Shaw had taken the Reflex, waited until it had kicked in, and braced the guy. They found a warehouse with nobody home and went inside. The place smelled like stale burlap, and was dusty, but it had plenty of room to move around in, and was well lit from a series of big skylights open to the sun.

Shaw circled to his left, deliberately moving slow, watching the hulk across from him. The man's name—at least insofar as the Flex was concerned—was Marlowe Wong. He was big—a head taller and twenty kilos heavier than Shaw—and his face looked like an airless moon after an asteroid shower. He was ranked 106th as a player, and

Shaw figured that was due to a high pain threshold. He had hit Wong a few times, full-power shots to the body, and the man had just grunted and kept coming.

M. Wong was a mouth-breather, and noisy about it.

Shaw stopped. Watched the bigger man gather himself for a charge, then launch it. There was no threat in it, he could take a nap before he got there, *Jesu damn*—

Shaw v-stepped to his right and threw a low, underhand punch, elbow tight to his body, pivoting to get his hip into it—

The force of the hit was enough to deflect the bigger man, and he felt muscle tear and a rib crack under the strike.

Wong shook it off, turned, and swung a back fist that would have knocked over a tree had it connected—

Shaw ducked, and did a quick one-two-three to the broken rib, hard punches, they *had* to hurt!

Wong bellowed like some kind of angry beefalo and lunged for a grab.

It wouldn't do to grapple with a guy this big and strong. They went to the ground, Shaw's speed advantage was gone. Shaw spun away, out of range.

A stick or a blade would have taken away much of what the man had. But since Shaw had been the challenger, Wong had the right to choose it bare or armed, and he had gone for bare. Easy to see why, now.

Well. He could pound on this sucker all day and do nothing but get tired. Time to finish it.

When Wong lumbered in the next time, Shaw broke his knee with a kick, slammed his throat with an elbow as he fell, and delivered a hammer fist right between the eyes as the man hit the ground on his back. The thug was still conscious after two head shots, damn, so he gave him two more hammer fists, as if pounding on a drum, and the light finally went dim in the man's eyes.

Shaw stood, feeling very tired suddenly. It had taken much longer than he had expected.

Or so he thought. Later, when he looked at the recording cam he'd set up beforehand, the total elapsed time for the fight was less than he had thought:

All of eighteen seconds from start to finish.

He was disappointed. Shit. If that was all he had to do, it wasn't gonna be nearly as much fun as he had hoped.

Well. Competition would get better as he went up the ladder.

Ago's Moon was a frontier world; tourists came to see its high waterfalls, and the main industry was mining, everything from iron to bauxite to bird guano. Miners tended to be a self-sufficient bunch by and large, and big on minding their own business. Sola had been to the planet once before. While there weren't any huge cities, it was big enough to hide on, since asking a lot of questions, whether you were Confed, a private cool, or even a reporter, tended to earn you more glares than information.

Sola and Mourn caught a boxcar from deep to the surface, a ground-effect shuttle from the island spaceport to the mainland, and an electric hack from the terminal to a house Mourn had rented during the boxcar's drop.

It was a pleasant, balmy day, temp about two-thirds body heat, a little breeze blowing, it felt and, to judge from the foliage, looked like early fall. She recorded some footage for background, then shut the cam off. Which turned out to be a mistake.

The hack pulled away, leaving them in front of the rental house, a nice quiet neighborhood of everlast-plast buildings not too faded by sun and rain. She wasn't really paying enough attention. It didn't register that two men coming down the street from a few houses down and two more coming from the other way, had anything to do with each other. Not to her.

Mourn said. "Stay in the street, behind me."

"What?"

"We have a problem."

Sola looked again. The four men? They didn't look particularly dangerous. They looked like miners, on their way to or from work; they wore hardskin overalls, boots, had helmets crowed to their belts, lunch boxes.

Mourn put his guitar and travel bag down, and as he did so, the four men sprinted toward them. One pulled a short stick from somewhere, sunlight glittered on a blade in another one's hand, then they were there—

Her hand wand was in her locked travel bag. She'd never get to it. Sola backed away, into the empty street—

Mourn didn't step back. He attacked, leaped at the nearest man—the knifer—did something so fast she couldn't follow it, and the knife flew through the air as the man fell—

Mourn kept moving, spun into the man with the club. There was an exchange of blows, too fast! and the clubber dropped—

Cam, shit, I have to get my cam working—

The third man moved toward Mourn, thought better of it, slowed, but Mourn went to meet him—

Jesu Christo, cam, get the fucking cam on-line—!

Three of them were down, dead or dying, when Mourn saw the fourth one's gun come up. He had time to recognize it for what it was, a compressed-gas bullet-pusher, probably using hydroshock-expanding composites or explosive slugs. There was no place to go, no cover, the shooter was ten meters away, and he'd never get there in time to stop the first shot.

He was next to his guitar case. He grabbed it.

He yelled at Sola: "Run!" and charged the shooter. He held the case in front of him.

He was three meters away when the first round hit, and the shock and noise told him it was a popper, which was good. It wouldn't penetrate as well as a solid or even a hollow point.

The second and third rounds smashed into the hardshell, but he was there, and he just plowed into the guy at full speed, hit him with the guitar case, and knocked him down. He skidded to a stop, raised the case and brought it down on the man's head, once, twice, three times, watching with interest but no regret as the man's skull deformed under the heavy case.

After the third impact, there was no need to continue. The shooter wasn't going anywhere or doing anything else without a direct hand from God.

Nor were the other three.

Sola came up behind him. "Mourn? You okay?"

"I thought I told you to run."

"I did. But after you squashed him like a bug, I didn't figure I had to keep going." She waved at the other three. "They aren't going to be bothering anybody, either."

Mourn looked around for more trouble, didn't see anybody. He knelt, checked the shooter's pulse by touching his throat. Nope. Guy was chilled.

He laid his guitar case on the plastcrete. There were three large holes in the front. He thumbed the latches, and opened the clamshell lid, hoping for a miracle.

Apparently God had dispensed all the miracles he intended to pass out today.

The front of the Bogdanovich had a splintered, fist-sized, ragged hole in it, and the thin and ancient polish was completely shattered and spiderwebbed all over the rest of the sound board. Another round had hit the neck and chewed it in half. The third shot had gone through the lower curve on the left and eaten through the front, side, and back.

The guitar was mortally wounded.

Ah, fuck!

Mourn felt a sense of grief, much more for the loss of an irreplaceable instrument than for the men he had just killed. Assassins—and that's what they were—were a demistad a dozen—there would never be another guitar like this one. *Fuck.*

Mourn stared at the ruined instrument. Even a talented luthier couldn't fix that much damage, not and make it sound as it had before. You'd have to replace the front, back, one side, and the neck and fretboard. Basically build a new guitar.

Damn.

He allowed himself another moment of grief, then closed the case and stood. "Let's go," he said. "Shooting brings cools, more often than not. I'll dump this in a compactor somewhere. We need to get off-planet again."

"I'm sorry about your guitar," she said.

"Thank you."

They hurried a few streets over, found a public com, called a hack. While waiting for it, he saw that she was shaking.

She needed to talk. He understood; he did, too. To blow off the pressure that still remained in him, even after taking out four men.

"It's okay," he said. "We're alive. Not likely to be any more of them around. Not here, anyway."

"Jesu damn," she said.

He nodded. "Yeah."

"What was that all about?"

"Weems," he said. "Got to be. He sent them to rattle me. White Radio, lucky guess, maybe he has more like these at every stop. I underestimated his anger."

"Wouldn't he rather do it himself?"

"Probably. And maybe he thinks I'll survive and give him the chance. They weren't very good."

"You were . . . gone, Mourn. You looked like some kind of . . . of . . ." She ran down.

"Animal?" He nodded again.

"No shit."

He shook his shoulders, let the move carry to his arms and hands, down to his fingertips. It was an old yoga loosening exercise, co-opted by martial artists thousands of years ago.

"It's limbic, hindbrain stuff. Around long before the overlay of all our wonderful cognition and reasoning abilities. Reflexive baring of the teeth, goose bumps to erect the hair to make you look bigger in the face of a deadly threat, hormone dump for fight or flight, all like that. The dark rage. The part of me that wants to kill whatever it is that frightened me. It's blind, unreasoning, ungoverned. Everything subtle goes away. If a move hasn't been done so much that it is almost a reflex, when the darkness comes, I can't use it."

He was definitely talking too much. Adrenaline aftereffects, he knew. There was something to be said for betablockers, but he'd never liked the side effects—

"Remind me not to frighten you," she said.

He shook his head. "If I had been calmer, I might have taken them all down without killing any of them. If I had been more efficient, I could have gotten to the last one before he started shooting. Thing is, the darkness doesn't have a governor. It's on or it's off."

"When you fought Weems . . . ?"

"Didn't happen. I saw him coming, knew what to expect, had my training ready. With those four, I was surprised. I shouldn't have been. I didn't have time to think much about it, I just reacted. My fault, a fairly big mistake."

"You're telling me it's a bad idea to sneak up and go 'Boo!' at you."

He smiled. He liked that, that she could make him smile even when he was still ragged with hormones and breathing too fast. And his beloved guitar was now in thousand of tiny bits in the belly of a disposal grinder, case and all.

"Probably," he said.

"Boy, if you could turn that off and on like a switch, you'd have something."

He nodded. "Yes. Fighters have been trying to do that forever. Lot of them can let it out—the Viking Berserkers, the Moros, the Mtuan Zelawali—but controlling it once it is loose is something else."

"Well, there you go. Something to work at."

He smiled again. "You know, I could get used to having you around."

She smiled back. "Well, of course you could. I'm a wonderful human being."

The hack pulled into sight.

"I hope you enjoyed your visit to Ago's Moon," he said. "Not a good idea for us to come back here for twenty or thirty years."

"I hear you," she said.

15

Azul did some shopping, though most of her new clothes were bought offworld and the purchases back-dated by CI. She had decided that Azul the artist would be somewhat conservative in her dress—basic, nothing too frilly or outlandish. She had CI pick up several silk or-thoskin suits, from simple black to dark maroon to navy blue. Some nice cloned-leather jackets, dressy trousers, shirts, the kind of thing a young artist might choose if she was more interested in letting her art make a statement than her outfits. The package needed to be attractive, but not over the top.

With her newly gained knowledge of art, she did a tour of some of the city's galleries and familiarized herself with the local art scene, from the expensive shops that catered to the rich to the street artists who worked the tourist trade with pulse-paint caricatures done on the spot in a few min-utes. She took in a display of Mtuan micromodels, tiny cities so small that you needed twenty- or thirty-power magnification to see the details. She learned about solid carbon dioxide sculptures that required pressurized freezers, or they'd just evaporate. She watched sandpainters finish mandalas that took weeks of effort, then watched them drag a finger through the fine grains, destroying them.

Some arts were more ephemeral than others.

She learned her own catalog, of paintings and drawings she had supposedly done, and received by special CI courier her latest works in progress, along with the paints, brushes, and other supplies she would have needed to create them.

One of the two mostly done projects was of a pair of ancient gladiatorial types, men who were mostly naked, sweating, bruised, and bleeding, locked into a dynamic wrestling pose. The piece came with detailed instructions on how to finish the background, which colors to use, how to mix them, how to apply them. She memorized the lesson, practiced on a blank canvas until she was satisfied, then destroyed both the practice canvas and instructions. She could stand in front of the fighters and, with somebody watching her, work on it and complete it so that her efforts would match that of the real artist who had created it.

The history of her fake brother arrived, with holographs and background details, based on a real player in the Musashi Flex. The player, CI had discovered, had been killed in a maglev train accident on Spandle, in Mu, two years past. Having no known relatives, M. Voda Clee's body had not been claimed, and he had been cremated by the city authorities. Clee had, at his peak, been rated Thirty-One in the Flex's ranks. High enough to be interesting, not so high that there would be a profile that could not be altered. Voda Clee bore a superficial resemblance to Azul, enough so somebody comparing images of them would not find the idea that they were related to be unbelievable, and his history had been adjusted so that his real name was Azul, and stats dovetailed so that he had a sister,

Luna. A fambot released into the galactic web would make the connection, and there was no longer any information that would gainsay it—Clee's true identity had been completely scrubbed from all records that CI had been able to find.

Azul sometimes wondered: How many people had CI remade thus? Hundreds, to be sure, maybe thousands or even tens of thousands. Kill a man, you took his body; scrub him from the records, you took everything he had ever been.

Well, that was not her worry. She had another brother now, conveniently dead, so he wouldn't show up and spoil her game, and a point of interest to her quarry.

Next, she needed an event. Something that M. Shaw would attend at which he could happen across her. It needed to be large enough that she could blend in, small enough that he would find her without her having to make any obvious moves—public events of any note were always recorded, and a security agent going over those tapes must not see Azul doing anything that looked as if she were angling herself into Shaw's path.

After examination, Azul found an art show that should serve. It was an annual affair, had been around for four years, was invitation-only, and Shaw had attended all of them. A dressy function, expensive work would be on display, and one of the artists that Shaw collected would have new pieces hung. He might decide to skip it this time around, that was always possible, but it was the best bet she could see.

It was too late to have any of her pieces accepted, and she did not wish to arouse the slightest suspicion, but that was not really necessary. Once she told Shaw that she was an artist, he would check her out. He should find her work interesting, at the very least. A door would be opened, even if just a hair. That would be all she needed.

The art show was to be held in but a few days. A coded

com to CI would provide her with a legitimate invitation—
there were enough people attending so that one sneaked in
would not raise any alarms, and it would be as legitimate-
looking as any.

Azul walked to the full-length holomirror and stripped.
She turned and examined herself critically. She was tight,
lean, and fit—she worked hard enough at it so she should
be. Her hair, dyed a pale blond for her prior assignment,
was long and could use a trim. She would have the dye removed, allowing her normal dark brunette and slightly
curly locks to return to a more natural state. She could
change her eye color with droptacs, but the blue-gray of
her own eyes went well enough with the dark hair. Nothing
else needed any particular attention. She would start to
think of herself as beautiful, and with a little care in her
makeup and dress, would become that. M. Shaw might be
rich, good-looking, and powerful, but he was a heterosex-
ual male. Whatever he might be, he was about to become
Luna Azul's prey . . .

Again, they were on a starliner, and this time, the only
accommodations available on short notice were first class.
So they had a monster of a suite, including two bedrooms.
It cost what Sola made in a good year. When she sold her
documentary, she could get used to traveling this way. Intended to do so . . .

Leaving in a hurry was a good idea, given that Mourn
had killed people who were not Flexers back there. Yes, it
was legally self-defense, but as he had pointed out, spending time in the local jail while it all got sorted out wasn't
real appealing.

She had been recording again, getting his thoughts on
that fatal encounter, realizing how little she really knew
about such things. She had thought she'd known more than
she did, the reporter's conceit.

She had seen, but until that encounter with Weems, she had never participated. Those four would-be assassins? That was scarier still.

And now it was Mourn, asking her: Had she ever been in a fight before? Following up on his idea of teaching her.

She shook her head, remembering the two players she had recorded on Earth, just before she had seen Mourn for the first time. How she had felt when they had started talking about using her for sex, that icy fear that had frosted her to her bones.

She said, "I've watched a lot of fights, but I don't know how to do it myself."

"You have the hand wand," he said. "Use it much?"

"Just that once, on Weems."

He nodded. "It's not as easy as they make it look in the entcoms, is it? Several things get balled up together— when you perceive real danger to yourself, you get that whole spectrum of fight-or-flight reactions, like we were talking about earlier. It's hardwired stuff, goes back before the first men. You can dull it with drugs, beta-blockers and such, but you can't get rid of it. So the first thing is, you have to learn how to deal with what the syndrome brings to the table and how to use it to help you. You need to know."

"All right."

The suite had a central room that would have seemed big in a planet-based house. Mourn started moving the furniture—not much, a double seat, small table, a chair, all of which were crowed to the floor, in case of a gravity failure—to give them more space.

Once he'd cleared the area, he said, "Okay, here's the deal. You have your wand where?"

"Back pocket."

"You practice drawing it in a hurry?"

She shook her head. "Not really."

He nodded, serious. "That's the first thing you have to change. If you are going to carry a weapon and depend on

it, you have to be able to get to it in time to do you any
good. Inside six or seven meters, if you wait until you see
me move, I can get to you and break your neck before you
can pull that wand, even if you have it in a belt sheath. If
you have to dig around in your pocket looking for it, I can
cover more ground than that." He backed away until he was
across the room from her, six or eight meters away. "From
this far away, if I go for you, you'll never get your weapon
out in time to stop me."

"You're kidding," she said.

"A demonstration," he said.

Sola frowned. "I don't want to hurt you."

"Two things. First, a hand wand on stun isn't going to
permanently hurt me. Second, you won't get off a pulse
anyhow."

He seemed so confident. Well, of course, he would be.
He was among the top fighters in the known galaxy. Lack
of confidence wasn't going to be a problem for him. But he
was all the way across the room. She could get her wand
out, surely? She had managed to shoot the number one
ranked Flex player in the galaxy, hadn't she?

"All right—" she began.

He leaped, and she froze. Frantically, she jammed her
hand into her pocket, touched the wand—

—and he tapped her lightly on the body, just under her
sternum.

Her heart was pounding, her breath held, and panic enveloped her like a heavy coat of ice.

He took two steps back. She started to breathe again,
but quickly and without any depth.

He said, "If I'd had a knife in my hand, you'd be bleeding from a heart wound. See how you feel? Your heart is
racing, your breathing is shallow, and you feel as if you
need to find a fresher to pee, right? And when you saw me
move, you couldn't see anything else but me, and even
though you don't remember it, you couldn't hear anything

else. I was the threat, and everything you had was focused on me."

Dumbly, she nodded, not trusting herself to speak.

"My move was unexpected, and you froze for just an instant, too. That's a built-in protective behavior. Don't move, maybe the predator won't see you—most of them see movement better than if you are real still. Not everybody does that, but if you do, that's part of your wiring."

Her mouth was dry, as if she had tried to swallow a bowlful of hot sand. She could only nod again. How could he know exactly how she felt?

"That's the pattern. You can't control it once it kicks it, it comes out of the hindbrain and was there before people learned how to use tools, or weapons, or language."

"Then I'm going to die if I'm ever really threatened," she said, finally able to manage speech.

"Not if you work on it."

"But you said it can't be controlled."

"No, I said you can't control it once it kicks in. What you can do is keep it from kicking in. Suppose I back off, and run in that direction, away from you toward the picture wall? Watch—"

He did a short and fast sprint toward the wall. Stopped when he got there. He turned toward her. "Not the same as when I charged you, is it?"

"Not the same."

"Because you didn't perceive a danger. I wasn't a threat. Take out your wand."

She did so.

"Set it to the minimum charge. Got it? Okay, now shoot me. Go ahead."

Still feeling the echo of her fear and on some level pissed at him for making her feel that way, she pointed the tube at him and pressed the recessed firing stud.

Mourn collapsed unconscious on the floor. For some reason, this surprised her.

"Jesu, Mourn!"

She ran to him.

She was wiping his face with a wet cloth ten minutes later when he woke up. He looked at her, managed a weak smile.

"Are you okay? I'm sorry."

"Don't be sorry. What if I were a rapist and serial killer? Got a headache, but I'm fine." He sat up, and came to his feet. "So, now you know your wand works. You just knocked one of the Flex's toughest players on his ass with it set on minimum. Second one—you did Weems, too. If you ratchet it up to max, or even midrange, there's nobody human it won't drop."

She nodded.

"So, if I back off across the room again and you already have the wand in your hand and ready to shoot, you know you can stop me."

"Yes."

"Because you just saw it work."

"Right."

"So, no reason to be afraid. No threat."

"In theory."

He smiled. "A few practice runs, the theory will be real enough, though I'm not inclined to be the dummy anymore today. Maybe we'll pick up a spatter-spray practice wand later."

"But I'd still never get the wand out in time."

"Right. And that's the other part. The fastest draw is to have the weapon in your hand when trouble arises. As soon as you think you might be at risk, you get the wand ready to work. There's not a man alive who can cover seven meters against a drawn and aimed weapon before you can trigger it. One step, zap, end of attack."

She took a deep breath, less ragged now, and let it out. "You are saying that I can short-circuit the hard wiring."

"Yes. If you pay attention, if you see any possible threat,

if you are prepared to deal with it, should it come to pass, you can stay a step ahead of the lizard-brain reflexes. Heat works, but cool is better."

"And what if I don't have a hand wand? Or the charge is depleted?"

He smiled again. "Ah, well, that's a whole other bag of tricks. If you don't have a wand, or a stick, or a knife, you have to use the tools you do have. I'll show you some of those ways—but after I use a derm for this headache . . ."

Sola smiled. She was sorry he had a headache, but she felt as if she had learned something important, and that felt pretty good.

Mourn had taught slower students than Sola, men and women who had gone on to become pretty good fighters. But his method was usually similar. There were so many misconceptions a new student had, more when they had some experience, because they had learned the wrong way and had to go back and undo that before they could begin to go forward.

Teaching was good. You had to go back over basics, things you hadn't thought about in a long time, you'd been doing them so long, and when you did that, sometimes a new ray of sunlight would lance down and illuminate something you hadn't seen in quite that light before.

He'd been having some odd thoughts lately, and if not exactly new, they were at least somewhat tangential to his norm.

Some of what kept coming up had to do with a shift in perspective. Some of it had to do with ideas that seemed, on the face of them, counterintuitive.

Most martial arts Mourn had learned taught you to stay away from an incoming knife. A razor-sharp blade was dangerous, even in the hands of the untrained, and a mistake cost blood. Running away fast was the smartest response.

But if you couldn't get outside of effective range fast enough, then what?

Some of the arts he'd played with, like *silat,* taught that going *in* against a knife was sometimes the safest move you had. Like the two-bullet experiment or the walk versus run thing, at first glance, it seemed obvious that backing away was the smart money bet, and that going in was suicide. But things were not always as they first appeared.

Take a slugthrower, put it into a rest so it can't move, and aim it dead level. Hold up another bullet so that it is the same height as the muzzle. Fire the gun and drop the bullet at the same instant.

Which round hits the ground first?

When Mourn had heard this the first time, he'd thought the answer easy: the bullet you dropped.

He was wrong: They both hit the ground at the same time.

Gravity is a constant in the scenario, it's working on the chambered round even as it sits there, and since the fired bullet and the dropped one start at the same level and are the same size and weight, they hit the dirt together. Even though the fired one will travel farther, it is falling exactly as fast as the other one, unless it reaches escape velocity, which bullets from ordinary weapons don't do on an Earth-sized world.

Mourn was no physicist, but he'd had this explained to him by somebody who was, and he believed it.

The other one he liked was the walk versus run. Run a couple klicks. Then walk the same distance slowly. Which one burns more calories?

They both burn the same amount. Work is force through a distance. If you burn ten calories a minute running and it takes you six minutes to run the two klicks, it's sixty calories. If you burn a mere three calories a minute walking, but it takes you twenty minutes, it's still sixty calories. Running might benefit your heart and lungs more, because of the aerobic effect, if you are going several kilometers, long enough for it to kick in; but it won't burn any more fat than walking the same distance.

At their hearts, martial arts were all about motion. In the simplest instance, if somebody came at you with mayhem in mind and you weren't where they expected to connect with you when they got there—you moved out, in, sideways, wherever—then you had the advantage. If you devised a system of motions that would allow you always to be somewhere else when an attacker charged, and you were able to capitalize on your position before he or she could recover, you'd win the exchange. One battle did not a war necessarily make, and certainly any motion would have to account for all kinds of variables—distance, size, local gravity, terrain, and so forth—but if you could get to the most efficient way of moving at a particular instant, you'd have something there . . .

A lot of fighters Mourn had met over the years had come up with combinations of arts, or created their own, using others for a base. Sometimes these were better, sometimes not. The temptation was to take an old established fighting system and throw out everything that you saw as useless, keeping only the best moves. Some systems, this was a mistake—what you thought was a worthless move might have real value down the line when you were able to see the system as a whole. Monostylists got to the top just as often as eclectics; it depended on the style and the player.

Mourn had a sudden memory. He laughed.

Sola looked at him. "Do I look that funny?"

He shook his head. "No, I was thinking of something else. I used to be in a fighting class, and every time the teacher would show us a move, we had a guy who would say, 'But Instru'isto, where is the *power* in that?'"

"And this is funny because . . . ?"

"All moves don't rely on power to be effective. Hit a hundred-kilo bodybuilder in the chest with your fist, you'll probably break your hand. Poke him in the eye with your finger, you get a much better result. Precision in this instance is better than power."

"But how easy is it to do that? Poke a hundred-kilo bodybuilder in the eye?"

"That's the trick, all right. There are a lot of guys out there who think they can do it, but the map is not the territory."

He looked at her. "Bend your knees and drop your weight a little more," he said. "You want your center of gravity lower than your opponent's if he's coming in fast . . ."

Mourn watched her and considered the idea of counterintuitiveness. There was definitely something there he needed to explore.

16

"Was it a fair match?"

Here was the question for which Shaw had been preparing, and when it came, he was ready—it merely had to be framed in his own mind correctly: *If by fair fight, you mean, did I break any of the established rules for the Flex? Was it a fair match by those regulations?*

With that thought held firmly, he said, "Yes."

The two showrunners, a man and a woman, never took their gazes from Shaw; each of them had one hand out of sight, in a pocket, under a jacket, and Shaw knew that in those hidden hands were gripped weapons. Even if they were only stunners, he knew he would wake up dead if they used them.

People who lied and knew they lied gave themselves away—there were microexpressions that flitted across one's features, and vox patterns that changed to reveal a specific kind of stress. Beating the sensors at the hands of an expert was close to impossible.

If the tech told the runners that Shaw was lying, and even if he'd had Reflex coursing in his system—which he didn't—it would be iffy that he could have done much before they shot. And even if he avoided being cooked, and managed to get away, he'd still be a dead man—it would only be a matter of when another Flex showrunner could get a sight on him. Aside from which, the point was to stay in the game, not be on the run.

The tech running the stress scanner and face reader said, "Clean."

Shaw felt himself relax.

"Congratulations, M. Shaw. You are now ranked"—the tech looked at the little instrument he held, waved his thumb over a sensor and watched the holoprojic image—"One Hundred and Six. You may challenge any player ranked Ninety-Six or higher, and the list, updated frequently, can be found at the infostat log available on every planet and all major wheelworlds, available to your coded query."

"Thank you," Shaw said.

"Our job," the tech said. So far, neither of the showrunners had spoken a word.

Shaw nodded at them as he stood and headed for the door. This was a low-rent office in a seedy area of town, and likely as not after a day or two, would be abandoned. Showrunners tried to stay a step head of the local LEOs—better that the cools didn't gather up any more information than they already had. If Shaw stuck around on this world and waited for another challenge, he probably wouldn't be coming here for the tag transfer, and probably wouldn't see this trio again in any event. Showrunners and techs moved around, so as not to present targets for the local cools themselves.

Somebody could challenge Shaw, now that he was near the Top Hundred. He had hoped to climb a bit higher, and had merely taken over the slot of the man he'd beaten, but he wasn't going to wait for challenges. He had agents out looking for the ten ranks above him, and the ten above them, and the next ten, all the way to the top. Any or all of those might change, but with any luck, he could move to within challenge range of the Top Ten fighters with another eight or ten fights, depending on the arcane scoring system. His next victory would almost certainly put him into the Hundred, and after that, it was just a matter of going for the highest rank allowed, assuming he could find them. He might have to zigzag a little, but with the kind of money he had at his call, if a player was to be found, Shaw's agents would find him.

Servo stood waiting by the flitter, and Shaw ambled that way, feeling a mix of emotions. One the one hand, he had gotten into the system and past the showrunners, which were good things. On the other hand, the relative ease with which he had done so made the feats somehow not as . . . joyous as he had hoped. Of course, Marlowe hadn't even been among the Hundred, and Shaw knew that the lower the number, the more adept the player. He had trained with men who'd been in the Teens—and had been soundly beaten by them—and with his new edge, he was certain he could beat any of those players now. He did have some skill; without that, he'd hardly be able to compete, no matter how fast he was; still, it wasn't just that he wanted to *be Primero,* he wanted it to be an accomplishment of which he could be justly proud. He wanted to be the best, but he wanted it to *mean* something. He wanted to have to work a *little* . . .

Servo opened the flitter's door as Shaw approached. Shaw nodded at his bodyguard and stepped into the flitter.

Sooner or later, there would be a fight with witnesses, maybe even recorded. He wanted people to see him as skilled. If you had more relative time than your opponent, then you should be able to choose techniques that would showcase your ability. It was not only important to *be* good, you needed to *look* good . . .

"Sir?"

"To the ship," Shaw said. "Who is the closest and lowest on our list?"

Servo said, "Barnes d'Fleet, Ninety-Eight, is on Mti, in Ndama System. Teel Cotta ToDJonCam, Ninety-Six, is on Nazo, in Nazo. Mti is three day's transit, Nazo is eight days."

Shaw nodded. D'Fleet was closer, JonCam lower. Was it worth the extra five days' travel for two ranks?

No, he decided.

"Call the ship, tell Carter we're going to Mti."

"Sir."

Shaw leaned back in his seat. If there was game to go with the name, then he would have it. If not, at least he would have the name. Richest man in the galaxy. Best fighter. After that? Well, he'd just have to see, wouldn't he . . . ?

He'd have to do this one quickly. The annual art show was coming up soon, and he wanted to get back in time for that. Fremaux had some new stuff, and there might be some other artists he'd find interesting.

There were perhaps 350 people in a grand ballroom that would easily hold twice that many. The walls were hung with paintings, there were pedestals here and there bearing sculptures, freestanding mechanicals, and carefully placed lighting to showcase the art. Very nicely done, Azul thought.

She drifted around the ballroom, sipping good champagne from a tall thincris flute, into her persona as an artist looking at other artists' works. Her newly learned critical abilities came into play. Some of what was displayed here was good, some of it was great, and some of it was simply pretentious and awful. Much of what demanded the highest prices was, in fact, the worst art. Money covered a multitude of sins.

Several times men or women had attempted to strike up a

conversation with her. She was fairly stunning herself: She wore a black orthoskin suit that fit her like paint, matching slippers, and nothing else. The suit had a faint dusting of pulse-dust, so that under the right lighting, she shimmered with a barely perceptible rainbow glitter. Sexy, but tasteful, everything covered but revealed. Subtle was good.

As far as Luna Azul the artist was concerned, there was no such person as M. Ellis Shaw. She was a professional here to take in the work of other professionals, that was her mind-set, and thus her moves fit it naturally.

Eventually, she wound her way through the crowd to the paintings of the artist that Shaw collected. These were watercolors or something that looked enough like them to fool her, and very dynamic. Athletes, most of the subjects, in motion. A woman runner leaning at the tape just ahead of the other racers; a weightlifter under an impossibly large barbell, halfway up from a squat; a dancer just leaving the floor in a leap that you could almost see would soar to a great height. She nodded. The artist, one Fremaux Fremaux, had a nice touch with color, a mastery of human anatomy, and an eye for composition. His prices were not low, but neither were they at the top of the scale compared to other painters in this show. She knew from her research that he was relatively young, only forty T.S. or so, and with continued practice, could someday be a master painter. These were things she might have painted herself, in her persona, so she tried to appreciate them suitably.

"Which is your favorite?" came a deep male voice from behind her.

That would be Shaw.

She did not turn to look at him, but continued looking at the paintings. "The dancer," she said. "He's captured the potential. You can see how she is going to rise, how she will unfold, and even how she will settle."

"You have an artist's eye yourself."

Now she did turn to look at him. He was tall, dark-skinned, handsome, and fit. He radiated a power not evident in his holographs. He was in a smartly cut formal suit, the drape of the jacket perfect, the cling of the trousers precise, the dress slippers expensive but simple. A man comfortable in his demeanor, with no need to show off his riches, just as she had figured from her research.

"I hope so," she said. She gave him a polite, but uninterested smile. She had brushed off other people who had wanted to talk, and she was not going to show any particular interest in him, either. She turned back to the watercolors.

She could almost feel his amusement at being dismissed. Obviously she didn't know who he *was*.

"I take it thus that you are an artist?"

"I like to think I am."

"Would any of your work be on display, Fem . . . ?"

"No. I've only been on-planet for a short time. Nothing of mine is here." She ignored his attempt to coax forth her name.

"Are you any good?"

This was a challenge, and her persona would not allow such to slide by. She turned back to look at him. "Am I as good as this artist? Maybe. There are works here that I would not claim to match. Others that I find . . . less than inspiring."

He laughed. "Isn't that always the case?"

"So it seems. Please excuse me, sir, I came to see, not to, ah . . . visit."

He smiled broadly and gave her a slow nod. "Enjoy yourself, F. Azul."

She frowned. "How did you know my name?"

He tapped his ear, indicating the hidden com-button.

"But—who *told* you, sir?"

"I am a man with some connections," he said. "I have people in my employ who are paid well to know everything I need to know. Ellis Mtumbo Shaw, at your service."

She pretended not to recognize his name. "An artist yourself?"

That got another laugh. "Of a kind, perhaps, but not one with these skills." He waved one hand to encompass the ballroom. "I am in business."

She shrugged, flashed the polite smile. Business did not interest her.

"I should like to see your artwork, F. Azul."

"I am sure that a man with connections can find my catalog easily enough."

"I expect that you are right. Are you staying on our world long?"

"Maybe. I have a couple of paintings I want to finish before I leave. A week or three. However long it takes."

"Perhaps we'll meet again," he said. He raised his glass to her, then turned and sauntered away. People watched him, some of whom were surely security, some because of his looks, his grace, some for his wealth.

Inwardly, Azul smiled. That had gone as well as she could have hoped. She would bet her last stad that she would be hearing from Ellis Shaw again. And soon . . .

Mourn was in bed just drifting off to sleep when the door to his room slid open. It was quiet—first-class doors didn't squeak—but he was fully awake before the door was fully open.

Sola stood in the doorway, and the faint backlight of the room behind her spilled around her form bright enough to show that she was naked.

She didn't say anything.

Mourn said, "Come on in."

She did, the door sliding quietly shut behind her.

He sat up on the bed as she approached, opened his right arm to gather her in. She sat next to him, slid in close.

"You sure you want to do this?"

"I wouldn't be here if I wasn't," she said. She smiled, then leaned in to kiss him.

It had been a while since he'd been with a woman. She smelled clean and fresh, she was passionate, and she felt good pressed against his nude body. He was quick the first time, but slower the second, and she still called to him, yin to his yang. Her orgasm came just a hair before his third, he hadn't gone for three in ten years. She shuddered for what seemed a long time, milking him with a velvet pulse, strong at first, but one that gradually ebbed.

"Wow," she said.

"Yeah."

Side by side, she propped herself on her elbow and looked at him. "I've been wanting to do that since you first showed up in my hotel room in Spain," she said.

"I know. Me, too."

"Why didn't you make a move?"

"It wouldn't have meant as much then as now."

"That's important to you?"

"Yes."

She reached out with her free hand to rub lightly at his chest. "You have a lot of scars. You could have had them revised."

"What would be the point? Mostly nobody sees them but me and assorted medicos, and if somebody else does, they don't care. Or sometimes the scars make it better for them."

She nodded. "What now?"

"You want more?"

She laughed. "No, I meant generally."

"If we are going to finish your documentary, we probably need to get to a place where Weems or his hirelings either can't find us, or can't get to us if they do."

"You know a place?"

"Yeah. We can talk, work out, and if you are interested, play this game some more."

"I'm interested."

He smiled.

"Can I stay? Sleep with you?"

"Sure."

She lay back and relaxed.

It had been a while since he had allowed that, too. Sex was one thing, sharing your space afterward was something else. But he liked her, truly. She wasn't a child, but she was still young enough so that the galaxy was her oyster. There was a fine energy in being with somebody who felt that way.

As he drifted off to sleep, the thoughts he'd been having lately about fighting arose. There was something just outside his grasp, something very important. The more he reached for it, though, the more it eluded him. He had to let it go. Maybe it would come back, maybe not. But it was important, he knew . . .

Sleep claimed him and pulled him deep. He did not dream.

When he awoke six hours later, she was still asleep next to him. He got up to go pee, and she stirred a little, but stayed asleep.

She was so young and so beautiful, smart, too, and the sex had been good. He smiled. He could get used to having her around.

Careful, Mourn. This could turn into some heavy baggage, maybe too heavy to carry . . .

17

The Bruna System Hub station was crowded, hundreds of people milling back and forth, changing from starliner lighters to system hoppers, to be ferried out to other starliners, or to local planets. The place smelled of unwashed bodies—a lot of starships carried steerage passengers, and the cheap beds didn't always allow easy access to even the sonic showers, whose best efforts at cleaning didn't get close to soap and hot water. Too many people in the hub probably hadn't bathed in days, and the station's overworked scrubbers couldn't keep up with the odor. You tuned it out after a while, but a first whiff, it was potent.

"Farbis?"

"Yes." There were four organic worlds in the system— Farbis, Pentr'ado, Lagomustardo, and Muta Kato, plus one large wheelworld, Malgrand Luno. The latter was where Mourn and Sola were headed, to catch a local boxcar down the gravity well.

"Never been there," she said. She searched her memory, he could see her hunting for it. "Agro world?"

He nodded. "Much of the temperate zones."

"Why there? Don't think Weems will look for you on a farm?"

"That. Plus I know it—or I used to. I was born there, spent my first eighteen years on the planet."

She blinked. "You were a *farmer*?"

He smiled at the wonder in her voice.

"I have trouble picturing you driving a harvester among the rows of cottonwood or giant corn."

"Everybody has to be born somewhere."

"So how does one go from being a farmer to a fighter?"

He glanced at the ship schedule holoproj floating above them. The transport to the wheelworld station wasn't due for boarding for another hour. There was a food kiosk just ahead. "Let's get something to eat. I'll tell you a story."

She raised an eyebrow. "On cam?"

"If you want."

The day after Lazlo Mourn turned twelve was the day his life changed direction. Up until then, he hadn't thought much about what he was going to do when he grew up. He and Ma and Da worked on a giant communal farm in the NorthWest Quarter, living in a prefab that was old when his father was born. Both sets of his grandparents, along with a dozen aunts and uncles and twenty or thirty cousins, all lived in the Quarter, too, as had *their* parents and grandparents. The NWQ co-op covered 270,000 acres, dotted by four villages full of others who worked it. The main crops were export cereal grains—wheat, rice, oats, giant corn— but they also grew legumes, beans, peas, and root vegetables, and had several herds of milkers from which they made cheese and butter and yogurt. The work was hard, even for children, but it was simple, and Mourn had assumed he would continue to live in his village, eventually meet a girl, get married, raise a family of his own. That was how it went.

Normally, on their twelfth birthday, children went to town and registered as citizens. It could be done from the village, of course, but the tradition was, you went with your da or ma to the Confederation Center, had your holo made, your retinal patterns, fingerprints, and your DNA scoped, and got your first ID cube, which was really a kinda squashed square that looked more like a mint than a cube. Some places, they liked the implants, but on Farbis, most people just got cubes. If you didn't have a reader for a transfer, it was hard to lend your implant to somebody who needed to borrow a few stads from your account. Then again, an implant didn't get lost . . .

From then on, you were no longer just a child, but a citizen, even though you didn't get full rights for another six T.S. years.

But on *his* birthday, there had been an accident at Wheat Storage Four. One of the silos collapsed. That wasn't supposed to happen, the extruded everlast-plast structure was supposed to be rated for twice what it could hold, but somehow, a crack developed, and the weight of all that grain, piled sixteen stories high, had blown the base out and spewed however many hundred tons of grain across the surrounding plastcrete like a volcano blasting apart.

Nobody had been caught in the tsunami of wheat except a couple of trailers and a flitter, but the damaged silo fell over, and it came down on the computer/communications shack and crushed it like somebody stomping a size twelve down hard on a jik egg. The ten people inside, six men and four women, had been squashed into the wreckage.

Lazlo had been out with his father in an inspection flitter, checking on the giant corn seedlings in Sprout Nineteen, when the call came. They had planned to make a quick pass, then Da was going to take him to town for his registration. But Da was in the Emergency Corps—pretty much every grown man was, and he was a supervisor, so those plans got canceled, and there was no time to drop his son off. He cranked the fans up to full and leaned the flitter hard toward WS-4.

The place was pretty much in chaos when they got there, and by the time it all got sorted out, it was well after midnight.

Nobody in the shack survived, but they had to dig them all out to be sure, and it was a big fucking mess, the whole area knee deep in wheat. Of course, Lazlo had known the people who'd died, though none of them were relatives.

The cleanup crews took over, and Da and Lazlo went home to bed. In all the excitement, he'd pretty much forgotten all about registering.

But the next morning, Ma got him up early and told him they were going to town.

Not that "town" was much more than the village. It was bigger, of course, they had a boxcar port, some shops and pubs and things, plus the government offices, local and Confed. But there were maybe ten thousand people in Ship City, while his own village had half that many.

Ma parked the flitter in a public lot and they got out and headed for Registration. The day was cool for spring, but the sun was shining, and the smells of town were different than the village. More machinery lube, hydrocarbon dross, a lot less crop stink. It was exciting, Lazlo felt as if he had to pee, and his belly was fluttery. You didn't get to register but once, after all. Everything seemed much sharper than usual—the sights, sounds, smells, everything.

They had just crossed the street behind a four-trailer grain carrier, a forty-wheeler loaded to the canvas, and gotten to the sidewalk when Lazlo's short life took a sudden turn.

He heard the music first. At the time, he didn't con-

sciously mark it for what it was—somebody playing solo
finger-style guitar—he didn't realize that until later. Of
course, he had heard music before, it wasn't as if the co-op
didn't have entcom, and there were people who got together in groups to play. He had a cousin who was a pretty
good keyboardist, and an uncle who played rumblestik.
And he had heard guitars, though not quite like this one.
The song was bright, melodic, and catchy. But of a moment, there was a crash, as if a door was slammed open,
and the music stopped.

To their left, a surge of people flowed out into the street,
coming from a building with neon and pulse-paint signs
that ID'ed it as a pub. There was a score of folks, at least,
mostly men, a few women, and at the center of the collection's attention was a short and compact man in lube-
stained freight hauler's blue coveralls with the sleeves cut
short to reveal thick and muscular arms. On one shoulder
he had a tat that Lazlo couldn't quite make out, something
that looked like a long sickle or a knife.

It was obvious that the short man in blues had done
something to piss people off, and it looked as if he were
about to get his ass seriously kicked, because there were at
least six men moving in on him as if they wanted to plant
him head down in the plastcrete.

Flitters and haulers hit warning horns, but nobody in the
crowd paid any attention, and the vehicles fanned or rolled
to stops. With traffic stopped, everybody focused on the
men in the street.

Ma grabbed Lazlo's shoulder and tried to steer him
away, but he didn't move. He was almost as big as she was,
and he wanted to see this.

"Lazlo—"

"A second, Ma."

The hauler dropped into a fighting crouch.

Jesu, he's gonna get his dick knocked in the dirt!

The first attacker got within range and swung a wide,

hard, looping punch at the hauler's head. The puncher was big, twenty centimeters taller and probably fifteen kilos heavier, and if he hit, that would be the game. Lazlo had seen enough fights in the village or fields to know that a big fist to the head usually ended the dust-up pretty quick, and the bigger guy almost always won, too—

The hauler ducked the punch, moved in so fast Lazlo couldn't really tell what he did, and the bigger man *flew* backward and slammed into two men behind him and all three of them went down—

And then the guy just *danced* into the others, not waiting for them, attacking the other five men as if they were nothing, as if he had all the time in the world.

It would be ten years before Lazlo had the wherewithal to reconstruct what he saw that day. It was no more than a learned skill, what the hauler did, but on that spring morning in Ship City, the twelve-year-old version of Lazlo Mourn saw what appeared to be magic. Those six men might as well have been carved from stone. None of them laid a serious hand or foot on the hauler. Time slowed to a crawl for them, but it sped up for the man facing them.

Lazlo couldn't believe what he was seeing.

It took but a few seconds before it was done, and when it was over, it was . . . *astonishing*.

The hauler stood alone in the street. Six men lay around him, and the rest of the crowd had hauled ass to the sidewalk, fast. You could almost smell their fear from where Lazlo and his ma stood.

Two of the people on the walk, a man and a woman, began walking away in a hurry as a siren announced that the local cools were en route and closing. The couple passed by Lazlo and his mother.

"Lazlo!" his mother said. "Come on! The authorities will be looking for witnesses! You'll not get registered! Let's go!"

He nodded and allowed himself to be hurried along.

The man and woman who'd passed them were only a meter or two ahead on the walk. The woman said, "Who the prong was that guy? How could a hauler *do* that?"

And the man laughed, and said, "He's not a hauler, he's a dueler. Musashi Flex player. Tattoo right there on his shoulder. Stupid. Their own fault, messin' with a man like that."

Lazlo had never heard of the Musashi Flex; but at that moment, he realized that he wasn't going to spend his life on this world, working the farms. He had just seen something amazing, and however the man had managed it, Lazlo was going to learn how to do it, too. Such power, to be able to move like that. Such power . . .

Sola shut the recorder off. "Wow."

Her food—such that it was—sat congealing on her plate. This was not the background she would have picked for Mourn. A kid attracted to the Flex by a street fight in some back-rocket farm town. Great stuff. She could do it as a voice-over while she ran CG images of a re-creation. The entcom audience would eat it up.

"And you haven't been back since you left?"

"Nope."

"Twenty-five years."

"Twenty-seven."

"Your parents still alive?"

"No. My father died in a flitter accident a few years ago, a repellor blew, he crashed into a field. My mother apparently developed malignant silicosis and passed away six months after he did."

"You kept track of them?"

He shook his head. "Not really. I thought about going to visit them last year. I did a records check then, that's what it said."

She didn't say anything, but she knew he got the unasked question.

He said, "It wasn't an amicable parting. My parents couldn't understand how I could even consider the idea of leaving the farm. None of our family ever had before. And the idea of becoming a professional *fighter*? We had big and loud disagreements about my future. Said things that couldn't be taken back. I was young and full of myself, I had no patience for what they wanted. Day I reached my majority, I took off."

She nodded. She could understand that. Her father thought the idea of her becoming a reporter was insane. She was supposed to be a medico, as he was, as her grandfather and her uncles were. Writing tales for entcom? That was no kind of life for a proper-caste woman . . .

"So, you're going home."

He shrugged. "Not exactly. I figured we'd go to one of the other farms, where we wouldn't run into anybody who might know me. We'll use alternate IDs, lie low, pretend to be a couple on their honeymoon. I'm a farmer from the next world over, you're an office worker."

"You think you can pull that off?"

"You never forget the smell of wheat dust," he said. "I can pass for a farmer."

She nodded. A little quiet time would let her work on the documentary. There were worse ways to spend your time.

18

They could have taken a transport directly from the port to their destination, a country inn in the farming community three hundred klicks away, but Sola wanted to buy some clothes.

"I'm a bride," she said, holding on to his arm. "I should have some newlywed weeds."

He had smiled. "I suppose that's the least a good groom can do."

So they caught a local into the city, a fair-sized town called Juneallo, the local province capital that also catered to the port trade. They stopped in several shops, and Sola purchased a few items.

Mourn didn't like to shop, particularly. If he wanted something, he knew what it was. He would go and find it and buy it. If the first pair of slippers he tried on fit well, he bought those—no need to try on sixteen pairs, then wind up buying the first set, was there?

Sola laughed at him.

As they were leaving the last shop and heading back toward the transport station, they came out into a crowded
street.

"A political rally," Sola said.

Mourn nodded. Half the crowd, maybe five hundred
people, carried signs, the garish and bright pulse-paint
throbbing out their candidate's name and their earnest slo-
gans: SHAKE UP THE SYSTEM! DOWN WITH FASCISM! FREE-
DOM NOW! ELECT PREBENDARY JOSLIN!

"Let's go," he said. "This way."

"Don't you want to mingle with the people? Get a feel
for the electorate? Participate in democracy?"

He caught her hand and started up the sidewalk, away
from the rally.

"What's the hurry, Mourn? These things can be a lot of
fun."

He kept moving. "This one won't be."

"How you figure that?"

"You see the cools over there? See that short man in the
gray coverall and jump boots?"

He nodded at the line of police officers past the demonstrators. There were sixty or so of the cools. Their dark
blue uniforms were almost black where they showed in the
gaps of the not-quite-matching dark spidersilk armor plate
and helmets and boots they all wore. Some of them started
to put their thick, clear lexan face shields down. The civilian stood out.

"Yeah?"

"Hundred to one says he's Confed, sent to break this up,
and the local police have their marching orders. You'll see
the shockstiks come out in a minute, and they'll wade into
the crowd and start breaking heads. We don't want to be
here when that goes down."

"You aren't serious," she said.

"Serious as a ruptured air lock in deep vacuum."

They were a couple hundred meters away from the main

part of the crowd, which had begun to spill from the sidewalk into the street.

"They just started blocking traffic," he said. "That's all the excuse the cools need." He kept moving. The crowd flowed into the street as more people joined it.

Five hundred civilians and only a few dozen cools, but a mob was only as bright and focused as its leaders, and this one, he thought, didn't look very collected.

A deep and loud amplified voice said, "Attention! This is the police. You are creating a street hazard. This group has violated its permit. You must disperse immediately!"

Sola stopped, and Mourn either had to stop or jerk her off her feet, so he halted. They should be safe enough here—he didn't see any cools behind them who might cut off a possible retreat.

"One more warning is all they'll get," he said.

She looked at him.

"I've seen this before. If they left now, they'd be okay, but they won't. They never do."

"You are in violation of a lawful police order," came the augmented voice. "If you do not disperse immediately, you will be subject to arrest."

The crowd seemed to pause and mill about. A few people began to walk away, but the majority held their ground. *They were, by God, citizens, weren't they? Not doing anything wrong. The police were blowing smoke, right?*

When the cools moved, they did so in a hurry. No slow line advancing to push the people back. They looked like a pack of starving wolves going after sheep. Shockstiks and riot batons rose and fell at speed, smashing whatever they hit. You could hear the first impacts this far away, before the mob found its collective voice and drowned out the strikes with terrified screams.

Now the sheep tried to run, but the predators were all around them. If each cool could club three or four demonstrators, the work of a few seconds, then half of the crowd would go down in a hurry.

Some of them got past the line, scrambling in full flight up the street toward where Sola and Mourn stood. The cools didn't pursue the ones lucky enough to escape; they continued to work on those trapped in the ragged corral.

"Jesu damn, Mourn—!"

He nodded, watching the beating with a professional's gaze. Some of the cools were just whaling away, no real technique, bashing at anything in range; some of them had more skill, they were targeting collarbones—those broke easily, then you could hardly lift your arm to protect your head, which was the next target.

A few showed real expertise—they worked the body in combinations—a jab to the solar plexus or an underhand shot to the groin, and when the target bent over in pain, a smash to the back of the head or spine that flattened the target facedown on the plastcrete. Very efficient.

"Fuck!" She looked at him, and he read her face.

"I might be able to take the clubs away from a few, but you don't resist a riot squad—you either scram or you get bashed—if you fight back, they kill you. We can't stop it. Come on. We'll get run over if we stay here."

Once they were a klick or so away, listening to the sirens fade, he saw how much she was shaking. "Take slow and deep breaths."

"That wasn't right," she said, her voice ragged. "If they had wanted to break up the crowd, they could have used puke gas or tensmus bombs!"

"If all they'd wanted to do was break up the crowd, yes. That wasn't the point."

"How can they do that?"

"You weren't born yesterday. The Confederation does whatever it wants to do. You can't stop the rain by holding your hand up and wishing it would quit."

"But it was a peaceful rally!"

"And somebody didn't like what it stood for. Or maybe somebody thought the prebendary running for office was an irritant. Why doesn't matter. A message got sent. You get free expression as long as it doesn't cross a line. When it does, you pay for it, and it isn't cheap." He nodded back at the direction from which they had come.

"It isn't right."

He shrugged. "No. But that's how things are. Once upon a time, the Confederation had a real purpose—to explore, discover, and settle new worlds, to be prepared to defend us if we ran into some nasty aliens who wanted to fry us.

"We've found most of the habitable worlds within easy reach and put down settlers. Aside from some artifacts of the Zonn, a race that appears to have been long gone when humans were still living in trees, we haven't run into anybody with any kind of intelligence to challenge humans. So the Confed has gotten fat and lazy, and now what it does best is perpetuate itself.

"The three-hundred-kilo rock ape sleeps wherever he wants—especially if there are tens of thousands of him and they are heavily armed. That's how things are."

"I don't need a fucking lecture!"

"Yes, you do."

She didn't say anything for a while after that. And what was there to say? She knew what he said was true. Nobody had to like it, but there was no getting around it. With the Confed, you went along to get along. If you stood in its path, you got stepped on.

A smart man would move out of the way. Saved you a lot of trouble doing that.

A few days after the art show, Azul's com chimed. She was having lunch at a Perenesian restaurant, enjoying a dish of stir-fried shrimp and green crab with enough fireweed laced through it to cause tears and to clear her sinuses. Not bad for a planet light-years away from the source of both the crab and the spice.

She'd had CI make several calls from various "friends," just in case anybody checked her communcations records, but she knew who it was before she tapped the ear inset com to life—there was no need to check the caller ID sig.

"Yes?"

"Fem Azul. Ellis Shaw."

"Ah, M. Shaw. The . . . businessman."

He chuckled. "The same. I was wondering—do you have any works in progress that will be finished soon?"

"I have—but I also have twelve or fifteen paintings in my catalog that are still available for sale."

"Well, that's not so, F. Azul. All of your finished paintings seem to have been purchased."

"Really? I spoke to my agent last evening, and such was not the case."

"That was last evening. As of 1100 this morning, that is no longer the case."

"And you know this . . . how?"

"I bought them."

It was not hard to put surprise into her voice. "All of them?"

"Indeed."

"Your business must be doing well, sir."

"I get by. I like your work."

The fifteen paintings in question had been priced from twelve to twenty-five thousand standards each, and the total retail cost would be about a quarter of a million stads. Not even a drop in Shaw's ocean-sized bucket. Still, it was an impressive gesture: She had figured he would buy one or two, not all of them.

Too bad she wouldn't get the stads herself.

She smiled. "I can see that." This was the time for her to be intrigued, impressed, or both, and what artist could brush off a man who had just purchased all of her available output? "Perhaps we could arrange for you to view my work in progress, M. Shaw."

"Please, call me Ellis. And I would love to see what you have."

She smiled. No missing the double entendre in that comment.

Well on the way to another victory for Operative Azul, it seemed.

"Let me check my schedule and get back to you."

"You have my private number in your ID log," he said. "I'll wait to hear from you."

Shaw smiled at the com as he waved it off. He hadn't gotten the idea that Luna Azul was that impressed by great wealth, but buying all of her paintings and drawings? That had been a clever stroke, no question. And she was as intriguing to him as she had probably found his action to be. He did like the work—it wasn't fantastic, but it did call to him, both in subject and in execution. She was beautiful, though beauty alone was not something he had trouble obtaining. She found him attractive, he was pretty sure, but had not fallen all over herself to make a connection at the show, which was good. A nice blend of talent and personality. Rare enough to be treasured.

Cervo had done a full background check on her, and she seemed to be what she appeared: a young, beautiful, up-and-still-rising artist. And she had a brother who had been a Flex player, so one might expect her to have an interest in that, as well. Somebody worth exploring a little further, at least. A man in his position could have all manner of women. There were those who would sleep with him because of his wealth and power, eager to warm their hands at his rich fire. He could have exquisite company, paid for or not, women who were experts in the art of sex, but the ones who didn't know who he was, or didn't care if they did? Those were more fun. Like the medico, whom he'd paid, but who would have slept with him for free . . .

Buying her collective works? That was a cheap enough trick, and it made things easier. He'd used a cutout, so there wasn't a direct link to him, a thing he often did. People thought Ellis Shaw was interested in an artist? Prices went up. He could afford anybody's work, but why spend money he didn't have to spend?

Even if she wasn't awed by his money, even if she suspected he had bought the art just to get her to consider him in a good light, it was a smart enough move that the doing of it would make her stop and think. That a man would spend a quarter of a million stads to do that? How could she *not* find him intriguing?

He smiled again. It was good to be rich and powerful. It was better to be smart—a smart man could always become wealthy; a wealthy man could not always become smart . . .

He was looking forward to their encounter. It should be most amusing . . .

19

The fifth time Mourn stepped in and slapped her on the face, Sola was *really* starting to get pissed off. He wasn't hitting her hard, just taps, not even enough to sting, but no matter how she tried to block, it didn't seem to help. He got her no matter what.

The sixth time, she didn't try to block or parry—she took three fast steps to her right.

"What are you doing?" he asked.

"Not getting hit," she said.

"But what if you are in tight quarters?"

"And what if a passing starliner drops out of the sky and falls on this broke-sprocket village? I have room, so I moved."

He shook his head.

"Isn't it better to avoid a hit than to block it? Didn't you tell me that?"

"Yes. But you might not always have the space."

"But I do. Why shouldn't I use it?"

"Because—" he started, looking exasperated. But then he stopped. Blinked a couple of times, and went into that somewhere-else head space she'd seen him in before.

"What?"

"You're right. Having a punch miss is better than blocking or even parrying—it takes less effort, and if you do it right, you can off-balance an attack. And you should use what you have."

"See, I'm a genius."

He didn't smile.

"That was a joke."

He nodded.

"What?"

"If there was a way to duck or dodge or slip an attack in a very small space, just by moving a little, either your feet or your body or maybe a combination of both? That would be good."

"Right. So why aren't you teaching me that?"

"That's exactly the right question. Why aren't I?"

"And the answer is . . . ?"

"I'm not sure. Old thought patterns, old habits. But I could. I know enough to figure it out."

"Call me when you do. Maybe I'll go take a walk down to the grain silo and watch the bovines make cow pies."

"No, wait, we're onto something here. Put your hands into a basic high/low guard position. When I step in to punch this time, step with your right foot and put it down *there.*" He pointed to a spot on the floor. "Angle it out about forty-five degrees. At the same time, slide your left foot on the floor to there. Don't try to block at all, just keep your hands in position. You don't need to take two or three steps, one small one will do. Like you're moving along one leg of a triangle, with the base running back there."

"I'm not supposed to block? You're gonna slap me again."

"Just try it, okay?"

He stepped back and set himself for an attack. He nodded, then stepped in, fast.

She did as he had told her, stepped slightly forward and to her right a hair, and scooted her left foot up.

His slap missed her cleanly.

He grinned. "Good."

"Yeah, but you are almost on top of me, and like you have been saying since day one, you aren't going to throw one punch and then stop and wait for me. What about the other hand?"

"You move again. I'll be throwing a left, or turning and trying another right, maybe a kick or knee, so, let's see, you pull your left foot over behind your right foot, that *sempok* crossover step I showed you. Then when I throw the third attack, move the right foot across in the front version, the *depok* step. I'll go slow."

He did, and with the two steps, he missed both strikes again.

"I like this not-getting-hit stuff better," she said. "It's more like dancing."

"Exactly. And that's what martial arts are, dances. After each of your steps, you could counterattack, a punch, an elbow, a knee, depending on the range, you don't just have to dodge. Once I miss, you get a shot. And you are in balance at any point."

She nodded. "But what if you didn't just punch, what if you threw an elbow or a knee or whatever?"

"Doesn't matter. If you have the proper position, I won't connect. The trick is to be sure you are in the proper position relative to whatever attack I might throw."

"The possibilities are infinite," she said.

"No, not really. There are only a relatively few ways I can attack effectively and efficiently from any given stance. If you can see how I'm standing and poised, you can avoid my attack. If I am here, there can't be but a few ways to move my feet and get there."

"Yeah, after thirty years of practice I might get it."

"No, I think you could learn it pretty quick!"

He was as excited as she had ever seen him. Her action had triggered something in him, he had made some kind of connection in his thinking, and she could almost hear the wheels in his mind turning at speed as the idea took hold.

"Ninety, maybe a hundred moves, they would cover just about any attack from any angle."

"Only ninety or a hundred? Jesu, that's a lot, Mourn."

"No, no, no, it isn't! I've learned thousands and thousands of attack and defense patterns, and they start to duplicate each other pretty quick. When you get right down to it, there aren't that many ways for somebody to come at you effectively. All you need is one or two good responses for each one."

"Why didn't I see this before?" He shook his head.

"Maybe you didn't have the right teacher," she said.

He looked at her as if seeing her for the first time. "You're right. Pure truth sometimes comes out of the mouths of babes. Man! I can do this. I can put together some sequences that will cover anything that can come at you. Link them together in a system. Damn!"

She liked it that he was so excited, and that somehow, even though she wasn't sure how, she was responsible for it.

The meal was superb, and Azul expected no less. A billionaire with taste doesn't have to eat less than the best, and whoever the chef was here, she or he was top-grade. The fish they'd had was probably swimming around unaware of its fate an hour before it was prepared, and the vegetables picked and rushed to the kitchen from a garden behind the place. Only the wine was aged, and the vintage was a very good year indeed.

That they were the only patrons in a room designed to

hold eighty didn't surprise her, either. Shaw could own the restaurant, or merely have rented it for the evening. The superrich were different from ordinary folks—not only did they have more money, they knew how to spend it to their advantage.

A waiter materialized at her elbow with an icy bottle of sparkling wine and topped off her glass, a thincris flute that probably cost a couple hundred stads all by itself. The wine was pale straw in color, the bubbles very tiny, and it was the best sparkling wine she had ever tasted.

It would be hard not to be impressed, and Azul was well aware that Shaw had pulled out the stops to do just that. But her persona had to have some resistance—artists would not be artists without a few quirks.

He lifted his own wineglass. "To art," he said.

She raised her glass and nodded. "To art."

"Your meal was satisfactory?"

"Of course. It was perfect. You won't have to fire the chef. Are you renting, or do you own the restaurant?"

He smiled. "As of this morning, I own it."

"Just how wealthy are you, M. Shaw?"

"Business has been pretty good to me. I can't complain."

"Would you like to come to my hotel room and look at my paintings?"

"I would like that, yes."

She returned his smile. She'd show him those, but that was all he was going to get from her tonight. Of course, she was going to sleep with him, there was never a question of "if," but only "when." She had pronged a lot less attractive men a lot faster when the need had been urgent, a couple so ugly they'd scare a carrion beetle. It went with the job. He was handsome, rich, and she expected him to be an adept lover, which would be a bonus; however, to resist him for one more meeting would raise his interest in her yet more.

She would make it apparent that she wanted to bed him, but that he would have to wait at least a little while longer. Men could be impatient for sex, but a man like Shaw would enjoy the hunt as well as the capture. They wanted to win, but they also wanted at least a little challenge.

She had something he wanted, he had something she wanted. With luck, they'd both get there. A fair trade.

Unbidden, the waiter returned and quickly set before them fine china coffee cups, into which he poured a hot and fragrant brew. Probably roasted the beans and ground them here this very day.

It was the best coffee she had ever tasted.

"Just like mother used to make," she said.

Shaw said, "Ah. And are you an only child?"

She took another sip of the coffee. "Had a brother. Voda—he died two years past. Some irony in that—he was a Musashi Flexer—ranked in the top fifty or so players, off and on. Used the name Clee. Fought many duels with weapons, survived those, only to be killed in a maglev accident on Spandle. We didn't find out about it until months after it happened."

He would already know this from his background check, but it would make her cover more real if she told it. If you were looking for wolves and you heard one howl, you were ready to believe that it was real when you saw it.

"Sorry to hear that."

She shrugged. "If not the train, some player would have gotten him eventually. He used to say that if you kept playing, you'd eventually lose. Only way to beat that was to retire, and that wasn't in his nature. He was destined to die young."

"You disapprove of the Flex?"

She took another sip of the coffee. "Not really. Everybody has to be somewhere. Some of us are artists, some of us fighters, some of us are businessmen. There is something to be said for having talent, no matter where it lies. Better to be capable in one arena than in none at all. Nothing wrong with physical prowess. It has its uses."

He smiled yet again.

He'd like her saying that, too. A man wanted to be admired for the things he enjoyed. Her persona wouldn't know about his dabbling in the Flex, so for her to offer such a thing in the abstract meant it could be applied to the specific. You like guys who can kick ass? Honey, here I *am* . . .

The trick to telling a lie was to always wrap it around the truth. The more truth, the better the lie. It was going as well as could be expected.

"Shall we?" she asked, putting down her empty coffee cup.

"By all means."

Shaw was amused when Azul showed him her paintings and then gently, but firmly, let it be known she wouldn't be sharing her bed with him this night. He was adept enough at the game to hear the promise that it wouldn't be impossible or even unlikely in the near future, and that was enough. A man of his experience could be patient, if the goal was worth waiting for, and he had decided that having this woman bucking under him was worth it.

They had a drink, he offered to buy her paintings when they were finished, she demurred out of hand, refusing to price them until they were done, then he took his leave.

As always, Cervo was nearby, along with a his team of two dozen armed and expert bodyguards who looked like anything but, scattered around the hotel and street outside. A billionaire not entirely stupid did not risk casual kidnapping. In a compound controlled by his people, Shaw felt relaxed enough to move about alone. In the city, there was no point in taking chances. He was usually covered, and Cervo had his telemetry monitored even when Shaw was out of sight. Shaw guessed that Cervo could tell when he was making love to a woman by the increase in his heart rate and respiration . . .

Of course, during the challenges in the Flex, only Cervo had his back. Nobody knew who he really was on those excursions, and certainly nobody would be able to follow him from home. And while on his speed-enhancing drug, anybody offering him grief would get what they deserved . . .

He smiled as Cervo opened the door to his vehicle.

"Sir," his man said, "we've found the next nearest available match."

"Ah. Where?"

"Right here on-planet."

"Outstanding! You have his location?"

"Her location, sir. Yes. In Shakha Town."

That close? Only a few hundred kilometers away? How great was that? Shakha Town was a ranching burg, grown up to deal primarily in livestock, trading in meats, milk, cheeses, various kinds of leathers and wools and the like.

He didn't have any Reflex with him, but it would take only a few minutes to fetch it from his private medical safe at the lab. With luck, he could be engaged in the match in a few hours. "Take us to the complex, Cervo. I need to collect my dancing shoes."

They didn't get to Shakha Town until nearly midnight, but Cervo assured Shaw that his prey was an owl, up nights and sleeping days, so he wasn't going to have to roust her from a bed, which was good. Not much fun in beating somebody half-asleep, was there?

As Cervo had said, she was out and about. Cervo's agents had trailed her to a pub and were watching her as Shaw arrived in town. They got directions and went to find her.

The pub was called The Naked Albino, a solidly middle-class ranchers' place, and it was bustling, twoscore patrons

drinking, toking, laughing, and talking, the air thick with
noise and flickstik smoke, some kind of music generator
playing in the background. Cheap fun for the masses, but it
held little appeal for Shaw. No quality control.

She was a tall woman, solidly built and not unattractive.
Black hair worn short, pale skin, blue eyes, in a loose, hip-
length tunic over orthoskins and boots, nursing a drink and
watching the other patrons. She looked bored.

It took her about five minutes to discern Shaw's interest in her, and, he thought, realize that it wasn't sexual but
professional. She put her half-finished drink down and
left the pub.

Cervo was outside watching.

Shaw followed the woman outside. By the time he had
made it into the warm night, she was half a block away,
walking quickly, but not running.

Ranked Seventy-Seventh, she was, and without the
background check, her name alone wouldn't have given her
sex away—Shaw wasn't sure what the origin of the name
"B'ahl Muth Tah" was and maybe if he had known, he
would have recognized it as female, but it didn't really
matter. Her rank alone indicated a certain level of skill, and
that was what really mattered. She was another rung on his
ladder, and his fourth fight.

He was flying on Reflex and not worried. Cervo stayed
well back, idling along in the flitter as Shaw followed the
woman on foot.

He finally caught up with her near a long row of storage
units filled with tark's wool in an industrial complex maybe
a klick away from the pub. The air was full of a barnyard-
kind of musty smell from the wool sheds. Various night insects swarmed the cheap lighting although it was supposedly
in a spectrum that wouldn't draw the night bugs. Plenty illu-
mination enough to see by, if a bit too blue for his tastes.

The place was her choice—she had led him here.

He moved in. "Evening, fem," he said.

"It is that."

"Want to dance?"

"Sure. Armed," she said. "Impact or cutters." She pulled a long-bladed knife from under her tunic and smiled wolfishly at him. The artificial lighting flashed bluely on the mirrorlike blade as she waved it lazily in front of herself. She was confident enough, didn't look afraid.

He returned the smile. He hadn't fought a match armed yet, and while he could have chosen weapons that would have given him great advantage because of his speed, he had wanted to make it more exciting, so he carried a folding knife with a blade about as long as his thumb, single-edged with an upangled *tanto*-style point. Not much more than a penknife, really, normally suitable for cutting twine or slicing a piece of fruit, not one most would take for a dueling weapon. Handmade and expensive, of course, not something that would fall apart after one stab, but small by knife fighters' standards.

She didn't smile when she saw his little knife. Smart of her.

A slap-cap, a Newton-bleak unidirectional shaped charge worn like a ring, would have probably been the best impact weapon for him. A slap to the chest would blow out a man's pump, one to the spine would crush bone and the spinal column and paralyze instantly, to the head, the brain would turn to mush. With his speed, he could dart in and make such a hit before most people had a chance to realize just how fast he was. A two-second fight, bam! end of match.

But where was the fun in that? It was about winning, of course, but it was also about at least a chance of risk; otherwise, why bother? He wanted to have to work for it a little. So far, that hadn't been the case. His matches had been walkovers, his speed simply too much for his opponents to deal with, and all three of his previous fights had been disappointing. By giving himself a self-imposed handicap, maybe he could spice things up a bit.

He was, maybe not so oddly, feeling a little horny. If Luna Azul had let him stay with her, he might not have met this woman whom he would soon be piercing with an altogether different weapon . . .

He smiled at the thought.

The woman circled to her right, keeping the knife in front of her.

He'd have to go around the blade, block it, or do a pass; otherwise, he could spit himself on her point, since she didn't even have to move it, only hold it in his way. She wouldn't be fast enough to track him with a stab or slash, and if she stepped back, he could just follow her in, no problem.

"My name is Ellis Mtumbo Shaw," he said. "I'm ranked Eighty-First."

She nodded, crouched lower behind her knife. "I'm guessing you know who I am and my rank." Not a question.

"Yes. Any last words?"

She chuckled. "Come and try, sucker. We'll see who has last words."

He went in, glorying in his ability. He could see her eyes start to widen as she realized nobody could move as fast as he was, as she understood she couldn't get away—

He stuck his free hand out for the block, to open the way for his thrust. He didn't want to kill her on the first pass, only to sting her enough so she could feel it, but not so hard as to put her down—

She cut at him, but so slow. He blocked the stab, rocked to the side a hair, punched her in the left shoulder with his knife, driving the blade in no more than a couple of centimeters, then jerked it out and jumped to his own right, to stop two meters away.

"Fuck!" she said, the fear filling her voice. She slashed wildly, but he was way outside her range.

"You see how it is going to go," he said. "Give me your tag now, I'll let you live." He was feeling perhaps a little more kindly toward her than he would have a man, after his pleasant and erotically promising encounter with Azul earlier in the evening. It would be almost a shame to waste this woman by killing her. Maybe if he didn't kill her, they could pass the time doing something else afterward?

What would it be like to have sex while on Reflex?

That thought made him chuckle. Would give a whole new meaning to the old joke about whem-bim-thank-you-fem. He'd probably feel like an electronic vibrator to her—

"No," she said.

She knew she couldn't beat him, she *had* to know after what he had just demonstrated, and yet she was willing to keep fighting. Brave.

Foolish, but brave.

He'd stick her again, shallow, go for the thigh this time, give her one more chance.

He blurred in as he had before, his knife aimed low—

—and she surprised him.

She cut straight down in front of her own thigh, a short slice. Her blade was half a meter away from any part of him, what was she doing?

He was moving so fast he didn't realize it in time. She had figured out where he was going to stick her, and she was moving in anticipation of his attack, not aiming for where his arm was, but for where she guessed it was *going to be* by the time her cut got there.

He was moving too fast stop his own attack, too much inertia. His point touched her thigh as her edge caught his forearm. When he snatched his hand back, her very sharp blade raked a long and shallow cut along his arm, over the radius, from midarm all the way to his wrist—

Damn!

He jumped backward.

The cut was nothing. Bloody, but not deep enough to cause any loss of function, no big vessels hit. A little orthostat glue, maybe a staple or two, he'd be good as new.

It impressed him, though. She had realized she couldn't match him, he was too fast, so she moved before he did, hoping he couldn't adjust in time, and she'd guessed right.

He saluted her with his knife, touching it to his forehead, even though he was pissed off about the cut.

"Good move, but it's not enough, sister. Give up your tag, walk away."

"That's your blood running down your arm and splattering on the ground, brother. Give up *yours* and walk away."

She sounded calm. Maybe she really thought she had a chance. Time to show her.

He leaped in, faked a stab at her face, moving slow enough so she could see it and raise her hand for the block, keeping her blade low to cover her belly and groin—

When her blocking hand was at the level of her chin, and her knife was covering her low line, he pulled his knife back a hair. There was an opening between her empty hand and knife big enough to drive a freight hauler. He put the blade into her throat and cut hard to his left, severing her right carotid artery. He danced back.

Too bad she hadn't given up. Not his fault, he'd offered her two chances. Still, it was a pity—they wouldn't be sharing a bed together this night. Nor any other night.

All he had to do was wait.

Two minutes later, he had her tag and was on his way to where Cervo was with the flitter. He had learned a valuable lesson from the dead woman. There was a way to get a jump on somebody who was a lot faster than you. Fortunately, all it had cost him was a nasty cut on his arm.

He wouldn't make that mistake again.

20

Back at his house, Shaw shooed the medico out and called for Cervo. Something had been bothering him, just outside his ken, and while the medic had worked on his arm, he recalled what it was.

"Tell me about that operative we lost," Shaw said. "Following Randall's man. What happened?"

If Cervo wondered why the subject had come up now, it didn't show on his face. "Somebody blasted her in the face with a shotgun. It happened in an alley near the port. She knew she was in trouble because the cools found her spring pistol out and next to the body, fresh prints and her DNA on it. She saw it coming, pulled her weapon, but she didn't get off a dart."

"They have anything else?"

"No. Zipple on anything linking the killing to anybody."

"Could it have been random? Street robbery gone bad?"

Cervo shook his head. "Unlikely. Our op was good. She wouldn't have put herself at risk without reason, and she was adept enough so your basic alley mugger shouldn't have been able to sneak up on her and take her out. Way I figure it, she was working, she ran into somebody better than she was, which almost has to mean a pro. She was on the job and following another operative. Too coincidental to think she got strong-armed by a drugged-out cutpurse."

"I don't like this. How can we find out more?"

"How bad do you want to know?" Cervo asked.

Shaw frowned. "Meaning?"

"If our agent was killed by Randall's op, finding out for sure involves certain risks. If we approach the man and buy him and he stays bought, that's the best thing, but we have no guarantees that he won't turn around and lay it out for Randall to earn another fat bonus. You have to decide if you want the PR to know we did that."

Despite his size and look, in his area of expertise, Cervo was no man's fool. Shaw nodded. "Okay. Go on."

"If we grab him and extract the information from him, we have to eliminate him to avoid that same risk." Very matter-of-fact, as if the man was talking about there being fog in the city this morning. Well. Given that he had killed people himself, it was not such an awful option as all that. You could get squashed by a van while crossing the street.

"Yes."

"This is assuming that he chilled our op. And that doesn't really make any sense that I can see. We have our people, Randall has his, everybody knows this. What would be the point in one of his killing one of ours?"

Shaw said, "Because ours discovered something that Newman really doesn't want us to know."

"Possibly." Cervo conceded the point.

"Best-case, worse-case scenario?" Shaw asked.

"Best case: We grab their man, squeeze him, find out what he knows. Tap him out, and we know what—if anything— they wanted to hide bad enough to chop our operative. We get a jump on the opposition. Leave a herring so they think their man spaced on his own, they don't know we did it.

"Worst case: We grab their man, squeeze him, and he doesn't have a clue what we are talking about. We still have to kill him, and they replace the known op with one we don't know, and we still don't get the prize. Doesn't cost us much, but it's not a win. And if our team steps on a bar of soap or something, or a convention of cools just happens to be passing by and grabs them, then we have to do some fast singing and dancing to make the problem go away. I don't mind spending your money to do it, but it could leave a trail to our door for a smart hound to track. What they don't know won't hurt us."

Shaw considered it. Sub-rosa field ops weren't cheap, not the good ones, but it wasn't as if he was going to miss a meal to pay for a new one—or a thousand new ones, if that was necessary. Newman would be in the same ship—he could replace his missing pawn without batting an eyelash.

"Collect him," Shaw said. "At the very least, he was in the vicinity when our woman went down. He might not have done it, but maybe he knows who did. If she saw something she wasn't supposed to see, there's a good chance he saw it, too. I want to know what it was."

Cervo nodded. "I'll put our alpha team on it."

"Do we have anything less than alpha teams, Cervo? Do I pay for betas or omegas?"

The bigger man grinned. Small and tight, but a smile nonetheless. Those were infrequent, and Shaw liked it that he could provoke Cervo into one now and again.

Once he was gone, Shaw repressed the urge to rub at the synthetic flesh on his forearm. The cut under it didn't itch or throb—the chem in the medicated patch stopped that. And the medico had matched his skin tone pretty well, too—if you didn't look closely, you might not even notice the bandage. A few days, the wound would be healed, the swarms of bioengineered bacteria and viruses would have done their job, and you'd have to know he'd been sliced to see any trace of it—no keloids would ridge up under Shaw's own pharmaceutical-grade synthetic flesh, no sir.

He glanced at the pulsing time sig on the office wall. It had been an interesting night. Azul, then the woman he'd fought. He smiled.

Life was good.

Mourn watched Sola walk to the fresher, enjoying the view of her naked backside. She was a beautiful woman, made more appealing because she was smart and ambitious. He would enjoy her as long as it lasted, though he didn't expect it to continue. Once she had what she wanted, she'd move on, and he wouldn't be able to complain—they had some idea of who each other was when they decided to take it to a sexual level. There was a built-in limit.

She was back in a few moments, and she took a couple of quick steps and leaped onto the bed like a diver doing a belly flop. He smiled at that. The exuberance of youth. Nothing like it.

"Well, sir, *that* was fun," she said.

"What, peeing?"

She laughed. "Yeah. That's what I meant. Peeing."

For a moment, neither spoke, and Mourn felt a tug on his emotions. He really liked her. More than he should.

"So, M. Combat Master, what are we going to do today. Go watch the grass grow? Or do you plan to teach me some more of this fighting dance you're working on?"

"Neither," he said. "There's a place I know about that you might find interesting."

"Lead on."

It took three hours in a rented flitter to reach the park. Even from a distance, it was impressive.

"Jesu, what kind of trees are those? They must be a hundred meters tall!"

"Called Methusalahs, named after a planet in a pulsar binary system in M4, I think, most ancient world anybody has ever found. The bigger trees are nearly five thousand years old."

Mourn piloted the flitter to a halt in the parking area half a klick from the start of the forest ring. He and Sola alighted and joined a line of walkers heading toward the trees. There were a hundred other flitters and a dozen chartertrans buses in the lot.

As they drew nearer the park, the huge size of the trees really became impressive. The Methusalahs were evergreens, kin to sumwins and fir, cone-shaped and pointed at the top, widest nearer the ground. The lowest branches of the canopy were thirty meters up, and the tallest of the trees was indeed more than a hundred meters from the needle-covered ground. Nothing grew under the dark shade save for Methusalah saplings and small ferns, and not a lot of either of those.

"The dead needles are acidic," he told her. "Kill just about any kind of plant trying to grow, and most animals that might try to eat them. Bark is poisonous to most pests, too."

There were many wide paths leading into the forest, and the widest and most used led to the biggest tree. Mourn and Sola followed other visitors along this trail, which was merely earth, but packed into plastcretelike density by the footsteps of all the trekkers.

The air was heavy with the scent of the needles, a sharp, piney, citrus smell. Methusalahs bore a reddish, flaky bark, brighter in color where the outer layer had peeled away, and the live needles were a dark blue-green, ten or twelve centimeters long. Some of them had seed cones, some didn't. Aside from the paths, the dead brown needles covered the ground knee deep on a small child. The largest fifty or so trees had names, and the biggest of all, called God's Umbrella by the locals, was thirty meters around and a hundred and twenty-six meters tall.

Standing at the base of that tree and looking up made you feel very tiny.

"Jesu damn," Sola said, her voice quiet.

"It gets better," Mourn said. "Come on."

He took her hand and led her on a meandering path away from the tree. The path wound along for another klick or so, then up a long and gradual rise. When they got to the top of the hill, he turned to watch her reaction.

Her eyes went wide at the sight, and he remembered the first time he had seen it himself, at the age of ten.

The Pit was three thousand meters deep in the middle, and thirty kilometers across, a more or less perfect circle, looked as if somebody had taken a giant scoop to the land, leaving a hemispherical hole softened and worn smooth around the edges by eons of time and weather.

It didn't take her more than a few seconds to realize what it was:

"It's a meteor crater," she said. "This isn't a hill, it's the splash lip of the crater." Her voice was still full of awe.

"About ten million years ago, a big something fell from the sky and hit here," he said. "Scientists say it probably was a comet, and it wiped out most of the plant and animal life locally when it landed—there would have been a big blast, and a lot of dust in the atmosphere, enough for an impact winter that changed life all over the planet. Hot enough to fuse most of the ground along the crater wall into a kind of very hard glass. They say there was some kind of residual radiation that lasted a long time, and that the Methusalah forest was a mutation that came from it. The only place the trees grow is the rim of the crater. They've found fossilized Methusalah wood going back at least eight million years."

She was held by the sight. "This is amazing. How come I've never heard of it before?"

"The locals try to keep it low buzz. Nobody here wants millions of tourists dropping round like they do at the Grand Canyon or the Deep Rift. It's not advertised, either here or offworld. I'd never heard of it, except from childhood friends who had seen it, until my parents brought me here as a boy. Not like it's some kind of state secret—there are offworlders who know about it and find their way here—but it is downplayed. 'The Methusalah Forest? Oh, yar, some old woods on an impact crater rim, I've been there, no major deal. You want to flit five hundred klicks to the middle of nowhere to look at a hole in the ground and some *trees*?'"

"Plus, it's not exactly a tourist planet anyhow. As you have pointed out to me several dozen times, watching cows make meadow muffins isn't the most interesting of activities."

"I still can't believe somebody hasn't done an entcom on this."

"They have. Pictures don't do it justice. You'd need a real big holoproj image to give you the feel."

"I can see why. It's—it's . . ."

"Yeah, it is."

She turned to him. "Thank you for bringing me here, Mourn. Really."

"So, how, uh, grateful are you? One of the big trees that died has been hollowed out, and there's a public fresher in it."

She smiled. "You keep telling me what an old man you are, how you are ready to retire, and yet you seem to have plenty of energy in that arena."

"Blame yourself, fem. You call, I but answer."

"Well. I do need to go pee. Which way is this fresher?"

"Let me show you."

* * *

The door's chime rang, and Azul went to open the portal.

"Fem Azul," Shaw said. "Are you ready for dinner?"

She smiled at him. She moved closer to where he stood in her doorway, leaned forward, and kissed him on the lips, probing a little with her tongue. He returned the kiss with passion.

After a moment of increasing heat, she leaned back. "What say we skip dinner and get right to the dessert? Unless you are really hungry?"

He smiled. "I'm sure we can find something to eat here that will satisfy us."

The trip to the bed involved a rapid removal of clothes, made easier in her case, since she had dressed with that goal in mind, and it took only three motions to go from clad to nude. They fell on the bed, he on his back, and she swung one leg over and settled down on him, already wet and ready. He slid into her smoothly to his base as she sat up on his crotch. She squeezed him with very fit muscles she kept toned for this very purpose.

"Oh," he said. "Very nice!"

She rode him, and he was quick, his first orgasm coming in less than a minute. She squeezed him until he stopped throbbing, then rolled off and lay next to him.

"Too fast," he said. "Sorry."

"You'll make it up to me."

He laughed. "Oh, yes, I will."

He moved down her body and began to use his lips and tongue on her mons, moving deeper, and he was good enough so that her first orgasm didn't take much longer than his. *Ah.* It had been too long.

As they lay facing each other and resting up for more of the same, she stroked his shoulder.

"I checked you out. I know who you are."

"I would hope you did," he said. "When?"

"Before we had dinner that first night."

"Ah."

She could see that pleased him. If what she said was true, she'd known how rich he was when she'd turned him away from her bed before. Which should mean that his huge fortune didn't matter that much to her. And the truth was, it *didn't* matter, not to Azul the operative nor to Azul the artist. For the op, it was a job, for the artist, it was the man himself. Had it been Azul on her own, playing neither part? The money wouldn't have mattered to her, either.

She saw the synthetic flesh patch on his arm. "What happened?" She touched the bandage with one finger.

"That? A woman cut me."

"Really? By accident?"

"On purpose. She had a large knife. You recall telling me about your brother? Well, as it happens, I have begun to play the same game he did."

Azul the op knew this. Azul the artist would not. And the next question could have come from either of them:

"What happened to her? The woman who cut you?"

"I killed her," he said.

Here was another crux. The artist could be repelled by this, taken aback that she was pronging a killer. Or she could be excited by it. Given that she had a brother who had been a ranked player, she would have more experience with such stories.

"Did it bother you? To kill her?"

"Some. I gave her a chance to surrender. She chose not to take it. She was trying to kill me." He shrugged. "It was on her head."

Excited, she decided. She moved her hand down his belly to his groin. He was ready. She scooted down and took him into her mouth.

She saw his triumphant grin as she began fellating him. He had conquered her, so he thought.

But now, he was hers . . .

21

On the way back from the forest, with a most enjoyable and exciting stop in the public fresher before they left, Mourn sat and watched Sola as she drove. She had a light touch with the flitter, which was a middle-of-the-lane sedan, not a particularly racy transport.

"That was fun," he said.

"What, peeing?"

He laughed.

"So, this is where I came from," he said after a moment of silence. "What do you think?"

"Everybody has got to be from someplace, so the man said. Better than some, worse than others," she said. "It's not where you were born that matters, it's where you end up. Only one you can control."

"What about you?"

"Me?"

"You came from somewhere. Want to share that with me?"

She thought about it for a few seconds. "Sure. Why not? I was born at a very young age," she said.

He shook his head.

"Sorry, old joke."

He waited, and she began to tell him her story.

There was never any question but that Cayne was going to be a medico, just as her father, uncles, and grandfather had all been, and as her older sister was training to become. It was the family tradition, and on her homeworld of Tembo, in CinqueKirli, tradition was no small part of the culture. The caste system was not legally enforced, but it was customarily observed, especially if you were of the upper classes, which full medicos were. If you were born working-class, you would almost certainly stay working-class, barring some stroke of fortune. If your father or mother dug shinies at the Strother diamond mines, then when you got old enough, you would, too—unless you found enough spare time to go prospecting in the Big Sands and happened across a vein nobody else had found. If you could circumvent all the obstacles in your way and file a valid claim, the Strothers would immediately buy you out, and you would be one of the storied people:

"Y'heard about Thistlewaite? Hit a meterwide seam two hundred meters long out past Dry Wells, sold out for six million stads."

"No feke?"

"Yar, a lucky bastard, him."

Yar, indeed. The lucky bastards were, however, few and far between on Tembo.

Being part of the elite was the chance of birth, and one of the advantages of high caste was that you had access to things the poor did not. Sure, everybody got basic entcom and edcom piped to their dwellings, and everybody had a shot at a mandated Confed–primary-level education. But if your father and his father were doctors, your caste got the perks: best neighborhoods and housing, high income, prestige. Plus access to First Tier education and full entertainment 'proj. More width, more depth, and that was what did it for Cayne.

At thirteen, she realized that the galaxy was a much bigger and grander place than even the highest castes on her planet could achieve there. There seemed to be no limits to what was possible away from her two-planet outback system.

By the age of fourteen, she was focused on the *possibility* of leaving her world.

By sixteen, she *knew* what she was going to do with her life. She was going to travel the galaxy as a reporter, go places, see things, taste foods that nobody in her family had ever eaten or even had the opportunity to consider. Her life was not going to be an endless ministering to miners coughing and wheezing from militant silicosis; nor delivering babies; nor doing cloned liver transplants on rich alcoholic retirees. No way. That didn't call to her in the least.

She began taking journalism and video-production courses via edcom, keeping them secret from her family. She found time to talk to people who worked in the news industry locally, made media contacts, all surreptitiously. The more she learned, the more interesting it became.

For a year, she got away with it.

Two months after her seventeenth birthday, her father came to her room. He closed the door behind him, and Cayne knew that she was in trouble.

Her father had never been one to dissemble, he came right to the point: "What the hell are all these edcom classes you have been taking, Cayne?" He waved a printout.

"They don't cost anything," she tried.

"That isn't the point! You should be studying premed

science by now—anatomy, physiology, pharmacology—not wasting your time on such trash." He held up the print-out as if the sight of it would wilt her into helplessness, like some entcom vampire confronted by a holy relic.

And in truth, she felt like wilting. On some level, she had known her parents would find out about her plans sooner or later. She had rehearsed what she would tell them, gone over it in her mind a hundred times, but she wasn't ready to deliver that speech yet. She had it in her thoughts that she would be eighteen, legally able to do as she wished, and that by then, she'd have a job waiting on a planet far away from this one. They'd be upset, but eventually, they'd accept it. That had been the plan.

"Baba—" She stopped.

"Go on."

"I want to be a reporter. A documentarian."

He blinked. Then he tried to put her statement into a framework to which he could relate: "Medical or surgical? There's not much call for medical cataloging or training vids here. Perhaps on the surgical end, but you'd need at least a fourth year of residency to become a good enough surgical diagnostician to know what to record—"

"No," she cut in. She took a deep breath. "I don't want to practice medicine. I want to report *news*!"

He stared at her as if her hair had burst into flame. "What? Don't be stupid, of course you'll practice medicine!"

She had never been particularly confrontational with her parents.

Her sister, Terah, had gone through a phase in which she and their mother were so irritated with each other over Terah's low-caste suitors that they barely spoke. And Terah and their father had yelled at each other about it more than once, full-volume shouting matches that sent Cayne scurrying to hide in her room, afraid her father would do something violent. Even so, those waters had calmed. Her sister's choice in male companions had provoked anger, but she had come to see the light about that and found a young man in the proper caste. Being *mated* to one of the elcee trash was not the same as using him to piss off her parents. And, of course, Terah had gone off to do her internship and residency at Tembo Medical on schedule, too—*that* had never been in question.

That was nothing compared to what Cayne was offering.

Cayne didn't want to upset her parents. But she also knew that their lives were not going to be hers. Knew it to the depths of her being. Either they were going to be disappointed or she was; they had chosen *their* lives, she was going to choose *hers*.

"You don't understand. I want to travel, to see the galaxy."

"You can do that as a doctor! I have attended conferences on a dozen planets, we have all taken vacations on other worlds!"

Her temper flared. "No! I don't want to have a few hours off from a conference on lung rot to hurry to some tourist gape, or spend two weeks a year trying to relax from fifty weeks caring for patients! It's not me, Baba!"

"You are *seventeen years old*, you have no *notion* of what you want!"

"I know what I *don't* want! I don't to be stuck on some galactic hind-arm smiling all day at people who are sick or injured or dying until I become one of them!"

It only got worse after that. They both said things that couldn't be taken back, hateful words that burned and cut and crumbled whatever relationship there was until there was no bridge left between them. Her father had stomped out, declaring that as long as she lived under his roof, she would do as he damn well said. And she had yelled after him that she wouldn't be living under his roof any longer than it took to pack her clothes.

So much for the plan and their grudging acceptance.

In the end, she had stayed until she was eighteen, her mother trying all the while to patch things up and bring her back to the family's path. But there had been slammed doors that couldn't ever be opened again. It didn't matter to Cayne. Her course was set, and wherever it might lead, however she might fail or succeed, it would be under her own direction, and not there . . .

The giant crop circles passed underneath the flitter as she finished her story. In the distance, a rain cell gathered into thunderheads, soon to offer water to the grains below.

"Sounds familiar," Mourn said.

"Doesn't it?" Sola said. "After a few years on the lanes talking to people, interviewing them, I realized that my story—and yours—aren't unique, not even unusual. Maybe one person in five or six has a similar tale. Gave the parents a good-bye wave and hit the road for their grand adventure."

"And has that been what it was for you? A grand adventure?"

"I've had my moments," she said, smiling. "I'd prefer to be a little further along my chosen path than I am, but I'm still making progress. Still better than the alternative."

"Let me guess. Someday, you plan to space back home and wave your success in your father's face," he said. "Pound him over the head with your credit balance." It didn't come out as a question.

"Pretty much."

"I wanted to do that, too, once upon a time. First week I hit the Teens as a player, I got a couple of nice contracts, some sponsors. I wasn't exactly rich, but all of a moment, I was making maybe three times as much a year as my father ever would in any year of his working life. I could have made him eat his words about never amounting to anything."

"But you didn't. Why not?"

He considered it for a second. "Because by the time I got there, it didn't matter. I'd been my own man for fifteen years, earning my way, enjoying my life, no regrets. Wouldn't have been any point to it."

She raised an eyebrow at him.

He continued: "Year before I left this world, I had an arm-wrestling match with my da. We used to do that a lot. As a kid, he could easily beat me, but sometimes he let me win. Once I got to be about sixteen, he had to work harder, and the matches were for real. By then, I had been lifting weights and doing exercises for a couple years to build myself up for the Flex when I got there. I had also begun learning how to box and wrestle with some of the locals, and I was almost as big as I am now and no weakling. He could still beat me, though. He was proud of his strength, but he was getting older, and he wasn't working out as much as he once had.

"Just before I turned eighteen, we had a match. There came a point during it when I knew I had him, I could win, no doubt about it. Knowing I could was enough for me, I didn't have to do it. It was important for me to know; it didn't matter so much to me that he knew it."

"You let him win?"

"It seemed right, for all the years when he pretended that I had beaten him. My father wasn't a bad man, he was just who he was, and that was limited to a world I didn't want to be part of anymore. Later, we had more harsh words, and I left with both of us angry. I might have been able to go back and smooth it over, but I never did. I regret that. Even though I hadn't seen him in more than a decade, when I found out he was dead, it was a shock. Once you realize your father can die, it changes things, even if you are in a job where you see a fair number of dead folks."

She nodded, and Mourn felt as if she were doing so unconsciously.

"You've been your own woman making your way in the galaxy for what, eight, ten years? You don't have to prove anything to anybody, you *know*."

"Yes. I do know. But he won't want to see it."

"Maybe not. Or maybe you might be surprised. Not as if you have anything to lose, right?"

She looked doubtful. "Maybe."

22

When Shaw left Azul's hotel suite, he felt pretty damned good. Nothing quite like great sex with a beautiful, intelligent, and artistic woman who knew exactly what to do to take the edge off your physical tension.

The usual contingent of bodyguards lurked about, disguised as hotel staff and patrons. He took the private lift to the rooftop parking level. When the door opened, Cervo stood there. Shaw smiled, but Cervo's expression remained blank. He had a puritanical streak, Cervo did. He never joked about sex. Never talked about it at all, come to that.

"Something?"

"We have collected Randall's op."

"Ah. And have you questioned him yet?"

"No, sir. I thought you'd want to be there to hear anything he has to say."

"Good thought. Well. I'm refreshed and relaxed. No time like the present. Let's go."

Randall's agent, whose name, Cervo said, was Belaire Cayliss, was being held at the compound in a room where no cams were installed.

The flight took all of five minutes. Cervo and Shaw went directly to the room.

Cayliss knew who Shaw and Cervo were, of course, and when he saw them his eyes widened, either in fear or surprise. Maybe both.

"M. Cayliss," Shaw said. He waved for Cervo to go and stand behind the man, who sat in a plain plastic chair in front of a bare plastic table. Shaw pulled the chair from the opposite side of the table, and sat. "Let's not waste each other's time," he said. "You know who I am, I know who and what you are. You have information I want. We need to come to an arrangement by which you will tell me what I want to know."

Cayliss blinked. He was quite the good-looking young man, if your taste ran that way. Tall, well built, a face that would be considered handsome by most.

"So the only question is, how *much* will it take for you to become *my* agent instead of PR Randall's man?"

Shaw could almost see the wheels turning in Cayliss's mind. He had been kidnapped and was probably worried about not getting out of the situation alive. Selling out put a happier spin on things.

While he was mulling this over, Shaw said, "I'm a very rich fellow, as you know. What say we just say a million stads, and you take your money and space for a planet far away from here, never to return?"

Cayliss relaxed a bit. Now it had come to dickering, and he understood this well enough. "A million is not that much for giving up my career and worrying that the Confed might be coming up on me from behind for the rest of my life. M. Randall has a lot of friends in high places and a long memory."

"True. Give me a number."

"Five million."

Shaw grinned. "What is it you think you know that is worth five million standards?"

Cayliss shook his head. "I don't have a pronging clue, sir, but if we are talking about *any* number of millions, then you must think it's pretty important."

"Two million," Shaw said.

"Four."

"Three."

Cayliss considered it. You could bank three million stads and live very comfortably off the interest forever without touching the principal. And certainly a sub-rosa field op would have another identity hidden away he could assume, just in case he had to leave town in a hurry.

"All right. Three million. But how do I know you'll pay me once you get the information?"

Shaw glanced up at Cervo, who produced a bank encoder. Cervo touched a number, then a record button. There was a small *beep!* as the device coded a credit cube. The cube was as wide as the tip of a man's thumb and half as thick. Servo handed the cube to Cayliss, who squeezed all four corners of it simultaneously with his fingertips and the tips of his thumbs. A small holoprojic image lit over the cube, showing a cash-value notation and the number GS 3,000,000, along with a Bank Galactica imprint holograph. It looked real, because it *was* real.

"So now you are a millionaire, M. Cayliss."

Nothing like haggling your way from maybe dying to three million stads to put a smile on a man's face. "What do you want to know?"

"One of my operatives was killed in an alley near the port recently. She was following you. Did you do it?"

Cayliss shook his head. "No."

"Cervo, the date?"

The big man rumbled it off.

Shaw said, "Why were you at the port that day?"

"I was working courier. I had an info ball to deliver. A woman arriving at the port from offworld, I don't know from where."

"Who was she?"

"I don't know. I had a temp-holo of her, but I'd never seen her before, and my control didn't give me a name."

"You know what was on the ball?"

"No. It was coded."

Shaw smiled. "You tried to see?"

The man shrugged. "Never know what might be important. But I couldn't open the file."

"Tell me about this woman."

"I only saw her for a few seconds to make the pass. Average height, maybe twenty-eight or thirty years old, plain-looking, blond hair, worn moderately long. Nothing special about her clothes, not carrying a travel case. I passed her the ball. We didn't speak. I cycled out. If your agent was following me, she was damned good, because I looked for a tail when I left, and I didn't spot her."

Shaw considered the information.

"What kind of work do you normally do for Newman?"

"Courier, surveillance, cam-set and collection, bug-sweeps, whatever he needs. Nothing heavy, nothing wet. If somebody on one of our teams killed your op, I didn't hear a whisper about it."

Shaw nodded. "Well. I guess we're done, then. Cervo, take the man to wherever he wants to go." He flicked a look at the bodyguard.

Cayliss started to stand, smiling. He was young, free, and now rich. Life looked pretty good to him at the moment.

Cervo wrapped one thick arm around the man's neck and braced it from behind with the other arm in a triangle choke.

Cayliss struggled, but after fifteen seconds, he was unconscious—the blood had been shut off to his brain. A knockout artery choke generally wasn't fatal. But if you continued to keep the air from the brain after the victim passed out, for three or four minutes? That would kill them.

The man dangled from Cervo's grip as if he weighed nothing. Shaw had already left the room by the time M. Cayliss was no longer among the living. The corpse would be fed to the recyclers, and the credit cube would be deposited back into the secret slush account from which Cervo had drawn it before the grinders finished reducing the dead man to parts beyond recognition.

Amazing what a cube worth a few million in a man's hand would do to convince him you were his friend and meant him no harm.

So his old pal Newman had passed some kind of information to somebody. They still didn't know who had killed their agent, and whatever the Confed's PR had sent on that info ball to whoever it was was as much a mystery as it was before they'd questioned the dead op.

Well. Some days that was how it went.

He could have Cervo do a scan of port cams on that date, but tens of thousands of people passed through the gates every day, and for all they knew, the mystery woman could have turned back around and gotten on the next boxcar uplifting for orbit.

No, probably she had not done that. What if the dead woman assigned to follow the late Cayliss had switched her surveillance from him—to the blonde? That might explain her demise. Maybe she got spotted and taken out. In which case, it was likely that the blonde was more than passing adept as an undercover agent herself. Blond. Average. Plain. Didn't sound like anybody he knew.

She could have come here for a thousand reasons, and all but one unconnected to Shaw in any way, but he needed to know. Just as knowledge was power, a lack of it was a weakness.

He'd have Cervo do some more checking. The port cams, passenger registration for single women arriving, like that. Maybe they could turn up something.

Mourn went through the pattern of steps he had established again, for the fourth time in thirty minutes since he had warmed up. It was more tiring than it should be, he thought, after what was only half an hour's effort.

He could do fifteen steps pretty well. The logical sixteenth step was a little tricky, but he could manage it okay. The next five were increasingly difficult, so that at the twenty-first step, he was almost always off-balance to the point where he nearly fell.

He reached the twenty-first step, and once again, his center of gravity was too far over his lead foot. He had to step out of it, and that was the wrong direction to be doing that. How best to correct that? Angle away?

No, he decided, what he needed to do was alter his position.

Lower, he decided. If he dropped his center so that his knees were deeply bent on the twentieth step, then the twenty-first . . .

Ah, yes, that would do it . . .

He considered what the twenty-second step should be. He had to decide from which direction a potential attack would be coming, either from a single opponent, or multiples. Obviously, you couldn't cover every angle with every move, but if the attack was coming from straight ahead, then a lateral shift would work, and if it was coming from a second opponent to the left or right, then a diagonal back step either way . . .

Mourn considered it. As long as he covered all the

possible combinations that were likely to arise, he'd be fine. Once you knew which way to move efficiently, it was just a matter of selecting the proper tool to do the job. All you had to do was mix and match. The real trick was in keeping to a set of principles that would allow enough flexibility to shift on the fly.

He had already covered basic punch-comes-kick-comes-knife-comes attacks from virtually any point on the circle, devised counters, and also built a set of attacks he could do that would short-circuit those. If you could get a beat ahead, you could win most fights.

He still had to deal with longer weapons—sticks, staves, maybe even swords—but those shouldn't take too much alteration if the basic positions were solid, it was more a matter of distance.

All right. What was the twenty-second step going to be?

Sola watched Mourn as he went through his dance, and marveled again at how fluid he was as he moved. The turns and twists, changing levels, going up and down, leaning this way and that? It required a dexterity she didn't have. She could do the first few steps, up to about ten or eleven, without falling down some of the time, but some of the moves after that were still beyond her. When she didn't *forget* them. Mourn had said he was going to put down some kind of markers, chalking footprints or something, to help in learning the pattern, and maybe that would help.

He was an intriguing man, Mourn. Exciting in ways, very comfortable in other ways. He was an adept enough lover—she had been with men who had been more sexually driven, able to go all night, providing and having multiple orgasms—but with him, once or twice was enough. She liked cuddling with him afterward, liked sleeping next to him. He had a solid feel, and Jesu knew she felt protected with him in the bed next to her. He was funny, smart, deadlier than a vat of nerve poison, and she liked him. She was pretty sure he liked her, too, and not just for sex. Hard to tell; she got the idea he didn't get a lot of practice in anything other than short connections. Being close to somebody for this long was unusual for her, too. Her job had kept her moving most of her adult life; there wasn't much chance of establishing a relationship with a civilian. And she hadn't met anybody among the rovers in her biz, the reporters she kept running into from world to world, system to system, that she had been drawn to particularly. Oh, sure, she'd bedded a few. Mostly men, a couple of women, but those had been slap-and-tickle, that-was-nice-let's-do-it-again-sometime kinds of encounters. Ambitious people in her field intersected, but you didn't need heavy baggage when you had to hop a liner for points spinward at a moment's notice and you might not get back for a month or a year—or ever.

This thing with Mourn? It wouldn't last, of course. She'd get her documentary material, then they'd go their separate ways. She'd put her stuff together and, with a little bit of luck, would be working the producer's circuit and getting ever higher into the lucrative end of the biz. Once you crossed into primecast intersystem with something for which you got writing, directing, *and* producing credits, even a documentary, you were looking at real money. Everybody in her biz knew the story of Takaki Seehm, a poor historian who borrowed enough to do a half hour throwaway on the Zonn for a local edcom net.

Core Systems Broadcasting had picked the little program up, deals were made, and the throwaway had turned into a six-episode educational series, two hours per. It was an instant hit. The edu boards of twenty-odd systems had made the series *required* viewing for 11 billion history students, and Seehm had, at twenty-four, gotten 6 percent of first-run net, 3 percent of the second, third, and fourth runs, one point thereafter. They were still showing the *Zonn*

Chronicles to the kiddies more than a decade later, hundreds of runs in some of the markets, plus outright sales for local copies, and Seehm's piece of the back end was supposed to have been worth over 120 million stads to her—*so far*.

Despite what Mourn had said about leaving the old arguments behind, of letting it all go and moving on with her life, Sola could still imagine her father's face if she had a sale like that. She'd want to record his reaction, so she could watch it over and over.

Yeah. Okay. She had an agenda.

Mourn would tinker with this stuff he was creating, and either use it in the Flex or set up a school somewhere and teach it. If Weems didn't hunt him down and kill him first. Mourn's path and hers, currently parallel and next to each other, would diverge, and that would be that. Enjoy it while it lasts, sweetheart, and wave bye-bye when the tide takes you.

Odd how thinking that bothered her. Made her frown, just a little.

And why should it? She was young, on the way up, and she was going to be somebody to reckon with, sooner rather than later.

Mourn was fifteen years older than she was, working his way toward retirement, and his best days were, according to his own lights, behind him. She was a journalist, he was a fighter. Aside from her documentary on the Flex they didn't have that much in common.

Well, okay, she *really* did like sleeping with him. And he was funny and wry and full of stories about things she found interesting. But still, it wasn't going to be anything permanent. No future there.

She knew this. Yet there was that frown that kept wanting to form.

Well, fuck it. She could buy a lot of smiles with a couple million standards, thank you, very much.

Mourn looked up and saw her. He waved her over.

"Ready to work out?"

No, not really, but it was interesting, this thing he'd come up with, and at the worst, it would help her make a better show. At best, she might be able to use the stuff to protect herself, and that would be something worth having.

"Always," she said.

23

"I have no idea what you just did," Sola said.

Mourn smiled. "I know the feeling."

"I'll never be able to learn this."

"Sure, you can. It just takes a little time in grade."

"Yeah, uh-huh."

He looked at her, remembering. "Back when I was young and stupid, only a couple of years away from home, I found myself on Raft, in Omicron. I'd heard about this mixed martial arts system, a bunch of different styles all working out together, coming up with an eclectic blend. I spaced there in steerage, got a job making enough to survive on, and signed up."

"Is this going to be a long story? Can I sit down?"

He laughed. "Not long. You'll just stiffen up if you sit. Walk around, stay loose."

"Yeah, right."

"So what happened was, the teachers would work group

sessions, with students from four or five different styles trying to pick up bits of their stuff.

"It was supposed to be an open and free exchange, but like everything else, there were always the politics and social order that had to be taken into account."

He shook his head at the memory. "Get a bunch of fighters together, a lot of whom are convinced that what they already know is better than what they are learning, the egos tend to get in the way. Guy's spent five or six years studying a style, he relies on that, and if somebody shows him a new trick that goes against what he knows, he tends to smirk a little at it, even if he doesn't say anything."

"Sounds just like the news biz," she said. "My way is the best way."

"Exactly. Anyway, one of the teachers was a local who specialized in a short-sword system—blades were forearm length, more like long knives than real swords. Broad, thick, single-edged, steel-basket handguards, like that. Called Espadita, which meant 'short sword,' 'little sword,' something like that.

"The Maestro was very good, I could tell, even though he didn't show off. He would demonstrate a technique, then indicate how you could adjust it so that it would work with or against a smaller knife or a longer sword. He was probably twenty years older than I was at the time, which would have made him forty or so, and of course, I thought he was ancient. The real serious stuff he kept for his senior students—but he gave us some decent basics.

"One night after his session, the last class that evening, we were changing clothes, packing our workout bags. I went into the office to debit my cube for next month's tuition. There were three or four other students in there, and the Maestro.

"One of the students, a tall, swarthy boy about my age who was a fairly serious Zhee-koondoh player, walked over to stand in front of the instructor. He had a practice knife stuck into his belt behind his back. He said, 'Maestro, what would you do if I did *this*?' whereupon he jerked the wooden blade from his belt and stabbed the teacher in the belly with it."

"Jesu. How smart was that?"

Mourn shook his head again. "Extremely stupid. But the student was cocky, he was sure his primary art was superior to this old guy waving his funny knives around in his funny patterns, and he wanted to show everybody he was right. His art put a big premium on being the first to strike, and he figured that poking the teacher in the gut would gain him some status."

"Did it?"

"It didn't go quite as he intended. The knife never made it to its target."

Interested now, she said, "What happened?"

"I was standing two meters away, looking right at them. One second, the student jammed the practice knife at Maestro's abdomen, the next second, the knife clattered on the floor and the student slammed into a file cabinet all the way across the room, hard enough to shake the office. If the cabinet hadn't been propped against the wall, I believe he would have knocked it down.

"Maestro hurried to the student, took him by one arm, and brushed his chest off with his other hand. He said, 'Are you okay? Sorry.' He sounded genuinely apologetic, as if he were worried he had hurt the fool."

"Christo."

"Yep. At the time, I couldn't begin to tell you what Maestro did. I saw a couple of his senior students who'd also caught the action, and they smiled at each other, as if they knew, but as far as I was concerned, it was like that first fight I saw at twelve. Might as well have been magic: Knife comes, attacker smacks into wall across the room, bam!

"It was maybe six or eight years later when I was practicing another art that I that I figured it out. We were doing a pass and disarm, and suddenly it popped into my head what the teacher must have done."

"You are saying I'll get it eventually."

"If you stay with it. Only so many ways to move efficiently, remember."

She nodded. "So what happened to the student. The teacher throw him out of the class?"

"No. Guy quit his primary art and became one of Maestro's best students—never missed a class long as I was there."

"Really?"

"If you have a skill and surprise, you use both against somebody, and he brushes you aside like a bothersome insect? You have any brains, you have to be impressed."

She sighed. "All right. I'm going to take your word for it. Show me the move again."

He grinned at her. He did like this woman. A lot.

Shaw and Azul were having lunch at the restaurant he had bought to impress her, and once again, the food was superb.

Just before he had gotten here, Cervo had told Shaw that he had located two more potential Flex matches. Neither of the fighters was on-planet, and in fact, neither was in-system. The closer of the two was, fortunately, ranked lower than the other, Sixty-Eighth, as compared to Seventy-First, but would still require four days' transit time each way— and that by personal starship. A scheduled liner would take ten days each way. So he was about to be gone from this world for a minimum of eight days if he took his yacht, and that assuming he found his match quickly once he got where he was going. But a win—and of course he *would* win—would very likely put him within two matches of the Top Fifty.

Oddly, he found that the idea of being away from Azul for more than a week was not all that pleasant a prospect.

Over dessert, which was some sort of sugary cookie wrapped around a frozen cream, Shaw brought up the subject of his pending departure.

"I've found a Flexer I want to challenge," he said, "but he's in the Centuri System, on Mason, so I'll be gone for a few days. A week, at least, maybe longer."

Azul took a bite of her dessert, made a satisfied expression as she tasted it. "Ah. Wonderful stuff." She looked at him. "Well, I have enjoyed our time together, Ellis, truly I have."

"A week is not forever, Luna."

"No, but my current paintings are almost done. I've been neglecting them since we've been seeing each other—not complaining, you understand, it was a choice I made willingly and would make again—but if you are gone, then I'll turn my attention back to them."

"So?"

"So, they won't take much time to finish. A few days. Once I'm done, I'll need to start a new project. There are some MuscleDancers in Rakkaus, a port city on the Holy World Koji, I have a mind to see and paint—they are reputed to have incredible control of their bodies."

"You are saying you'll be gone when I return?"

She smiled. "Likely so, yes."

He had to work to repress his frown. He didn't like the idea at all.

"Perhaps I could commission you to do a painting for me, here. One that would take, say, ten days or so to finish?"

"But I don't do commissions, Ellis. I paint what I must, and if the result is pleasing enough, somebody will buy it. Our time together has been wonderful, and I am grateful for it, but if you can leave to pursue your dream, then I must be free to do the same for my art, yes?"

"Come with me," he said, surprising himself.

She looked at him a moment, not speaking.

"Watch me fight," he said. "I'm sure you would find it stimulating. Maybe even enough to consider painting. I can take off my shirt," he said, smiling.

He had seen her face when he'd told her about the woman he had slain in a match. It excited her to be with a man who could do that.

"I've seen you with your shirt off," she said. "Your pants, too."

"Yes, but not from a distance, not in a fight that might be to the death."

She appeared to consider that.

He decided to press a little. "I could always drop you at Koji afterward if you still wanted to go there."

"That's a bit out of the way from Mason."

"My yacht spaces wherever I point it. I can afford the fuel."

She smiled. Took another bite of the cookie and ice cream. Smiled like a cat. She was delaying her answer to play him a little, he saw that. And he also saw that she was going to agree.

He felt a surge of triumph. *Yes.* When she saw him move? Surely that would make her want to capture him in acrylics. Surely it would.

And afterward? Well, that was another experience to imagine, wasn't it?

24

Mourn stood in the house's doorway, perturbed. Sola looked at the frown—something he didn't do much of—and wondered why aloud.

"Somebody has called me out," he said.

She blinked. "How is that possible? Nobody knows we are here."

"So I thought. But apparently Creestofer Cluster, currently ranked Fourteenth, does."

"How do you know?"

He opened the door, which was edge-hinged and made of cheap wood-grained plastic, wider.

Stuck to the door with a knife was a small piece of paper. On it, written by hand, it said,

Greeting M. Mourn—
    What say we dance? I shall be behind the large silo next
    to the empty animal pen a klick southwest of here at noon,
    if you've a mind to meet me.

With all sincerity,
Creestofer Cluster, Fourteenth.

Sola said, "What are you going to do?"

"Meet him," he said. "Find out how he knew where to find me. If he can, others can."

"Is that a good idea? Lose, you're dead, win, we still have to leave, right? Because the match will be recorded even if there isn't a body lying around."

"It's what I do, Cayne."

She nodded. And yet, she was afraid for him. She didn't want him to die. Well, that was only natural, wasn't it? He was a big part of her documentary.

Right, sister. You think that ship is gonna lift? You have enough footage of Mourn and then some. Who do you think you're fooling here?

She caught a flash of something in Mourn's face, just a passing hint. "You're *pleased* about this, aren't you?"

He tried to suppress his smile, but failed.

"You can't wait to try out this new stuff you've been working on."

He gave her a tiny shrug. "Only way to know if it works for sure is to do it against somebody skilled who's seriously trying to thump you."

"You could get killed if you're wrong."

"Would that bother you so much?"

Don't tell him, don't do it—! "Yes, it would."

Another big smile. "Thank you, I appreciate that. I'm the challenged party, so I'll keep it bare—no weapons."

"As you have pointed out more than once, Mourn, if somebody really wants to take you out and he's good enough, he won't need a weapon to do it."

"But M. Cluster doesn't have a grudge against me, and no particular reason to want me cold. He's just looking to move up."

"Maybe."

"Well. I've got a couple hours. I think I'll stretch and do a light workout, loosen up. Practice a couple of the new steps."

"Jesu, Mourn. Are you really that calm?"

"Maybe not quite—but I'm not afraid, Cayne. I'm good at what *I* do. And I've got a new toy to try out."

She shook her head.

"You gonna come along and record it?"

"Damn right I am. If you get beaten to a pulp, at least somebody will get some good out of it. I'm good at what *I* do, too."

He reached for the note.

"Leave that," she said. "I want to get it recorded first."

He laughed. "Aren't we a fine pair?"

Shaw's stellar yacht was not nearly as big as a commercial liner, of course. It was a mere hundred meters long, with but ten guest bedrooms, each with its own fresher; a dining hall, ballroom, library, exercise room; and several observation lounges in front of huge denscris view ports. Plus two kitchens, crew quarters, and, as Shaw said, "ample" storage. And since there was nobody on the vessel save for Shaw, Cervo, Azul herself, and the crew of twenty, it was much quieter, and smelled a lot better than a commercial ship, too.

Probably set him back two or three hundred million standards for the vessel, and operating costs had to run fifteen or twenty million a year, and that's if he didn't spend a lot of time system-hopping.

Being rich definitely had some advantages, she thought, as she stepped from her bath—taken in a two-meter-by-two-meter tub carved from a single piece of Cibulian black marble, and outfitted with twenty pulse jets that could deliver everything from a soothing massage to a screaming orgasm, if that was her bent.

She had gone with the massage.

Air blowers inset into the floor, ceiling, and walls went on automatically as she alighted from the tub, offering her a warm and drying breeze whose humidity was perfect and whose speed was not too fast or too slow, but just right.

She moved to stand in front of a full-length holomirror that offered a view of her from any angle she might choose, and fluffed her hair into shape as it and the rest of her dried.

She could get used to this. Could, if she wanted, make it her way of living. Shaw liked her, a lot—inviting her along to watch him fight told her that, when he thought she might be gone when he returned. She had played that well. Didn't ask to go, shrugged their liaison off as a nice diversion, but wasn't going to sit around and wait to be his plaything.

He liked that, too. Most men wanted a woman who could be a lover, sister, mother, friend. Strong men—those without big insecurities—often wanted somebody as smart and as talented as they were, to boot. Some wanted a challenge, some a slave, but a man like Shaw? He wanted an equal. Somebody with whom he could run and not have to hold back. She'd realized that early on. Yes, yes, the chase, and all the boy/girl games, but in the end, he wanted somebody into whom he could pour his joy, his worry, and, of course, his seed.

She could play him. Ditch her job as a Confed spy and go native. It had happened before, and usually the Confed was smart enough to let it go. Maybe someday the op would get bored and want to come back, and meanwhile, the Confed had a handle it could use on her. Having access to Shaw would be worth a lot to a smart handler.

She knew men. She knew what they liked, and she could keep Shaw happy. Maybe enough for him to marry her. He was of an age when he might start thinking about a legacy, a son or daughter to carry on.

Maybe she couldn't keep him from other playmates, a

mistress or three, but then, that didn't really matter. Love wasn't part of the equation; mutual benefit was.

It was tempting. She didn't really owe the Confed anything. It had used her as much as she had used it, a fair trade. She liked him, he was smart, handsome, rich, good in bed, and he appreciated her. What was not to like?

She waved at the mirror control to get a view of her hair from behind as it dried. Looked okay.

A year ago, she wouldn't have had the thought at all. Six months ago, she might have wondered, but would have dismissed it pretty quick. Now?

Now . . .

The door to the suite slide open and Shaw strolled in. He saw her standing there naked.

Well, from the look on his face, she guessed she was going to need another bath in a little while . . .

No question about, having Luna Azul around was definitely worth the effort.

Shaw was stretched out naked next to her, and she was also nude, but somehow more so than he was.

"All relaxed now?" she said.

"Pretty much."

They smiled at each other.

"So, M. Businessman, how is it that you came to all this?" She waved one hand at the suite, but meant more than that.

"I chose the right parents," he said.

"Ah."

"Well, perhaps not quite that easy, but it was the start."

She rolled up onto her side and looked at him. "Go on."

He thought about it for a second. Why not? She was an appreciative audience. "My grandfather was a pharmacist, SoAfrican tap, and he owned a small chain of retail drug shops, on Earth. He had ambition, so he started a pharmaceutical company and began to build it up.

"When he left it to my father—whose given name was Mnembo—to run, Shaw Pharmaceuticals was still a struggling concern. My father worked eighteen-hour days for years before the business turned around and began making real money. Until I was ten or eleven, I barely remember my father—he would generally leave for work before I got up in the morning and usually come home after I had gone to bed. I mostly saw him on holidays. I was a late baby—my mother was my father's segundo wife—he was polygamous—had six spouses in-residence before I was grown, plus two exes. I have no full siblings, but I did have seven half sisters and two half brothers by five different stepmothers. My biological mother was twenty-two when I was born, my father was forty-eight.

"He was a formal kind of fellow, my father, not mean, but not warm. He left most of the childrearing to his wives, but offered his advice and lessons now and then to the children. He remembered every slight anybody had ever offered him, and paid back every one he could. Once we got to be well-off, he felt as though we had almost become royalty, and that we had images and some kind of noblesse oblige responsibilies that 'ordinary' people didn't have. His children were expected to behave in certain ways, and if we did not, we were corrected.

"Papa plowed the money he made back into research, and his doctors and chemists eventually came up with a couple of things that became standard in just about everybody's medicine cabinet. One was a broad-spectrum antiviral, the other was a pill that increased female libido. The antiviral saved millions of lives, it would knock out stuff from the common cold to the flu to several kinds of pneumonia, and was one of the most useful drugs ever developed.

"The libido drug, on the other hand, got a lot of men

laid. You could drop it in your girlfriend's coffee and it would dissolve and she'd never know it. Thirty minutes later, she would start getting horny."

"You haven't put any of it into my coffee, have you?"

"I hadn't noticed a need."

She chuckled.

"Want to guess which drug sold the most?"

Azul smiled. "Libido, by two to one?"

"Try *five* to one. Thirty years ago, it was the number one selling drug in the galaxy, with the male version at number two. The antiviral wasn't even third—a rival's sleeping medication beat it.

"By the time the patents on those ran out, we had come up with others shifted a few molecules to the left or right, had studies showing they did something new, so we didn't lose much business.

"I started working there as a kid, doing odd jobs, stocking, running errands. All of the children did, sooner or later. A rite of passage. None of my half sibs still work there; most are 'retired,' living on their inheritances.

"By the time I was fifteen, I knew more things about pharmaceuticals than most of the other employees. When I turned eighteen, I took a full-time job as my father's assistant. When I was twenty-five, he retired, and I took over. I wasn't the oldest of his children, but I was the one who had the moves."

"Cause any friction at family dinners?"

He laughed. "Hardly. By then, I was making them too much money for them to care that the kid was running things. By the time I was thirty-three, I had increased our share of the market by four hundred percent, had opened branch factories and sales outlets all over the galaxy. Had to go public to raise the money to do it, but I kept seventy percent of the stock for our family, and I personally now own fifty-one percent. We have a board of directors, but it's my company—I run it.

"Our people were aggressive in all areas. We got several major contracts to supply various planetary health systems, and the big plum was a series of low bids for much of the Confed military. If you'd bought a thousand shares at a hundred stads each, the first week they were offered, and kept them, you'd have gotten three splits by now, and the stock is going for almost four hundred a share. You could sell them tomorrow and retire on what you'd make."

"That's pretty impressive," she said.

"Yes, it is, isn't it?"

"But."

He rolled up and looked at her. " 'But'?"

"It isn't just about money for you. There's something else."

He raised an eyebrow. "What makes you say that?"

She shrugged. "Nothing I can put my finger on intellectually. It's a feeling. Call it an artistic hunch. You run the company, sounds like you can't hire enough ships to haul in all your profits, you're good at it; but that's not what you really want to do when you grow up, is it?"

He leaned back. She was too clever by half, this one. She couldn't know, he had never told anybody, but she had a piece of it, somehow. Maybe it *was* artistic intuition.

"You don't have to tell me," she said. "It's none of my business."

Which was true, but she already knew about it, just not how important it was to him. What could it hurt for her to know? He was in it now, and it would come out soon enough, once he started wading through the high-ranked players and knocking them silly.

"The Flex," he said. "I'm going to become the top player in the Musashi Flex."

She nodded, as if the idea wasn't the least bit silly. "Are you good enough to do it?"

"I am now."

"You must have trained for a long time."

"I have. More than fifteen years, three major arts, half a dozen minor ones." He considered for a moment telling her about Reflex. No. She didn't need to know about that.

"How far do you have to go?"

"Not far at all," he said. "It's just a matter of time."

25

M. Cluster was waiting at the appointed place.
There were two men there, but Mourn marked the fighter
as soon as he saw him. Cluster was large, pushing two meters tall, and probably almost a hundred kilos, well built,
dressed to move, and probably ten or twelve years younger
than Mourn.

Aren't they all, *these days? Younger?*

Cluster looked familiar, but Mourn couldn't remember
seeing him before. Man must have come up from the ranks
recently, maybe while Mourn was training in Java. Happened that way sometimes. You thought you knew everybody in your shifting cohort, knew whom you could
challenge, who could come looking for you, but sometimes
you got a surprise.

The man with Cluster was younger still, maybe
twenty-five, and handsome to the point of prettiness. The
younger man seemed fit enough, to judge from the tight

and paint-thin orthoskins he wore, but he didn't stand or move like a fighter.

Boyfriend, Mourn figured.

Cayne looked at the pair. She said, "I ran a check on Cluster. He's been on a streak. A year ago, he was Seventy-First. Three months ago, he was Thirty-Fifth, and he's jumped twenty-one places since, took him six fights. He must be pretty good."

Mourn nodded. "Happens that way, sometimes. Let's go say hello."

They approached the two men and stopped three meters away.

"Ah, Mourn. And your lovely companion . . . ?"

"F. Sola," Mourn said. "A documentarian doing recordings."

Cayne waggled her cam.

"Really? I'd like a copy of the fight when we're done, if it isn't too much trouble?"

"Even if you lose?" she offered.

"Oh, *especially* if I lose, I'll need to see what happened. But I won't. Lose."

He turned and smiled at the younger man. "This is Jorjay, my . . . *intended.* Maybe if you and I kill each other, Mourn, Jorjay and Fem Sola can *console* each other."

Jorjay glared at Cluster. "Never going to let me forget it, are you? One time it happened, just the *once.*"

Cluster shrugged and gave the younger man a toothy, fake smile. "So you say. And of course, I believe you."

He turned back to Mourn. "I'm Fourteenth, as of this morning, at which time you were Tenth, so everything should be in order. If you want to check first . . . ?"

Mourn shook his head. "I'll take your word for it. I'd like to do this bare," he said. "If you don't mind?"

"That works for me. Hate to put blood on my new weeds."

Mourn smiled. He was aware that Cayne had switched on her cam and was moving to the side for a better view.

"A question first?"

"If it's not too personal," Cluster said. He smiled back.

"How did you happen to come across me here?"

"Ah. Well. Jorjay and I came to see the crater—we were in the neighborhood and thought it would be a . . . romantic stop. I have a new toy—it's not quite . . . legal, but it involves a piece of computer software that will scan and match faces against those stored in its memory. It's very good, this program, it uses fifty points of match, including the ears, which almost nobody bothers to disguise. I have the images of the Top Twenty stored and whenever I can get access to a planet's port security cams—which is actually much easier than you'd think, if you don't mind spending a few stads—I run the recordings through the program. Hard to do that on really populated worlds with a lot of traffic, it takes forever, but on a lightly settled planet like this one without all that many visitors, I can check back as long as a few weeks. You came up, and how fortunate for me that was. I hired an investigator to find you. You weren't trying to hide, so here I am."

Mourn nodded. "Clever."

"I must confess the computer program was Jorjay's idea, and his creation. He's a smart lad with such things."

Jorjay smiled, revealing dimples.

He got a real smile in return from Cluster this time.

Wasn't love wonderful?

Bad luck, but at least it wasn't something that Weems could do to find him—unless he figured out which planet Mourn was on. He might consider wearing a skinmask to hide his features when he spaced to new worlds. And he'd have to remember to disguise his ears, too.

Mourn said, "You ready?"

"Anytime."

"Let's dance."

Mourn turned to a forty-five-degree angle, bent his knees, and lowered his stance, watching the bigger man. For martial arts to really work, you needed for it to be almost reflexive, and he hadn't been training the new steps long enough for that. He was going to have to think more than he wanted, but if he was going to try it, that was just how it would have to be. If the new stuff didn't work, and he survived the clash, he could always revert to what he knew.

If he survived the clash . . .

Cluster did crossover backsteps to his left, circling toward Mourn's right side. Mourn turned to keep his angle, but didn't move otherwise. The man looked like a power fighter, and likely he would come in fast and hard if he was, but you couldn't be sure of that until you saw him make a serious move. Could be a boxer or a grappler, it was too early to tell. You had to be ready for either.

Cluster angled in and gained a little ground, then stole a full step, disguising it with hand motions to draw Mourn's attention, and leaning back, so that his upper body seemed to stay in one place as his lead foot advanced. Nice, but it didn't fool Mourn—he knew exactly what the man was doing, and likely he didn't really think Mourn would be fooled so easily—not at this level.

As Cluster shifted his weight forward onto his lead foot, just a hair outside Mourn's attack range, Mourn did a little scrunch with his feet and scooted back a few centimeters. Not much, just enough to make it necessary for Cluster to advance another quarter step if he wanted to reach his quarry in a step and a half.

A step and a half was knife-fighting distance. Any closer, and Mourn could attack; any farther away, and it would take too long for Cluster to reach him before Mourn could set for the intercept. In Mourn's new creation, position was paramount, more important than speed or power. He'd borrowed that from *silat,* along with the idea of step patterns, though he had created his own.

Cluster marked the distance and nodded slightly. He sidestepped and turned, to switch from a right hand and foot lead to his left side.

So far, Cluster was reading it right and not doing anything stupid. Mourn still hadn't marked him as a hitter or a wrestler. He could be either or both—a lot of the eclectic styles had been successful with the blend. In a one-on-one duel, with no need to worry about an enemy's confederates, grappling and going to the ground could be a sound move. If you could get a mount, do an arm bar and break, you could end a fight fast. If you did the shoot for a single- or double-leg and missed the takedown against a skilled player who knew what to do, though, you might not get another chance. Even if you got it, somebody who knew how to grapple could lock you into his guard, and it would still be anybody's fight . . .

Stop thinking so much, Mourn. Just relax and see what happens.

As Cluster was jockeying back and forth to try and sneak closer, Mourn helped him out: He scooted forward, to his range, which put him into Cluster's attack distance, since Cluster was taller. As Cluster bunched his muscles for the leap, Mourn watched his nostrils. They widened a hair as the man inhaled—

Mourn continued in fast, on Cluster's air intake, but stutter-stepped, long, then short, to retard his timing—

Cluster thought Mourn was moving faster than he really was—he set up his block, holding his ground, not backing away, but he moved too fast, because Mourn wasn't *there* yet—

Mourn threw the right punch he expected to be blocked, so that he could follow up with the left hand in an open slap, and then back to the right elbow, and he was in perfect position, just like on the pattern he'd been practicing—

The retarded timing messed Cluster up. He *missed the first block*! A quarter of a second too slow!

Mourn hadn't expected the punch to go through, but it wasn't a fake, just in case. His right fist smacked into the man's nose, and Cluster's head rocked back as Mourn's open left came around in a short gunslinger's draw from the low line hip, and caught him flat against the temple, rocking him to his left, dropping fast to cover low line, as Mourn's already-rising right elbow went to the opposite temple—

Bam, bam, *bam*—! Three shots, three hits.

Cluster sprawled, bonelessly. Out cold on his way to the ground.

Just like that, it was over. One of the fastest fights Mourn had ever had, one series, and done!

Son of a bitch! *The new stuff* worked!

Back in their rented cottage, Sola said, "You aren't going to submit the fight?"

Mourn was watching the recording of the fight on the room's holoproj. Even though he had been there and done it, it was amazing to watch. It looked so much faster than it had felt. He had hit it dead-on.

He paused the recording, just as his right elbow connected with Cluster's temple. "No. He was four ranks below mine, I won't get any real lift points for it, and I don't want to let the showrunners know where I am. Got to figure Weems has ears in there somewhere. Winner reports, and Cluster won't say anything, so it didn't happen. He's got a headache and no real injuries, a little concussion. I expect Jorjay will take good care of him."

She shook her head. Looked at him. Heard the pure joy in his voice. "If you were any more pleased with yourself, you would pop."

He smiled, real big. "Yeah. I confess, it's true. I thought

it would work, but you never know until the moment comes."

"You made it look easy," she admitted. She waved at the frozen image.

"It *was* easy. That's the part that's so funny—I could have developed this years ago, if I'd stopped to think about it. I never did. I owe it to you."

She said, "Not really. All I did was ask a question—you took it and did something with it. Ideas are cheap. I used to get approached regularly by wanna-be entcom makers. They'd say, 'I got this great idea—how about I tell it to you, you make the 'com, and we'll split the money?' "

She laughed. "Most people in my biz have a trunkful of ideas they won't live long enough to get done. It isn't the spark, it's what you do with it that makes it work. Be like somebody telling you, 'Hey, Mourn? Why don't you move better, you know, more efficiently? Then you'll win more often, hey?' "

He laughed. "That's true, as far as it goes."

"Yeah, but a long way from A to Z." She paused. "So what now?"

"Well, even though I don't think Cluster is going to tell anybody he ran into us here, I'd rather not take the chance. I still have some work to do on the steps. I'd like to finish that."

"You think you can make it good enough to beat Weems?"

He didn't smile when he answered: "I don't know. Maybe."

"So, where are we going?"

"I think Koji. That somehow seems appropriate. We can leave tomorrow, I'll book us a cabin."

Koji. The Holy World. Where, so it was said, if you sat on a bench in the park, you'd eventually see one of everything pass by. She'd been there once a couple years back, doing a story. It was a busy world. Sometimes, the best place to hide was in the middle of a crowd.

"Come on," he said. "Let me show you a new move."

"Really? A man your age?"

He laughed. "No, not that kind of move. A step I figured out."

"How many of them do you have now?"

"Seventy-four, for sure. Another five or six possibles I'm not certain about yet. I'll need maybe sixteen, eighteen more, I figure, to cover everything."

She nodded at him. A few minutes ago, he had been fighting a match that could have ended with him seriously injured or dead. Now? He was ready to practice, as if the match had been no big deal. Amazing man, Mourn.

They put the yacht into orbit around the world of Mason, sometimes still called Alpha Point, and took Shaw's personal lighter down the gravity well to the surface. Azul wondered how the poor people who traveled commercial ships then got packed into boxcars like grunion for the drop were doing. She watched the lights of the world go on when they crossed the terminator and onto the nightside. Always enjoyed that view as the tiny, bright dots began to sparkle in the night . . .

The yacht's runabout put into a private berth at the port, the local customs agents made a cursory appearance and did a less than thorough check of their identifications, and a rented flitter was already standing by to transport them to a nearby hotel. Billionaires got treated differently from the riffraff—hardly a surprise, that.

Shaw frowned at the need for the hotel room. The fighter he had come to find had apparently dropped from sight—his agents had lost track of him, and until they found him again, Shaw would just have to wait.

Azul wouldn't have wanted to be the operative who had lost Shaw's quarry; likely, that one would be looking for a new job even as she thought it. And if the man got offworld before they regained contact? All of the ops involved would be needing work, she was sure. Shaw wasn't a man to reward failure.

Well. It didn't matter. While she was looking forward to seeing how well Shaw actually could fight, her purposes would be served whether he did or did not. As long as she was in proximity, she could continue to work her skills on him. He had already opened up with her in ways she suspected he never had with anybody else, and she was just getting started.

The flitter put down on the roof of the hotel, and it was a very short ride in the lift to the top floor, all of which had been reserved for Shaw and his party. Cervo went off to instruct the local bodyguards. Shaw decided he needed a shower. Azul went to the hotel's shopping kiosk on the ground floor. She wanted to buy some sexy underwear, and to replenish some cosmetics.

"Charge whatever you need to our rooms," Shaw said.

"You think you can afford it?"

"You want the hotel? I can have it wrapped and delivered. Might be hard to get it through its own door."

She laughed. He was funny.

At the shopping center, she wandered around and found what she wanted, including a pair of panties made from silk so fine they were almost invisible. It was not so much the material as the idea that made them exciting. She presented her cube for payment. The clerk, a tall and thin woman of fifty or so, smiled. "Find everything you needed, F. Azul?"

"Yes, thank you."

"Have a nice visit."

When the clerk handed her the bag with her purchases, she pressed a short-term flimsy into Azul's palm along with the bag. The greasy feel of the quikrot sheet under her fingers was unmistakable. Azul smiled. "Is there a fresher nearby?"

"Through the front there and to your right," the clerk said.

"Thank you."

Trying to hurry while looking as if you were strolling was a trick, but having to pee might do that. She knew she had a pair of bodyguards assigned to watch her, a man and a woman—she had spotted them pretty quickly when she'd come off the lift. Shaw wouldn't want anybody trying to grab his paramour. But since she had maybe ninety seconds left before the flimsy just triggered degraded into a puff of dust, she couldn't wait to get back uplevels to her floor to read it.

In the fresher, she took a stall, shut and latched the door, and checked to make sure there weren't any obvious cams watching her. She pulled her orthoskins down, sat on the toilet, and peed, and as she did, she unfolded the flimsy and read it.

"REPORT" was all it said.

A few seconds later, the sheet curled, dried, and fell apart. She dusted her hands into the toilet as she stood and pulled her pants back up.

Well, well. Planetary Representative Randall was apparently not a patient man. And this little demonstration made it perfectly clear that she was only a small cog in his large machine, one that he could crank as he wished. That he had a clerk installed, however temporary she might be, and a note ready to be passed would certainly be impressive to the uninitiated. Azul had more than a little experience in such matters, and knew how it could be done, but still, it did indicate a pretty good level of function to be on top of it this way. He wanted to know what she knew.

The thing was, she didn't have anything to tell Randall yet.

There were ways, then there were ways, but the simplest and easiest was to use the conduit provided to tell him.

She left the fresher, went back to the kiosk.

"Forget something?" the clerk asked.

"Yes. I don't know where my brain is this evening. I needed some clear droptacs, completely slipped my mind."

"Ah, well, here you are. That it?"

She pretended to think about it. "Let me search my poor memory . . . no, I can't find anything else rattling around." She looked directly at the woman. "Nothing else to report, I'm afraid."

The woman smiled. Azul smiled back at her. Message received and message answered.

She turned and left the shop.

Whatever this Reflex was that Randall wanted to know about, it must be very valuable, indeed. She'd have to figure out a way to get Shaw to tell her about it. That would be a trick, since she couldn't just drop it into a conversation.

Well. Shaw was unfolding, it was only a matter of time until she got what she needed. Randall would just have to wait. She might not be able to paint, but she was, in her own way, an artist. Just in a different medium.

26

The starliner was fast approaching the port for download to Koji, the lone habitable planet in the Heiwa System. Sola and Mourn were in their cabin aboard the liner *Athena's Tears,* occupying a small, middle-class unit that would, theoretically, draw less attention.

Lying next to him on the bed, naked and sated, Sola said, "The unexamined life is not worth living."

"Really? Who says?"

"Some Terran philosopher, prestellar-space travel," she said. "Socrates? Plato? Lennon? One of those."

Mourn said, "And you bring this up why?"

"Seems appropriate, given where we are going. A lot of the folks there are doing a lot of examination. I don't think it means picking lint out of your navel, but that if all you ever do is put one foot in front of the other and never worry about where you've been or where you are going, you miss things."

"Ah. So we're talking about goals?"

She propped herself up on one elbow and looked at him. "Yeah. And maybe more. My biggest goal when I met you was to get my documentary done, sell it, see it on the entcom net, and become rich and famous. Pretty much that was it, but when you think about it, it's not a long-term reach. Say it takes a year, or even two or three. Then what? I've achieved my heart's desire, where do I go from there?"

He said, "Another documentary. Or maybe you branch out, do fiction. Write books, maybe."

"Yeah, I could do that, but it would be more of the same, wouldn't it? More money, more fame, and once you get to a certain point, what *is* the point? You can only sleep in one bed at a time, right? Once you can afford the best food, clothes, shelter, transportation, then how is a bigger pile of money going to help?"

"Point taken. So what are you talking about? Some higher purpose?"

"Maybe. Maybe I start some kind of foundation, feed the hungry or help educate the poor."

"Admirable activities."

"Yeah, but again, so what? The poor and hungry will always be with us in some form. And even if I had trillions to play with, which I'm guessing won't be the case, I can't cure that. I'm helping folks, sure, but to what end?"

"You aren't trying to convert me to your religion, are you?"

She laughed. "Right. Like I have one. Though that question does come up, doesn't it? What's it all about? Who is in charge? You ever think about such things?"

He rolled over to mirror her position. "Not much. We're born, we live, we die. That's how it has always been. I'm guessing it will be that way for a long time. Maybe someday we break open the secrets of time and space, skip into alternate universes where we can be pure energy, live forever, and have godlike powers, but that's not something I can get too excited about. Nobody has come up with answers to the big questions, at least not any that can be proven. Is there a god or gods? If you have faith, that's what you believe, but if you don't, nobody has a titanium-clad proof that stands up. Philosophers have been arguing about what it all means for ten thousand years, and there's never been any kind of consensus acceptable by all. A lot brighter men than I have broken their minds on the problem. Why spend your life worrying about questions that can't be answered?"

"So you don't believe in God?"

"Not a hands-on kind. If there is one, look around—he's doing a pisspoor job. Might go for one who set the top spinning, then went on his way."

"Maybe that's on purpose. Gives us something to work on."

"Not how I would do it."

"So you do just put one foot in front of the other?"

He sat up, crossed his legs. "Works as well as any of the others, far as I can tell.

"My life's goal, since I first walked into a school where people took swings at each other, was to get to be *Primero* in the Musashi Flex. I'm forty-five and slowing down, and even with the new moves? I don't know if I am going to get there. I aimed high, and got pretty high—in theory, as of yesterday, there are nine players between me and what I started out shooting for, and out of the thousands of people who also want the job, that's not a bad record. I could have done a little better, but I could have done a whole lot worse."

"But what if you had gotten there? Beat all comers, taken the title? Then what have you done?"

"Moot, isn't it? I didn't, so it wasn't a bridge I had to cross. And probably won't."

"Humor, me, Mourn."

He thought about it. "I'd have probably worked it until I got beaten. Maybe retired before that, I don't know. I could have lived off endorsements the rest of my life, I expect, or saved enough from them to manage it. Could have opened a school and done pretty well."

"Until one day you fell over dead."

"As lives go, that's not bad. We-all-die is how the game works for everybody, Cayne, unless you know something I don't?"

She shook her head. "No, I don't. And that's part of the point. If I got my documentary up and aired, and it made me rich and famous, and I got to roll for another eighty or hundred years in luxury, so what? What would I leave behind when I went into the final chill? Would the galaxy be any better for me having been here?"

"I would," he said, "be better for you having been here." He reached out to touch her shoulder, and she sat up and faced him.

"That might be the sweetest thing anybody ever said to me." She smiled.

"But . . . ?"

"That philosopher, Lennon, he said things that people still remember eons after he said it. People go to churches and study the words of Jesu, thousands of years after he was gone, he is revered, worshiped, adored by millions. As are the Buddha, the Prophet, the Three Ameli."

"You looking to be the next Jesu? Going to try walking on water?"

"No. But I look around and I see a lot that's wrong with the way things are. That demonstration we saw back on your birthworld, where the cools waded into the crowd and cracked heads. The daily repression that the Confederation offers to everybody. That's not right."

Gently, he said, "No. But you can't fix that."

"Not by myself. But I could be part of the solution. Instead of turning a blind eye and being part of the problem."

He said, "This is pretty deep stuff for a ragged old fighter. Not much I can offer to help that."

"Don't give me that 'ragged-old-fighter' crap. I just heard you say things that tell me you've thought about all this. Maybe what you know is exactly what people need."

"Beating players up? I honestly don't see how that would help the galaxy much."

"Maybe it depends on who *does* the beating versus who *gets* beaten."

Watching her sit there cross-legged and nude, he couldn't help but smile. So intense. So young. So beautiful. "You sound like a revolutionary."

She shook her head again. "No, I don't think that's the way to go, not now. I don't think things have evolved enough to revolve. The wheel is stuck in the mud, and it needs to be rocked onto dry ground before it has that kind of traction."

"Nice metaphor, but what does it mean?"

"I don't know. Maybe entcom is the wrong way for me to be aiming. Maybe I should be thinking edcom."

"Lot of call on the education channels for documentaries on washed-up old fighters?"

She gnawed at her lip. "I don't know. Maybe I should find out. I—I just feel the need to do *some*thing, Mourn."

So earnest. For a moment, he thought about it. How would it be to have a statue of you as a bird-perch somewhere a thousand years from now, with people studying your life? Because you were the axle upon which the galaxy took a turn for the better? It was a nice fantasy, but that's all it was. You wouldn't be there to see it.

Or maybe what they'd be doing was shuddering at the awful atrocities you committed, and using stories about you to scare children into behaving themselves properly.

You wanted to be a force for good, but instead became one for evil? Like the Confed had become?

A slippery slope, that one. No risk, no gain, but no loss, either.

"Mourn? Where'd you go?"

He smiled. "Daydreaming," he said.

"You think I'm crazy, don't you?"

"Not at all. I was just remembering another old saying. I dunno who gets the credit for it, but it's something to the effect of 'The journey of a thousand kilometers begins with one step.'"

She blinked at him. "What are you saying?"

"Everybody has to be somewhere, Cayne. You wanting to do good for your fellow humans is a lot better place than some you could be."

She leaned forward. "Well, thank you, sah. And I suppose I could do some good for one of my fellow humans right here and now, hey?" She dropped her hand into his lap.

"Oh, yes. No question about that, fem . . ."

Shaw was in the office at the end of the hall on the floor they had at the hotel, dealing with stock reports when Cervo came in. He was carrying a plastic folder.

"Tell me you've found my fighter," Shaw said.

"Yes, sir. He's with a woman on a game preserve outside of town. They've been spending a lot of time inside a yurt, watching giant saber cats. They apparently like to, uh, do it while they watch the cats do it."

Shaw grinned. "I don't know what I'd do without you, Cervo."

Shaw saw the pensive look on the big man's face. "What else? He didn't get stoned and break something so he can't fight?"

"Not that we know about."

"What is it, then?"

Cervo hesitated, and since he almost never did that, Shaw felt a twinge of worry. "What?"

"I've been on the White Radio with home security. About our operative killed at the port."

Shaw waved one hand. "That? It can wait until we get home."

"I don't think it can," he said. "They came up with a slate of possibles on the woman Randall's courier went to see. Eighty-some women traveling alone arrived at the port from offworld during the time frame the courier mentioned. I got them to steganograph security cam holos of those. There's one you need to see."

Cervo put a low-rez hard copy flat photograph on the desk.

Shaw picked it up. A plain woman, a blonde, what—?

Then he recognized her. *Jesu Christo!*

Had he seen the picture without being alerted, he would have gone right past it. The woman in it seemed so different, but there was no question, once you looked carefully:

Luna Azul. *She* was the dowdy blonde at the port.

The implications fell on him like a collapsing wall. "Fuck," Shaw said. *Fuck!*

"Yes, sir. What do you want me to do?"

Shaw sighed as he stared at the picture. Oh, she was not just good, she was outstandingly good! He thought he had picked her out at the art show, had pursued her, and she had offered him a lack of interest, had rebuffed him, intriguing him to keep after her. How clever was that?

He was extremely pissed off—and beset with a grudging admiration. She had gulled him completely! He'd never had a clue, there had never been a hint she was anything other than she seemed.

She was Confederation Intelligence, had to be. Cervo's background checks were very thorough. The only way to fake a history as thick and rich as Azul's? Had to be done

officially. Right down to the dead brother who'd been a
Flex player. She had gotten his number cold and worked it
perfectly.

Damn . . .

"Boss?"

"Huh? Oh, nothing. Don't do anything. I'll deal with
this."

"Sir, uh . . ."

"If she had wanted to kill me, I'd be long dead by now.
She didn't get past our defenses—I invited her in the front
door. I need to figure out who sent her, and why. Two can
play this game."

"Randall," Cervo said.

"Yes. But I need to be sure."

"What now?"

"Now, we do what we came here to do. That will give
Azul something to look at and report back on, won't it? Randall will pee himself once he hears how fast I can move."

"Sir."

"Oh, and Cervo? Start looking into ways that PR Randall might have a fatal accident. If Azul is his, he absolutely will not benefit from it."

"Sir."

After Cervo was gone, Shaw stared at the picture.
Amazing how different she looked now. It wasn't just the
hair color and style, it was her whole carriage. Whoever
she really was, he was going to find out.

And then what?

Normally, you deleted spies—he had done so several
times over the years. Send them over to the other side, and
no regrets, they knew the risks. But this woman? Ah, she
was a conundrum, wasn't she? Even as he hated her for
fooling him, he admired how well she had done it. Never a
false note. What a shame it would be to kill her.

He put the picture into the drawer and closed it.

What a shame it would be to kill her.

27

Azul was stunned. She had never seen anything like it. She had trained with the Confed's best, had seen men and women who were experts in fighting, shooting, running, and jumping, and none of them had ever moved like Shaw had just moved. He had literally danced a circle around the other fighter, a man his own size, and at a speed that was superhuman.

The fight had never been in question. Shaw had moved in and out at will, smashing the Flex player and avoiding hits in return. He had beaten the man down into an unconscious heap in seconds, and could have done it much faster had he not been showing off for her.

So this was what it was all about. A drug that gave you this. Shaw had created it, or had it created, and was using it to climb up the ranks of the Flex. It was new enough so that it wasn't illegal to use. Eventually somebody would figure out what he was doing, but if Shaw hurried, he could make it to the top before that happened.

No wonder Randall wanted it. The Confed, already the dominant force in the known galaxy, would be unstoppable with soldiers tanked on this stuff.

Shaw had the martial arts moves, and he looked pretty good—when she was able to follow what he'd done—but this was his edge, and it was sharp enough to cut through steel plate—certainly other Flex players, at least.

He was sweating a lot when he came over. Cervo approached with a bottle of something that looked almost phosphorescent green, and Shaw drank most of the liquid down in a few swallows.

Some kind of nutrient solution, with electrolytes, she figured. Moving at that speed had to burn a lot of energy in a hurry.

"So, what did you think?"

She didn't have to pretend amazement. "That was incredible. How can you move like that?"

"Clean living," he said. He drained the rest of the drink, tossed the container to Cervo, wiped his face with a towel. "My labs have developed a kind of . . . metabolic enhancer," he said. "Legal to use, since nobody has passed a rule against it."

"I'm impressed."

"Are you? Well, good. I have something else I want to try before the chem wears off. Involving you and me." He smiled. "We can use the yurt—our friend there won't be needing it."

"He's dead?"

"Well on the way. His woman has departed, and Cervo will deal with him. Come on." He took her hand and started toward the yurt.

This should be interesting, she thought.

And it was. He was like a vibrator once he got going . . .

Afterward, she said, "Wow. Now what?"

"We're done on this world. You mentioned Koji. Why don't we drop by there and take in the sights? We'll go back to the hotel, pack up, and leave. That sound okay to you?"

"Sure. Why not?"

Cervo knocked at the door a few minutes later, after another very fast session of vibratory sex. They took the flitter back to the hotel.

In her room, Azul packed her things. The cases were hauled up to the roof and loaded into the vehicle, and, in short order, they were ready to go.

Shaw and Cervo went to the roof, but Azul needed to make one more pass by the fresher first. She did that, and was heading for the lift, when one of the hotel maids came out of the office Shaw had been using, down at the end of the hall. The maid held a hard copy sheet in one hand.

"Fem?" the maid said.

"Yes?"

"M. Shaw must have forgotten this. I found it while cleaning.

She handed the sheet to Azul.

Her bodyguards were at the other end of the hall, trying to look inconspicuous. Azul glanced at the image, then handed the picture back to the woman. "Oh, this isn't anything. Just drop it into the shredder, thanks."

Azul smiled, but what she was thinking was, *Oh, shit!*

She was burned! Shaw *knew!*

How had he found out? When?

Was she going to make it to the yacht, or maybe take a high swan dive from the flitter into a large body of water on the way there?

This was bad. Shaw was a man who could kill with his hands and wasn't overly disturbed by such a deed. He had dispatched at least two people she knew about, probably others. And he knew she was some kind of sub-rosa op. Very bad.

She could get to the emergency stairs pretty quick. Lose the bodyguards, and if she could make it to the lobby and outside, she could get to the local Confed HQ—she'd be safe there—Shaw wouldn't be able to muster enough muscle to get to her once she was there, at least not in the short run, and they'd spirit her away pretty quick.

Prong it all!

That would be the thing to do. Get gone, fast!

But: How long had Shaw had that image of her? More than a few hours, and he could have already killed her a dozen ways if that was his intent. He could have poisoned her, strangled her in her sleep, and had Cervo dump her body like he had the Flex player's. Nobody would have known she was gone, not for a long time. Maybe he was still planning to do it, but was waiting until he figured out what she wanted, who had sent her. Maybe he was going to work her, try to figure it out, then delete her. If that was the case, she had time left . . .

The smart stads said bail, right now—hit the stairs running and full out until she was clear. But she wasn't *done* yet. She'd never failed a major assignment, not when it was her fault, and if she had a chance, she could still pull this off. Maybe he wasn't even planning on taking her out.

Wouldn't be wise to bet her life on that, but her intuition told her she was still okay, at least for now.

How long might that last?

What to do?

She smiled at the bodyguards as she headed their way.

Nothing ventured, nothing gained.

The steps were coming easier now, there was a natural flow to Mourn's moves that hadn't been there before. Now and then, he found himself reverting to a step he'd already figured out, but the good thing was that he realized it immediately—it felt wrong. When he found a new one, it felt right.

So very strange that in all the years he had trained, he had never come up with this before. Pieces of it, sure, but not a coherent system, one principle connected to the other. It seemed so simple, how could he have missed it?

The house they had rented once they reached Koji was a bungalow-style building in a quiet neighborhood of similar houses, three or four klicks out of Shtotsanato, the Holy City that nestled inside a ring of old and weathered mountains. The house was adequate, if small: one bedroom, a fresher, kitchen, a living room, but with a high wooden fence surrounding a nice-sized yard. Plenty enough room to practice his moves.

The air was warm, maybe three-quarters body temp, and it seemed to be late spring here, small plants and trees blossomed, new growth waving in gentle breezes, colorful flowers amidst the verdant leaves and needles.

Peaceful, calm, quiet. It *felt* like a holy place—whatever that really meant.

Mourn and Cayne had taken an airbus from the port to this suburb, though there was, he'd found, a thriving business in caravans from the port to the city for those who felt up to a two-week walk. Apparently a lot of pilgrims wanted to do that; see the sights, clear their heads, arrive in a proper contemplative mood.

When they'd arrived on the planet, Mourn had been skinmasked, with his ears altered by bits of synthetic flesh, too. Along with using one of his fake identities, he figured it should keep him from being found, at least long enough for him to finish his work.

The city itself was rather small—probably three or four hundred thousand people, laid out for foot or cycle traffic as much as it was for wheeled or air-cushion vehicles. Open, broad, a lot of smiling folk, many of them dressed in religious garb—ranging from loincloths to enveloping robes, hues from black and somber to flaming red or orange. A city, an entire world, of pilgrims, come to seek and maybe find something beyond themselves.

In the cottage, Cayne worked on her editing. Outside in the clean light of the warm day, Mourn trained. It felt very comfortable, as if they had been doing it for years and had grown into it together. Like an old mated couple, secure in their own intersecting orbits . . .

As Mourn took the eighty-ninth step of his new dance, he had a sudden vision of himself bumping into Weems. A few months ago, the result of such a meeting would have been easy to predict: Weems would've creamed him. Exactly what went down on Earth when that meeting *had* happened.

Mourn had been defeated before he made his first move.

But now? Even now, he wasn't sure he had all the moves he might need, but Mourn knew he had *some* of them, maybe *most* of them, and if he and Weems went at it? Maybe he could run with *Primero* and not fall down. He had something new, and against a pretty good player, it had worked a lot better than he'd expected. What worked against one could be made to work against another.

He imagined himself standing over a defeated Weems . . .

He lost his balance and fell out of the step. Grinned at himself. Well, it sure wasn't gonna work if he didn't keep himself focused on it . . .

He backed up five steps and began the sequence again. *Concentrate, Mourn. You got something here. Finish it up, smooth it out, who knows what you might be able to do with it?*

The monkey brain wasn't giving up so easily. It kept chattering: *Beat Weems, and you take his place. Number One.* Primero. *What you've always wanted!*

A happy thought. And, having achieved your life's goal, you run into Cayne's viper-in-the-garden: *Then what? When you reach the top of the heap, where do you go from there?*

He missed the eighty-ninth step again.
Crap!

Sola sat at the console, watching the images of fights blur
past. "Play normal speed," she said.

The fighting slowed.

She'd had an idea when she had started the project, a
pretty solid one, of how it would go, what she wanted to
accomplish. Early on, that had remained clear, and the
footage of combat and the interviews had flowed toward
her goal. A general overview of the Musashi Flex, how it
worked, who the major players were, then more specifics
to illuminate answers to the ever-basic questions: who,
where, what, when, why, and how.

But then she had met Mourn, the game had gotten way
too personal, and now she was much more deeply involved
than she had ever expected. First-person journalism was
valid, of course, people had been doing it since the first
caveman came back to the fire and told a story about the
monster he'd fought. The first thing you learned in school
was that total objectivity didn't exist—by the very nature
of choosing what to tell and show, you made a subjective
decision. Still, a tale needed to be respun once the teller became a player in the program.

"Replay last ten seconds, quarter speed."

The holoproj images snapped back in time and began to
crawl. She watched them with a practiced eye.

The shift had come to her gradually, and when Mourn
had beaten Cluster so fast and decisively, it had gelled in
her thoughts. The general rule in telling a story was to start
as close to the end as possible and backfill what was necessary to keep things rolling. What had started out as a general overview of the Flex had fined itself down. She had
realized that, aside from a relatively brief intro to the Flex,
its rules and history, what would make her documentary

work was going to be the players themselves. Who they were, why they did it, what it took and cost them, how they trained, where they met, how they felt before and afterward . . .

Which brought her to Mourn. Mourn had to be the centerpiece. An old, established player, a man who had been around a long time, the consummate professional. The weary player who had seen most of it, done most of it, and was thinking about leaving the game when a sudden idea had galvanized him, made things fresh again. She had a part in that, small, but definite, and she'd have to speak to it, acknowledge it, break the frame and step into view, but that was okay.

Mourn, the tired old gunslinger who had, in his realization that it was time to quit, discovered a way to oil his stiffening joints, to gain that edge that had always been just out of his reach . . .

"Freeze image," she said. She chuckled at herself. *Starting to sound like a voice-over, hey, Sola?*

But she couldn't shake the rightness of it. The length was still open for discussion, but the arc was there. Open with Mourn fighting Weems—she had some outstanding imagery there. Getting beat, hurt. Cut to a CGI history of Musashi Miyamoto, real atmospheric, all brown tones, sword fighting as a teener, a montage of his duels. Fade to the present, some of the other fighters, the voice-over telling them about the Flex. Do some interviews with various players, eyewitnesses, cross-cut that with more fights, plenty of action. Back to Mourn, show him all beat up, run some of the early interview material with him.

Too bad she didn't have that street attack in the can, that would be a nice touch. Well. No point in crying over missed shots.

More fighting, more interviews, more history. Get to Mourn's moment of realization, have to CGI some of that, but that was okay. His new direction. The fight with Cluster.

She could end it there, make it about renewed hope. It didn't matter if Mourn ever went any higher, though that wouldn't hurt, the point was that he had been ready to leave, had realized he was never going to get what he wanted, but then there had been a flash and it had opened up the possibility again . . .

She had it, she had it *nailed*. She could see it all in her mind, from start to finish. Whether it was two hours or twenty, that didn't matter, she had plenty of material, she had everything she needed already. A stand-alone or a series, the arc was there, and all she had to do was flesh it out.

She felt a surge of joy well within her. This was how it should be. This was how she'd felt when she'd first started in the biz, full of ideas she couldn't wait to make manifest. She could show and tell her story, grab watchers and pin them to their seats, make them see what she wanted them to see. Make them laugh or cry or wince in pain, hold them in a place where they didn't exist separate from her tale, where they were so lost in it they couldn't get up to go eat or drink or pee . . .

It was a great fantasy. But even as she gloried in it, that little nagging voice in her head was there: *So what? Then whaddya do, huh? Build a big place to showcase your awards, run out and spend your money? So fucking what?*

"Go away!" she said aloud.

28

Shaw sat in a massage chair in his yacht's main office and tried to relax as the knobs of the shiatsu-style unit dug into the muscles on both sides of his spine, cycling from his low back to his neck and down again, hard enough to push his entire upper body forward. It was the state-of-the-art system, full of biofeedback sensors and bio-mechanicals that offered therapy as good as most human experts could manage. Not as good as his personal thera-pist, Liana, of course, but she was at home—he should have brought her—and the chair was available. One made do.

Physically, it *was* relaxing. Mentally, he was still tied into a Gordian knot. What was he going to do about Azul, his little spy? It would be so easy to shove her out an air lock and watch her pinwheel into the cold vacuum, freez-ing solid in a cloud of her own fluids, to drift alone and undiscovered forever. Well, maybe that wouldn't be so easy to watch—up until he had discovered she was not what he thought, he had enjoyed her company more than that of any woman he had ever had. That vexed him. Her facade was a lie, but it was most convincing. And he couldn't believe that she hadn't enjoyed rolling around on various beds with him—there had been too much evidence to the contrary. When you brought a woman to an orgasm that caused tears? He didn't believe she was good enough to fake that. A spy needed only to be fairly good in bed to convince most men she enjoyed it; but Ellis Shaw was not the average man. For sure, he had touched the real woman under the disguise during those sessions, he knew he had. The question was, how much more of her had he reached? What connection had been made when you stripped away the phony artist?

He sighed. Of course, that was the problem, wasn't it? The real reason she was here. The more he thought about it, the more he was sure she was Randall's cat's-paw. The PR wanted Reflex, and there was no limit to what he would do to get it. Bringing in a Confed agent to get next to Shaw? That was nothing. Confederation Representatives wielded great powers—he could summon the best spy with a snap of his fingers.

Randall was going to get the drug anyhow, eventually, but a man like that wouldn't leave anything to chance on something so important. That was not how you got rich and powerful, leaving anything to chance that you could control.

Shaw could have Cervo sit Azul down in a chair and try to pry information out of her, but that might not work. A field operative so skilled had to be valuable. She might have implanted fail-safes that would blow her head up, or mental blocks that would hold under the most rigorous tortures. You had to assume the Confed wouldn't want its secrets being extracted easily, and that they would take pains to keep that from happening. Lay a hand on Azul, she might curl up like a plastic flimsy in a hot fire, poof!

On the one hand, she deserved that, for her charade.

On the other hand, he wasn't ready to see her dead just yet.

She had gotten to him in ways no other woman ever had. He needed to sort some things out before he did anything that couldn't be undone.

It was a thorny forest, and Shaw wasn't happy to be standing at the edge, planning to enter it. But that was the situation, and he had to figure out what he was going to do.

"Massage off," he ordered. This wasn't helping.

The chair shut down.

Somebody knocked at the door.

"Come in."

Cervo entered. Shaw raised his eyebrows.

"Good news. There are sixteen Flex players in the Top Hundred on Koji."

"That many?"

Cervo shrugged. "Guys got philosophical, maybe."

"Go on."

"Two are in your immediate upreach, one eight places away, one four. Nine are ranked in the Seventies to the mid-Nineties, but probably won't get you any real points. Beat the one eight digits lower than you, it puts you in range of two more. Beat them, it puts you in the cohort of one more here. Beat *him,* you can go looking for whoever is ranked Twentieth."

"My. Four fights on the same world that gets me that far? Amazing."

"Nobody on-planet in the Twenties . . . yet."

Shaw caught the hesitation. " 'Yet'?"

Cervo fought to hide a grin. Something was up.

"Yeah, here's a funny thing: My searchbots and BOTG spies have found seventeen upper-ranked players in transit around the galaxy, and six of them, Twenty-Second, Seventeenth, Ninth, Fifth, and Second—are all on their way *here.*"

Shaw frowned. That was way past any reach of coincidence. Those players had a reason for coming here. What could it possibly be?

Hold up a second. "You said six were heading here, but you only listed *five*."

Cervo couldn't stop the grin now. "Yes, sir, that's right. The other one? It's Weems."

Shaw let that sink in for a second. Six top players, heading here? Why would—?

Then he understood. "Ah. *Primero*. And potential challengers have figured out he's heading this way. They are coming to try him."

Cervo nodded. "Where the alpha goes, so do those who would eat his dinner."

Shaw smiled. "Several players who can go against him directly, and some who can get there in two. Makes strategic sense. But I don't think any of the challengers can defeat Weems. I, on the other hand, can beat *them*—then *him*."

"If you don't burn out from using the juice too much."

"Oh, that won't happen. Eight, nine fights. If I space them out right, I can do it in two weeks or less. Truly this *is* a holy world, to have such a thing happen. A miracle, dropped right into my lap. There must be a God." And in that moment, Shaw felt as if this might be close to true. His goal was about to be reached, and it was being *delivered* to his doorstep! How amazing was that?

"When?"

"Starting tomorrow, over the next week and a half. *Primero* will be here in ten days, if he comes direct. Others may follow."

"Perfect."

Cervo said, "What about Azul?"

Shaw smiled. "What about her? If I can pull this off in a few weeks? I won't care what happens to the drug then. Let

the Confed have it. I might even be feeling so magnani-
mous I'll let Randall have it and not kill him."

And maybe let Azul live, too.

Or not. *We'll just have to see how that feels when I get
there.*

The Confed mostly left Koji alone. It might not be the
smartest beast, but somewhere along the line, the idea of
alienating a number of the major religions must have come
into its collective thought, and something sparked back
what a bad idea that would be. The Confed had the men and
guns to win against any world or even a group of worlds,
but holy wars were nasty, because some of the more zealous
religions were willing to die to the last man, woman, and
child, if it came to that. If you pissed off eight or ten of the
major religions to the point where they were willing to call
jihad? You might win, but the cost would be incredible.
Somebody would pay it, and the men or women who were
considered most responsible for such a folly would be the
first called on to address the debt.

Not a career path a politician wanted to go down.

Accommodations were made. Koji paid its taxes, and in-
fluential ministers, priests, monks, brothers, sisters, imams,
rabbis, and other spiritual teachers and leaders got and
gave favors that kept things quiet and peaceful. Most of
them didn't want a long and debilitating war, either. Bad
for harvesting souls when the bodies got all shot up before
you could convert them.

Which, as Azul walked along the city streets, smiling
back at passersby, didn't mean that the Confed had no pres-
ence on Koji. Just not an obtrusive one. No armed troopers
wandering around, no armored vehicles rumbling down the
streets, no big imposing embassy sticking out like an eye-
sore in the middle of town. Low-key was the ticket. There,

but incognito. Anybody paying attention knew they were around, but as long as they didn't make it too obvious, people shrugged it off. Some religious folks had worldly concerns, but many did not. As long as a problem wasn't in their path, they could pretend it wasn't there at all.

She could, Azul knew, stop at a public com and get hold of whoever was running things for the Confed here. Her ID would get her a fast pickup. She could do it now. The bodyguards shadowing her—four new ones who were pretty good, but not great—probably wouldn't even try to prevent her from doing it. And if she wanted, she could lose them fast enough. She had a military-issue confounder in her jacket pocket that should stop dead any bugs she might have picked up. Trigger that, duck into a shop and out the back, she'd be gone. And if they were good enough to stick, even so? She also had a dart gun in her pocket that she'd assembled from innocuous-looking components—a makeup stick, a light pen, a couple of small jars of vitamins—that would give her five shots. One more than she'd need . . .

But—not yet. She wasn't sure what Shaw was going to do, but she didn't think he wanted to take her out, at least not yet. Their lovemaking the day after they'd had gotten here hadn't seemed any less enthusiastic—he certainly wasn't faking that. Really hard for a man to fake orgasm. And once she took that first step to run? That would end things. And she wasn't ready to end things.

She wanted to see him fight again. He'd be doing that soon, and from what he'd said, several more times in the not-too-distant future. She wanted to see how high he would get before the showrunners of the Flex figured out what he was doing and took steps to prohibit it. She guessed that would stop his rise; if he could have gotten as high as he had without the drug, he probably would have done it on his own. He was good, but among this company, good wasn't anywhere close to enough.

Whatever else it was, it was interesting. And she wasn't likely to have the Confed stomping in and leaving bodies in any case, which was a pleasant change from a lot of her assignments.

Was there a risk? Sure. But life was about risk. Without that, how boring would it be?

So, she wouldn't fly. Not just yet.

Mourn was working on the ninety-first step, enjoying the sweat and ache in his muscles from getting something new and different just right when a sudden thought came to him:

Kiley, the old man. He had moved to Koji five or six years ago. Was he still around?

Of a moment, he felt a desire to know. He couldn't say why, exactly, only that it seemed important.

He went into the cottage. Cayne sat in front of her computer, a one-sixth-scale holoproj lit over the desk. She looked up. She appeared tired to him.

"You okay?" he asked

She rolled her head, stretching her neck. "Too long sitting in one spot. I need a break."

"Me, too. Is the house com working?"

"Far as I know. Who you gonna call?"

"An old friend, if he's here."

Mourn went to the com and lifted it. "Directory," he said.

"Go ahead," a pleasant and probably artificial female voice said.

"I need a listing for Akeem Kiley."

The pause was almost imperceptible. "We have an Akeem Kiley, Bladesmith, listed in Shtotsanto. Would you like me to connect you?"

Mourn grinned. "No, that won't be necessary. Just an address will do."

The pleasant voice said, "Forty-four Artesian Row,

street-level shop, second-level, personal residence, Hotai District."

"Thank you."

"You are welcome, sir."

Cayne looked at him. "Want to go visit a local store?"

"Something I can use in my project?"

"Oh, yeah. The best knifers in the Flex all own blades made by Akeem Kiley."

He saw the interest replace the fatigue. "I'll get my slippers on."

"I'll call a hack."

Sola enjoyed the ride—it really was a pretty town, in a quiet, back-planet kind of way. As many people walking or riding trikes or spinwheels as were in flitters or wheeled carts. Lot of them smiling. Lot of children, too.

Well, when you had a connection to your god, little things didn't worry you all that much, at least not that you could tell by looking around here. No sign of brewing religious wars evident.

"We have arrived," the human driver said.

Mourn paid the man with a handful of hardcurry coins, was thanked for the large tip. They got out.

The shop front was small, maybe five meters wide, with a single window to one side and a door to the other. Natural wood, or something that looked just like it, almost blond, with some kind of oil or shellac on it as a protectant.

The upper level looked to be much larger, though it was hard to tell from the front how much of it belonged to which street front.

No sign identified the place, not that she could see.

She mentioned that to Mourn.

"He doesn't need to advertise. People who know who he is and what he does, they can find him. Anybody else? He doesn't want their business."

In the window, on a block covered by what appeared to be black velvet, was a knife. It had a white handle that looked like some kind of ivory, the blade was a striated gray, watery patterns in the steel. The guard was black, a small oval as thick as a ten-stad coin, probably ceramic, maybe denscris or metal. The knife was small, just big enough for a medium-sized hand to grip the handle, and the blade no longer than Sola's middle finger.

"Nice," she said. She had seen a few blades since she'd started this project.

"Nice? Seven or eight years ago, it would have cost you maybe two thousand stads. Probably two, three times that now."

"Five or six thousand standards for a *knife*?"

He laughed.

"Who has that kind of money to spend?"

"You'd be surprised. But just having the money isn't enough. Doesn't matter how rich you are—he won't make you a knife unless he thinks you deserve it."

"Deserve a *knife*? Who the fuck does he think he is?"

"He's a man who can sell every knife he builds for thousands of stads—and who has people lined up on a waiting list that's ten years out. Last time I checked, anyway."

"No way."

"Come on. I think you'll enjoy meeting Kiley. He's an . . . unusual character."

If the outside of the shop was bare, the inside was more so. The room was empty, save for a small workbench, some tools, and an extremely old man sitting on a three-legged, saddle-shaped stool at the bench. He didn't look up as Mourn and Sola entered.

Mourn held a hand in front of her. Sotto voce, he said, "Wait a second. We don't want to break his concentration."

"We could be here a while, Mourn," she whispered back, "before he ever notices us."

"He knows we're here. And he knows who we are—at

least he knows me—otherwise, we'd never have gotten through the door."

She looked at him.

"Frowning like that will give you premature lines in your face," he said. "You'll see why you don't want that in a minute."

She looked at the old man. He was white-haired, what there was left of it, and his skin was very dark, almost bluish. He wore a ragged coverall and moccasins, and a leather apron. He held a partially finished blade on the bench and applied a file to it in long, slow, even strokes. She could hardly see his face from this angle, but his hands were knobby and scarred.

A minute or so passed. He put the knife down and turned, the saddle seat pivoting, so that he faced them.

God, he looked to be about five hundred years old—had enough wrinkles on his face to make a busload of teeners look aged.

"Mourn."

"Maestro. This is Cayne Sola. Cayne, Akeem Kiley. Best knifemaker in the galaxy."

The old man smiled, and the wrinkles deepened. Seamed, lined, creased, as if his face was pliable leather folded into a grin a million times, so many times that any other expression would seem not quite right.

What a strikingly handsome man he must have been in his youth, she thought.

"Careful, the old fart will try and seduce you, and if you buy that smile, he's halfway there already."

She looked at Mourn.

"He's right," Kiley said. "What does a woman with your beauty and obvious charm see in a wastrel like Mourn? He doesn't deserve you." The gigawatt smile flared again. Great teeth for a man his age.

She grinned back. Kiley had to be eighty, ninety years old, and he exuded a smoldering, smoky pheromone so

thick you could almost touch it. At his prime, she expected
he would have had her out of her pants by now—all he'd
have had to do was ask and she'd have shucked them as
fast as she could.

She'd felt that energy a couple times in her life. Once, it
was when she'd interviewed a famous pornoproj entcom
star, a man noted for several things, not the least of which
were his physical endowments. Another time, that flare of
primal do-it-now sex had come from a woman about whom
she was doing a story, an athlete who was a champion
sprinter. Both times, it had been all she could do to keep
herself from leaping upon them in pure lust. Neither time
had it gone any farther than the unspoken and unacted-
upon desire she'd felt. How would it feel, to have that kind
of effect on people? You'd have to know it was there, and
you'd have to think about using it . . .

"What are you carrying?" Kiley asked.

Mourn pulled the curlnose case from his belt and
handed it to the old man.

Before Kiley opened it, he inspected the outside of the
leather case. "Nice work. Joseph Tandy?"

"Chas Clements, Earth."

Kiley nodded. He opened the case and removed the little pair of curved, ring-ended knives. Mourn had showed
them to her, and told her what they were—she had it in her
recordings—but the name escaped her.

Kiley put the case down and examined the little knives,
turning them individually, putting them together, slipping
his forefinger through the rings, spinning them around the
digit in unison.

He put one in each hand, gripped them lightly, and
closed his eyes. A small smile played. "Shiva Ki," he said.
"Cable pattern weld *kerambits*. Ki puts good combat into
his stuff. First-rate."

Mourn said, "Yep. Knowing I got the case on Earth
gave it away. You did miss the case's maker, though."

"Leather isn't my area of expertise, Mourn."

"Just pointing it out."

"I heard you were on Earth a while back, studying *silat*. Fine knives in that art."

He wiped the blades with some kind of oiled cloth that gave off a musky, pleasant scent. Sola reached for the memory: sandalwood? Kiley put the knives into the case, shut it, handed it back to Mourn. "I made a *keris* once, as an experiment. Not a very good weapon for real-time work, though you can do some nice patternwork for the magicks. Did a little *pisau* once, too. Never tried *kerambits*, nobody ever asked."

"What are you working on?" Mourn asked.

"Drop-point hunter for a guy wants to stalk great cats," he said. "Probably wind up on the floor of a bamboo thicket somewhere."

Mourn chuckled.

Sola said, "I'm missing the joke."

Mourn said, "The Maestro doesn't think that hunting great cats with a knife is a survival characteristic."

"So you think your handmade expensive knife is going to be found next to the remains of the guy who bought it?"

"Great cats don't leave many remains, as I understand it," Kiley said, "and it might never *be* found, but, generally, yeah."

"Isn't that a . . . waste?"

Mourn laughed and shook his head.

"What?"

"Start the old bastard down that road? He'll talk your ears off."

"Pay no attention to Mourn, he can barely crow his fly shut after he pees without pinching his willie. You being a bright and beautiful woman, I'll tell you my secret: I make knives for people who will use them. Fighters—like Mourn used to be—hunters, soldiers, cools, field medics, emergency workers. I expect my blades to be pulled and used frequently, and if you plan on mounting one on a wall in a trophy case and pointing at it when company comes? I won't make it for you."

"How can you tell?"

Again, the dazzling grin. "That's the right question, fem. Not 'Why?' but how I can tell.

"How it works is, you come and see me and we talk. I believe you are right for the blade, I'll make it for you. Well, at least that's how it used to go. Now, I'm slowing down, I have to finish the orders I have, so I'm not taking any new ones."

"But even so, if you know the man who buys your knife is likely to die?"

"That's his choice. He wants to go against a cat half again as big as he is, using only a knife? He deserves the best tool he can get for the job."

"And that's your knife."

"Yes. If he fails, it won't be because his blade couldn't do the job. So it's the try that counts. Win, lose, draw, doesn't matter what happens after, only that he was willing to *try*. Those are the people who deserve my work."

"Do you mind if I include this in my documentary on the Flex?"

"We can talk about it," he said. "Over dinner, maybe?"

"Will you stop hitting on my woman?"

Kiley kept looking at Sola, as if willing her to himself. Even as old as he was, she could feel the pull. What really struck her, though, was what Mourn said: *my* woman? She almost grinned at how much she liked the sound of that, despite the possessive nature of it. She wasn't a slave, she didn't *belong* to anybody. Still, she understood what he was saying. And liked it. A lot.

Kiley said, "From what I hear, you might not be around much longer. Shame for the gorgeous fem here to be all alone after you're gone. She needs somebody who'll appreciate her."

"Somebody who has the *capability* to appreciate her, which would let you out," Mourn said. He looked at Sola. "He has three wives he can't keep happy."

"Four, now," Kiley corrected. "Ask them if they have any complaints." Again the fat-cat-happy grin.

Mourn shook head. "I take it that you've heard the story of my match with *Primero*?" Mourn said. His voice was dry.

"One version of it." Now he turned from his come-hither look at Sola and looked at Mourn. "You don't even know about the Gathering, do you? Crap, Mourn, you're getting careless in your old age."

Mourn said, "A Gathering? Here?"

"What is a Gathering?" Sola asked.

"When a bunch of high-ranked Flex players wind up in the same place at the same time," Mourn said. "Could be accidental, but usually, it's intentional. Lot of fights generally ensue."

"Numbah One Hisself is coming to our world, and where the shark swims, so swim the remora."

"Weems can't know I'm here."

"*Primero* has access to a lot of information," Kiley said. "And it could be just a coincidence, though I have to say, given what I've heard about your last meeting, I doubt it." He looked at Sola. "You were there. Did you get it recorded? I'd love to see it."

"We'll leave," Sola said. "Be long gone when he gets here."

"Ah. *That's* how it is."

"What?" she said.

He just gave her a tiny version of his magic smile. "Some lines even I won't cross."

"No," Mourn said. "I'm almost ready. Maybe four, five more steps."

Kiley lifted his eyebrows. "Steps?"

"I've been working on a system," he said. "Something new. It's positional."

"Good enough to take *Primero*?"

"In theory. Won't know until we get there."

"Well, if my information is correct, you have a little over a week to get ready. Assuming he can knock over a few folks who might get in his way, which he can certainly do." He looked at Sola. "You be sure and record it, luv, and you can show it to me after we hold Mourn's wake."

The idea of Mourn being dead did not go down well at all.

"We don't have to stay," she said to Mourn.

Kiley laughed. "You survive, you want to hang on to this one. Damned if she doesn't *care* about you. Count your blessings. While you can."

29

Mourn's first fight was only a day after he and Kiley had talked. He could have avoided it, but having decided he was going to stick around for Weems's arrival, he thought *Fuck it* and put his real name into the local com directory. Anybody wanted to talk to him, all they had to do was call.

He was in the kitchen in the rented cottage, preparing lunch, Cayne behind him at the table, staring through the window.

She didn't say anything out loud, but he felt it from her.

"You don't want me to do this, do you?"

"I'm not the person to tell you what you can or can't do, Mourn."

"You are afraid for me."

"Is that so awful?"

"No, I appreciate it. But you know the story about the viper?"

"Refresh my memory."

"A viper got caught in a snowstorm. Being cold-blooded, this was a death sentence. A man passing by saw the snake. The viper said, 'Please, sir, pick me up and warm me against your body, else I'll freeze to death.'

"The man said, 'No fool I! You'll bite me and I will die!'

"'No, I promise I won't! Please!'

"So the man collected the snake and put him in his pocket. After a while, the viper warmed, and then he bit the man through his shirt.

"'Viper! You have poisoned me! You lied!'

"And the snake said—"

"'You knew what I was when you picked me up,'" Sola finished.

Mourn smiled. "Are you planning on coming along and recording the fight?"

"Yes."

"And if I start to lose, will you stop recording?"

"I take your point, Mourn. We are what we are. You fight. I record. Those are our roles."

"For now, yes." He shrugged. "Who knows what later will bring?"

The fight was against Wim Diversela, an HG mue who was one of the best heavyweights in the game. He was ranked Ninth. Even though Mourn was one rank higher at Tenth, Diversela challenged—and let it be known he was doing it for a warm-up—he wasn't interested in cutting Mourn to pieces with his bowie-knife variant, a Texas toothpick, so he'd appreciate it, even though Mourn was the challenged party, if they could do it bare. Diversela expected that he would beat Mourn and that the match would help ready him for lower numbers—maybe not Weems himself, but somebody in the Top Five. You wanted to keep your edge, you had to work it against skilled players as much as possible.

Mourn understood this and was happy to oblige.

They met behind Mourn's cottage.

The match took four seconds—Diversela charged, Mourn moved and tripped him, and caught him with a kick on the back of the head on his way to the ground. It was the fastest match he'd ever had in all his years in the Flex.

"Jesu, Mourn," Cayne said, "I hardly had time to turn my cam on!" But she was relieved, he could see that.

Truth was, he was a bit relieved himself. Beating Cluster, that could have been luck. Winning a second fight made what he had seem more real.

Cayne, on the other hand, was definitely turning into more baggage than he would have guessed. Still, it didn't feel *all* that heavy. Just not something he was used to having.

Mourn didn't figure the match would do much for his ranking, and he was right. He and Diversela swapped places, that was it.

Still, Ninth was the highest he had ever been.

Three days later, Ali Muhammed Mather, ranked Fifth, arrived on-planet. What the hell, Mourn figured, in for a demi-, in for a stad. He called Mather. Mather was hoping for Weems, but Weems wasn't there yet, and if he declined, he might lose a place or two, and while it didn't really matter in the Ten vis-à-vis who you could challenge, his ego didn't want the knock. Mather agreed. He also chose bare.

That match took, by Cayne's count, nineteen seconds, and that only because Mather had a pain threshold high enough to keep hobbling around with a broken ankle. It took a second sweep-and-stomp that broke the other ankle to keep him down.

At that level, you generally took the place of the man you beat, so Mourn moved to Fifth.

By now, word had gotten around. Orleans Plinck had retired at Third, and Besimi Besimi, a Vishnuan, of all things, had moved into that spot. He came to see what Mourn had.

This fight, also bare, took longer. Besimi, a light heavy, was cautious, and he kept trying to bait Mourn into

an attack, so he could counter. Mourn wasn't going to give
the man anything to work with, so they spent four or five
minutes circling and feinting, nobody offering any real
threats.

Besimi's patience was shorter than Mourn's. He finally
thought he had an open head shot, and he took it. It was
a trap. The forty-seventh step worked perfectly, and Besimi hit the ground hard enough to knock out both his air
and his consciousness.

Just like that, Mourn had risen and defeated three of the
Top Players, without working up a sweat on any of them.

It was awfully hard not to be overconfident. He knew
better, but even so, either he'd encountered three top fighters when they were all having really bad days, or he had
come up with something worth having.

Once the art he was working on got out, once people saw
it and began to understand it, there would be countermea-
sures devised against it. That was inevitable. But for somebody who had never seen it before, somebody who expected
Mourn to fight as his old recordings might indicate, the
surprise had, thus far anyway, proven to be overwhelming.
Such things had happened before, many times in many
places. Two foreign cultures came together, they didn't
know what arts the other had devised, and some nasty and
painful surprises came out of the meetings. Eventually, once
you understood what your enemy had, you could figure out a
way around it; but "eventually" was the key term. Eventually, everybody died, and eventually, the universe would spin
down; it was what you did until your time came that mattered.

Mourn and Cayne lay in bed after making love, and she
said, "So, how does it feel to be Third, Mourn? Two men
away from the top? You excited?"

He considered it for a moment before he spoke. "Not really," he said. "How weird is that?" And that was the truth
of it. He wasn't excited. He was more interested in testing

what he had built than in the ranking he had achieved. Doing it right, win or lose.

"Goals change, Mourn. You grow, and things don't seem as important as they once were."

Out of the mouths of babes. Yeah. He was beginning to see that.

He wasn't sure that he liked it. You get to the top of the mountain you've been climbing most of your life and once there, you decide you don't like the view?

How crappy was that?

He wasn't at the top yet, and he still might not get there, but he was close enough that it didn't seem like such a long haul. And the view? Better than at the base, but . . . not really all that special . . .

"Who the fuck is Lazlo Mourn?" Shaw was irritated, and the question was rhetorical—he was alone when he said it.

This guy, had to be five or six years older than Shaw, came out of nowhere after having bounced around in the low Twenties and high Teens forever. A solid fighter, better than a lot, but nothing to make the Top Ten lose any sleep until lately, when he started to tear through them like a needler punching holes in tissue paper! How?

Could it be that Mourn had some kind of chemical aid, too?

Could it be? And if so, was it better than the one Shaw had?

No, that was not possible. Shaw knew his field. He was at the cutting edge and everybody else was far behind. Nobody could have come up with Reflex on his own without leaving a wide trail, and he had people looking all the time. It was something else. Some new trick, and it had to be pretty good for Mourn to have beaten the players he'd defeated.

It would be nice to know what the trick was.

A rumor had it, somebody had recorded Mourn's recent fights—a documentarian, from what Shaw's agents could determine, but nobody seemed able to find her to make an offer for her footage. Nobody had a name or location for her, only that she had been there and caught the fights.

It was vexing. But *Primero* was coming, and Shaw had improved his own position among the contenders so he was only two fights away from being able to challenge anybody in the Top Ten. Win those, and it didn't matter about this Mourn asshole. No matter what skill he had, he couldn't beat Shaw's speed.

"Cervo!"

The big man appeared as if by magic.

"Yes?"

"Find out who the woman is who has recorded the fights between Lazlo Mourn and the guys he beat this past week. Pay her whatever she wants for the footage."

"Okay."

"And where is my next opponent?"

"He'll be arriving here tomorrow."

"Good."

He was rising fast, faster than he'd hoped. By the time Weems got here, he'd be almost ready. Another match, two, and he could challenge *Primero*. Getting so close he could almost taste it . . .

When the op bumped into her on the street at the outdoor market and passed her the info ball, Azul felt a sudden premonition grip her in its cold fingers. The woman was good—she was a short, round, young-mother type, complete with two preteen girls in tow. The children looked to be about nine and seven or so. Nobody would look at her and think "Aha, a sub-rosa operative!"

The day was warm and sunny, the smells of sugarbread frying and harmonic incense crystals sharp, and the walla of the shoppers attending the vendors soft and nonthreatening.

The exchange was quick, and the four bodyguards shadowing her wouldn't have caught it if they'd been five meters away, much less half the block to the front and back of her.

"Oops, sorry," the op said.

"My fault entirely," Azul said. "Have a good day."

"You, too." The woman smiled and said, "Come on, girls, Dads is waiting!"

With the warm steel marble palmed and hidden, the bright and happy day took a nasty turn, and her sense of danger grew.

How had they found *her?*

Shaw would have filed a flight plan for his yacht, and they had moved into a very large dwelling near the edge of town, a walled estate. Shaw had rented or leased it—for all she knew, it already belonged to him, or he could have bought it on the spot. Billionaires tended to shine like novas wherever they went unless they were making great efforts to keep their light hidden. But Shaw *was* trying to maintain a low profile, because when he went out to fight in the Flex matches, he didn't want a crowd. So while he wasn't wearing a skinmask and skulking about after dark, he also wasn't advertising who he was.

Of course the Confed could have tracked him. He could have a bug on his ship, a WR transmitter that would allow somebody to home in on it from light-years away. But even so, tracking the ship was not the same as tracking *her*. If an op was able to casually walk up and deliver a message as the woman had just done, that meant something else. The Confed would have to have a team of agents tailing her— they'd need more than one—and she'd have long since spotted the woman with the little girls, had that been the woman's primary role. She had been keeping a sharp eye tuned for the shadows Shaw had on her and she hadn't seen anybody else. Even the best around had to be in line of sight most of the time, and she would have picked them up. She knew the moves, and she'd used them.

The second, and more likely, possibility was that she was bugged. No need to keep contact if there was some kind of caster in her clothes. She hadn't been running her confounder, which was the top-of-the-line model with a built-in wide-spectrum radio scanner, and even if she had, there might be new bioelectronic transmitters that a confounder wouldn't shut down. She'd heard rumors that CI had developed some that used viral-molecular biologicals that generated IR or microwave sigs instead of common radio bands, and produced enough power to run forever from ordinary motions.

There were ways to check it, and as soon as she could find a place where she'd be unobserved, she would do just that.

She went into a public fresher. It was one of those cutesy places using one-way plastic. Mirrored from without, but you could see through the walls from inside. She put a coin into the booth's slot once she was inside and closed the stall's door.

She lit the confounder, thumbed the scanner on, and let the computer run the scan. It took ten seconds for the device to latch on to the sig, flashing a red dot in the air a centimeter over the confounder. The field strength meter narrowed it, and drew her a schematic:

It was in the heel of her left slipper.

She pulled the slipper off and looked at it closely.

Nothing to see.

She remembered when she had bought the shoes. It was during her setup for the artist persona, part of an order that had been shipped to her. Of course.

Her first reaction was that it was CI who was behind it. It was always wheels within wheels in the biz, nobody trusted anybody, and in their place, maybe she'd do the same thing.

But maybe it wasn't CI. It could be PR Randall. He

knew who she was, and he had contacted her directly once before. Maybe he was keeping tabs on her.

Or maybe it was Shaw. He knew who she was, too. Could be he'd borrowed the slipper, had it reheeled with the bug, stuck it back into her closet.

Azul put the slipper back on. Better the tracer you knew than the one you didn't; she could always run the confounder or lose the shoe. What the confounder could spot, it could shut down.

Unless, of course, the caster she'd found was one they expected her to find, and there was another one not so easily detected?

Wheels and wheels, cogs and gears.

None of the options were happy news. The immediate purpose of a bug was to be able to find the person upon whom you had implanted the device. The reason why you might want to do that? That was the more important question.

Who needed to keep such close tabs on her?

The answer to that question was in the little steel info ball tucked into her pocket. She needed a reader. She had one in her room at the mansion, but she didn't want to use that instrument.

Time to find an electronics kiosk, she decided. And maybe buy a nice new gadget for Shaw while she was there.

30

"Mourn? You might want to take a look at this."

Mourn was about to go outside to train, although he had to confess that his heart wasn't in it: A thundershower had drifted over them, and a steady rain pounded on the roof, punctuated now and then by flashes of lightning and subsequent thunder. He turned around. Cayne sat at the desk, the three-dimensional holoproj lit over the computer's console.

"What's up?" He ambled that way. The rain was probably warm enough, and one needed to practice in varying conditions, but still, no need to hurry . . .

"Look at the stats here on one E. M. Shaw."

Mourn glanced at them. His eyebrows went up.

"Yeah, interesting, huh? I did some background on him, and this is the fun part—the guy is a billionaire. He's the Shaw in ShawPharm Corp."

"Jesu." And while that was interesting, it wasn't nearly

as interesting to Mourn as the man's record as a player. A couple years down in the high Hundreds, up, down, no real movement, and then all of a sudden, he's riding a Bender ship straight up at FTL speed, into the Teens—in a matter of a few weeks. Something not right about that.

"What's a billionaire doing playing the Flex? And, all of a sudden, doing it so well?"

Cayne nodded. "That's the real question, isn't it? Probably a good idea for you to find out, since, as you can see from his last couple of matches, he's here in town, and at his current position, of Eleventh, he could drop by."

Mourn shrugged. Whatever the guy had, he couldn't do anything about it. All he could work on was himself. He had ninety-six steps in his art now. He had gone over and over it, and that seemed to be the number he needed. Any conceivable attack and defense sequence he could come up with, some combination of those moves would cover it. Might be somebody who'd leap up in the air and bark like a dog while slapping himself on the head as an attack, and he didn't have anything specifically for that, but, then again, he didn't really think he needed anything for that.

Ninety-six steps, that seemed to be the sum of it all.

And while the rain hadn't slackened any, he wasn't going to get any more skilled with his new art standing here looking at the holoproj. Time to go work out . . .

The electronics kiosk had, despite this being a holy world and theoretically not as concerned with such things, the latest technology on sale. As Azul was examining various toys, it was easy to slip the info ball into one and arrange it so nobody could see what it revealed.

Which was another address, in a neighboring city a few kilometers to the east of Shtotsanto. No names, but Azul was pretty sure who the sender was. It would be interesting to see if PR Randall had come all the way here just to have a chat.

She removed the recording, felt the marble heat up as it destroyed its contents. She bought the reader, along with a couple of other items. Just in case the reader had some kind of spyware in it, it was going to go away at the earliest opportunity.

Hmm. Now, she had to lose her shadows, get a vehicle, and go see who had sent the message. None of these ought to be particularly difficult.

She bought a new pair of slippers at a shop next door and left her old ones in the trash can outside, just to be safe. Probably it was Randall's bug, but "probably" could get you killed.

A few minutes in a crowded mall was enough to shake her surveillance team. It wasn't that hard to lose a tail if they didn't want you to spot them. It was when they didn't care if you knew they were there that it was tricky—they could stick closer that way.

A hack ride to a flitter-rental place, a phony ID and credit tab, and she was in the air and headed for Three Rivers, which, she learned from the rental flitter's nav-comp, was a small and scenic retreat about half an hour away, on the western edge of an inland sea shaped like a bean that was almost a thousand kilometers long by six hundred wide at the midpoint. This little ocean, the Somber Sea, was home to a number of species of colorful fish, aquatic mammals, and seafaring birds, including the very dangerous diamond-head slasher, which swam in large schools, looked like a cross between a tiger shark and a manta ray, and would eat virtually anything that was unfortunate enough to swim into its path. Boaters were warned not to swim in waters where the churning of diamond-heads could be seen during feeding frenzies.

What kind of idiot would swim where predators were in a feeding frenzy? The nav-comp was silent on that point, but Azul figured it was another kind of person that the gene pool was probably better off without. Swim, fool, and get what you deserve.

Three Rivers, she also found out, had been named not for the local geology, but instead for branches of religion that had come to exist together in harmony there. Population was about twenty-five thousand, and the average income was fairly high, so it was a place where people with money hung out. There were four four-star restaurants, a four-star hotel, and assorted recreational activities . . .

The flitter's computer directed her to a rustic but large building a little ways out of the town. There was a recent-model luxury sport flitter parked near the house, with the top down. Azul spiraled her ride in and landed next to the sportster.

She approached the house, and decided that, once upon a time, it had been a hunting or fishing lodge. Might still be.

She climbed a short flight of steps to a broad, wooden porch. The place had large windows, but they were opaqued a dark and smoky gray.

The front door opened at her approach, rattling a little in its track as it slid back.

She walked inside, her hand in her jacket pocket, the little spring gun assembled from innocuous parts gripped and ready to fire. She didn't expect she would need it, but it was better to have it than not.

There was a large room, dressed with distressed and probably natural leather couches and chairs, a giant fireplace against one wall. Heads of various game animals adorned the walls, and stuffed and mounted fishes hung here and there.

A hunting *and* fishing lodge. How baroque.

She noted a hall to her left, turned and headed down it. At the end of the hall was an open door.

The room was more of the same, smaller, with a large desk made of some striking and attractive striated wood, edges all gently rounded, gleaming dully under what looked to be a thick coat of wax. Another fireplace was inset into the wall to her right, a set of heavy-looking steel fire-tending tools racked upon a stone apron in front of the grate: a shovel, brush, tongs, and a poker.

Burning wood for heat was apparently a serious business around these parts.

Behind the desk, peeling the last bits of a skinmask from his face, sat Planetary Representative Newman Randall. No real surprise there.

"Ah. My spy. You've seen to your appearance, quite lovely, you are. Come in, sit." He waved at an overstuffed leather chair in front of the desk.

Azul sat, removing her hand from her pocket and smiling at the PR. The smile stopped before it got to her eyes.

Randall finished picking the synthflesh from the tip of his nose and dropped it upon the desktop. "Nasty stuff," he said. "Never comes off quite as easily as they say. I expect you've worn these a time or two."

"A time or two, yes."

"Still, a mask is much less cumbersome than having to drag one's bodyguards around, and much less likely to draw attention, which the Confed frowns upon if you visit the Holy World. Incognito is the order of the day."

Azul said nothing, waiting. It wasn't long in coming.

"So, tell me about the Reflex."

No point in taking the long and slow route, since he already had flown most of it. She said, "While he is on the drug, Shaw is the fastest human you've ever seen. He can run circles around a champion sprinter, can pound the best fighters into the ground in the blink of an eye. It's incredible to watch. I've seen it half a dozen times."

"Side effects?"

"Makes him tired and dehydrates him. Nothing else I can tell to look at. Both are easily fixed. A good night's sleep, electrolyte fluids, he shows no other signs of stress or wear."

"Excellent. Duration?"

"Varies a little. Hour, hour and a half. I don't know if that's dosage related or not—I'm not sure how he takes it."

Randall nodded. "I'm sure our scientists can tweak that, come up with longer half-life. Easier to add or subtract once you have the basic model."

She shrugged. Chemistry was not her area of expertise.

"Well, this is what I needed to know. He's sitting on it, dragging his feet, but that's about to change." He reached for a comset lying on the desk.

"What are you going to do?"

He looked at her as if she were a puppy that had just peed on an expensive rug. "Do? I'm going to have CI move in and take it over, of course. Production, supplies, whatever he has on it. It's too valuable to risk losing. What do you care?"

"I don't care about CI. But if you eminent-domain the drug, that will get out. Somebody always talks."

"So . . . ?"

"The showrunners for the Musashi Flex always have an ear to the ground for this kind of chem. They'll make it illegal there."

"And . . . ?"

"Shaw won't be able to use it anymore."

"And . . . ?"

"That will . . . disappoint him."

Randall laughed. "Life is full of disappointments, fem. Do you think I am going to risk losing a major potential weapon in the Confed's arsenal because it might *disappoint* M. Shaw? Hurt his *feelings*? He's a big boy. He'll get over it."

She shook her head. "I've gotten to know him. Winning the Flex is a big thing for him. A major focus."

"Well, that's tough, isn't it? He'll have to come up with some other game to play. He can afford to buy himself a new toy. Whatever he wants." He smiled at her and picked up the com.

She pulled the spring pistol from her pocket smoothly, pointed it, and squeezed the firing stud. The titanium-boron dart, designed to pop out angled, sharp-edged, and flexible whirling ribs that would increase its diameter by a factor of six on impact, hit him in the left eye before he could blink, then screwed a channel bigger around than her thumb through his brain until it was stopped by the back of his skull. A great close-range weapon, if you could place the dart properly.

PR Randall was pretty much brain-dead before he had time to be surprised.

But Azul had plenty of time for that emotion. She hadn't known she was going to *pull* the pistol until she fired it.

Oh, shit, girl! What did you just do?

31

The rain was pretty warm, but even so, Mourn was drenched, and his clothes were binding as he moved. He had just decided he was going to shuck them and finish his workout naked when he looked up and saw Cayne appear in the doorway. She walked out into the yard, and the rain started to soak into her hair and clothes. She looked as if she'd just seen a ghost.

"Cayne?"

She walked to within a meter. She was holding a com. She handed it to him without a word.

He felt his breath catch as he took the com from her. He didn't need to ask. He held it to his ear.

"Hello, Weems," he said.

32

Done was done, there was no way to take it back, and now the problem was how to slow the inevitable pursuit. And it would come, the only question was, when?

Even if Randall had told no one he was coming to meet her—which she didn't believe—any CI op-supervisor worth his boots would make the connection soon enough. Azul was on Koji, Randall had come to Koji. She was working for him. All this was a matter of Confed record. He had come here incognito, and why else if not to take an ears-only report from his spy?

If they found his body in this lodge with a spring dart in his brain, at the very least they would want to have a long chat with operative Luna Azul. Dead PRs roiled a lot of waters that CI wouldn't want to see disturbed. They'd need to catch the killer, fast, and even if she hadn't done it, she'd still be a good goat for it. That was moot—they'd strain her brains, and when they got done, what was left probably wouldn't object to whichever way they wanted to execute her. Game, set, match. Better luck next incarnation, hey?

If, on the other hand, PR Randall wasn't found dead—if he wasn't found at *all*?—then the investigation would start later and proceed slower. Rich men had been known to take off suddenly for all kinds of reasons: chem, fems, or midlife crises; worry over being caught for some criminal act, bad marriages, or just an urge to chuck it all and try a simpler life—all kinds of reasons caused otherwise upstanding people to vanish. First, they had to notice he was missing; then they had to try and trace his movements, and in both cases, they had to proceed with caution, because nobody would want to cause a scandal that might reflect badly on a rich and powerful man's reputation. What if he wasn't in any danger, but had sneaked off to experiment with illegal drugs or forbidden sex? Would you want to be the cool who brought that information to light about a man who could buy your whole planet and blow it into atomic dust if he wanted?

Dead was bad, but gone was less so.

There were spare bedsheets in the linen closet next to the fresher, and Azul used one of them to wrap up Randall's corpse. It would be nice if it were dark, but waiting a couple hours for night entailed risks she didn't want to take—he might have another appointment, or somebody could drop by unannounced.

She looked outside, didn't see anybody. She hoisted the dead man over her shoulder and carried him to her flitter, put him into the passenger seat, folded over so he wasn't visible.

She hadn't touched much in the lodge. She went back in and wiped everything she had laid hands on, using a spare towel soaked with cleaning fluid, so there'd be no prints or DNA. The eye shot hadn't produced much blood, and all of that had been soaked up by Randall's clothes.

A final check, and she took the towel, cleaning fluid bottle, and Randall's com unit to the flitter. She got in, cranked the fans, and lifted. Somebody might see her vehicle, but she couldn't help that. Even if they could trace it, the ID she'd used to rent it was now as dead as Randall.

She headed out into the Somber Sea, angling away from touristy-looking beaches and pleasure sailboats that dotted the calm water near the shore.

It took forty minutes to find what she was looking for—a frothy patch of water ninety kilometers out. She dropped lower, and saw half a large fish burst from the sea and fly through the air a meter or so above the water. A large, toothy head emerged to snatch the falling remainder before it touched the water again.

That would be a diamond-head slasher, she reckoned, along with its brothers and sisters, feeding on a school of unfortunate fish.

She circled the flitter around, opened the passenger door, and shoved the late M. Newman Randall, Planetary Representative for the Confederation, out. The body fell fifty meters and hit flat in the middle of the frothing water, creating a large splash.

More churning quickly surrounded the impact spot.

Gather round, boys; dinner is served . . .

Azul pulled the flitter up to cruising-lane altitude and set the autopilot to take her back to Shtotsanto. Unlikely that enough of Randall would ever be found to identify him, but even so, all she had done was delay what was coming. A week, a month, CI was not always bright, nor fast, but as an organization, it did usually grind fine. Once you were caught in between the millstones, there was little chance you would escape intact. You had to get gone before they caught you.

Her years in the biz had given her some not-inconsiderable skills and contacts. She had identities she hadn't used yet, some completely unknown to the Confed. She had a high hole card, too, an ex-CI programmer who'd sold her an ID worm she'd kept updated, along with

a limited, but theoretically adequate, access to the Confed's protected ID systems. If the worm worked, it would
eat through her own files, leaving them intact on inspection, but subtly altering her DNA and retinal patterns in the
records. If it worked, what would ID Luna Azul and all of
her official incarnations would shift. As soon as she got to
a galactic-linked system, she would loose the worm. By the
time anybody got around to looking for her, it would be a
done deal. She wouldn't be setting off any alarms when
she walked through a reader looking for her.

She knew how to run and how to disappear. With enough
of a head start, she had a chance to survive.

Why had she done it? Thrown her career, and maybe
her life, away? She knew the answer, even if she didn't
want to admit it: She'd gone native. Allowed herself to get
involved with a civilian in the worst way. She'd put his wel-
fare above her own. Stupid.

Now, she would have to run, and once the Confed had
you on its list, you didn't get to stop running until you died
or they found you.

*Well. That's how it goes, Azul. You screw up, and you
pay the price. Like the late Randall said: Tough.*

"Let me get this straight," Shaw said. "You're a Confed
spy, but you just killed the man who sicced you on me?"

They were in the largest room of the estate, just the two
of them, though Cervo was outside the nearest door. Shaw
sat on a couch; she stood in front of him two meters away,
her hands held behind her back, almost as if she were
standing in a military parade-rest pose.

Azul smiled. "Afraid so. You knew about the spy part,
though, didn't you." It was not a question.

"If you knew that I knew, why are you still here? I could
have deleted you for that."

"In your place, I probably would have done that as soon as I found out. Why didn't you?"

"My question first: Why did you kill Randall?"

She nodded to herself, a small gesture, almost invisible. She looked at him, took a deep breath, and relaxed a little as she let it escape. "You have no reason to believe me—I wouldn't, in your slippers, not after all I've done—but the truth? He was going to screw up your chance at winning the Flex."

Shaw didn't speak for a few seconds as he absorbed that. "And you killed a Planetary Representative for *that*?"

"I would say it seemed like a good idea at the time, but that wouldn't be true. Soon as my brain kicked in, I thought it was a crappy idea. Gets worse every time I think about it again."

"But you did it anyway."

"Yeah."

He wanted to believe her. Oh, he *really* wanted to believe her. And, on the face of it, if she had killed Randall, he couldn't come up with any other reason that she'd do that. Then again, everything she had told him before this moment had been pretty much a flat-out lie. So buying this would be stupid and risky and *really* stupid. Except—

—except that he could feel, at some deep and totally illogical level, that she really did care about him. He didn't believe in his heart of hearts that it had all been a lie. Some part of it had been real. He had gotten to her.

Yeah. And she had gotten to him, too.

The cautious part of him screamed a warning. But that magical piece that sometimes gave him the future and the truth, *that* part of him that just *knew* things, was nodding. Of course. The woman threw away her life just to keep Randall from fucking up his chances to win the Flex.

He believed her.

What the fuck must *that* mean? He stared at her.

"Why didn't you kill me, Ellis? I saw the holograph of

when I arrived at the port back on your homeworld. You knew I was a spy."

"I knew, yes. Why didn't you run when you realized that?"

"No, it's your turn. I answered your question. Answer mine."

And he knew why—he didn't *want* her dead. He wanted her to live, and he wanted her around. She had laid her cards on the table, what did he have to lose?

"I couldn't do it," he said.

"Why not? You've done it before."

"Not to you," he said, his voice almost a whisper. He came to his feet. "I could never do that to you."

She blinked, stunned, he could see that. And her feeling was no more surprised than his at having said it. It was true.

"I need you," he said.

He opened his arms. She came into his embrace.

Son of a bitch!

33

"You coming?" Mourn said.

Cayne shook her head. "No."

"No?" That caught him flat-footed. "This could be the best footage you've gotten, Cayne. *Primero* against *Tercero*—it would make your documentary!"

She looked up at him. "I don't want to watch it. If you lose—if you die—I couldn't use that footage. I wouldn't want to have it. I wouldn't want to have seen it happen."

"That's a great confidence builder, fem."

"You can joke about it, you want, but I'm not laughing."

He saw the tears welling. They bothered him, more than he wanted to acknowledge.

"I have to do this."

"I know you do. This is who you are. You're the snake I came across in the snow. Go, do it. I'll be here. If you don't come back, I will miss you, Mourn."

"I'll come back."

The tears flowed. "You promise?"

"Yes. Of course."

They hugged, and she clung to him with such a fierce clutch that for a moment, he considered not going. Packing up and taking off. If he really quit the Flex? Weems probably wouldn't be able to track him. Go someplace far away, new name, new face, leave it all behind . . .

And never know if what he'd uncovered could have withstood the ultimate test . . . ?

That was not who he was. Not the kind of person who would be able do that and then look himself in the mirror of a woman's eyes and see what he wanted to see. Win or lose, he couldn't quit until he had tested himself.

A man had to do what a man had to do. Cliché it might be, but that's how it was.

The place Weems had picked was in the back of a public school, closed for the season, and, Mourn knew, chosen because it was the kind of place he and Weems had encountered each other when last they'd met.

There was a grassy sports field, grown or mowed short, a hundred meters behind the buildings. The rain hadn't returned, and the sun shone through a partly cloudy sky. Warm, pleasant, nobody else around. As days to die went, it wasn't bad.

"Weems," Mourn said.

"You've come up in the galaxy, Mourn. Third? I don't see how that's possible. Your opponents all have sudden heart attacks?"

Mourn took a deep breath, held it for five seconds, then let it out. What he had developed and taught himself had worked against other men who had been better than he was. In this, he had the advantage—his opponent had never seen what he could now do, and he *had* seen Weems move. Still, this was *Primero*. *Numero Uno*. And a man who had beaten him bloody and broken the last time they'd seen each other. They both knew that.

"Gone mute?" Weems circled to his left, five meters away.

Mourn tracked him, stood his ground. "Nope. Nothing I can say to make you turn around and leave, is there?"

Weems laughed. "Oh, I can't *imagine* anything that would do that. I owe you big. After I'm done, I'm going to hunt down that slit of yours and pay her back for blasting me with that wand, too. I'll make it last a long time before I get done with her."

Mourn smiled. "You trying scare me unconscious with trash talk?"

Weems twirled his cane. "Tools or bare, sucker?"

Mourn shrugged. "You pick. You're not planning on me surviving it either way, are you?"

"I take it back, Mourn, you're not entirely stupid after all. But you know how I can wave my magic wand." He jiggled the cane.

"I know. It doesn't matter."

A quick frown flashed, but Weems brought the smile back up to hide it. "Really? You *must* have a new trick."

"You figure? Don't really believe that my opponents all had heart attacks?"

Weems's face went hard. "I'll use my stick." He spun the cane in one hand, rolling it around his fingers like a magician doing a coin trick.

Mourn pulled the pair of *kerambits* from their curlnose leather sheath. He transferred one of them into his left hand.

Primero was too canny to be tricked by what had worked on Harnett.

Weems laughed again, louder this time. "That what you brought? Those little claws?"

Mourn gave him his best smile. "All I need."

Again, the frown flitted by, staying longer this time.

Mourn should be scared, halfway to losing already, that's what Weems would be thinking. But he didn't look scared, and he wasn't acting scared. Why not?

"Whistling past the graveyard, Mourn?"

"Maybe."

Dueling had a psychological edge that could cut both ways. Weems was *Primero,* the best in the game, that was a major weapon to his arsenal. Anybody who came to dance with him knew this, and certainly he knew it—when you stood at the top rung, you didn't lack confidence.

But, here Mourn was, having come from Tenth to Third in a very short time. You could ascend the list by leaps and bounds if you were at Two Hundred or even One Hundred, but once you got into the top dozen or so, things moved slower. Fighters were too evenly balanced in their skills. More than a few times, matches had ended *ai-uchi*—mutual slaying—because of that. Moving up as fast as Mourn had? Wading through people who'd have stomped him a few months ago with relative ease?

Koji had become very interesting to Flex players and fans. Mourn would be very high on the list of men to watch. Especially since he had been in the game so long. It wasn't done—he was a known quantity, not some hot-hand who had blown in out of nowhere and started kicking ass. Mourn had been around, and he was what he was, so his jumping ranks like he had meant *something* had *changed,* and you had to take that into account. Failure to do so could be fatal.

And even taking that into account didn't give you every-thing. Mourn was what he was—but that wasn't what he *had* been the last time Weems had seen him.

That was *his* edge. The pattern he had discovered, all ninety-six steps' worth. He had been practicing them three hours a day. He'd have to get around to naming the new art—assuming he survived this encounter. The steps were based on everything he had learned, with some things he had only discovered as he had started to put them together. The art was the sum of it all, old and new, and if he did it right, he could beat Weems.

Of course, if he screwed it up, he was a dead man.

He shrugged mentally. Well. Sooner or later, that was how it went for everybody. It would be a shame not to be able to pass the new stuff along—the positional aspects of it were not like anything he'd ever seen. But it wasn't entirely up to him.

Weems brought the cane around and laid his other palm on it, holding it with both hands, pointed at Mourn's right eye, like a *katana* fighter. He waggled it a bit, to loosen his hands and shoulders.

Weems had some fancy one-handed moves with the carbon-fiber stick. Mourn had seen vids of the champion doing them in combat demos, but that wasn't likely to happen here. Weems was confident, but he was also cautious. Mourn had come up too fast for it to be luck. He had beaten men who had given Weems trouble. He had something new. At their level, the first man to make a mistake would pay dearly for it. They both knew that.

Weems edged toward him, centimetering forward, right foot leading, knees bent, cane still aimed at Mourn's face.

Mourn turned a hair, angling himself. Weems could cover a lot of arc with his stick. He could stab or cut with it, striking from the head to the ankle. His first move, he'd expect Mourn to dodge or block. He'd give up the second move, too. But the third move—

Weems came in, fast, and swung the stick in an overhead cut at Mourn's head. He was expecting Mourn to back away, to go left or right, or to hold his ground and block with one of his knives.

Mourn stepped in, using the sixth step of his new dance—

Weems shifted the downward strike, twisting the cane

in an arc to his right and down, aiming to shatter Mourn's
left knee—

Mourn kept going in, but angled away to Weems's left,
the tenth step—

Weems reversed the cane, up, over, and around, to catch
Mourn on the opposite side, aiming for the temple—

Mourn reversed and cheated the tenth step to the left,
skating as much as stepping, raising his left blade to hook
the incoming cane as he moved to meet it, and dropping his
right blade for a low line strike at Weems's ribs—

The cane hit the little knife, and the shock vibrated
Mourn to his teeth, but the block held. The slash with the
second knife went in, caught a rib, dug a furrow through it,
the muscle between it and the next rib, and scored that rib
before Mourn retracted it.

He took two steps to the right as Weems shifted the cane
and managed to catch him across the thigh with the end. It
hurt, but did no damage.

Weems glanced down, saw his wound. It was bleeding
but Mourn knew it hadn't done any real damage. Not physically.

But: Nobody had gotten past that cane to lay a blade on
Weems in a couple of years. That had to be a shock.

"I hurt myself worse with beard depil," Weems said. He
circled to his left.

Mourn turned, but didn't back up. "You ought to buy a
better brand. Or maybe grow a beard."

"I'm going to pound you like a demon drummer on
crank, sucker."

"Anytime you're ready, *Primero*."

Weems gathered himself to attack. Mourn watched the
man's nostrils. When they widened a hair, as he inhaled,
Mourn leaped, timing his move to the other man's breath.
It was an old trick, though he had used it recently, and
probably nobody had tried it on Weems in a long time.

Weems brought the stick around, but Mourn had timed

his move so that he caught it on his left side. It rocked him, it hurt, probably broke a rib, but that didn't matter, because he snapped his raised left arm down and trapped the cane. Just for a second, but that was all he needed. Weems twisted and turned for the disengage, to free the stick, using both hands. Mourn followed the tug in, dropped to his knee, cut with his right *kerambit,* and sliced a deep gash across Weems's left thigh. He continued the motion, diving, doing a shoulder roll, and coming up with a half turn, so that he faced Weems—

He didn't have long to set himself; Weems charged in, full-bore straight on, determined to finish him with a hard attack and lots of momentum.

Mourn did the v-step he had practiced as part of the pattern, angling out but toward Weems. If he had backed up or gone in, Weems would have run over him.

Weems tried to adjust, but he was moving too fast—

Mourn cut, right high, left low, right high—

Weems should have dropped the cane and blocked, using both hands, but he didn't. He held onto the weapon that had brought him so far and used that, swinging it one-handed.

He was very good and he was fast. He blocked the first cut, deflected the second—

—but he missed the third.

The short and curved steel snagged Weems's right eye, buried itself in the socket, and gave Mourn a handle. Weems's momentum kept his body going forward, but his head stopped. Mourn twisted and finished his step in, did a foot drag and, using the handle in Weems's head as an opposite lever, slammed him down onto his back. Mourn dropped, and smashed the back spine of the second blade into Weems's forehead, just above the knife jammed into the man's eye.

Then he let go of the one stuck into Weems and slashed the tendons of the man's wrist with the other knife. When

Weems's hand opened, Mourn grabbed the cane and jerked
it free. Before Weems could move, Mourn used the cane,
twice to the head, then to one knee. Bone cracked and
broke with every strike.

Z. B. Weems might survive, but he wasn't going to be
walking away from this.

The best fighter in the Musashi Flex had just lost.

However arcane the scoring system was, when you beat
Primero, you *became Primero.* There was nowhere higher
to go.

And now, Mourn knew for sure that he had come up
with one hell of a martial art. And that was more important
even than winning. He had created something of real
value.

He reached for the com he carried, to call the medicos
for Weems. If they showed up in the next fifteen or twenty
minutes, Weems had a good shot at surviving.

Oh, yeah, and the tag. He wanted to collect that. Maybe
it wasn't as important as it had been once, but if you went
to meet the best and you won? Might as well take the win.

After he took the tag from Weems's boot, he hurried
away.

He didn't want to keep Cayne waiting.

34

"He beat Weems?" Shaw couldn't quite wrap his mind around that.

"Yes, sir," Cervo said. "Weems is in a docbox at the local MCU being pumped full of chem, cut up some. Medico wasn't talking past that, but he was in the Healy overnight. Got to figure it was bad."

"He beat Weems," Shaw said again. Who the fuck *was* this guy?

Shaw said, "Where am I?"

"Ninth."

"Find him. Do it fast."

"Sir."

Cervo left, and Shaw paced, thinking. Well, it wasn't in the script he'd constructed, he hadn't thought anybody could beat Weems, but it didn't really matter who it was, did it? Whoever held the title was the guy to beat, that was the important thing.

Azul came in. "Something?"

"Mourn just beat Weems."

She nodded. "So you go up against Mourn."

"As soon as Cervo can find him." He paused. "What about your situation?"

"I did some checking. My control, Pachel, said he didn't know what Randall wanted me to do for him. Far as I can tell, that's true. I was supplied with a background, clothes, and supplies, but I never told anybody what they were for. A bright op might be able to make the connection—if they know what kind of art you like, but otherwise, I don't think so. They'll start looking for me here and in Chim City. They don't find me, they'll spread out on Tatsu, and the rest of the Haradali System. But it's a big galaxy, and I won't look like I did, plus my scans won't match what they have in their records. Even if they know I rascaled the files? They won't have the right data."

"I've been thinking about moving my corporate headquarters," he said. "The weather in Chim City's been lousy. In fact, I don't much like the weather anywhere in Haradali, come to that."

She smiled. "You'd do that?"

"Why not? I can. I can run things from anywhere I want."

"And where is that?"

"Anywhere you are," he said.

They both smiled.

"Soon as I take care of this one little thing," he said.

She frowned.

"What?"

"This Mourn guy worries me."

"You've seen me move. Nobody can match me."

"But he has something—something he didn't used to have. To jump from the Teens and high digits into the top spot after having lived there for so long? That's not how the game works, is it?"

"It doesn't matter what he has. It won't be enough. My juju will beat his."

She didn't say anything, but he could feel her doubt.

"Don't worry," he said. "Start thinking about places you'd like to live."

"Boss?"

Shaw looked up.

"I got him."

"That fast?"

"He's in the com directory."

Shaw smiled. "Let's make a call, shall we?"

"So, you're the man who knocked off Weems. I heard it was pretty bad. He die?"

They were at a public park in a quiet section of the city. The grass was a deep green, bordered by a ring of evergreen trees, the sun shining. A great day to achieve your dream.

"No. Got a new eye and some cosmetic work, some bones glued, but he'll survive."

Shaw shrugged. Weems didn't matter anymore, he was history.

"What's your trick, M. Mourn? I tried to get footage of you, but it wasn't to be had."

"No trick," Mourn said. "I put some things together is all."

"New way of moving?"

"I don't think so. Different attitude. I didn't create it, I just discovered it. It was always there."

Shaw moved a little closer, but still outside Mourn's immediate attack range. Mourn had gone for bare. With Shaw's speed, he could go in from three or four steps away faster than Mourn could stop him. "It won't be enough."

"You could be right." He circled to his left, angled at

about forty-five degrees toward Shaw. "I've seen your record. Impressive."

"I'm a few seconds from what I've wanted my whole life."

Mourn smiled.

"Something funny about that?"

"No. Until day before yesterday, I could have said the very same thing myself."

"Can't say you sound all that happy about it. Not all you hoped it would be?"

"Not really. You might find out in a minute."

"Oh, I will, you can bank on it."

Shaw felt the Reflex dancing him, wanting to sprint, to *move*! He had it all, now. That conversation with Azul rolled around in his head. She was something, the partner he had never even known he had wanted. Smart, beautiful, brave— a woman who would risk her life to protect him, who had done so. Had met his enemy and taken him out. He had her. And in a few seconds, he would reach the top of his personal mountain.

Life could not get any better than this. It just couldn't.

Mourn stepped back and came up from his crouch. "How important is this to you? Being *Primero*?"

"You have to ask? I couldn't begin to tell you."

"You can have it."

"What?"

"We can go call the showrunners, and I'll give you the win. I'm going to retire anyhow."

"No!"

"No? But I thought you wanted this more than anything?"

"I want to *earn* it!"

Mourn shook his head. "Fairly? But you can't, can you?"

Shaw glared at him. "What are you talking about? The runners have called all my matches fair."

"But they weren't, were they? I talked to a couple of the guys you beat. I know what your trick is. You've kicked your speed up. Given your background, I'd guess it was chemically augmented, some kind of metabolic enhancer, with something the runners haven't seen before, so they haven't banned it yet. Probably you can beat me anyhow, so why bother?"

"Why would *you* give up what you worked *your* whole life to get?"

Mourn laughed. "Because it doesn't really matter. Along the way, other things got to be more important. I got where I wanted to go. I thought it was the top of the galaxy. It's not even the summit of a foothill. I have seen the view. It's not so hot. I don't need to stay here. It's yours, and welcome to it."

"No. I don't want you to give it to me. I want to take it for myself."

"What if you can't? What if you can't beat me? You want to risk it? Word gets around, somebody will pass it along to the showrunners pretty soon. Somebody will complain, and when enough of them do, you'll get called in for a chem scan. They might not know what it is, but they'll see something, and they'll forbid it. You don't get where you want to go soon, you won't get there. I am your last chance. You aren't good enough without the crutch."

"But I can beat you now!" Shaw said. He felt a red rage, joined to the Reflex. And a realization that Mourn was probably right. Time was running out. This might indeed be his last chance.

"Come on, then. Show me what you got, rich man. Cheater."

The insult stung. The rage blew through his controls. Shaw leaped—

Mourn had never seen a man move as fast as Shaw did. If he'd been inside a step and a half, Mourn wouldn't have gotten his hands up in time. As it was, he barely did. If his position hadn't covered his lines, he wouldn't have had time to block. Shaw essentially ran into Mourn's hands, literally hitting his body against Mourn's fists. The speed was enough to make it a pretty good impact without Mourn doing any extension at all.

It wasn't as if the man was a blur—Mourn could see his motions—but his own moves weren't going to be able to keep up. If Shaw moved first in close, Mourn's reactions were going to be too slow.

Shaw bounced back, cursing, still moving at that inhuman speed.

Mourn backed a couple quick steps away, to give himself more time to react. If ever there was going to be a test of position, this was it. He had to read Shaw's attack the instant it was launched, then ignore it, hurrying to get himself set, or he'd never make it. He had to be enough ahead of Shaw to make up for the man's incredible quickness, and he had to have distance to do it. Most of what he had been discovering went in or angled to one side. Here, if he didn't give himself room—

Shaw barreled in, changed levels, and Mourn reacted, reaching for the block—*bad idea*—!

Shaw slapped Mourn on the left side of his head, a little bit above the temple, so the strike rocked him, but didn't gray him out—

Shaw punched again with his other hand, and all Mourn had time to do was tense the muscles of his belly for the impact—

If Shaw stayed there and kept pounding away, Mourn would have been in deep shit—he turned, managed to get a low elbow in the way, but the counterattack with the other elbow to the high line was a full beat behind—

Shaw laughed and leaped away.

That was a tactical error. He wanted to damage Mourn, back off and look to see, then come in again, striking like a shark or a dire-wolf, rather than staying and clinching. If

Mourn could catch him, grapple him still for long enough, he could hit back—

Shaw bore in again, and since he was depending on his velocity, he left an opening, the solar plexus. He wasn't worried, probably was sure he could cover it in time.

Mourn started his punch when Shaw was still a meter and a half away, at the same time, covering his face for the high punch that Shaw's lowered shoulder promised was coming—

Mourn's block was good, it deflected Shaw's attack so it missed. His punch was better—it hit Shaw solidly, aided by the terrific speed of the man's attack—

Shaw reeled away, gasping for air.

Mourn bore in, moving as fast as he could—

Too slow, he could see, but he threw one of the attack *sambuts,* high to the face, then low with the same hand changing the line halfway through, going for the belly, and the other elbow horizontally for Shaw's head—

Shaw blocked all three attacks, but they kept him off-balance enough so that he couldn't generate a counter—

Shaw broke away, retreated to gain himself room—

He's too fast to trade techniques with.

How do you beat a man who can fly rings around you? You can't move quickly enough to swat a hummingbird . . .

Shaw came in, and this time, Mourn knew he wasn't going to throw a couple of punches and back off, he would stay and use his superior swiftness to try and end it—

How do you swat a hummingbird? You don't—you have to . . .

Shaw fired off a kick and a punch, and Mourn knew what he had to do—

He didn't try to block either attack. He opened his arms wide, as if to offer himself up for the slaughter—

The kick caught him on the thigh, it hurt and it would slow him, but that didn't matter now—

The punch smashed into his left cheek—the bone

cracked and his vision flashed red and gray, but Shaw was there—

Mourn wrapped his arms around Shaw, pulling him in tight.

It didn't matter how fast he was, *if he couldn't move—!*

Shaw's instinctive reaction was to try and push away, but Mourn wasn't having any of that. He snapped his head forward, twisted his neck slightly so that the head butt was where his horn would be if he'd had any, and slammed Shaw's nose—

Shaw's nose broke, and the impact stunned him. He struggled to escape—

Mourn butted him again, slightly higher and to the left, and felt the impact jar him as he smacked into the orbit of Shaw's right eye—

Shaw went slack, dazed even more—

Mourn slid his left foot forward a hair, hooked his instep around Shaw's right ankle, and butted him again, forehead to forehead. His vision swam with Brownian motes—the impact was nearly enough to knock himself out, but not quite—he had the momentum and the intent, he knew it was coming—

Shaw almost collapsed. Mourn let his bear hug go, threw a short elbow to Shaw's upper chest, and pulled inward and upward with his left foot, sweeping Shaw's leg clear of the ground, leaving him no support on that side—

Shaw fell, hard, and Mourn dropped with him, bringing the point of his elbow straight down and just below the xiphoid process. The nerve plexus there was not very well protected, and the impact knocked Shaw's breath from him—

Mourn twisted, and used his left elbow, a strike to Shaw's right temple, to finish it. Shaw went limp, out cold.

When he managed to slow his own breathing, Mourn got back to his feet. He had won the title he'd wanted. He had defended it against a man who should have beaten him. He had added a ninety-seventh step to the art he'd discovered.

Not a bad couple of days, when you thought about it.

"If he's dead, so are you," a woman said.

Mourn turned and saw a beautiful brunette standing there. She had a spring gun in her hand, pointed at him.

"He's not dead, just unconscious," he said. "He'll have a headache, probably a concussion when he wakes up."

"Back away."

Mourn did so.

The woman kept him covered, the pistol rock-steady as she moved toward Shaw.

"Put it down, sister, or you'll be taking a nap, too."

Mourn looked to his left. Cayne stood there, her hand wand aimed at the woman who was bending over Shaw.

The woman looked. She tossed the spring gun to the side and reached down to touch Shaw's face. Shaw groaned. The woman smiled.

Cayne walked closer, stiff, her weapon still pointed at the woman.

"I thought you weren't coming to any more of these."

"Yeah, well, I changed my mind."

"Why?"

"Because if you died, the man who did it wasn't going to be walking away."

He smiled.

"What now?"

"Now? I'm going to put in a call to the runners. I'm retiring."

"You serious?"

"Yes, fem, I am serious. As serious as an old guy like me gets."

Her face lit with a big grin.

"Ellis?" the woman cradling Shaw's head with one hand said.

"What happened?" Shaw said, his voice just above a whisper. He turned his head to the side and vomited.

Now it was the woman's face that shone with a smile, even as she wiped puke from his lips with her bare fingers. Mourn nodded to himself. Cayne had come to avenge him, if necessary. The woman with Shaw must have had the same idea.

He hoped Shaw was worthy of that kind of care.

He hoped he was, too.

"We're done here," he said to Cayne. "Let's go."

35

Cayne came into the cottage. Mourn had heard her return once she'd cleared the courtyard's gate and noticed that her steps weren't quite even. He saw why she was off-balance as she stepped into view:

She was carrying a guitar case.

"Happy birthday, Mourn."

He blinked. "How did you know that?"

"I'm a trained journalist, remember?"

She put the case on the table. It was, like his previous one, spun-carbon fiber—light, but very strong. He unsnapped the six latches that held it shut.

Inside was a cedar-topped classical, with a Gilbert-style bridge and tuners, the fretboard made of what looked like rosewood instead of ebony. Mourn carefully removed the instrument from the case.

The sides and back were a rich, striated, beautifully patterned brown.

"The wood is something called claro walnut," she said.

"Not exactly the same as black walnut, but in the same family."

He nodded. Inside, the maker's label was old and somewhat faded, the script ornate, but legible: Jason Pickard. The serial number was "2," and the date "2003."

Lord. So old.

Mourn strummed an open D-chord. The deepness of the basses and the resonance of the box filled the cube. It was tuned down a full step, and the high string was a hair flat. He adjusted it, belled the twelfth string harmonic, wow—!

"It's tuned down a full step," Cayne said. "And that just exhausted my entire knowledge of the thing. The guy I got it from didn't know anything else about it."

He played a scale. A wonderful instrument, almost in the same class with the murdered Bogdanovich. Almost.

He smiled at her. "This is the best present anybody ever gave me. Thank you." Then the smile faded. "You can't afford something like this," he said.

She shrugged.

"Cayne . . ."

"I sold my camera," she said.

He stared at her as if she had just levitated on her own. "What?"

"I've stored all the footage I'll ever need," she said. "Not that it matters—I'm not going to produce the documentary anyhow."

"Why?"

"You know why. Because there are bigger things going on here, Lazlo. You know it, I know it. Something more important than an entcom show on Flexers. I can get a new camera if I ever need one, you can find those anywhere. But this guitar? There's only one of them just like it, and you need it."

He nodded. "You can't know how much this means to me."

"Yeah, I can. I—I love you, you know?"

He smiled. "Yeah. I know. I love you, too."

Her face became radiant.

"What, you didn't think I was going to say it?"

"Well, I couldn't be sure," she said. "I mean, I *knew* it, but it's nice to hear. Sometimes men can be dense. You more than most."

He laughed.

"So, what now?"

He nodded. "I think maybe I'll open that school. But it needs to be about more than just teaching people how to fight. It needs to be about teaching them why to fight—and who."

"You think?"

"Your idea. I've got a little money, enough to get started somewhere. We develop a curriculum, hope we can attract the right kind of students."

"Who would be . . . ?"

"Those with a lot of patience. I'm guessing we won't be ready to go out and change the galaxy for a while. I don't think I'll live to see the day, but maybe I can teach somebody who might, or who can then teach somebody else who might. Got to start somewhere."

"Big step."

"Just a first step. Not that big."

There was a knock at the door.

"We expecting anybody?" she asked.

"I think maybe so."

It was Shaw and the woman who'd had the gun. Shaw didn't look all that much worse for wear, given the fight they'd had.

"Mourn. This is Luna Azul."

"Shaw. F. Azul. Come in. This is Cayne Sola."

Shaw and Azul entered. The two women inspected each other briefly.

Cayne was leery. "Mourn, I have to point out that this guy tried to stomp you yesterday—and his girlfriend here pointed a gun at you."

"I recall. That was yesterday. Things aren't the same today."

"I need you to teach me your system," Shaw said. "I had a cheat that should have let me win against any normal fighter, and you beat me even so. If I'd had what you know, I wouldn't have needed the drug."

"Maybe," Mourn said. "No guarantee that's so."

"But I know it's true," Shaw said. "I have to learn it."

"And if you do, you'll try again?"

Shaw shook his head negatively. "I don't think so. I realized something. I wanted to have the skill to be the best, and I couldn't get it, which is why I developed the chem. But you *have* the ability. That's what I want. It doesn't matter if I get the title, as long as I know I *could* win it fairly if I wanted. If I *knew* . . ."

"I understand."

"Lazlo . . ."

He turned to Cayne. "We're looking for students, right? Why not M. Shaw? And what about you, F. Azul?"

"I go where he goes."

Cayne said, "But can you trust him?"

"He gave me the ninety-seventh step, the last one I needed to complete the art. I don't think I would have gotten it against anybody else. He has something we need."

"What?"

"What we talked about. Going down a road other than the one we're on. *Doing* something."

Shaw looked at her. "I can lube a few gears," he said. "I have a fair amount of money. It comes in handy."

"For what?"

"Anything you want. As long as Mourn will show me his art, I'll fund whatever he wants. I can buy a country and make him king."

Mourn laughed. "Could be a whole new game. We could put together a place where we can educate people, teach them the things they'll need to know to get the galaxy's wheels out of the mud and onto dry ground. Isn't that what you wanted, Cayne?"

"Maybe. You think we can do it?"

"Who can say? Worst that can happen is we die trying."

She was silent. "What the hell," she said. She looked at Azul.

Azul said, "I, uh, know a few tricks that might come in handy. We can probably keep these two on track."

Mourn felt a sense of something in the air, something he couldn't quite put his finger on, but it felt *right,* whatever it was. What the hell. Might as well give it a shot.

The legend begins...
The *New York Times* bestselling author's
acclaimed Matador series

STEVE PERRY

THE MAN WHO NEVER MISSED

Once a ruthless soldier, Emile Khadaji
has disappeared from the
Confederation—with a secret plan to destroy
it all in the name of freedom.

0-441-51918-0

MATADORA

She's one of the best martial artists in the
universe. One of the finest bodyguards alive.
And she's back.

0-441-52207-6

THE MACHIAVELLI INTERFACE

Khadaji and the Matadors mount an
offensive to bring down the Confederation
once and for all.

0-441-51356-5